The McMurry Girl
by
David L Porter-MacDaibheid

The McMurry Girl
© David Leslie Porter-MacDaibheid [2016]

Paper edition – ISBN 978-0-9532221-2-4

Published by D L Porter-MacDaibheid, United Kingdom
e-mail **dportermacdaibheid@yahoo.co.uk**

Cover Illustration
A Woman Victorious by Jennifer S Blake
© Jennifer S Blake

Acknowledgements

The late Richard (Dick) Douglas Boyd — his advice and encouragement has been invaluable.

My thanks to Hugh Manson for making me a couple of terrific guitars, and by doing so, inspired me in the writing of a couple of chapters. And also, my thanks to all the guys, past and present, from the guitar shop and works for their unfailing welcome and expert advice — which, incidentally, has also gone some way in inspiring me to write the aforementioned chapters.

To those who I have come to know through my time as a voluntary ambulance car driver, in particular, to those who have not only listened to my ideas but have actually encouraged me to complete this novel, thank you!

My thanks to Jennifer Blake for the use of her painting, **A Woman Victorious,** for the cover.

Chapter 1

The milky-blue radiance of the night subsides as a solitary cloud drifts lazily across the face of the full and bright October moon.

With the lunar glow having all but gone, the sleek and sprightly wood mouse has broken free from the relative safeguard of her hidey-hole and now scurries between stones and tufts of vegetation in her desperate search for food.

Although preoccupied with her need for sustenance, she is instinctively cautious and, as such, remains ever-vigilant and acutely primed — lest there be a need for her to execute a hasty flight.

On locating a fallen berry, she stops — and then, whilst sitting on her haunches, and with the dexterous fingers of her tiny paws, she eagerly examines her find before promptly pushing it into the secure confinement of a cheek.

Scouring the ground for yet another prize, her translucent ears twitch and turn to every sound of danger; she is naturally wary and ever-alert.

Success. Another is grasped and then safely stored alongside the first.

Looking for signs of peril, she scans the area. After all, she has a need to ensure that all is safe before she can move on to find herself a place of sanctum — a place where she can relax and take her time to fulfil the needs of a near empty belly.

Seemingly unaffected by the muted sounds of music which drift out from the adjacent village hall, and strategically positioned amid the branches of a twisted and ancient oak, a plump and mottled tawny owl keenly watches on.

Although the night is his time, he is, unlike the foraging wood mouse, grateful for the added assistance of nature's night lantern; for his eyes — large, black and mysterious — make good use of the shine as he scrutinizes the ground in search of something which will, to some degree, satisfy the immediate demands of his own voracity.

So as not to alert potential prey of his presence, he waits silently as he tunes in to the most minuscule sounds of motion. Sounds which can so often betray the presence of a life which, when preoccupied in the industrious pursuit to ensure its survival — somewhat ironically — manages only to increase its susceptibility to being deprived of that very right to exist at all.

A rustling of activity detected from far below captures his interest. With due care and purpose and in readiness for a quick and silent release, he repositions each foot. Then, whilst slowly flexing an armoury of menacing, sabre-like talons, he tilts his head to one side … and focuses.

Self-disciplined and with single-minded resolve, he waits; for it is through the experience of having partaken in successful, and unsuccessful, predation that he has learnt the worth of espousing to the arts of patience and stealth.

Although having had the benefit of camouflage whilst foraging in the undergrowth, she is now edging towards the open expanse of the car park and so, as the security of her cover lessens, the risk to her wellbeing increases significantly.

Meanwhile, suspecting that she has either obtained sufficient fare to fulfil her immediate needs or, if not, that she has decided to widen her scope and search elsewhere, he can sense that she is becoming more vulnerable by the second; the time for action has all but arrived.

Experience has taught him that she will in the next few moments make a break from the relative safety of cover and — with the draw of the overflowing, galvanised dustbins which crowd, somewhat untidily, beside the kitchen doors — will then, almost certainly, make a sudden dash across the car park.

Silently, he waits.

Self-restraint ensures that he will not permit himself to give way to the compelling impulses of anticipation. Instead, he will continue to watch until he detects the first shivers of her rush; only then, when the time is right, will he break his vigil and take to the air in what he hopes will be a swift and clinical procedure.

But, as always, there are no guarantees. After all, primeval instinct will not allow her to take the risk of being in the open for too long; in the interests of self-preservation, she will assume the shortest route, deviating only to take refuge beneath the undercarriages of the parked and unattended vehicles.

It is only then, when she has safely achieved the crossing and can thus embrace the haven of the shadows once more, that she will be able to take advantage of the cover which disguises the well-trodden path which skirts the building.

She hesitates, and whilst hovering at the edge of the asphalt-covered plain which, somewhat enticingly, stretches out before her, she checks for signs of danger.

With all appearing to be clear she, without warning, throws caution to the wind and, as if risking all in a moment of recklessness, seizes her opportunity and darts forward — her tiny legs carrying her as fast as they are able.

Once away from the density and darkness of the forest, she scurries across the open expanse of the car park, her tiny heart throbbing powerfully as it pumps the oxygenated blood around her body, thus ensuring that her muscles are adequately fuelled for the task.

Intuitively she knows that she is now at her most vulnerable but the risk is weighed and in the end, her desire for food proves to be too great.

With the security of cover no longer within reach, a spur of adrenalin boosts her metabolism, firing a last-gasp effort to quicken her pace.

This is the moment that he has been waiting for. Targeting her, the owl releases his grasp and moves quickly from his vantage and into the air.

Swooping downwards, he measures his approach with the precision of a military marksman — his presence betrayed only by the whoosh of the air which races past the soft, streaked plumage of his broad, rounded wings as he swiftly gains speed.

With feathered talons suspended and primed, *he*, the hunter, prepares to make his snatch whilst *she*, the hunted, is sprinting across the tarmac.

On this, his final approach, he — whilst simultaneously emitting a loud and distracting **kee-wick, kee-wick** — instinctively tweaks his aim.

In little more than an instant, the light of the moon is smothered by the fast-growing shadow of this predatory angel of death, and it is only now, with the fatal strike an almost certainty, that she is fully alerted as to the imminence of the threat to her very being.

Many would freeze — but not her!

With an appetite for life which debars her from resigning to the fate of being subjected to a painful and gruesome end, whilst being torn asunder from beneath the confining cover of a soft and feathery cloak, she, spontaneously and evasively, zigzags across the tarmac.

It's too late! Ambushed by a thunderous tsunami of sound and an eruption of bright, pulsating lights, the darkness is ousted and the peace destroyed as the by-product of human revelry escapes through the rupture of the opening doors.

This sudden and unwelcome distraction skews the exactitude of his focus and — although his talons brush frustratingly close to their mark — they miss their quarry by little more than that of a whisker.

With his mission thwarted and his patience and efforts having garnered no reward, he can do no more than to career past whilst trapped within the momentum of flight.

Carefree, holding hands and laughing, a young couple — with their hips still swinging in time with the pounding beat and infectious hook of Van Morrison's *Brown Eyed Girl* — step into the night.

Equally enrapt as the other, they are far too occupied to have noticed the conclusion to nature's dramatic episode.

The wood mouse — living on, and with the threat of her demise no longer dire — reaches the relative safety of the building; whereas her would-be assassin, unsuccessful and still feeling the nagging pangs of hunger, climbs gracefully up and into the night.

In a display of petulance which seems to echo the frustration and reluctant acceptance of failure, he fires a determined and powerful beat of his wings, propelling his ghostly silhouette up and away before it twists and turns as it arcs back towards the gnarled and familiar oak.

Disappointed? To a degree, maybe, but then, he has learnt how to put his frustrations behind him. After all, he knows through the wisdom of experience that the darkness will continue for a good while yet; so it will only be a matter of time before another unsuspecting rodent makes its presence known as it, too, starts to scavenge through the discarded foliage, thereby, unwittingly reopening a window of opportunity for him, the predator, to finally satisfy his own need to be fed.

Muffled by the closure of the doors, the volume of the music is no longer able to assert its presence, and so, with the sounds of nature daring to reclaim their authority, the courting-couple take advantage of the darkening shadows.

With an air of confidence, she flicks her hair away from her face, allowing her luxuriant mane of raven tresses to tumble, abandoned and free, over her shoulders and gracefully down the length of her back. As she dips her head to one side and reveals the amber glow of her pendulous, teardrop earrings, her sparkling blue eyes peer deep into those of her suitor.

Gently and seductively, she bites a grip on her lower lip and leans backwards, so as to accept the firmness of the building as her support.

Ensnared by her mysterious beauty, he is at the mercy of her sensual allure, and, as such, he makes no attempt to resist the draw of the most primal of animal instincts.

Facing her, with his hands pushed up against the wall so as to rest above her shoulders, he gazes into her eyes. Then, no longer able to disguise his lustful intent, he closes in to claim a kiss.

She can easily drop down and duck beneath his arms to avoid him, but she sees no reason as to why she should deny herself the pleasure and excitement of participating in this brief, and somewhat surreptitious, experience of having a no-ties session of carnality. Enticingly, she smiles, and then, with a none-too-subtle show of her lustful intent, she runs the tip of her tongue along the length of her moist and silken lips. He returns the smile and readily accepts her unspoken but, nevertheless, clear invitation with nothing more than a gentle touching of his lips on hers.

Although only just eighteen, she is mature and in her prime.

What's more, she knows exactly how to provoke a reaction!

As his chest presses firmly against her breasts, she feels a shiver of excitement tumbling, uncontrollably, through the length of her body. Energized with a rush of recklessness, combined with the need to satisfy her own desires, she allows herself to court the precipice of danger and, in doing so, take the risk of being swept away by the almost magical sensuality of this unplanned for, but wonderful, experience.

Readily surrendering to the lure of each other, they kiss … as his hands

— sensing not even the slightest hint of resistance — slip freely over the satin sheen of the newest and most elegant addition to her wardrobe. The thrill of the encounter, heightened by the sumptuous feel of the silky softness, causes his grip to tighten, and with the added input of a wild and irrepressible drive firing his deepest desires, he pulls her, firmly and tenderly, from the waist towards him.

Her hands, mirroring his, cannot help but to slide down the contours of his body and then assist him in pulling them closer and tighter together.

Her eyes start to close and with her four-inch, high-heels raised off the ground, she adds an extra inch to that of her natural stature. Then, whilst on her toes, and as if in harmony with the increasing intensity of the moment, she readily submits to her desires. As the fires of passion stake their claim, she releases the last of her inhibitions and kisses him with a fervour that knows no bounds.

Fearing that any distraction, however small, may break the spell, he resists the need to adjust his clothing but, instead, tenses for a moment whilst a slight, but not wholly unpleasant, feeling of discomfort is experienced as his manhood reacts naturally and autonomously in response to such close and sensual contact.

She, too, feels nature's response as their bodies remain clasped; and whilst embracing a feeling of excitement and expectation, she senses the last fragile strands of self-control snapping as the pulse of raw and natural animal instinct threatens to override all acceptable rules of behaviour. With her somewhat licentious desires brought to the fore, her heart pounds out its rhythm, and as her breath is drawn from deep within, she prepares herself for the eruption which will, like the antithesis of the lull that awaits the oncoming storm, precede her willing submission to the most final act of her infidelity.

The moment is shattered!

With the glare from its headlamps illuminating all that stands before it, a vehicle glides into the car park.

Releasing each other, as if they had been simultaneously stung by the thorns of guilt, they instinctively turn their heads away from the unwelcome intrusion. Their faces, ill-defined whilst veiled within the shadows of the night, desperately reflect the hope that they have not been seen — but if they have, then at least it would have been with insufficient clarity for them to have been properly recognized.

The car draws to a halt.

As he wraps his hand around hers and gazes into her eyes, he, with the added enchantment of a playful beam in his own, wills her to join him in maintaining the discretion of silence.

Intuitively, she reads the allusion, and with a hushed and nervous giggle, she blankets her lips — discretion is thus assured.

Looking down, and clearly unimpressed by yet another, untimely, disturbance, the owl releases his grip, and with there being nothing to be gained from an exhibition, or an utterance, of complaint, he pushes his bulk away from the branch. Then, with a powerful down-stroke of his wings, he takes to the air and melts into the anonymity of the night.

Chapter 2

The pair, hushed and inconspicuous, watch with interest as the car's engine is silenced and its lights extinguished.

It is only now, when their eyes have been able to readjust to a darkness which has already replaced the dazzling and intrusive glare, that they can focus their attention on the identity of this late arrival.

Although it is night, the unmistakable blue dome which is mounted on the white moonlit roof of the Ford Escort saloon identifies the newcomer as being the local constable.

He is of the old fashioned ilk — a country copper — the type of man who knows his manor inside out. He is also the type of man who can feel the draw of a free cup of tea and, if he's lucky, a slice of homemade cake, from more than half a mile away.

However, careful to maintain an air of impartiality, he has always tried to ensure that he remains professional, and, accordingly, he has not allowed himself to be seen to be *too chummy* with anyone on the *patch*. After all, he is not one to be the instigator of gossip; instead, his preference is to listen to the idle chatter of others and, whilst doing so, gather and sift through each snippet of information — whether it is likely to be of immediate significance or otherwise — before discreetly storing it away for some future reference.

Baptized Robert John Russell, the moniker of *Shep* had attached itself to him a couple of years after he had enlisted in the Constabulary.

His old section-sergeant, having seen how he had seemed to routinely *round up his flock* whenever they had started to get out of hand, and, also, how he would pursue an investigation tenaciously — and in a manner which was akin to that of an old mongrel doggedly, gnawing at a well-chewed bone — he had likened him to a trusty old sheepdog, and so, he had dubbed him *Shep*.

With only thirty-nine paydays remaining before the scheduled date for his retirement, he has no wish to rock the boat. And so, as far as he is concerned, a city posting at this stage of his service would be about as welcome as a kick in the groin.

This is definitely not on any *bucket list* of things to do before *he* retires.

In truth, all he wants is to be able to continue to enjoy the *fruits of his labours* whilst being left, unhindered, within his post as the parish's *resident bobby*.

After all, more often than not, he is free to execute his own form of rural policing; a style which successfully combines the use of modern technology with good, old-fashioned values, rather than just simply replacing the one with the other. The thing is that, although not always achieved by complying with the approved, but ever-changing, procedures of the times, his ways have brought a much-envied tranquillity to his country patch.

He is also a man who has, throughout his service, possessed the ability to empathize with the victims of burglary and violence; for, as a young child, he had experienced the terror of witnessing the presence of two masked figures, stealthily and systematically, foraging around his darkened home whilst they had relieved his sleeping family of their possessions. Having been frozen with fear, he had been unable to utter a sound and so he had sounded no alarm.

Understandable?

Of course it was, but, all the same, the guilt of his silence remains with him even to this very day.

Despising the predatory ways of the parasites and lowlifes who burgle and rob, he has made their kind a career-long target for his attention. What's more, he makes no secret of the fact that he has both the resolve and the power to hound them off his patch.

However, the seriousness of his calling does not prevent him from maintaining a hint of rebellious independence, which — when combined with a somewhat dry and subtle sense of humour — does not make him altogether popular with the hierarchy. Once, when told, somewhat pointedly, by his superintendent that the recently-appointed *chief constable* did not like his officers to have beards, he made it known that he would be happy to shave his off — but *only* when the incumbent of the top post publicly declared it to be compulsory for each officer to have one.

This did not go down well at the time, but then, the very fact that he had remained in his post suggests that the message may not have been passed on.

Normally Shep works alone, but sometimes, as is the case tonight, he has been given — or in his view, been saddled with — the company of a young and enthusiastic special constable. These *hobby-bobbies*, as he and his colleagues often discourteously label members of the unpaid volunteer force, are well-meaning, but their presence can sometimes interfere with his routine and, subsequently, disrupt his well-established, on-duty social life.

His tea-stops have always been jealously guarded and they are not willingly shared with his colleagues — be they paid or otherwise.

It's late!

"Come on, Sunset, I reckons 'tis time to show the flag!"

He opens the door and hauls himself out from the sunken and well-worn driver's seat.

Being in *shirt-sleeve order*, his body succumbs to a shiver as it reacts to the substantial differential in temperature.

The long, summer evenings have gradually, but noticeably, given way to the ever-lengthening nights, which will, over the next month or so, usher in the bitter winds of winter.

In contrast to the warmth of the day, the air now carries the subtle hint of a chill; a stark reminder that in just a few short weeks the broad-leafed sycamores and the majestic horse chestnuts will compete with one another as they prepare to display a belated, yet glorious, exhibition of warm, earthy, russet shades before releasing their fruit and stripping naked in preparation for their long, winter rest.

With one hand pushed into his pocket and the other clutching the radio, he ambles towards the main entrance with Sunset following, dutifully, at his heels.

As they approach the building, neither of them can fail to spot the courting couple who are, albeit unsuccessfully, trying to remain discreet whilst hidden within the shadows.

Shep acknowledges their presence with nothing more than that of a polite, but knowing, "Good evening."

The *special*, being vaguely familiar with both parties, does not wish to be seen to be rude, so with just a smile and a nod, he echoes the civility of his mentor. There is no need for the officers to hesitate or, for that matter, to make conversation, and so, without further ado, they continue towards the entrance.

Peering in through the small wired windows of the double doors, it is clear that the hall is packed and the bar staff are busy.

As is normal for this type of event, it is run by the licensee of the local hostelry and, as such, it is customary for a representative of the local Constabulary to show a presence.

This serves not only to be a sign of good community liaison, but it also acts as a gentle reminder to all those present that, although they are away from the familiar surroundings of the Stone Cross Inn, the celebration of the joining of two young people in matrimony does not negate the necessity for the guests and bar-staff alike to adhere to the licensing and *drink-drive* legislation.

The businessmen and the less energetic of the two newly-merged families chat — some with their ties and jackets discarded, and some, as if trapped within the traditions of always having to maintain an air of politesse when in the public eye, remain fully clad in their suits.

There is also the younger and somewhat sportier group, who, whilst still celebrating the success of their team, enthusiastically discuss the two goals which had been instrumental in maintaining the *Grecians'* positive start to the season. The result has brought joy to both fair-weather and diehard supporters alike, and even though it is early days, there are those who already dare to think the unthinkable, and that is ... promotion!

Others, who have no interest in the ritual of following the fortunes of the local league football team, prefer to discuss business and the attributes and performances of their latest company cars. Wedding or not — they will not dance. After all, where there are people, there are potential clients, and for them to miss out on a valuable opportunity to put out feelers for a future deal would be, to say the least, rather wasteful.

The men who do make the effort to take to the floor are, in the main, the semi-inebriated young, who, like parading peacocks, appear to be advertising their availability to *any* woman who cares to take notice.

There are those of middle-age who, with their inhibitions having tumbled in proportion to the quantity of alcohol consumed, dance with arms and legs firing randomly and in all directions — actions which are much to the annoyance of their wives and their offspring.

Then there are the ladies and teenage girls who, being away from the practicalities of having to be clothed in the earthy garb of everyday rural life, are delighted to have this rare opportunity to air some of the treasured contents of their wardrobes and their, seldom opened, jewellery caskets. Gleefully displaying their bracelets and necklaces as adornments to their beautiful dresses, they move rhythmically with the variance of music which has been taken from the decades of the past and the so-called new-romanticism of the present.

Those who abstain from such vigorous activity catch up on the family gossip — reliving the scandals and rumours of the past yet, sometimes, not too sure if they recall things *exactly* in the manner in which they are now being related.

There is the well-spoken lady who — as her cheeks glow redder by the minute as they reflect the measure of her steady intake of Chianti — uncharacteristically makes eyes at, and consequently embarrasses, the male consorts of her nieces and daughters.

Her husband, glimpsing her behaviour from across the hall, shakes his head, then gives a wry and knowing smile before ignoring her and continuing with his socializing.

Confident in his assumption that it would be unlikely for her to be the object of desire for these young bucks, he is not particularly concerned.

Sat quietly at the fringe of the dance floor, a young bridesmaid, still wrapped in the taffeta trappings of the ceremony, struggles to stay awake as she snuggles up close to her equally tired grandmother. Under normal circumstances she would have already been home and tucked up in her bed, but today is an exception. After all, tomorrow is Sunday. She will be able to slumber undisturbed and then, once recharged, she will be able to waken in her own time. With cheer and vigour, she can then embrace whatever the new day has in store.

Conscious of the fact that their presence, along with the purpose of their visit, could be misinterpreted by minds which have been clouded by the effects of alcohol, the officers are careful to maintain a semblance of discretion.

Whilst they make their way around the dance floor, they can see that, with the almost non-stop pouring of drinks and the taking of cash, the barmen and barmaids are, without doubt, earning their wages.

As they near the bar, Shep focuses his attention on the licensee.

He is standing at one end of the bar, and whilst, somewhat robotically, wiping dry the freshly-cleansed beer glass which is clasped firmly in his left hand, he appears to be in a world of his own as he stares out and across the dance floor.

It seems evident by the direction in which John, the licensee, has fixed his focus, that he may well have become captivated by the presence of such an abundance of attractive young women who, figuratively speaking, have let their hair down.

Spotting the arrival of the officers, he is jolted from his musings, and on seeing the expressions on both of their faces, he guesses that they may well have read or, for that matter, misread, the nature of the thoughts which had been lingering behind the wander of his eyes. But still, without the slightest hint of shame or guilt within his smile, he averts his focus and concentrates on them.

"Good evening, gentlemen. So, what can I do for you?" Noting the uniforms, he adds, "I take it 'tis business then?"

With the accompaniment of a nod, Shep, in his characteristically slow, yet precise, Devon drawl, confirms the licensee's assumption. "Yep, you'm quite right, John, 'tis just routine. So, unless 'e's gonna be telling me different, then them's nothin' for 'e to be worrying yourself about."

He looks across towards the revellers and then back to the bar. "I trust all's going well?"

"Yep. All's fine. No problems at all. The bride and the groom have just gone, and they are, as we speak, on their way to the airport. Then they'll be off to the sun and the sandy beaches of the Med. It's all right for some. Anyway, do you boys fancy a drink? A coffee, maybe?"

Shep wavers for a moment as he glances at his colleague.

"No ... Thank you for the offer though, but we'm still on duty. Another time, maybe."

He sees no point in breaking the rules, especially with Sunset as a witness. Although the youngster is known to him, in as much that he has worked with him before, his discretion has not, as yet, been tested and, what's more, Shep has no intention of testing it now.

As Shep steers his eyes towards those who are just simply enjoying the party, he, with a somewhat non-too-soft touch of subtlety, makes it known that he did, indeed, observe the way in which the licensee had looked at the womenfolk.

"I must say 'tis nice to see all they young 'uns enjoying 'emselves. What d'you reckon, John? I mean, now that them's all done up in their finery an' all I reckons some of 'em's scrubbed up pretty good!"

Before John has a chance to either agree or to differ, Joe — the son of Jack Hardy, a local farmer, whose family can be traced back as having lived in and around the village for at least a couple of centuries — interrupts. "I's sorry to butt-in, John, but I was just wondering whether you've seen Lucy on her travels?"

The licensee, as if he needs to confirm to himself that he is not mistaken before giving his reply, scans the faces in the hall. "No, I'm sorry Joe … I don't think I have. Not recently that is. Mind you, if I sees her, then I'll be sure to tell her that you'm looking for her."

There's a look of desperation in Joe's face; a look which suggests that he's been searching for his girlfriend a little too long for comfort. What's more, he appears to be at a loss as to where he should start looking next.

As he turns away from the bar, his eyes linger as they meet and then fix on those of the two officers.

Shep, having overheard the interaction between the two men, is not slow to echo the essence of the licensee's response. So, with little more than a shake of his head, he answers Joe's question in silence and before it has even been posed.

Joe, with rather more than just a hint of his disappointment being revealed in his expression, quietly expresses his thanks, and then, without further delay, he moves off and into the throng, so as to resume his search.

Sunset, appearing to be somewhat bemused as he watches him move away, turns back towards his colleague and, daring to question the inference of Shep's response to Joe's enquiry, casts his line. "I don't know her particularly well but I'm pretty sure that could have been her outside. You know, I think that was her with that Marcus Warren, guy. What d'you think?"

"Well, maybe it was her an' maybe it wasn't. But then again, even if it were her, I reckons that sometimes what one knows, an' what one sees, 'tis often best kept to oneself. You see, bu'y, there's nothing to be gained in us stoking up fires which don't need to be stoked. So, whatever needs to be found out, will be found out in due course and I's pretty sure it'll be without us meddling" Shep pauses, then continues. "Anyway, we'm done our duty. The flag's bin flown an' I guess 'twil soon be time for us to be clocking off. So bu'y … with that in mind, I reckons we'm best be on our way. Don't you?"

The look on the face of the *special* suggests that he is not altogether happy with the decision for them to leave. After all, if Joe finds the two *lovebirds* together, then there could well be trouble. Now *that*, he believes, is something which *they*, as police officers, are meant to prevent.

But then, Shep's decision has been made … and it is final. So, without wavering, he turns back to the licensee.

"Well, John, I reckons all's in order 'ere. So, I reckons we'm gonna be making our way back to the nick … so, I'll be bidding you, goodnight."

"Yep," he replies, and then adds, "I'll see you again. Oh, and gentlemen … have a good night yourselves."

Having returned to his duties, he takes an awaiting customer's order.

The two men in blue, taking care to maintain a look of no more than that of routine, make their way around the perimeter of the dance floor and, pausing only to nod politely as they acknowledge the presence of those who eye them, head out of the hall and into the car park.

"Shep?"

"What now, bu'y?"

"That John bloke … The barman."

"Go on. What about him?"

"Don't you think it's a bit unhealthy? I mean, the way a man of his age was eyeing up the young women?"

"Look, bu'y. Even I can admire a Bentley, but then that don't mean I's gonna wanna nick it, do it? Anyway … maybe 'tis not the look which is in the eye of the admirer which 'tis important — I reckons, 'tis more the look in the eye of 'e who needs to turn away when 'e's been spotted that shows up the guilt."

Sunset hesitates before responding. "Yeah … I suppose so. Maybe, you're right."

Although uncertain as to whether Shep has, indeed, made the right judgement, he has decided to save on having an argument and has, thus, decided to *let it ride*.

"There's no *maybe* about it — I's right … and that's all there is to it. Now then … unless you know something I don't about the man, then I reckons 'tis best we leave it there!"

Sunset nods, and having been admonished, decides to say nothing. The matter is closed; from now on, he will keep his own counsel.

As they arrive at the vehicle, Shep stops, then glances back towards the hall.

Eyeing the young couple who are still making the best of the seclusion of the shadows, he notes how they, whilst engrossed in the sensuality of their reciprocal exploration, fail to notice the presence of either he or his colleague.

Shaking his head with disappointment, he is clearly saddened, but also resigned as to how the acceptable ways of modern-day youth would have been considered to have been totally inappropriate in the days of his own adolescence.

He is also well aware of the fact that it will be only a matter of time before Joe catches up with Lucy and discovers her, still rapt in the excitement of exploring her new-found interest.

He does not condone acts of infidelity, and, with this in mind, he, uncharacteristically, opts to go against his professional judgement. He will, by his absence alone, permit a window of opportunity for the forces of natural justice to find their own way. Even though he feels the pangs of guilt as he pushes his crime-prevention duties to one side, he is resolute in his decision, and so, without further ado, he hastens their departure.

"Let's be off … 'else there's bound to be some strife which, if we's not careful, will be keeping us from our homes."

Sunset looks at him rather quizzically, and then, with just an edge of protest in his voice, asks of the older man, "But what if there *is* trouble?"

"Well … Then they can give us a call! You see bu'y … even out here, them's got such a thing as a telephone, an' likewise, we've got this." He taps the radio handset, and his questioner is, accordingly, silenced.

But then, Sunset's look of disbelief, having not gone entirely unnoticed, fires the older man to continue.

"Look, bu'y …" Shep explains in his sage-like manner, "… 'tis a fact that dust settles best without the aid of a broom …" He pauses, and then, allowing Sunset sufficient time to absorb the wisdom of his words, he continues. "I reckons there be no need for us to be gettin' involved when we'm not needed."

Again, he allows a moment for his words to be absorbed. "What I means to say is … 'tis just a splash of water that does the settlin'. So, maybe … you could be prayin' for a bit of rain … I's always thought that a good Devonshire downpour 'tis better than twenty bobbies when it comes to encouraging people to go back to their homes. So, bu'y … you pray for a bit o' rain, an' then that'll be doin' the trick."

Somewhat pensively, they stare into the clear, starlit sky.

It is blatantly clear that neither of them will have the need to seek out the talents of a weatherman to help them deduce that the signs of an imminent arrival of precipitation are, without any doubt, nonexistent.

Sunset glances back to the older man and waits for further enlightenment. There is none. Shep has elected to say nothing, and with just a shake of his head, he acknowledges the irrelevance of his wise words, which have already dispersed into the oblivion of the night.

"Oh well …" He jolts himself back into the reality of everyday parlance, "… no doubt them 'ill sort 'emselves out. Come on bu'y. As I says, 'twil soon be time to book off, so I reckons, that maybe, 'tis best we go."

With the nonchalance of a shrug, he opens the car door and drops into the driver's seat.

With the turn of the key the engine fires.

Quietly, but purposefully, they head out of the car park. With the redden glow of activated brake lights having momentarily illuminated the trees, they turn to the right before accelerating off through the long and winding country lanes.

Chapter 3

Whilst the music plays on and the dancing continues, Joe canvasses both his family and his friends for knowledge as to the whereabouts of his girlfriend. Standing tall, and with a partially consumed pint of lager in one hand, he surveys the sea of faces.

As he scans the hall, he eyes a pair of teenage girls who are fast disappearing behind the closing door of what is rather quaintly referred to as being … *the ladies room.*

Knowing that this is the one area of the building in which, by the fact of his gender alone, he is barred from entering and has, therefore, not searched, he wonders if this may be the place in which Lucy is hidden.

Maybe, he supposes, she has consumed a tad too much of the alcohol and is now suffering the inevitable consequences of her actions. So, bearing the possibility in mind, he deliberates as to whether or not he should break the rules of etiquette and enter this space, which is, by convention, prohibited to men.

He edges his way closer towards the door, and then, with a clear and uninterrupted view, he hovers and watches. If only to distract himself from the passing of time, he finds himself speculating as to why so many young women seem to feel the need to have a friend to escort them to the *ladies.*

Maybe, he surmises, it is because it is guaranteed to be man-free and is, therefore, a place where young ladies can be free to discuss topics which are not meant for the ears of the opposite sex. Of course, he will never know. Besides, he does not consider his wonderings to be of any more significance than that of an idle distraction.

All he wants to know is whether or not Lucy is behind that door.

After a few drawn-out minutes, the girls emerge, their grins suggesting there having been a juiciness within the content of their tête-à-tête.

With still no sign of Lucy, he approaches and asks if there is anyone else who is yet to come out.

With the insistence that there is, indeed, no one occupying the ladies room, his anxiety intensifies.

Purposefully, he resumes his search elsewhere, and as he becomes evermore frustrated at having to squeeze and push his way past the jumble of uncoordinated and intoxicated dancing obstructions, his concerns rapidly become weighted with annoyance. He has no time for pleasantries. So, disregarding the need for civility, he bulldozes his way through the crowd as he seeks her out from amid the mass of faces which fill the hall.

Glimpsing Lucy's mother standing in the midst of a group of her family and friends and obviously engaged in the politeness of conversation, he pauses.

Ah! She'll know where her is, he whispers as he deviates from the directness of his quest and makes a beeline towards her.

The slight bulge where her dress stretches tightly against her tummy is barely noticed. Although she is in her late thirties, her unexpected pregnancy has given her a healthy radiance which, to the uninformed, may well suggest that she is far younger than the actuality of her years.

He is not certain as to the actual date on which Lucy's sibling is due to make an appearance, but even though he is lacking experience in such matters, he is of the opinion that there will still be a few months of development before she can no longer claim to be an only child.

The passing of time has not been as kind to Geoff, Gina's husband of twenty-eight months, for the excesses of his so-called good life have clearly taken their toll. Reddened and somewhat puffy, his pockmarked complexion reflects a lifestyle of overindulgence. His penchant for the high-calorie cuisines of pub-meal fare, along with an excessive consumption of both spirits and beer, have left him with a haggard look which belies the fact that he is, with some three years of separation between their respective ages, the younger of the pair.

Together, however, they appear to be content and happy, no doubt excited by the advancing prospect of a new addition to their family.

As Joe approaches, her eyes meet his. She smiles.

Noticing that his returning smile is forced, short and obviously unsuccessful in its attempt to disguise a deeper concern, her expression becomes more questioning.

"Have you seen Lucy?" His tone, although polite, conveys an undercurrent of urgency.

"Oh, umm… Yes. I'm sure I saw her. It must have been a just a few minutes ago … Yes … I'm certain I did."

Her disjointed reply, along with a look of concern as she attempts to locate the familiar face of her daughter amid the gathering of guests, suggests an element of self-doubt.

Suddenly, distracted by movement at the main entrance, he stops, and, with a sense of relief, he identifies the figure as being Lucy. "Hang fire … I think I've found her."

Satisfied and relieved that she has not disappeared without a trace, he relaxes, deposits his glass and then steps towards her.

His new-found sense of calm falls short as he notes the way in which she has, somewhat cagily, sidled into the main hall, having made her appearance from beyond the partially-opened doors.

His pace slows as he allows himself more time to observe.

Seeing that she has an excited yet restrained look about her, his trust begins to wane as a growing and uncomfortable uncertainty returns to the fore.

He stops and watches as she checks the faces across the hall.

Failing to see him, nor readily identifying anyone who might be sufficiently watchful to have noticed her return, she glances back at the doors from which she has just emerged.

Her cautious and secretive demeanour is again noted as she mouths her private message to an unseen *other*.

Unobtrusively, he continues to scrutinize her actions, whilst she focuses on the mysterious *other* who, frustratingly, remains hidden from view.

With a hint of self-consciousness, she waits ... and then, as if not wishing to betray anything which could shed light on her recent conduct, she attempts to remove any evidence of misdemeanour by discreetly palming away the rumpled creases from the lustrous fabric of her dress, whilst at the same time, readjusting the fall of its skirt.

With her words apparently answered, she takes a deep breath and, adopting an air of composure, she turns about before nonchalantly stepping into the fringes of the main hall.

Having allowed the spring-loaded doors to release and then gently close behind her, she moves further inwards.

His desire to approach her is strong, but he waits — evermore intrigued as to the identity of the recipient of her words.

Catching sight of Julia, her close friend and confidante, she immediately, and with some purpose, propels herself towards her. As she approaches, their eyes meet, and without stopping, she ushers her friend to join her as she hurries towards the sanctuary of the ladies room.

Detecting further movement at the edge of his vision, he refocuses.

The main doors have opened. With an air of smugness, edged with more than just a hint of guilt stretched across his face, in walks Marcus.

Joe's eyes fixate as he watches him strut around the edge of the dance floor and then join up with a group of young men from the village.

Marcus, unmistakably on a high, laughs loudly as one of the group tells a tale — speaking as much with the animated movement of his hands and body as by the actual use of words.

His periodic glances across the hall towards the ladies room do not go unnoticed.

Joe's festering suspicions take on a spurt of growth as his thoughts race through the reasons as to why there should be a need for Lucy to have acted with such caution and guilt.

He wrestles with the rush of adrenalin which fuels his muscles as he consciously, and in order to disguise the true extent of his anger, makes an effort to control his outward appearance.

Marcus glances across the floor, and as he becomes aware of the icy attentiveness which radiates towards him, he is abruptly dismounted from his position of contentment.

Their eyes momentarily lock, and his complexion flushes with culpable embarrassment.

Alert to the likelihood of a violent confrontation, his heartbeat quickens, and, whilst he feels his new-found confidence swiftly ebbing away, he prays that Joe will fail to become aware as to the true scale of attention that has been paid to his girlfriend.

The foolhardiness of any test to Joe's temperament is fully understood; for a pen-pusher in the accounts department of the local agricultural merchants store against an aggrieved rugby playing herdsman does not suggest a close contest.

Even though there are no records of any violent incidents involving Joe, his fitness and strength is well known to all within the village. What's more, it is more than evident, through both his occupation and his prowess on the sports field, that he would always be more than a match for anything that the likes of Marcus could throw at him.

Submissively, he drops his gaze, and, adopting the adage of discretion being the better part of valour, he assumes a position of anonymity by trying to remain hidden within the sanctuary and company of his chattering friends.

Distracted by the sudden emergence of the two girls, Joe, determinedly and single-mindedly, refocuses his attention.

As he approaches them, he breaks his silence, and, raising his voice in order to compete with the rhythmic blast of the disco, he demands, rather accusingly, "Where've you been?"

Julia steps away. She has just been made privy to Lucy's actions and has no wish to be pulled into the quagmire of an embarrassing row.

"To the loo!" Her reply is abrupt.

"No!" he snaps, before following on with a clarification of his questioning. "Before that!"

"I can't hear you!" she responds, whilst cupping her hands over her ears, suggesting that the volume of the music is too great.

He needs an answer, and as she turns towards Julia, he grasps her by the arm and pulls her back.

"We need to talk!" With the volume of his voice increasing and the severity within his look, it is obvious that there is no room for refusal.

She nods in reluctant compliance, and, with a hint of nervousness, she permits him to lead her by the hand and towards the exit.

Conscious that she does not, as is normal, allow her hand to grip his in return, he knows that all is far from well.

Once in the car park and away from prying onlookers, he questions her with a progressive and inquisitional intensity. Her feeling of discomfort increases as she becomes subjected to a *grilling* which leaves her in no doubt as to the detail of his earlier observations and, more significantly, the suspicions that had ensued.

He wants an explanation, yet she makes every effort to avoid having to give him one.

"What were you doing with that Marcus bloke?" he demands.

"Nothing!" Again, as her vision blurs with the tears which have started to well up and engulf her eyes, she lies.

His questioning has pushed her into a corner and the prospects for a successful escape are few.

Assertively, she quickly changes tack and turns on him.

"How dare you talk to me like that!" This is not a question, it's a warning.

Although she knows her earlier indiscretion was, at best, an error of judgement which, incidentally, she is already in the process of regretting, she realizes that if she were to implement the old adage of *attack being the best form of defence,* then she may well be able to create a situation where she will be able to wriggle out of her predicament and, thereby, evade having to be entirely truthful.

Before he has a chance to regain his position, she fires another round. "You just don't trust me! If I knew you were going to be jealous and possessive every time I left your sight, then I'd have dumped you months ago!"

"I's sorry, *Luce,* I's just tellin' you what I saw, that's all."

His apologetic explanation suggests that he is already on the defensive. The tactic has worked.

She has the advantage, and so the interrogation stops.

She continues. "It's too late for that … It's over … It's finished!"

As she speaks, she knows that, deep inside, she does not mean it, but it will stop any immediate resumption of any oppressive questioning.

It's certainly a risk, but she is quite confident that it will only be a matter of time before there will be a healing to this glitch in their relationship, and she will have at least succeeded in evading having to divulge the truth.

"Look … I think we should take some time out. That's all."

"Time out? What d'you mean by that?" His voice becomes raised as he tries to wrestle with his confusion.

"You know exactly what I mean."

"Do I? Explain. Why d'you need time out? What's going on?"

Feeling no need, nor desire, to give a reply, she pushes past him and then marches back into the hall.

"You'm just bein' a bitch, maid!" His comment hits home before she has a chance to walk far enough away so as to be out of earshot.

Halted by the insolence in his words, she turns back, and with an irrepressible rush of anger, she glowers at him. Then, turning on a heel, and with a heightened purpose to her step, she strides away as she makes her way back into the hall.

"Nobody calls me a bitch and gets away with it!"

He senses that he will have to pay for the insult, and knowing that she has not the patience to exact retribution in accordance with the maxim of *revenge being a dish best served cold*, he is more than certain that she will ensure that the response is nigh on instant.

Whilst still in a state of confusion and shock, he stalls; then, revitalised with a sense of urgency, he moves forward and rapidly gains ground on her as she wends her way through the writhing throng. He watches intently as she obviously has a strategy in mind.

Suddenly, with an added burst of speed, she puts a little more distance between them both and then continues, single-mindedly, towards the unsuspecting, and otherwise preoccupied, Marcus. Marching directly and resolutely towards her target, she pauses; then as if to confirm that Joe's full attention has been fully gained, she glances back through the assemblage of dancing revellers.

Obstinate in her focus, she moves forward — the unwavering fix of her gaze firmly planted on her unsuspecting quarry.

They meet … and then, with both hands, she wrenches him away from the triviality of his gossiping with his friends and pulls him sharply towards her before kissing him firmly and ardently on the lips.

Stunned, yet pleasured, by this public show of intimacy, he, without objection, submits to the sensuality and the delights of this unexpected *assault*. Savouring the moment, he glances over and past her shoulder. Then, having eyed the piercing and unwavering glare of a man who is so obviously struggling to restrain the furnace which rages within, he freezes.

Marcus's joy dissipates as speedily as it had arrived; the display of passion was not a show which had been put on for him … it was just a means to ignite a fervent reaction from another. He tries in desperation to push her away.

Joe is not only saddened, injured and wronged but, additionally, he is humiliated in front of his friends and his family. This steady, easy-going man-of-the-land is seething. He has moved far beyond the state of jealousy and is now hunting for retribution.

Forging forward, he pushes through the horde of celebrants, while rapidly closing in on his target. As the gap shortens, he is soon within arm's reach. Taking it on himself to physically and personally separate the pair, he grabs Marcus by the collar. Then, dismissing the presence of the group of young men as being of little significance, he pulls him away and drags him through the crowd, barging past those who fail to make clear his way.

Blinded with rage and a desire for vengeance, he is oblivious to the feelings of those whose faces contort with anger and disgust as he forces them aside. His eyes — cold and clinical — are devoid of even the slightest remnants of compassion; for when he takes a beast to slaughter, there is no time for feelings of guilt — nor is there room for the indulgences of sentimentality.

Yanking the doors wide open, he hauls his rival out and into the car park, then, without ceremony, hurls him to the ground.

As the doors close behind him, the light which had flooded out and across the tarmac has diminished; but, with the glow of the full moon and the remaining illumination from the windows, he can still clearly see the look of terror etched on Marcus's face.

The light brightens as the doors are re-opened and they are joined by those who are concerned as to the welfare of the accused ... along with those who, somewhat morbidly, wish to witness this potentially brutal episode of unscheduled entertainment.

Marcus tries, unsuccessfully, to stagger back up and on to his feet.

With just one hand, Joe grabs hold of him by the shirt front, and then, with a jerk, he lifts him from the ground and drags him off to the side of the building and shoves him violently up against the wall.

He leans forward and, whilst staring into Marcus's eyes and with their noses almost touching, he demands to be told exactly what has been going on between the two of them.

Marcus is afraid ... He is very afraid!

Feeling the breaths of Joe's rage gusting against his face, he is now fully aware of what is meant by the words, *hovering between the devil and the deep blue sea.*

The dilemma for him is straightforward — if he tells the truth he will be punished, but then, if he lies, then the consequences will be just the same.

In an attempt to wheedle his way out of the situation, he adopts the defence of having diminished responsibility and declares, "I think maybe I's had a bit too much to drink ... Look, I didn't mean anything by it — it was a mistake ... a big mistake. Please ... Believe me when I tell you ... I's sorry."

"A mistake? What was a mistake?"

"I've told you I'm sorry. Let's just forget it, shall we?"

"You'm not answering me — so, I'll ask you again ... What exactly did you mean when you said it was a mistake?"

He hesitates, but then, knowing that he has no option other than to be up-front about it all, he takes a deep breath and continues. "Okay, I'll tell you … It was … Lucy and me. Now I know I was wrong … and I shouldn't have done it. But, if it helps, then believe me when I say, I really am sorry."

Albeit sheepishly and without detail, he has admitted his trespass; but then, having reassessed the look on the face of his adversary and thereby realising the potential for disaster, he wonders if he would have been wiser to have denied the whole thing.

He is becoming increasingly uneasy as he, yet again, glances into Joe's eyes as if he is in a desperate search to find even the slightest sign of forgiveness.

The returned glare is measured, cold and mean, and the signs which are sought are nonexistent. With an image of the predatory stare of a *bull shark* gripping his mind, he — like a rabbit blinded by the glare of a searchlight — freezes as he prepares for his impending doom.

Suddenly, the instinct for self-preservation cuts in. And, as a natural and subconscious sign of his willingness to submit, he averts his gaze — no doubt, in the forlorn hope that his decision will not exacerbate his already precarious situation.

Appealing for clemency, he, yet again, offers his apologies. "I'm sorry."

"Sorry for what?"

There is no reply.

"Now … You best be telling me exactly what you two were up to?"

The eyes of the wronged have narrowed; a natural mechanism which, in anticipation of any potential violent conflict, instinctively protects them from suffering injury.

Marcus knows that he is unlikely to be believed, but, nevertheless, he attempts to emphasize his innocence.

"Nothing — I promise you … nothing happened!"

Joe stares intently at him as he waits for more.

"Honestly … I've told you … nothing happened."

Marcus's voice rises both in volume and pitch as he tries, without success, to convince his assailant.

Still gripping his victim by the front of his shirt, Joe loses his patience and fires his fist hard and powerfully into his belly.

Marcus buckles as his diaphragm gives, forcing the air up and out of his lungs.

Accentuating every word, Joe insists, "Now … I thinks you'm telling me porkies. So … I'll give you one more chance to tell me exactly what's been going on!"

The lack of an immediate reply suggests there may be a need for further encouragement.

Joe pauses. Again, he smashes him heavily against the wall before following through with another forceful, breath-stopping punch into his stomach.

Winded, in pain and with tears filling his eyes, Marcus squeals out his response, "Nothing's been going on — I promise you!"

Impatient with the sound of whimpering, and clearly no longer anticipating a full and frank confession, the disabling effects of Marcus having a broken jaw, and the consequential loss of his facility to speak, is no longer to be considered to be an issue of any significance. So, yet again, Joe pulls back his fist and — without even the slightest of hints of him having any feelings of compassion — smashes it, soundly and determinedly, into the face of his pathetic adversary.

The muddle of impassioned voices which noisily urge him to stop are disregarded as being little more than an irrelevance. As he, hard-heartedly, ignores their pleas, he, once more, pulls back his fist in readiness to repeat the action.

From behind him, and in an attempt to hold back and prevent the strike, a pair of hands grasp tightly at his right bicep. Keeping his attention firmly on the object of his rage, he tries to wrench himself away from the sharpness of the fingers and thumbs which insistently squeeze and dig into his muscle. The hands are irritatingly persistent in their refusal to release their grip, so, without warning, and without looking to identify the source of this intrusion, he blindly swings his arm backwards and smashes the irritant in the face with the back of his forearm.

Instantly, he sees the look of shock and horror on the face of Marcus.

The shouting and screaming of the gathering stops momentarily as they are stunned into a worrying silence.

Something is seriously wrong!

He turns his head and looks behind.

Aghast at the vision before him, he is sickened by his actions; actions which he knows have resulted in the most terrible of outcomes.

Shocked and motionless, he absorbs the sight of Lucy clutching her face whilst she lies, crumpled and in pain on the hard and unforgiving tarmac.

Releasing his grasp on Marcus, he dismissively pushes him away as he turns his full attention towards his injured girlfriend.

Stunned and bewildered, she lies silent; then, as she starts to regain her bearings and the pain begins to filter through, her tears begin to flow.

Whatever her misdemeanour, she certainly did not deserve to be struck by him; apologetic, appalled and visibly devastated at the result of his actions, he crouches beside her.

Gina, horrified and distraught by the incident, rushes to her aid. And then, with a venomous rage fuelling her actions, she shoves him away; for it is her, not him, who should be the one to fulfil the role to protectively console her injured daughter.

Though visibly concerned and full of apologies, he backs off and edges away.

Suddenly, a voice shouts out from the enlarging crowd.

"Someone! Quickly! Get an ambulance and call the police!"

Joe has never caused any trouble in his life, and with the thought alone of him being locked up in a bleak and cold police cell, he is filled with terror.

Although he is strong in both body and mind, he has, like many a proud man, his own *Achilles heel*. For him it is a fear: a fear of confinement.

As a young child, and whilst he had been playing alone in the largest of the barns, he had tried to scale a stack of hay bales which had been piled up within. As the stack had moved and then collapsed, all but burying him beneath its bulk, he had become trapped by the legs. His cries, muffled by the weighty covering, had gone unheard, and it had been almost an hour before his absence had been noticed and he'd been rescued. The loneliness of that experience, which had been exacerbated by the fear of him not being found, even now, finds the occasion to haunt him in his nightmares.

He feels the grasp as someone tries to grab him.

He does not hit out this time. Instead, he shakes him off and, once free, runs across the car park towards his Land Rover.

He opens the door and fumbles as he pushes the keys into the ignition.

The ignition light is on. He flicks the key, and the engine fires. With the tapping of his foot on the pedal, the engine revs, thus, giving sufficient warning to those who may consider blocking his exit.

The way is cleared.

With the headlights blazing and on full beam, he accelerates off and out of the car park.

Lucy, tearful and in a state of shock, is grateful for the assistance of her mother as she walks gingerly from the car park and is guided into the light of the hall.

Her face is reddening, and although she does not recall putting her hand out to break her fall, it carries the evidence of the event … her left palm is grazed, bleeding and sore.

The state of her dress — having been torn and scuffed — serves only to compound her misery.

Marcus makes his faltering approach, but he is intercepted by her step-father. "Don't you dare go anywhere near her!"

"Is she all right?" he asks — with his own face cut and throbbing with pain.

"You've caused enough trouble tonight, so I think you ought to do us all a favour and shove off!"

"Go!" Another voice joins in from the midst of those who have gathered.

Marcus looks at the source of the command and detects facial expressions that suggest he should move away before being physically forced to do so.

He has no stomach for further conflict.

Wisely and in anticipation of an excessive consumption of the local brew, he has left his vehicle at home. So, albeit with a tinge of reluctance, he stumbles his way out from the car park … homeward-bound.

With only his thoughts to accompany him, he staggers along the lonely Devon lane. The few lunar beams which have managed to break through the treetop canopy give little light, but although the shine is barely sufficient for him to make safe progress, he moves forward. As each step takes him farther from the illumination of the hall and its precincts, he increasingly permits himself to self-indulge on a journey along a path of unforgiving vengeance.

Allowing himself the luxury of a smile whilst he embraces his feelings of absolute privacy and solitude, he begins to feel the onset of a strange, inner satisfaction as he catches his thoughts which — as if echoing the menacing darkness of the forest that borders his route — are sinking, effortlessly, downwards and along a path which leads to the blackest and most sinister of depths.

Chapter 4

Shaken by the ferocity of the episode, she is left trembling and unable to walk unaided, and so, having gratefully accepted the offer of a supporting arm from her mother, she allows herself to be escorted across the crowded hall so as to find refuge within the privacy and calm of the ladies room.

This is the place where she is not only able to avoid the prying of the many, but also, where she can, with the assistance of her mother, gently and without hindrance, commence the delicate and somewhat painstaking task of washing away the grit which has become embedded within the grazes of her palm.

Standing in front of the mirror, she considers the extent of the damage to her dress, whilst her mother … with her hand cradling hers … tenderly but determinedly tweezes out the fragments which have stubbornly resisted being released by the steady flow of warm water.

As each minute particle is carefully removed, Lucy winces with the pain.

She is, without any doubt, distraught.

With the welling of tears reflecting the mixed emotions of both her hurt and her loss, she examines the soiled and torn, satiny sheen of the silken fabric. This was a dress which, only a few minutes earlier, had not only been luxurious to the touch but had also been faultless to the eye.

"It's ruined! It's completely ruined!"

Her words are not shouted out in an outburst of uncontrollable anger, but rather, they are spoken softly and with a mood of melancholic acceptance … thereby adding to the pathos of the moment. The heartbreaking fact is that whilst her contemporaries had whiled away their time on trivialities, she had worked hard in her role as a weekend sales assistant so as to save sufficient funds from her meagre earnings to have been able to afford to indulge in the purchase of this beautiful and stylish creation. But now, having put in more hours than she would care to count in order to make the purchase, she has been made aware as to how easily and quickly the rewards of her toil can go to waste. As she examines the damage, her thoughts start to race. She knows that her outward appearance of calm is in danger of erupting … and that she is on the verge of being catapulted into a state of irrepressible rage.

"Guess what?" She spits her words with a fury which could put the fear of God into the toughest of adversaries. "… He's not going to get away with this. I'm going to make sure he pays!"

"How do you mean … *you're going to make sure he pays?*"

Gina tries to remain calm as she awaits an answer, but there is no immediate response from her daughter. She tries again, this time with a change of tack towards trying to clarify any ambiguity within her statement. "To pay monetarily or punitively?"

Lucy snaps back, "What?"

"What I mean is … financially or—"

Midstream, she's interrupted as Lucy, having only just registered her question, replies, "Oh, I don't know! Maybe both. In fact, I think he deserves to pay in *every* way. Don't you?" Lucy's reply carries a sharpness which shows no sign of an impending sweetening.

"Yes … Maybe he does." Although, on the face of it, her answer suggests that she is in agreement, there is more than a touch of hesitation in her reply; so, in an attempt to douse the mounting flames of her daughter's rage, she adds. "But, I must say, when it comes to it, I don't think he really meant it. I mean, he didn't even know it was you, did he?"

Lucy is unconvinced. With the inherent traits of defiance cushioning her from having to accept any possibility of there being any truth in her mother's words, she listens in silence.

Endeavouring to prevent the opportunity for a furtherance of any conflict, Gina offers her help. "But still, if you wish, I can go 'round in the morning and see if he'll pay for it … if that's all right with you, that is?"

"There's no need!" she snaps, "I can sort him out on my own!"

Waking up to the fact that her mother is only doing what any caring mother would do — and that is to make every effort to give help — she pauses and then, with a conscious and almost apologetic softening of her tone, acknowledges the sincerity of the offer. "… But thank you anyway."

She is, in truth, always grateful for her mother's assistance, and although she is, at present, desperately trying to keep the lid on what could well be a *Vesuvial* eruption of rage, the thought of having to face Joe so soon after the event fills her with an overwhelming dread. Of course, she knows that, realistically, she cannot hide from him forever, and, as her father has advised so many times in the past, she must never be afraid to challenge her dragons; she must, with nothing less than that of an unwavering and confident gaze, stare deep into the oily blackness of their predatory eyes until they submit to her greater strength. Yes … although the temptation to delegate the task to her mother is great, she is in no doubt as to the fact that she must take her father's advice and then, once dealt with, walk away with her head held high.

"I suppose, if you like, I could go with you. Of course, I won't interfere … I'll just be there to give you a bit of moral support if it's needed, but then … only if that's what you'd like?" As her offer is being deliberated on and before there is a chance for her daughter to give a negative response, she continues. "And, if — I'm sorry, I mean … and *when* he pays for it, then you and me will just have to force ourselves to trawl around the shops and get something really special for you to wear. How does that sound?"

With the reward of some retail therapy in the offing, she starts to feel the gradual easing of her distress — and, thus, having now begun to put some distance between her and the shock of the episode, she reflects on how her mother can always be relied on to rein in an uncomfortable and distressful situation and then place it firmly under her control.

"That sounds good, thank you." Lucy clearly finds the idea of looking for something new an attractive prospect, and so, with a confirmatory nod and the welcome return of a sparkle to her eye, she augments her response with a broad and engaging smile.

Whether it's down to her natural equanimity, or whether it is merely due to the almost musical intonation of her soothing Welsh accent, it is of no consequence; for the fact is, her mother has yet again managed to pacify the brewing winds of an approaching storm, and by putting the things which matter into perspective, she has returned their world to an even keel.

Gina, delighted to see that her daughter has lost neither her sense of humour nor her desire to make herself feel good, looks at her and smiles. "Come on, Lucy McMurry … let's get you ready. Then we can go out and face this big bad world together."

The special and sacred closeness which exists only between a mother and daughter has healing powers which are far greater than that of any medicine. It is a relationship which is greatly treasured and is, therefore, jealously guarded by both.

Her mother, now standing slightly behind her, peers over her shoulder, and as they both look into the mirror, they cannot fail to see that, although not quite like peas in a pod, they each reflect the unmistakable lines of their Celtic roots.

With tissues at the ready, they work together, removing the tell-tale smudges of tear-stained make-up from around her eyes as they attempt to mask the extent of her distress. A careful re-grooming of the hair, followed by a touch of expertly-applied colouring to the lips, initiates a much-needed boost to her self-esteem. She again looks at her reflection and smiles. "Not *quite* perfect, but I think I'll pass."

Relatively satisfied with the results of their efforts, she turns and faces her mother.

A reassuring glance from Gina as she straightens the fall of the beautifully-crafted amber pendant of her daughter's gold necklace, confirms the accuracy of her self-assessment.

With shoulders back and backbone straight, Gina stands upright. And then, with the adoption of an air of dignity, and the slightly exaggerated display of self-confidence, she invites Lucy to do the same.

Instinctively, the pose is mirrored. A technique which was, no doubt, developed in the cradle, when, as a baby, she would have learned that by mimicking the expressions of her mother, there would always be a favourable response in return.

She pulls open the door and allows her daughter to walk through. With her pride intact and her head held high, Lucy holds onto her mother's arm and, as if they are joined together as an indissoluble entity, they merge with the energized mass of revellers who fill the main hall.

They are greeted with welcoming and reassuring smiles from those who had only just previously witnessed the sight of her pain and suffering, along with the innocent indifference from those who did not.

Geoff approaches the couple. As he assesses their expressions and tries to read the answer to his forthcoming enquiry, he hesitates. It looks safe, but then again, looks can be deceptive. With Lucy, he can never be sure. But still, he plucks up the courage and, with the risk of becoming the victim of her wrath, he asks anyway, "How are you?"

Lucy hears the question and, apart from a glancing look of disapproval directed towards him, she ignores it. She has never fully accepted his presence. After all, she still blames him for instigating the break-up of her parent's marriage; a chain of events which had consequently led to her father moving away to start a new life in France.

Gina, sensing the animosity targeted towards her husband but, equally, wanting to maintain the peace, answers for her. "She's sore … but then she'll be all right. What I mean to say is … at least there's no bones broken. Anyway, thanks for asking."

The message conveyed through the look in his wife's eyes is understood. He will question her no more.

"Good."

Pleased that she is, in the main, uninjured, he is still slightly disappointed with the knowledge that he will never be accepted as being her stepfather. However, he does wish that she would at least make an effort not to hinder his marital relationship and, maybe, even learn to acknowledge him as her mother's spouse. It has been a long, drawn-out seven years which has often been fraught with tension and a near constant feeling of him having to walk on eggshells. The likelihood of there being a change of heart on her part is, at best, remote.

His silence is short-lived as his feelings get the better of him and he shakes off the restraints of wisdom.

"With an attitude like that, it's no wonder she gets hurt." His words appear to be aimed at Gina, but the volume suggests a hidden agenda in that, in reality, they were also meant for the ears of her daughter.

Lucy reacts instantaneously and quick-marches right up close to him. Her face, reddened with rage, almost touches his and, in doing so, ensures that there can be no mistake as to whom she targets her venom.

"I despise you — I always have done and … if I'm honest … then I think I always will!"

He tries to interrupt her and take control. He fails. Before a word is released, terrier-like, she snaps at him. "No! Now you listen to me you jumped-up little squirt!"

Shocked, he makes no further attempt to interrupt. The control is now all hers.

"I've had to put up with your self-opinionated attitude for years. You're always bitching about my Dad to my Mum. Yes, I've heard you. You didn't think anyone could hear you — but I did!"

He looks stunned as she continues to release her previously pent-up feelings.

"Don't you try to deny it. Behind closed doors, you thought no one else could hear. Well, I've got news for you — I heard!" Drawing a breath before looking him straight and piercingly into the eyes, she adds, "I've heard you. My father is worth a hundred of you … and you know it!"

Gina tries to separate them but Lucy pushes her away. "No! Leave it Mum. He's got to hear this."

She turns back towards Geoff and, without respite, resumes her lecture. "You feel threatened by my father. Just remember, he's a large part of me. So … when you insult him, then you insult me, too!"

Again there is a pause as she grasps onto the significance of her own words. "Ah… That's it — that's why you treat me with so much contempt?"

She nods her head as if confirming her own revelation. "That's got to be it! Every time you look at me, you see him! And guess what? I don't think you can handle it! The truth is, I'm always going to remind you of who was there first!"

He shakes his head in denial.

"No, I know I'm right." She rebukes him for daring to suggest otherwise. "I'm a constant reminder that you were not the first."

"Well, it's a pity he didn't want you enough to fight for you then, isn't it?"

His response is sharp, and she is, in an instant, silenced.

As his retaliatory broadside cruelly hits home, Gina cannot fail to detect the deep hurt which lies hidden behind the veil of anger which now fills her daughter's eyes.

She intervenes. "That's enough! Both of you!"

Separation is a policy which has met with success in the past, and she sees no reason why it should not work now.

"You stay here!" She barks the order to her husband.

He knows better than to argue, and so, reluctantly, he complies.

She looks at Lucy. "And you, young lady! You come with me!"

Holding on to her arm, she guides her, somewhat forcefully, out of the hall and back into the car park, where — away from the prying ears of bystanders, who so often relish any opportunity to seek fuel to feed the fires of idle gossip — she takes command.

"Lucy! Listen to me!" She demands her full attention. "Now, I want you to calm down."

"But—"

"No buts — you just listen to me. Okay?"

"But Mum … He shouldn't have said what he did about Dad."

"I know, but people say things in anger that they don't always mean."

"He meant it. I know it … He meant every single word of it!"

"*Sticks and stones.*" She reminds Lucy of the old adage in the hope that she will concede that no injury has been caused.

"No Mum!" She shakes her head and shrieks, "That really hurt! Dad would never have given up on me!"

Gina instantly recognizes the inaccuracy of the old saying, in that, although the damage of words may not be physical, they can often leave a wound that even *time* struggles to heal.

"I know. It wasn't a nice thing to say, and I will be speaking to him about it."

As is so often her role, she is the advocate for peace.

Lucy nods, assured that her mother will not now be taking the side of Geoff.

"Look … It wasn't that your dad *didn't* want you. You do know that, don't you?"

Lucy again acknowledges her mother with a nod.

Her faith in her father's love for her is unquestioned as she recalls the way he has always welcomed her with a sparkle in his eyes, a big wide smile and a tight hug … followed by a fatherly kiss on the forehead. She clutches her pendant lovingly, treasuring this precious gift from her father; a gift which he had presented her with on the anniversary of her eighteenth birthday. She remembers it well. Geoff was away on business — or rather, that was what she had always been told when they had both argued and he had then vacated the house for a few days — and she had been out for a one-off celebratory meal with her mother and father. She recollects how they had behaved impeccably and unselfishly, putting aside any historical feelings of animosity to each other, as they had made every effort to make her birthday special.

"It was because he loved you enough to know what was best for you. That's why he didn't start a custody battle. Your dad's a good man. Really, he is."

"I know that. It's Geoff. He just winds me up. Sometimes he's just plain nasty."

"Maybe, but I do think he has a point though."

She looks at her daughter in the hope that she would accept some responsibility for the disharmony.

Sensing the imminent arrival of an attack on her behaviour, Lucy's reply is abrupt. "About what?"

"About your attitude. You always get stroppy when things don't go your way ... and there are times when I think you should grow up and try to be a little less tetchy."

"Me? Stroppy?"

Her Taurean anger re-ignites, and her voice immediately rises in volume, thus, reflecting her view as to the incredulity of her mother's accusation. "You want me to be a little less tetchy? It was him! He wrecked our family! If he hadn't come along you'd still be with Dad."

"I very much doubt that."

Her mother shakes her head, suggesting that the failure of her marriage to Lucy's father was inevitable.

Teenage selective hearing chooses to ignore the comment as Lucy continues to lay the blame on Geoff.

"Dad was away." She pauses, and then, accusatorially, she spits out her words. "It was *HIM*. He took advantage of *YOU*."

"No Lucy! It wasn't like that at all. Your father and me had just gone our different ways ... that's all it was."

She does not believe her.

"No, I think that maybe you're right. It wasn't just Geoff, was it? It was you! It was *you* who did the dirty on Dad!"

Gina wants to snap back at her daughter in self-defence, but knowing that there is an element of truth in what she has said, she decides not to add fuel to the already raging fires. Besides, any needless escalation of the conflict would not only be pointless, but it would also be far more damaging to their relationship than any point-scoring could ever be worth.

After all, the records show that her marriage was dissolved as a result of her adulterous liaison with Geoff. It is true, he had taken advantage of a situation; but then, she had allowed the advantage to be taken and, therefore, she had no option but to accept her share of culpability.

"I've had enough of this! I'm going!" Lucy turns, and as she starts to walk away and towards the road, her mother calls after her.

"And where do you think you're going?"

Without turning back to face her mother, she shouts the reply, "Home!"

She hesitates as she allows wishful thinking to overrule practicality, then turns around and adds, "Maybe to the home where I'm really wanted ... the one where my *real* dad lives!"

Unable to argue with the sentiment, Gina is silenced.

Standing as if tethered to the spot, she watches as her daughter stomps off and, with an air of arrogance, heads towards the forbidding darkness of the lane.

She glances back towards the hall and starts to feel an inner rage brewing as she notices the way in which Geoff unconcernedly watches the departure of Lucy. Standing alone and silhouetted against the lights of the entrance, he coldly displays a self-satisfied smile as he seems, for the moment, to be relishing in the upset. But then, seeing the eyes of his wife focused in his direction and realising that he has undoubtedly been sussed, he shakes his head as if in disbelief. He turns about and, with an air of nonchalance, strides back and into the hall.

Although she wants her daughter nearby, the reaction of her husband suggests that he would be *more than* happy if she were to move out and return to her father.

It is not often in a marital break-up that one of the parties can be considered as being truly blameless for its failure, but this was one of those rare exceptions.

Tom, when he had not actually been working, had been spending an increasing amount of time abroad — that is to say, in Spain, Portugal and France — as he had been searching for a suitable premises in which they could have a home with sufficient and suitable land for a business enterprise to keep them solvent. He had hoped that, with a little bit of luck and a lot of hard work, this would eventually lead to a better life for the family as a whole. With many of his extended family still in their homeland, he could easily have returned to his Irish roots, but it was the attraction of sunshine and warmth which had spurred his desire to avoid the often excessive precipitation of the Emerald Isle.

Gina easily recalls her feelings of excitement over the prospects of the new venture, but she also remembers her sense of caution — in particular, with regard to the timing. Her maternal instincts had, quite reasonably, prioritized her concerns for Lucy. And with the importance of her education being paramount, she had subconsciously held back from giving Tom the final encouragement to take the plunge.

In retrospect, she now realizes that Geoff, as her employer, had, to some degree, abused his position and had readily taken advantage of the fact of her having doubts as to the wisdom of a move abroad. Moreover, what with her husband spending so much time away, he had homed in on her ever-increasing sense of loneliness.

It had begun with no more than the occasional, no strings attached, pub lunch, which was, as far as she was concerned, just a distraction away from the office. But then, once alcohol had been consumed and defences had been dropped, the form of their relationship had started to alter.

She had confided in him, and he had responded with both

understanding and support. After all, he could see the reasoning as to why she had doubted the wisdom of disrupting Lucy's education. In fact, he had even suggested that Tom had been acting irresponsibly when putting his own dreams above the practical needs of both Gina and Lucy.

Although she had not, at that time, realized that he was trying to undermine the credibility of her husband, nor had she allowed any physical relationship to develop, the rumours had already started. Once started, they had spread like wildfire and had become progressively more difficult to quash.

It was the anonymous telephone call to Tom which had instigated the visit to his lawyer. Then, with her having received a letter from his legal representative, she'd had no option but to seek legal advice for herself. As a consequence, one thing had led to another and it was not long before there were the inevitable preparations for a divorce. Gina had often wondered how the caller had managed to get hold of Tom's work number — but then, that was in the long and distant past, and so a witch-hunt for the culprit would have served no purpose. She'd let it go gracefully — as she'd done her marriage.

With Tom and her at loggerheads, her relationship with Geoff had developed more out of habit and circumstance than from any romantic spark. In spite of this, she had accepted his proposal, and a short while after the granting of the *decree absolute*, they had moved in together. It was, however, only after a series of many unconvincing excuses as to why the time was not quite right that — in order to shut him up — she finally relented, and they went through with the formality of a wedding.

Had she been more honest with herself, she would have recognized that she did not really love him … and that the idea of marriage was entirely his. However, her acceptance and compliance was, she now believes, more of a case of her just having *gone with the flow*.

Chapter 5

With the raging fires of teenage intransigence fuelling the strides that take her away from the glow of the hall, her thoughts — whilst still muddled by the tumbling of mixed emotions which now inhabit her topsy-turvy world of sorrow and rage — are left to ricochet around the medley of events which have ruined, what should have been, the most joyful celebration of that of her cousin's wedding.

As she reaches the junction where the car park meets the opacity of the unlit road, she hesitates. Then, with no more than a cursory glance over her right shoulder, she again turns away, ensuring that she is seen to brush aside her mother's appeals for her to cede to her calls … and effect an immediate return.

Looking first to her left and then to her right, Lucy assesses the wisdom of leaving the security of the light for the vulnerability of the tree-lined tunnel which carves through the heart of the forest.

She peers into the lane. A way which will take her to where the shadows of the night have merged into a mass of inhospitable blackness which is broken only by the occasional moonbeam which has been successful in forcing itself through the highest branches of the overlapping trees.

This forbidding, twisted thoroughfare offers no alternative, for it is the only route by which she can reach the sanctuary and light of the village, and so … home.

Little comfort is offered in the knowledge that in less than a quarter of a mile the lane will curve once more, then it will straighten … as if reaching out to embrace the warm, amber shine of the village's lights. This is where the wilderness of the forest has, over the years, had no option but to give way to the demands of order. It is also where the old Norman church, standing proud at the heart, is nestled within a colourful array of lovingly tended gardens which serve to give character, depth and privacy to each of the assortment of ancient and individually styled, stone-built cottages.

Primordial caution hones her senses, and as her eyes become accustomed to the diminished light, the range and clarity of her vision expands, so strengthening her confidence.

Her first few steps are taken with the utmost of care. Urging herself forward, she finds herself slipping deeper into the debilitating constraints of the darkness, and with each tentative step, she becomes increasingly aware as to how tuned her hearing has become.

As much as she tries to reason away the *whys* of the snaps and the *wherefores* of the rustles, she cannot help but to listen to the echoes of movement; for as they reach out from deep within the forest, they have managed not only to have taken precedence over the fading rhythms of the pulsating disco, but — by accentuating the feeling of there being no refuge within the loneliness of her predicament — they have also succeeded in preying on the most primal of humankind fears.

As if clinging to the hope that the raised volume of each crack of her heels striking the neglected and uneven tarmac surface will, in some way, act as a means of defence, she quickens her pace.

In doing so, her steps grow heavier and markedly louder.

Whether or not her actions succeed in convincing an unseen menace, earthly or otherwise, that she is larger and, thus, more of a threat than the truth could ever admit to, is immaterial; for it is merely the show of confidence which may be enough to put doubt into the mind of a predator.

To her right, she hears the snapping of a twig and the rustle of something bulky kicking its way through the first of the fallen leaves.

She stops, holds her breath and listens ... her focus on whatever is hidden within the shadows.

As if echoing the hush of her stillness, the sounds abruptly cease.

She sees nothing ... breathes again ... and then, convincing herself that she may well have become too sensitive, nervously resumes her journey.

A few short paces and the sounds restart. Again, she stops and listens ... but, the forest — as if *it* is watching her — immediately and ominously returns to a peculiar and unnatural state of noiselessness.

Fully aware of the dangers of her self-imposed solitude, she calls out; and as she hears each of her words drift away, unanswered and to a place where even light — a force which has travelled across the vast distances of space — appears to have had its entry so emphatically denied, she trembles with trepidation.

"Joe?"

She waits for a reply.

There is none.

"Marcus?"

She pauses to allow for a response.

Again, there is none.

"Is that you?"

There is more than a hint of uneasiness in her voice as she senses the presence of a danger lying hidden within the silence that prevails.

Fearfully, she looks back towards the car park and then forward towards the village. Equidistant from safety, she wavers, and then, having weighed her options, she decides to continue onward. The thumping of her beating heart resonates through her body, further accentuating the self-awareness of her isolation.

There is no one to turn to.

Her *fight-or-flight* instincts sharpen and her pace accelerates as the latter becomes the chosen option.

She breaks into a run and, after a few paces, falters as the sudden turn of her ankle, and its accompanying sharp and sickening pain, throws her into the roadside embankment.

Looking down at the offending shoe, she is enraged by the spectacle of its heel hanging precariously and uselessly loose.

With her anger overriding her fears, she damns the forest with its veiled and secret mysteries — the insistence of her protestations having instantly shocked its anonymous inhabitants into an uneasy silence.

It is a motivating response. So, satisfied that a semblance of control has now been regained, she glares upwards, and then, with a mounting confidence, she curses equally at the night whilst simultaneously endeavouring to alleviate her pain with a soothing massage of the ankle.

Tentatively, she lowers her leg and eases her weight back and onto the injured foot.

She stops.

The pain is severe.

Hauling herself up and onto the earthen embankment, she settles on the moss-covered buttress-root of a rather aged and silvery beech.

Resting her back against the smooth support of the trunk, with her knees pulled up tight towards her chest and both arms wrapped around her legs, she continues to caress and support the tender and rapidly inflaming joint.

In spite of her vision being impaired by the reflexive emergence of tears, she carefully feeds the soft leather strap backwards and out through the buckled fastening as she tries to relieve the pressure. Grimacing in anticipation of a surge of further agony, she tenses and then pulls the strap tight against the swelling. The securing pin frees and the pain eases, thus, facilitating the final removal of the ruined item of footwear.

The newly-resumed sounds of the forest are, yet again, abruptly drowned when — with the subtlety of the strike of a thunderbolt — a dark and powerful cervid mass, muscles and smashes its way through the thicket and out towards her. She spins her head and stares; unable to fully gain her focus, she gasps for breath whilst the stall of sheer terror captures and silences the screams which are about to leave her body.

The beast — startled by her presence as much as she is by its — stops, and, as if frozen in time, stands with its forelegs halted, and trembling, on the embankment beside her.

Cautiously, she wipes the tears from her eyes, and as the clarity of her vision is reclaimed, she peers up at the rapid puffs of condensing breath which, through the flaring nostrils and gaping mouth, escape from the heat of internal respiration into the coolness of the air. Following the line of his head, she peers deep into a wide and wild eye which — illuminated only by a rare and thin shaft of moonlight which has determinedly prised its way through the treetop foliage — reflects the torment of a soul that has run for its very life and now rests for a moment, contemplating the level of this new threat, whilst considering the route for flight.

Relieved by the realisation that he is as fearful of her as she is of him, terror steps aside to admit the positives of her witnessing the majesty of nature, untamed and in the raw; for she rarely sees red deer in the wild, and, what's more, she has certainly not experienced the magnificence of seeing one at such a close proximity.

In the hope that she can allay his obvious feelings of apprehension towards her, she whispers, "It's okay … I'm not going to hurt you."

Enchanted by his strength and beauty, and so as not to cause him to panic, she sits motionless … and then — with time standing still as if it were to be for an eternity — they both, with uncertainty marring their thoughts, eye one another as if they are awaiting the first signs of intent.

The scent of raw sweat rising from his steaming coat, drifts into her nostrils. And as he cranes his long neck rearwards and watches along the length of his body — his ears, erect and twitching — he listens intently as the most minuscule of sounds that hail from deep within the forest are analysed for further signs of threat.

Turning back, and satisfied that he has been successful in outrunning his pursuer, he flashes a fleeting glance towards her and then looks out and across the lane.

His hind legs, quivering as if in preparation for a further burst of action, are, in turn, hauled up and onto the embankment as they join those of the fore.

Suddenly, he moves forward and drops the four-foot descent to the road, pausing for only a moment as the powerful limbs of the rear take the strain. Then, with an upward spring, he propels his majestic form over the opposite ridge and, almost mystically, disappears into the darkness … to be seen no more.

With the distraction of the encounter having made her disregard the weakness and throbbing ache of her swollen ankle, she tries to stand.

As she attempts to regain her equilibrium, her ankle sends a sharp reminder of its injury; instinctively, she adjusts the distribution of her weight back and onto the uninjured foot.

Without warning, and as it yields to the force of the piercing presence of a single four-inch heel, the loose earth starts to crumble and break away, impelling her into making a desperate attempt to regain her balance by shifting her weight back and onto her injured and painful limb.

She fails. Then with the sudden agonising effects of the injury shooting up and through her body, she staggers … and then falls backwards, tumbling down the hard and uneven inner slope and into the gully.

Having lost control, and now in the hands of destiny, she feels the thud and the jolt as the momentum of her fall is abruptly halted with the side of her head crashing against a protruding and firmly-set boulder.

The pain is sickening. She puts one hand to her injured temple and dabs the wound with a finger. Moist and sticky, she pulls the finger away and, tentatively, puts it to her mouth. The taste of blood confirms the injury.

Knowing that treatment is essential and that she should return to the village hall for assistance, she attempts to stand.

Unsteadily, she forces herself up, and then, feeling faint and increasingly nauseous, she stumbles, only to fall back and into the ditch. Unable to move, she is afraid, lonely and tearful. Suffering alone, she has come to rue her decision to storm off from the natural and protective devotion of her mother.

The trickle of blood which seeps from the wound and into the earth that pillows her head, is a sign that all is far from well.

Feeling numb, yet also aware of an uncontrollable shiver as the adrenalin pumps through her body, she stares into the sky. Unable to do more, she watches as the few faint traces of light from the moon weaken until they are finally swallowed by the darkness.

Her eyes ... no longer functioning ... slowly close. Yet, in her desperation to maintain a state of consciousness, she manages to summon the will to force herself to listen to the noises of the forest ... until they meld into an indistinguishable fusion of sounds, before finally fading away ... to become forever lost in the deafening silence of non-existence.

Chapter 6

On edge and impatient, Gina flits between the car park and the foyer … the expenditure of her nervous energy being far outweighed by its adrenalin-fuelled creation.

She hesitates as she stands beside the payphone, questioning herself as to whether or not she should contact the police. But then, not wanting to be seen as being an *over-reactive* and *panicky* mother, she decides otherwise and opts, instead, to wait and simply trust that all will be well.

Again, she checks her watch. The elapse of time suggests there to be no likelihood of an imminent reappearance. She returns to her spouse, enraged and primed for confrontation.

"I saw you and your self-satisfied grin!" Her angst has readily transmuted to ire, and as she watches his face redden, she concludes that this is, in itself, a reaction which is sufficient to be taken as being an admission of his guilt.

"So, tell me! What was all that about?" she snaps accusingly, not really expecting or, for that matter, wanting to hear the answer that she believes she already knows.

"Nothing … I was just—"

Mid-sentence, his explanation is halted and then overruled as she vents her fury.

"I suppose you're proud of yourself!"

"No. It's not like that. I—"

She cuts him short before he is able to justify himself. "I don't want any excuses! Now you just get yourself out there and find her! Do you understand me? Find her!"

Recognising *the look* — the look which accepts no insubordination — he chops a sardonic salute and spits his response, "Yes, Ma'am! Anything you say!"

Storming out of the hall, he strides, unswervingly, across the car park and then onwards towards the road, before turning to his right and disappearing from sight.

Half-heartedly, he calls out into the night. "Lucy! Where are you?"

Then, with a barely audible aside, he adds, "You spoilt little brat."

There is no reply.

His calls, as if synchronized with the upsurge in the level of his irritation, reverberate in the darkness as they are met with the silence of before.

Surmising that she is out of earshot and therefore not too far from home, he makes his way back to the hall.

Gina watches expectantly from the entrance, and as she sees her husband return alone, her hopes take a dive and her worries edge upwards.

"Well? Where is she?" she snaps, as he approaches.

Other than that of a simple shake of his head, there is no answer.

As he nears, she repeats the question.

"So where is she? How far did you go?"

"Look, she's probably got home already. I'll just get the car and then I'll go and check. Okay?"

"I'll come with you."

"No!" he barks, "You stay here until I get back!"

He takes a deep breath, and then, with a little more composure, he adds, "I think it's better for you to stay here. Just in case she comes back on her own … okay?"

Seeing the sense in the suggestion, she complies.

"Okay. I'll stay — I'll wait for her here. Now, please … just go and find her."

He certainly does not relish the thought of being on the rough end of any further ear-bending, especially with her sitting in the car beside him, so with haste, and before she has a change of heart, he strides off towards his car.

As he takes his seat within the vehicle, he jerks the door tight, thus, ensuring a measure of uninterrupted seclusion before driving off towards the village.

With headlights on main beam, illuminating both the narrow road and its adjoining embankment, it would be impossible for him to fail to see a pedestrian. He rounds the bend and heads towards the lights of the village; it's clear that no one is walking along the road.

***

Again, Gina stands at the entrance of the car park and peers into the blackness.

Stepping a few paces into the lane, she stops and listens.

With the sound of their car having faded into the distance, the sounds of nature, which can so often bring about a feeling of life to an otherwise still and somewhat sterile ambience, have already returned.

She calls out.

"Lucy!" She pauses and calls again, "Lucy! Are you out there?"

With even the sounds of the disco in the background, her words carry easily on the air.

She ventures farther into the darkness and repeats her calls.

Hushed by her invasion, the sounds of the forest are quickly replaced with the white noise of silence — a noise which serves only to exacerbate her feelings of unease as she awaits a reply.

As her thoughts start racing through the darkest of possibilities, she begins to fear the worst.

"Lucy, my love..." she whispers, "...don't do this to me. Please!"

As she stands in the darkness, she tries to fight off her negative thoughts by urging herself to envision an image of her daughter sitting at home whilst having a good, old-fashioned, sulk.

She calls out again, and, deep within her, she pleads for a response.

But there is only a lengthening of the dreadful silence.

The thought that maybe Geoff was right and that she had stormed off homeward, gives some respite to her worries, but on the off-chance that she is hiding and still within earshot, she calls out one more time.

Having received no response, she turns and, in resignation, makes her way back towards the hall.

***

The gentle glow which radiates through the living-room curtains, along with the brighter light from the kitchen, which shines across the driveway, suggests habitation.

Geoff parks the car and approaches the house.

With the turn of the key, he enters his home.

Hearing the sound of raised voices within, he pushes open the living room door and checks for life. Confronted by faces which, contorted with anger, shout out from the television speakers to a non-existent audience, he knows that all is as it should be.

This is just how it had been left — a deception of occupation to deter any potential burglar.

Methodically, and in order to satisfy his need to be certain, he checks each room of the house as he calls out for his step-daughter.

The pulsating light on the telephone answering machine indicates the presence of a new message. He presses *play* and listens ... *You have one new message* — the pause which follows the long tone precedes the voice of Gina — *Lucy! It's Mum. Pick up the phone! Oh, come on Lucy ... Stop playing about* — *I'm worried for you.*

With no response forthcoming, Gina had replaced the handset.

Concluding that she had not been home, he returns to the car and sits quietly, contemplating as to whether he should continue his search of the area or accept defeat and return to face his wife.

An image of her — with the look of her having been fired with anger — flashes through his mind. Decision made, he reverses out from the driveway and then accelerates through the village.

He will widen his hunt.

***

Standing alone outside the doors of the hall, Gina, anticipating the early return of her husband and daughter, checks her wristwatch.

With the advance of time seeming to run too slow, her thoughts hurriedly flit through the events of the evening. She fears that the remaining hours of the encroaching night will be long.

She checks her watch again. Barely a minute has passed since last viewed.

"Hi Gina. Is everything all right with Lucy?"

She turns to focus on the concerned and friendly face of her sister, the mother of the bride, and then flashes a quick smile in return.

As if trying to hide the detail of her unease behind a façade of flippancy, she replies, "Oh yes … Thank you — it's just a teenage thing. You know Lucy … on and off, like hot and cold water."

Annie's expression reveals that she has readily recognized the shallowness of her sister's smile, and, furthermore, the look in her eyes has failed to disguise the depth of worry which haunts her.

"No, I mean it," she adds, as if trying to lay another lining between the reality of her concerns and the likelihood of an over-reaction. "She's probably gone off home, and, no doubt, Geoff will be back in a moment to say that all is well."

Forcing another smile in an attempt to confirm that she is fine, she instantly betrays the sham by checking her watch anxiously before staring out and into the stillness of the car park.

She knows that the probability of her daughter having come to harm is minimal, but still … she just can't help feeling uneasy. It is as if she has activated a sixth sense … and that she knows that her daughter is in trouble and is calling out in desperation for her.

A comforting hand squeezes her shoulder. "Well Gina, if you want anything … then you know where to come."

The warm smile confirms the offer to be genuine, and it's followed up with a hug and a simple but, all the same, meaningful … "Thank you."

Her sister, careful not to be too invasive, quietly slips back into the hall, thereby, allowing Gina to be alone with her thoughts.

She checks herself — *Don't be so stupid Gina. This is the real world.*

She recalls how her late mother would often draw a prompt halt to the exaggerated fears of childhood with the reassurance that the shadows on the bedroom wall were not unwelcome visitors from a fantasy world … but rather, they were nothing more sinister than that of being plainly and simply — shadows!

Knowing that *mother was always right* and that this is unlikely to be an exception to that rule, she consoles herself with the thought that Lucy has only been gone for a short time and will, in all probabilities, soon return … apologetic and glowing red with embarrassment.

***

Geoff slows as he approaches the first of the two homes which he has listed on his unwritten itinerary. The living room light suggests occupancy, but with the only car in the driveway being that of the parents, Geoff knows that Marcus has already been and gone.

"Idiot!" he exclaims, recalling the condition of the lad.

Marcus may have been sufficiently wise to have decided not to have driven to the event, but it appears that he has since allowed his judgement to be clouded by the effects of alcohol and, regardless of the consequences, has irresponsibly taken to the road.

Geoff tuts in despair. For Marcus to have driven in such a state of inebriation would have been, at best, reckless ... and, at worst, a grave misjudgement; it could easily result with the destruction of the lives of others and also of that of his own. Geoff knows exactly what it's like to have failed a roadside breath test and to then have been subjected to the ignominy of being arrested and faced with having to supply further samples via the Lion Intoximeter 3000. On the occasion of his experience, he had been fortunate in that his reading — although slightly over the legal limit — was sufficiently borderline to result in no more than that of him being subjected to an informal but, nevertheless, harsh warning from the custody-sergeant.

Continuing slowly along the road, he double-checks the row of parked cars; Marcus's vehicle is nowhere to be seen.

Satisfied that he has gone, Geoff heads out of the village and along the winding lanes, away from the darkness of the forest and towards the more open and arable lands of Ashleigh Barton.

There is no need for a sign to mark the presence of the farm. The discolouration of the road which carves through the sprawl of outbuildings is sign enough in itself. After all, it announces the well-defined route of the livestock which, routinely and leisurely, snake between the pasture and the parlour.

He pulls up onto the verge and draws to a halt. Stepping out of the car, he peers, with some hesitation, into the courtyard.

The usual explosion of barking dogs alert the occupants to his presence, and as the yard suddenly floods with light, Joe's father opens the door and stares out ... and with more than an air of suspicion.

In an attempt to identify himself to both man and beast as friend and not foe, Geoff calls out, "Sorry to disturb you Jack. I was wondering if you've seen Lucy."

"Come 'ere. Ger in 'ere now!" The dogs immediately obey the dominating growls of their master and, with their barks diminishing to no more than that of a grumble, reluctantly slink into the house behind him.

With the threat of being subjected to canine savagery no more, Geoff moves closer to the light.

"Oh ... 'tis you Geoff. Come on in ... 'tis late. What's the problem?"

"I can't be too sure if there is one. We're looking for Lucy ... so I was just wondering if you'd seen or heard from her. I thought, maybe, she'd come back here with Joe."

Jack slowly shakes his head, somewhat perplexed as to the extent of concern. "Ah ... now them's bin at the do, an' 'em?"

Geoff nods silently in confirmation, not knowing whether to explain the extent of the troubles of the evening.

Jack continues. "Well, to my mind, I thinks them's probably sittin' up quiet somewhere. Perhaps enjoying the company of each other, if you know what I's saying. Bit of the old-fashioned courtin' if you ask me. Memories ... hey! Still ... those were the days."

Geoff ignores the intimated invite to reminisce on the times when they themselves had wooed their respective young ladies, and so, unwaveringly, he keeps to the point. "So Joe hasn't been home then?"

"That's right. Now ... are you sure you don't wanna come in?"

Lorna, his wife, steps into view from behind him. Her look of puzzlement quickly turns to relief as she recognizes the visitor.

"Oh ... It's you. Hello Geoff. 'tis a bit late. Is everything all right?"

"Hopefully. It's just that Lucy's stormed off and I'm trying to find her."

"Oh dear, I hope's there be no problem."

Her probing statement of concern invites further explanation.

"No, it's okay. Maybe Jack's right an' they'll be back later. No doubt they wanted to have some time together. Gina's just a little anxious, that's all."

"You'm sure you don't wanna come in?"

"No ... but thanks anyway."

He shakes his head as he starts to edge back towards the car.

"I ought to get back to Gina — you know, keep her updated and all that."

"Yea, I understand." Jack can see that he wants to get on, and then adds, "If they turns up, I'll give 'e a ring."

"Yea. Thanks for that, umm..."

He pauses for a moment, still undecided as to whether he should give the reasons for his worry.

He decides against an act of disclosure and, instead, simply apologises for the disturbance.

"I'd better get on back to Gina. You never know, Lucy could be back with her by now. I'll see you both soon. Goodnight!"

He returns to his car and then, having exhausted the immediate options, takes the direct route back to the hall.

Convincing himself that Lucy has either safely hidden herself away so that she can take time to consider her actions, or alternatively, and on her own volition, she has already returned to her mother, he presses his foot on the accelerator.

As he heads back, empty-handed, he visualizes the likely response from his spouse.

The clash with her daughter has already failed to impress, and knowing that his disastrous attempt to locate and retrieve her will serve only to exacerbate her anger, he braces himself for further castigation.

His search aborted, he gathers speed … and, with the forest on one side and a steep incline on the other, he rounds the bend.

The briefest image of movement at the nearside, followed by a sickening thud as a shadowy shape glances off the wing, shakes him from his wandering thoughts.

With the sudden slamming of the brakes, the wheels lock and the car grinds to a halt.

He looks behind; with the darkness encasing the already traversed course, he sees nothing.

Engaging reverse gear, the white lights at the rear automatically shine out and illuminate the previously unseen roadway.

With no obvious sign of a victim, he reverses and scrutinizes the tarmac for evidence of the impact. There is nothing whatsoever to assist him in ascertaining its identity.

Shaken by the incident, he stops and collects his thoughts before emerging from the car and then examining its front. The nearside headlamp no longer shines through the now broken lens, and yet, apart from a light depression in the wing, there appears to be little else of consequence.

Thankful that no major expense is likely to be forthcoming, the issue of the missing casualty is readdressed.

He listens for any signs of life from over and down the embankment. The lack of any useful light prohibits an immediate search, thorough or otherwise, and so — with no sounds of distress or cries of pain drifting out from the darkness — he assumes the victim to have been no more than that of a hardy young roe which has, by now, run off and disappeared into the valley.

Comforted with the thought that, whatever it was, it may well have survived, he re-examines the damage to his vehicle and then resumes his journey back to the hall.

Chapter 7

The persistent chirrup of the telephone demands a response.

Shep glances up at the clock. The positioning of its hands show that he is now in his own time. Although his wish to disregard the intrusion is strong, his dedication to his patch and, therefore, the welfare of its people, overrides his personal desire to be on his way home.

He lifts the receiver. "Police — P.C. Russell."

"Oh, Thank goodness I've caught you. I'm worried about Lucy. She's gone off. We can't find her."

"Lucy?" he questions, seeking further information to confirm identification.

"Oh, I'm sorry. My daughter. Lucy … Lucy McMurry."

He puts a face to the name. "Of course … Lucy. Now then, what did 'e mean when you said, *she's gone off?*"

He pauses; then, as if to double-check that he is, in fact, thinking about the right girl, he asks, "Didn't I see 'er up at the hall a while back?"

"Possibly … but then, there's been a bit of trouble since you left."

Sunset strolls through the front office and, being careful not to interrupt the call, he waves a goodbye as he opens the front door.

With a hand cupped over the microphone, Shep delays the exit. "Can 'e hang fire a couple o' minutes, bu'y?"

Sunset nods and waits for Shep to complete his conversation.

"Sorry 'bout that … now, where were we? Ah, yes … A bit of trouble you say."

As Gina gives her account of the evening's events, Shep listens in silence.

Although Lucy has been gone for a only a short period and she is of an age and capability that cannot be considered as being particularly vulnerable, he senses the genuine concern of her mother.

He makes his decision.

"Give us a few minutes an' I'll be over … okay?"

"Thank you. I'll wait at the hall."

With the handset settled in its cradle, Shep leans back and utters a weary sigh, and as his legs straighten and push against the floor, his chair wheels backwards and thumps against the wall.

He turns his attention to Sunset and makes his enquiry. "You'm workin' in the morning?"

"No. But I've gotta take the car to a mate's first thing. He's gonna check it out for its M.O.T."

"Well then, I reckons you'm best be off … an' I'd better be ringin' comms an' tell 'em I's gonna be a bit late booking off."

"Why? What's up?"

"Well, that phone call was from Lucy McMurry's mother. It seems like her young maid's gone off somewhere ... and now her's a bit worried about it."

"Gone off? D'you mean ... she's missing?"

"I don't know about that. Her's probably just had a bit of a tiff. I very much doubt whether there's goin' to be much in it. Anyway ... I reckons she'll be back by the time I gets there."

Sunset nods, and Shep continues. "Now then ... whiles you'm on your way home, perhaps you could take a little detour for me? If you don't mind, that is."

"Yea, sure. Where?"

"Maybe just a quick scout 'round the area ... see if 'e can see the maid. If so, maybe you can get her to go back home and save us all a lot of bother. Do 'e mind?"

"No, I don't mind at all. It'll be no problem."

"Thanks bu'y. Well don't just stand there, I reckons you'm best be off then. Oh ... an' maybe you should take a spare radio with 'e ... just in case."

"Yea, Sure. I'll drop it back tomorrow."

Sunset, feeling encouraged that his presence has, at last, been appreciated by the old hand, grabs a radio with a spare battery and then bids farewell.

Shep nods, and makes his call to the control room.

***

Gina, relieved that the local police officer has taken her call seriously and not dismissed her as being an overreacting mother, stands at the entrance to the hall and, with a mixture of anxiety and anger, looks out.

With the festivities not too far from drawing to an end, one or two of the guests have started to collect their coats before venturing into the chill of the night air.

As they pass by, uttering their *goodnights*, she asks each in turn if they would keep an eye out for her daughter whilst they journey home.

Unwilling to engage in a full account of the evening's events — which, she considers, would only feed the appetite of rumour — she repetitively spills out the same line. "Oh! It's nothing really ... it's just that, with her dress being ruined and everything, she's had another upset ... and now she's stormed off."

Before a question can be posed, she adds, "I'm just a bit concerned in case she's walking in the lane. You know — being out in the dark and dressed the way she is, she could easily be hit. A driver might not see her in time and there could be in an accident."

Her explanation is, on the face of it, readily accepted by all, and so the warning of a potential hazard on the road is heeded.

She juggles with the possibilities that may explain the reason as to the delay in Geoff's return. Either, he has found Lucy and is now in the process of talking her into returning, or, alternatively, he is yet to find her and is still diligently pursuing his task. Whichever it is, she finds it difficult to be able to cope with the loneliness of not knowing.

***

A clattering from the overhead camshaft as the motor splutters into life does not indicate the presence of the County's only diesel-fuelled, two-litre Ford Cortina; rather, it tells the tale of a petrol engine which, with its gunged-up oil-ways and leaking gaskets, is unlikely to survive the winter.

Additionally, with the signs that rust has already taken its hold in the wheel-arches, and the tell-tale bubbles in the paintwork of the sills suggesting its spread, the durability of the engine may well be a matter of little relevance.

Whether or not the car is to be scrapped will be subject to the success or failure of Mondays Ministry of Transport Test. Only then, will Sunset be forced into making the final decision.

After just a few hundred yards, the circulation of what little oil remains, succeeds in quietening the groaning beast.

He welcomes the opportunity to try and enhance his standing within the Constabulary. He is happy to make a systematic search of the narrow lanes which snake through the rural and forested expanse of the patch.

***

As the celebrations draw to an end, the steady exodus of family and friends exacerbate her sense of isolation.

She checks her watch; an action which seems to be more out of habit than that of a genuine need to verify the time. She looks away, then almost immediately, checks it again.

A flicker of lights moving briskly through the tree-lined lane alert her to the approach of a car. As it pulls into the car park and swings around towards the hall, anticipation and worry serve to hone her senses.

Her interrogative stare forces its way through the blinding dazzle of the single headlamp. As she steps forward, she prays that she will see not only her husband, but also, sitting somewhat sheepishly beside him, her daughter, Lucy.

As the engine stops and the lights extinguish, the driver's door opens … and, as if stalling the arrival of the inevitable, Geoff stretches and straightens himself beside the car.

She concentrates on the unopened side.

The door remains still. He's alone; her hopes are dashed.

Lucy has not been found.

Gina approaches, assessing and reading his expression before she utters a word. "Where is she?"

The shrug of his shoulders, with his hands held open, is sufficient to confirm his inability to give a satisfactory answer.

Her anger, now tempered with an overriding concern for Lucy's welfare, has diminished.

Reading her signals as well as she reads his, he steps forward and gives her the comfort of a reassuring embrace.

"Oh..." she adds, as if he were unaware of the fault, "one of your lights isn't working."

"Yes, I know. I think I may have hit a deer. I've checked the damage, but don't worry ... there's nothing much. I'll sort it in the morning."

Under normal circumstances, she would have been livid at the inconvenience of them having to face the expense of having to repair the damage to the vehicle — but, for the time being, she has more important things on her mind and, so, dismisses it as being insignificant.

Her worries certainly override the triviality of a broken headlamp. So, whilst feeling the comforting warmth and security of his embrace, she endeavours to put aside the emotional strains of the evening, trying instead to adopt a mindset of cold and hard-headed logic. She knows that there can be no room for the distraction of sentiment if the whereabouts of her daughter is to be established; therefore, she has no option other than to adopt a more rational and clinical approach.

Chapter 8

His return to the hall is obviously no longer just a routine exercise in public relations. On this occasion, when he alights from the car and approaches Gina and her husband, he carries a worn and battered briefcase — a sign that he considers that there may well be a need for documentation.

"Shall we go in?"

Without delay, Shep has taken control, and, with a smile, he steers them into the privacy of the committee room. He knows his way. On the third Thursday of each month, his presence is required to answer the queries of both the parish councillors and the regular few who attend to witness the conduct of the meetings.

Instinctively, they take their seats — Gina and Geoff seated beside each other and Shep sitting opposite.

The policeman breaks the silence. "Now then … you'm told me there's been some problems, and that 'e can't find Lucy. Is that right?"

"Yes, that's right … she's gone off?" Gina responds nervously.

"So, tell me … why do you think her's gone off?"

"Why? Well, because I saw her! That's why!" Gina's answer suggests a misunderstanding of the question.

"I's sorry, I think you misunderstand me. What I meant to say was … what reason did her have to go off?"

"Oh, I'm sorry. There was a bit of a tiff … then she got upset and went storming off."

Geoff then adds, "I've been home and checked around the lanes, but there's nothing. There's just no sign of her anywhere."

"So tell me, how old's she?"

"Eighteen … she was eighteen last April."

"Mmm… And how long's her been gone?"

"Oh, I don't know … a couple of hours, maybe. I can't be sure. What's the time now?"

Geoff looks at his watch. "Yea, that's about right … two hours … maybe a little less. I can't be too sure either."

"Okay. Now, as her's gone off on her own accord then, although it's been stressful for 'e both, it were obviously her decision to go. Anyway, to my mind, that's less of a worry. You see, she were in control of her movements … and that means she weren't under the control of someone. What I's saying is … 'tis likely her just don't wanna be found … yet."

Acknowledging, but not necessarily accepting his line of thinking, they nod.

Shep continues. "Now tell me, what's you being doin' to find her?"

"Well, as I said, I've been home and she wasn't there … so then I went to see if Marcus was home — that's Marcus Warren. I couldn't see his car, so I assumed that he'd gone off somewhere."

"Why was 'e checking on Marcus?"

"Well, there was a bit of bother earlier, and he'd gone off in a strop. He wasn't happy — in fact, he had his tail between his legs. Anyway, I thought that maybe she'd met up with him."

"Okay, we'll get back to that. So … what then?"

"Well, then I went over to the Hardy's place. I spoke with Jack and Lorna.

They hadn't seen Joe. But they'd thought that maybe he was with Lucy, and that the two of 'em had probably gone off together somewhere."

"Okay. I reckons that seems to be a fair assumption. Maybe 'tis possible that he is with her and they'm gone off, just as his parents have said. What d'you reckon? I mean, do you think that's what could have happened?"

There is no reply, other than an air of uncertainty which hovers behind the shrug of his shoulders.

"You'm got your doubts?"

A glance between spouses, accompanied by a further shrug of the shoulders, confirms his observation.

"Right then … so, then what?"

"Well, then I came back here to be with Gina. You know, to check if Lucy had come back and, of course, to give her support."

Gina is agitated. She can sense that maybe her worries are being considered as a little premature. After all, even *she* is wondering whether she has reacted prematurely. Nevertheless, she is not too happy with what she sees as an apparent lack of urgency in the situation. In fact, she feels that the police officer appears to be doing nothing more than just going through the motions of an investigation … and so she feels the need to express her feelings.

"I know you think that I'm overreacting … and I know it seems like I'm just a fussy old mother, but I can't help it. I just feel, in my heart, there's something wrong. No! What I mean is … I *know* there's something wrong. If I'm to be frank with you, I don't think we're doing much good by just sitting around chatting, do you?"

"In what way?" Shep remains calm. He has an old-fashioned trust for gut-feelings — whether they're his own or those of another.

He clarifies his question. "What makes 'e think there's somethin' wrong?"

"I don't know! I can't put my finger on it, but I'm really worried about her."

"Okay, I understand that. So then, wha'd you reckons happened that was *so bad* that it made her wanna go off on her own?"

The couple exchange glances, not sure as to which of the two can best explain the circumstances.

Gina bites the bit and furnishes him with her account of the events which had preceded her daughter's disappearance.

"Well — Lucy has been going out with Joe for some time, but, tonight, things flared up ... especially after Joe started accusing Marcus of going off with Lucy."

Shep recalls his observations of earlier but, diplomatically, opts to keep his own counsel; instead, he waits in silence and allows her to continue.

"Now, Joe found out ... and, as a result, he had a go. That's when it all got a bit out of hand ... and Marcus got hit. In fact, if I'm to be honest about it, I think he actually took a bit of a hiding."

She looks at the police officer, and, having searched for a reaction and finding none to be evident, she continues. "Anyway ... during the fight — well maybe a fight's too strong a word for it ... it was more one-sided than that really. Anyway, as I was saying ... while Joe was having a go at him, Lucy tried to pull Joe off. But then ... he just turned 'round and hit her ... right in the face — he sent her flying!"

"Joe hit her?" The tone in the policeman's voice fails to conceal his surprise.

"Yes. He hit her ... and she fell!"

Seeking more detail, he continues. "When you say ... *he hit her* ... wha'd you mean? By that, I's askin' ... did he thump her? Was it a slap? What exactly?"

"Oh ... I don't know. I don't think he meant to hurt her. He just hit out. It seemed to be more like he was just trying to shake her off ... if you know what I mean. I think that when she'd grabbed hold of him, he didn't know it was her — so he just swung round and hit out."

He nods, confirming his understanding of her explanation of the incident, and asks, "Was she hurt?"

"Of course she was!" She is surprised and irritated at being asked a question to which the answer is so obvious.

"No, I'm sorry. What I meant was ... was she injured? Did she have any marks or cuts, or anythin' like that?"

"Oh ... Yes ... maybe, but I suppose it wasn't as bad as it could've been ..."

She realizes her description of the events may have sounded far worse than what was, in reality, no more than an instinctive response to Joe having being grabbed "... She had a few scratches, and I think she'll probably have a few bruises as well. To be honest, it was her pride being hurt more than anything. Oh yes, and her dress ... It was ruined — completely ruined."

"How's that?"

"When she fell, it got torn. It's beyond repair!"

The look of sadness on her face reflects the memory of that of Lucy's.

"She was so upset. Do you know? She'd worked really hard to save up enough to be able to buy it." As a smile starts to break through her look of sadness, she continues. "She looked absolutely gorgeous ... it was as if my sweet little girl had suddenly grown up and had blossomed into being a lovely young woman."

Shep, noticing the tears returning in her eyes, and recognising the importance of not allowing her to break down, moves on. "Okay, so what was happening to Joe and Marcus?"

Abruptly woken from her bittersweet recollections, and annoyed by the thought that concern was being given to the welfare of the instigators of the events which have subsequently led to Lucy's disappearance, she snaps back, "What do you mean? What happened to them?"

Sensing his wife's growing anger, Geoff speaks up, "I think what the constable meant to say was ... where did they go?"

He looks across to Shep for corroboration.

A nod affirms clarification as to the intention in his question.

Geoff, seeing that Gina is rapidly showing signs of switching off, assumes her role and answers on her behalf. "Well ... they both went off — Joe in his Land Rover, and Marcus ... he went off on foot."

He looks to his wife, and she confirms his account with a quiet, but abrupt, "Yes, he went down the lane."

"So they ... that's to say, Marcus and Joe ... went off separately and before Lucy — is that right?"

"That's right."

"So ... if the two lads had already gone, then why should Lucy have gone off afterwards?"

Gina, feeling uncomfortable with the progressive invasion into the detail of her family's private affairs, interjects with an air of annoyance. "Because we had a row ... Okay?"

"A row?"

"Yes! Well, maybe not a row — more of a tiff, I suppose."

"May I ask what 'twas about?"

She shakes her head. "Look, it wasn't important. It was just a family thing. Now, let's leave it there, shall we?"

"If you like ... but it would be of help if I could be gettin' the complete picture."

She does not react. Realising that there will be nothing to be gained by pressing her at this early stage, Shep leans back in his chair and sighs — a sign that signals that the questioning is over ... for the time being, at least.

"Look, I know this is going to be difficult for you," he continues, "but

Lucy is legally an adult ... and as I's already said, her's obviously gone off on her own accord. Her's only bin gone for a couple of hours ... so maybe, 'tis just that her needs a bit more cooling-off time. Now, maybe it's right an' maybe It's not, but the way we do things is ... that unless her's considered as being particularly vulnerable — by that I means, if her were elderly, sick or suicidal — we wait for twenty-four hours before officially recording her as missing. Gives 'er time to calm down and then go home ... under her own steam."

"So, you're not going to do anything, is that right?" Gina responds accusingly.

"No, I didn't say that." Understanding her distress, he remains calm and attempts to make clear his intentions. "Now then ... them's gonna be locking up directly. So, what I's proposing, is that the both of you go home and wait for your maid there. Her's more likely to have headed to her home than she is to have headed back here."

Allowing insufficient time for any protestation to be made, he adds, "And also, if you'm at home, we can keep you up to date by phone ... Okay?"

They each acknowledge his words with a nod, albeit seasoned with a hint of reluctance.

"Now, I's gonna make a log of the incident so the night shift will be aware of what's happened. If they see her, them'll get in touch with you and then get her home. But I's going to need to take some more details for the log. Full description, you know — height, build, clothing, etcetera. So, if you don't mind, I'll follow you back to your place and then we can double-check to see if her's returned ... Okay?"

He waits for acknowledgment, then adds, "You never know, she may well be sitting in her room ... practising her apologies. That 'ill save me a bit of writing, too ... Will it not?"

"Yes, you're probably right, and I'm sorry if I was short with you. I'm just really worried."

"That's no problem. I understand fully. Now I's back on tomorrow afternoon. So if her isn't back by then ... then we'm gonna have to up the enquiry. Now... regarding any assaults and damage to the dress, we can sort that out after young Lucy's been found. My priority is to find your maid safe an' well. In fact," he says, rising from his seat, inviting them to do the same, "... as we speak, my colleague, the special constable, is having a scout 'round the area in his own car before he goes off to his home."

Gina thanks him and, with her agitation lessened, forces a smile.

"Oh ... and whilst we'm on the way, I'll be radioing through to comm's to get they to check the hospitals ... and also for 'em to get the city patrols to check the railway station and the bus depot — 'tis just basic routine for this type of enquiry. Okay? You see, nine times out of ten, young 'uns turn up when 'em's hungry, and 'tis a fair chance her'll be back home before morning."

He opens the door, allowing them to leave before he follows them out and into the car park.

Gina and her husband are in for a long and fretful night — he knows that. After he has been to their home and has obtained the relevant details, he knows that he must then return to the station. He has a log to update and several phone calls to make before he can even consider signing off and then making his own way home.

Chapter 9

Steering the Land Rover through the gateway which separates the public road from the concrete expanse of the farmyard, he glances across to the sheds, hoping that he can avoid the need for conversation. His heart sinks as he sees his father emerging from the largest of the buildings. The older man, somewhat pointedly, looks at his watch before glaring straight back at him.

As Joe alights from the vehicle, his father, continuing his approach, speaks out, "I reckons, that one day, some *whiz-kid* will be inventing som'it that'll show'e the way home, bu'y!"

"I'm sorry. I needed some time to think …" He hesitates, then with no attempt to explain his absence, he adds, "… on me own like."

"I reckons them cows have bin doing some thinkin' too … them havin' bin on there own like. After all, them's 'ad plenty of time to ponder. Maybe them was thinkin' … *The sun's in the sky — 'tis eleven o'clock, so where's me feed?* But then, them's could have bin reckoning that perhaps you'm just gone off gallivanting … an' forgotten all about 'em! What d'you think? D'you reckon that's what them's bin thinking?"

"Come on, Pa, I can do without this right now. I's knackered, an' to be quite truthful with 'e, I really needs to be goin' to the bathroom."

"Now you listen y'ere, son. I dunno what you'm bin up to all night, but what I do knows is … them animals need lookin' after — an' that's your job! Robert's had to go on off and mend some fencing. Them damn sheep, them's bin an' got out again. So now, maybe you should be acting a little bit more like your brother and take your responsibilities a bit more seriously. Is I makin' myself clear?"

Joe walks off, annoyed by the intrusion, but also, irritated by the fact that he knows that his father is right. They all know their roles — he sorts the cattle, and his younger brother sorts the sheep.

"Anyhow…" Jack calls after his son, "… what did 'appen last night? Geoff Smale were lookin' for 'e."

Joe slows as he registers the question. He decides to ignore the additional intrusion, and, instead, he quickens his pace as he strides off across the yard and towards the house.

"I suppose you'm gone an' taken her home, have 'e?"

He stops in his tracks and, with a look of puzzlement, turns back and stares silently at his father.

As if to clarify the unanswered question, Jack continues. "I's talkin' 'bout Lucy? Have 'e taken her home bu'y?" He pauses, and having had no immediate response, adds. "Her mother's bin on the phone all morning, she'm gone an' worried herself daft."

"No, Pa … I haven't seen her … I haven't seen her since last night. All I knows is, we was at the hall, then I went off. All right?"

Joe's tone, still reflecting his anger as to the events of the previous night, sounds a little dismissive about the whole affair.

"Well bu'y, we'd best ring her an' let her know."

He heads towards the farmhouse and mutters, "Police is involved, so heaven knows what's 'appened to the maid. Her's bin out all night … an' if her weren't with 'e, then what I'd like to be knowin' is, where was she?"

"Maybe they ought to try speaking to that sneaky little git … Marcus bleeding Warren."

His words are wasted. His father has already reached the house and is, as a result, well and truly out of earshot.

***

"Another coffee?"

Gina shakes her head and looks at her watch.

"How about something to eat?"

"No! I'm not hungry," she snaps, "… and I'm not thirsty either!"

"I'm sorry … I'm just trying to help."

Unable to settle, she ignores him as she checks her watch yet again.

"It's nearly lunchtime … I wonder if he's on duty yet."

She moves to the telephone and commences dialling.

The recorded reply answers her question. Shep has not yet arrived for his shift.

"He did say two?"

"Yes, I know he did. But, maybe he's decided to go in early!"

Overtired and fractious from a night with little to no sleep, her response carries more than a little of a confrontational air.

Geoff dares not argue. He has managed to doze off on more than one occasion; but, being cognisant of the fact that she, too, is tired and irritable, he knows that for him to court an argument whilst they are both in their present moods would serve no useful purpose.

"Well, if you don't want coffee, then that'll not stop me … because I do."

He makes his way to the kitchen. Whether it is the coffee he wants, or whether it is a few minutes alone to escape the tension which has lodged within the house, he cannot be sure; but, while the kettle starts to heat, he spreads the Sunday newspaper across the kitchen table and, as if seeking some return to normality, hunts for the sports supplement.

As he checks the results and the up-to-date rugby union tables, he becomes aware of the presence of his wife. She is tetchy, but, although she is unlikely to admit the fact, she is still in need of his company.

***

The farmhouse table, solid and durable, has already outlasted two generations and is likely to witness many more as it naturally retains its position at the core of domestic matters. Mealtimes are not occasions purely for the satisfying of the individual's need for sustenance; they offer an opportunity for the family to come together and discuss and, by doing so, put to bed the trials and tribulations of the day. It has always been this way, and there seems to be no reason why it should change now.

With the table laid and her men seated, Lorna delivers the traditional Sunday roast: home-bred beef with crispy golden potatoes, a selection of vegetables, a bowl of horseradish sauce and a boat of rich, steaming gravy.

A home-baked loaf of crusty bread, unbroken and fresh, lays in wait. Although not the sort of thing to be condoned when in company, when within their own home, the use of bread to wipe the last smudges of gravy from their plates — and in doing so, reveal, once again, the patterns of each item — has become something of a tradition.

As they spoon out the fare and fill their plates, the silence of the less than harmonious atmosphere is broken.

"Well Robert. Tell me … how d'you get on with the fencing?"

"'tis all done, pa. I's had to fit a new crosspiece an' reset the upright …'twill be all right now."

Jack nods and, having tasted the beef, looks across to his wife. "Now this is 'andsome, maid."

She acknowledges the compliment with a warm smile.

"Wha'd you reckon bu'y?" He attracts the attention of the elder of his two sons. "Mother's done herself proud, as usual. Do 'e agree?"

Joe raises his eyes just high enough to make contact as he, half-heartedly, prods at his food with a fork.

"Well … what with all this y'ere thinking you'm bin doing, it looks as if you'm lost your appetite."

Joe glances back, responding only with a shrug.

"Worry can lose 'e your appetite, bu'y. So, what you'm worried about?"

"I isn't worried 'bout nothin'!"

"Well, if you'm not worried 'bout *nothin'*, then maybe's you'm worried 'bout *som'in'*!"

Lorna interjects by raising the subject — the subject that they all know is at the root of Joe's worries. "I wonder if Lucy's got herself home yet. They must be at their wits end."

"Well, she wasn't home when I phoned Gina half an hour ago," Jack announces before adding his opinion. "an' I can't see her coming home too soon either."

Ever the optimist, Lorna tries to bring hope back into the equation.

"She must be getting hungry by now. Maybe she'll go home for her dinner."

Robert, having decided to keep his thoughts to himself, sits quiet and steadily satisfies his appetite.

Jack turns his attention back to Joe. "What d'you reckon son? D'you reckon she'll make her way home, like you're mother says?"

"I dunno what she'm gonna do. Her's nothin' to do with me no more."

Joe pushes his plate of uneaten food away and strides off to his room.

"Joseph!" His mother calls after him as she rises to her feet in readiness to follow.

"Sit down an' leave 'im be. I's not having him ruin our Sunday roast."

She listens to her spouse and then, somewhat unenthusiastically, returns to her meal — her appetite having been doused by the disruption, along with her natural, maternal concerns.

***

The chime of the door bell awakens the butterflies in her stomach. She looks to Geoff, urging him to take the lead. Nervously, she hangs back and peers around him as the door is opened.

Dreading the worst, she scans the face of the police officer, trying to read his mind before he has an opportunity to speak.

"Afternoon — I thought I'd come straight 'round an' see if you've heard anything from her yet."

Shep's obvious lack of knowledge as to Lucy's whereabouts keeps Gina's emotions mixed — relieved by the adage of *no news being good news*, yet troubled by the fact that if she *were* well, then she should have come to light by now.

"Please, come in."

Geoff ushers him into the living room.

"Would you like a cup of tea?" Manners and hospitality go a long way towards trying to remain calm and focused.

"Now that'd be very nice. Thank you."

Although not particularly thirsty, he finds it easier to work in the relaxed ambience of people sharing in a social activity.

Geoff moves off towards the kitchen, whilst Gina remains with the police officer.

The tilt of her head and the appealing look from her eyes asks the question.

Shep responds, "Right ... I've spoken with comm's and them's had no sightings of her overnight. The hospital's bin advised and, no doubt, them'll contact us if they hear anything."

She nods as she absorbs each item of information.

"Now, I's spoken with the special."

Her look of puzzlement indicates a requirement for him to explain further.

"Do you remember? I said that he were gonna have a look around for her on his way home."

The prompt is sufficient to spark her memory.

Shep continues. "Well … he found nothin' of any significance. So … I can only assume she'd already gone, and to be honest, she could have, by then, been anywhere."

Shep keeps silent regarding Sunset's unsubstantiated and, it must be said, unlikely observation of there having been a large cat in the area. To burden her with thoughts of a panther-like predator prowling the vicinity would not do her state of mind any good, nor would it, if the suggestion comes from his lips, do any good to his own credibility.

Geoff re-enters with the welcome distraction of a couple of mugs of tea in hand.

"Have you heard from anyone, or maybe thought of anything else which can help?" Shep asks.

Gina replies, "No. We've phoned around her friends … but no, there's been nothing. Oh, the Hardys rang. They said that she wasn't with Joe. But we've still heard nothing from the Warrens."

"That's okay … I'll have to go an' see 'em after we'm finished with the forms in any case."

They look at him, equally assessing the relevance of the need for documentation. The completion of forms suggest the crossing of a threshold. It is a movement away from that of it being simply matter of a missing sulky teenager, to the more ominous state of it having become a fully blown police investigation.

He explains, "Well, she'm bin gone a while now, so I's gonna have to make it official … Okay?"

They nod as he opens his briefcase and takes out the appropriate documents. A threshold had been crossed.

***

She calls up the stairway and towards his bedroom, "Joe!"

There is no reply, so she tries again.

"Joseph! Can you hear me? I'm calling you!"

There is still no response.

She takes the first few steps of ascent.

She calls him yet again, "Joseph!"

She knows that he is aware of her presence, but, still, she gives him the opportunity to retrieve some self-respect, and to respond with a modicum of civility. "Come on Joe … answer me … please."

Jack, unsettled by the upset, rises and moves to support his wife. "Robert ... Do me an' your ma a favour will 'e?" He looks towards the remnants of the meal.

Having read the unspoken request of his father, he knows what is required of him — so he nods and, without dispute, begins to remove the dishes to the sink. It is likely to take the efforts of both of his parents to get through to his older brother.

Jack follows her to the first floor and observes the proceedings as she knocks on the bedroom door ... and then, without invite, pushes it open.

As she enters — her spouse in her wake — Joe, having been staring blankly at the tiny cracks in the ceiling, rolls away from his prostrate position on the bed and lies on his side, his back to the incursion.

Conversation will lead to him having to give an explanation — and an explanation will reopen the floodgates of pent-up emotions. This is not what he wants. So, by adopting a state of silence and, therefore, a resistance to any interaction, he makes his stand, albeit passively, against any interrogation — well-meaning or otherwise.

Perching on his bed, she rests her hand on his shoulder, and instinctively, her demeanour returns to that of the nurturing mother; caringly, and with an air of gentleness, she tries to eke out the worries from her son. "Come on Joe ... talk to me."

His body tenses as he fights the natural desire to respond and share his deepest feelings.

"Look ... You know we don't keep secrets from each other. We're family, and we stick together. You know that."

She allows her quietly spoken words to be absorbed before continuing. "Come on. Let's talk, hey?"

His eyes, reddened and watered with sadness, are careful to avoid making contact.

With a lacking in tolerance, Jack turns to leave the room and cannot help but to add his parting opinion. "I can't be doing with this ... You'm bin out all night, and now that young Lucy maid's nowhere to be found! They in the village will soon be reckoning you'm bin up to no good, and frankly, I can't blame 'em — 'cause if I's to be honest with 'e, I's beginnin' to think the same!"

He stomps down the stairs — the vibration of each step expressing the depth of his anger.

She waits, retaining her appearance of calm, until the footsteps are no longer heard, and then appeals to her son to break his silence and to speak with her.

"Joe, you know I can't help you if you'm gonna shut me out."

With tear-filled eyes, he turns towards her and says, "Pa reckons I's done something to her, don't he?"

"Of course not. Where d'you get that idea from? No one's done anything to her. She's just been a bit upset, that's all. She's laid low for a bit, and I reckons that her'll come out of the woodwork when her's good and ready."

As the tears overspill, he forces out the words, "He may not have said anything, but I know that's what he meant. He reckons I've done som'it really bad."

"Now don't be daft Son. Why would anyone think anything like that? Now you mark my words — Lucy'll be home soon , just you wait an' see."

"Ma … You do believe me, don't 'e?"

"Of course I do. What I'm worried about is why you'm so down-in-the-dumps."

He starts to explain. "Her was off with that Marcus Warren bu'y, so I lost it, an' I smacked him one." He lowers his head in shame as he adds, "I gave her a smack too — I didn't mean to, but I did, an' I reckons I hurt her."

Lorna pulls her hand away and sits up, shocked by the revelation that not only has her son been involved in a fight, but he has, in the process, hit his girlfriend as well. "Her parents didn't say anything about that when they phoned."

She gathers her thoughts. "Oh dear. I'm so embarrassed. How could you? You know you should never raise your hand to a woman!"

"It wasn't like that. I didn't mean to, Ma. I didn't see her — I just hit out when I was grabbed, that's all."

She mellows as she looks him in the eyes. "Was she injured?"

"I don't know. I just upped and run. I's sorry Ma, I didn't mean to hurt her. You know me, I wouldn't 'ave hurt her for the world."

She wants to believe him. Moreover, she senses that she has no reason not to. The support of her loving embrace confirms her faith in him. "I know son. You wouldn't have hurt her for the world."

"It was an accident! I just felt someone grab me, an' all I wanted to do was shake 'em off."

"It's okay, I believe you. Now will you stop all this 'ere fretting? If not for me … then, how about for yourself?"

"I can't — police will be wan'in to speak with me. What's I gonna do, Ma?"

"Now, you just settle and calm down. I think maybe 'tis best we keep this to ourselves at present, don't you? Probably find you'm bin worrying 'bout nothing, an' nothin' more will come of it."

He responds with an unconvincing smile.

***

Marcus, nursing his bruises, sits alone in front of the television screen.

The programme running is of no real interest to him, but, at present, he has little interest in anything else either.

With his parents out, he takes advantage of the privacy afforded by him having the house to himself. He has neither the desire nor the need to go out; nor does he wish to make any complaint of assault.

He had certainly taken pleasure in the sinister thoughts which had engulfed him whilst in the darkness of the lane, and he would still like to avenge his hurt.

However, he weighs up the possible consequences of any acts of vengeance and decides to avoid any unnecessary police involvement by playing the whole thing down. After all, revenge is a dish which is best served cold.

***

Shep, alerted by the familiar sound of his collar number being called over the radio, diverts his attention and listens. Sunset, although not on duty, has requested *talk-through*.

Shep responds, "Receiving. Go ahead."

"Re, the radio — I won't be able to get it back to you today. I've got no transport. I'll bring it in tomorrow … if I can get myself another car, if that's all right with you."

Shep allows himself a smile as he answers. "No problem — I take it her's beyond repair then?"

"Yep. It's off to the scrap-yard in the morning."

"All right, bu'y … Maybe 'tis best if you be bringing the radio back when you'm next in then."

"Roger! Out!"

Shep ends the transmission and lowers the radio.

"Sorry 'bout that." His apology for the interruption is followed by the briefest of explanations. "The special took the radio with 'im last night in case he found Lucy. I must say, 'tis nice to see that there are still some youngsters about who can demonstrate a bit of conscientiousness."

Gina nods in agreement as she clutches a photograph of her daughter. With a deepening sadness and a touch of reluctance, she hands it to Shep for him to attach it to his file for circulation among the patrols.

"Thank you. I'll see that it's returned when we find her."

Again, she nods as she mouths a barely audible, "Thank you."

Chapter 10

As if reluctant to yield to customary seasonal etiquette, the long, dry summery days of southern France continue to encroach well into the time of another, and, by doing so, the clear blue skies — broken only with the occasional smudge of white cotton cloud — leave the white-hot sun to burn mercilessly onto the baked and hardened land.

The chateau, modest in its own right, yet impressive amid the rambling spread of ancient ochre-topped outbuildings, emits an air of permanence as it watches over the vines and the groves of olives which provide income for both landowner and the handful of seasonal workers alike.

Bedecking the courtyard, the ornately-forged suite of matching table and chairs, along with the colourful and aromatic abundance of potted flora, exude a suggestion of attentive and intimate moments. But, it is the backdrop of pale and faded lichen-green shutters which lie flat against the cracked and scarred render of stone-built walls which complete this scene of artistic contradiction.

A warm and gentle breeze wafts across the delicate covering of wheaten powder, lifting and shaping it into a miniature column of twirling dust, which, like a vortex of delight, chases and dances haphazardly across the yard, only to abruptly cease and, as if not to disturb the slumbers of a resting beast, silently unfurl as it falls and settles like some discarded silken scarf.

Splayed out and reserving his energy, the German shepherd dog pants rapidly as he absorbs the heat from the sun, which, with the morning on the wane, furtively replaces the shade of the ever-shortening shadows.

Tom pauses, looks up and waits. Delaying the task in mind, he listens and watches as the car which — with a cloud of dust in tow and thus a suggestion of some urgency — bounces along the rugged and twisting track as it carves its way past the almost biblical and peace-evoking setting of olives.

Hearing the approach as it winds its way through the heart of the gentle, rounded landscape of Tom's revived and beloved vineyard, the German shepherd stirs.

Stretching his front legs out and to the fore, he acclimatises to the demise of uninterrupted tranquillity and the premature return to a state of vigilant consciousness. Having risen to his feet, he shakes the dust from his coat and trots across the yard to be at the side of his master.

Pulling up to an abrupt halt outside the main house, the Peugeot's engine falls into silence. With the dust still floating on the breeze as the pull of gravity slowly coaxes it back to earth, the door opens, and its uniformed occupant emerges with a welcoming smile.

Recognising the familiar face of the local police officer, the German shepherd moves forward, his tail beating with pleasure as if in anticipation of an affectionate fuss.

With the expected attention received, he breaks away and, with his nose scenting the ground, eagerly and purposefully hunts around the yard.

Tom steps towards his friend.

"Bonjour, Philippe."

"Bonjour, Thomas, ça va?"

"Ça va bien, et tu?"

"Oui, ça va bien aussi."

With the usual *hellos* and *how are yous* duly exchanged, they clasp each other's hand in greeting.

Distracted by movement from behind his host, Philippe observes the housekeeper, who, nonchalantly and apparently oblivious to his presence, is strolling towards the chateau with a wide laundry-laden basket in hand.

He calls across to her, *"Hé Rozenn! Ça va?"*

She could respond by acknowledging his greeting and then confirming that she is well, but instead she ignores him.

"Je pense que ma petite soeur m'évite."

Affirming the fact that she *is* avoiding him, and along with the explanation as to the reason why, she responds, *"C'est vrai. Je tu évite. Peut-être c'est parce que tu aves oublié mon anniversaire ou peut-être je suis trop occupé pour parles avec tu."*

Philippe knows that she is right, and he cannot blame her for ignoring him! After all, he *had* forgotten to acknowledge her birthday, and although he doesn't quite go with the additional excuse of her being too busy to speak with him, he accepts his guilt; so, duly admonished, he watches on silently as his sister steps indoors.

With a Gallic shrug, along with an impish smile and a dismissive flick of the hand, he makes his opinion audible only to his friend. *"Elle est parfois très querelleuse."*

Tom laughs at how the simplicity of the single word, *querelleuse* — or quarrelsome when translated into English — can so accurately sum up a person's character.

Tom, surprised, if not a little amused, that Philippe had forgotten his sister's birthday, seeks confirmation of her allegation — after all, she had, uncharacteristically, not mentioned it to him.

"Est-ce qu'il est vrai? Est-ce que tu vraiment aves oublié son anniversaire?"

"Oui. J'étais très occupé au travail mais je me suis souvenu de deux jours plus tard et alors je l'ai donnée elle présente."

It was true. He had been busy — and yes … he had forgotten her birthday.

With a large stone clasped in his mouth, the German shepherd returns, and by the way in which he stares up at Phillipe, he is expectant of play.

Without making even the slightest of eye contact, Philippe removes the stone from the powerful and masculine jaws and then hurls it as far as he is able, across the track and out into the rough.

The distraction, convenient in that it gives the opportunity for Philippe to change the subject, allows him to announce, "*Vos téléphone est en panne.*"

Tom responds in passable, but not necessarily fluent, French as he confirms the observation. "*Oui, Je sais. J'ai eu des problèmes. J'attends l'ingénieur.*"

His telephone has been out of order for several days. But knowing that the pace of life is much slower in rural France than it is in the United Kingdom, he is not particularly concerned as to the delay in the arrival of the engineer.

"*Je les téléphonerais pour découvrir combien plus long.*"

He smiles as he makes gentle fun of the fact that he would indeed call the company to establish when the engineer will arrive ... had it not been for the offending fault.

"*Oui, mais vos téléphone est cassé.*"

Philippe laughs as he, too, recognizes the difficulty in making a call to the company without a functioning telephone. Then, remembering the reason for his visit, his facial expression immediately adopts a look of formality and seriousness.

Retrieved, the dampened stone is proudly dropped at the feet of Philippe.

"*J'ai une demande pour tu téléphoner Inspecteur Dowsett à la Police de Exeter.*"

He hands him the piece of paper on which the number is written.

As Tom reads the message, Philippe picks up the stone and throws it as far as he can, hoping that the dog's search will be extended and thus allow sufficient time for him to complete his assignment.

The dog kicks up a cloud of dust as he rushes off in joyful pursuit.

"*Pourquoi est-ce qu'ils veulent qu'ils parlent avec moi? Est-ce que tu saves?*" Tom asks, concerned as to why a policeman from Devon would have a need to speak to him.

"*Est-ce que je pense c'est de vos fille! Lucy?*" Although Philippe has said that he *thinks* that the enquiry concerns Tom's daughter, Lucy — who, incidentally, he had met when she had visited France during the last holiday period — the truth is that he actually *knows* that it concerns her welfare.

"Lucy? What's the problem? *Quel est le problème?*"

Naturally, Tom is worried. Understandably, he needs to know what has happened to his daughter. She has not been in contact with him for a while. But then, this is probably due to the fact that his phone is out of order and, of course, the additional fact that she is a teenager.

"*Je ne sais pas. Peut-être il y a un petit problème avec la police.*"

Due to Inspector Dowsett's inability to communicate adequately in French, Philippe has not been made privy to the detail of the British enquiry. Nevertheless, he tries to minimize his friend's worries by insinuating that it may well be a relatively minor matter.

"Maybe. *Peut-être tu aves raison.*" Tom nods his head, hopeful that his friend is right, and then asks for a favour. "*Comment est-ce que je peux téléphoner?*"

"*Tu pouves utiliser le téléphone à le gendarmerie.*"

"*Merci.*" The offer to make use of the police station telephone is gratefully accepted.

"*Nous pouvons aller maintenant. Je tu rencontrerai à la station de police.*"

"*Merci. Tu es un bon ami. Je tu suivrai.*" Again, Tom is grateful to a man who has, over the past few years, become a good friend and confirms that he will, indeed, use his own car and follow him to the police station.

Philippe returns to the police car and waits. "*Je tu verrai bientôt.*"

"*Oui, d'accord.*" Tom gives his response before calling out to Rozenn.

Little more than a year ago, she had started working as his housekeeper, but since then, she has managed to have initiated the sculpting of a more meaningful relationship from out of what had been platonic origins.

Although assuming an image of casual indifference, her prompt arrival in the doorway suggests her appearance as being more of a response to her having been summoned by her employer-cum-companion than that of a mere accident of coincidence. She has, however, never possessed the temperament to show noticeable signs of subservience; so, persistent in her execution of the charade, she stands and silently peers out and towards him.

Whilst taking advantage of being able to luxuriate in the seductive warmth of the sun's rays which press gently on her face, she poses with one arm outstretched, upwards and against the pillar, and the other, somewhat flirtatiously, resting on her hip.

There is nothing for her to say, for it is her expression alone that tells him that she is awaiting an explanation as to why she has been interrupted from her activities.

Even though he is worried about Lucy's welfare, he suspects that, as is often the case, things will not be as bad as it appears to be at present.

For a moment or two, he is distracted from his thoughts … as he cannot help but to smile as he catches the enchanting image of Rozenn.

Maybe, he muses, it is the way in which she always knows how to look *at her best*. After all, even the most unassuming of her flowing cotton dresses can look stylish and graceful when draped over her smooth and tanned shoulders. But then, he thinks, drifting away from the romantic, it may be nothing more than the glow of that playful look in her eyes — along with the good fortune of having inherent attributes of beauty — that enable her ability to charm and, thus, disarm him from his thoughts.

Whatever it is that she has, he knows that she definitely possesses a certain look; a look of allure, which, he believes, is a trait envied and mimicked by many … but is, in the main, perfected only by those of Gallic descent.

He concentrates on the task in hand and tells her of his plans. "I'm going to the police station with Philippe. I need to use his phone. I'll be back soon?"

Unimpressed by his apparent lack of response to her need for attention, and failing to register the fact that he now has an urgent need of his own, she steps out and into the yard.

"*Quand est-ce que tu seres revenu?*" she asks, whilst throwing a brief, disparaging glance towards her disgraced brother as he — a little shamefacedly — fires up the engine.

As he starts to edge his way back along the track, he leans out of the window and calls back to Tom. "*Je tu verrai à le gendarmerie.*"

Tom nods in acknowledgment and then turns to Rozenn.

"I won't be too long." He pauses, then, continuing in the language of the indigenous, he corrects himself. "*Je ne peux pas être sûr. J'ai un message pour téléphoner Angleterre. C'est de Lucy.*"

Evidently troubled by the message, he explains that he cannot be sure as to how long he will be, as he has been asked to make a telephone call to England, concerning Lucy.

Like a flick of a switch, her attitude changes as she understands why he had failed to react to her provocative performance of a few seconds before, and then, sincerely and with compassion, she asks, "*Est-ce qu'il y a un problème?*"

"*Je ne sais pas. Le plus tôt je téléphone le plus rapide je saurai.*" He tells her that he does not know exactly what the call is in relation to, and emphasizes, with a suggestion of impatience, that the sooner he is allowed to make the call … then the sooner he will know what it is all about.

"*Philippe est allé. Je dois aller à.*"

With Philippe having already gone, Tom does not wish to delay his journey any longer.

"*Est-ce que tu prends le loup?*" With an affectionate smile in her eyes and a questioning tilt of her head, she hopes that simple charm will lessen his worry and, at the same time, override the need for her to turn a request into a demand. Even though she is sensitive to the fact that he is preoccupied with anxiety, she feels happier if she is not left alone with what she refers to as, *le loup!*

"*Il n'est pas le loup! Il est le chien!*" He corrects her, Sonny is not a wolf — he is a dog. Showing signs of impatience, he adds, "*Et Non! Le chien restera ici! Comprendes?*"

"*Il ne m'écoute pas.*"

She is wrong. *Le loup* does listen to her! It is simply that he is either unable to, or lacks the desire to understand her. Although of a gentle temperament, Sonny has always sensed her apprehension, but he can, at times, make her feel a little uncomfortable as he tends to take advantage of the situation.

"*Tu le prends, s'il vous plaît.*" Her disarming look of desperation which embellishes her plea for him to take the dog does not go unheeded. Exchanging glances with Sonny, Tom weakens and decides that he can waste no more time; besides, he knows that the innocent, uncomplicated company of a loyal German shepherd is difficult to surpass, especially at times when a person's stress has become distress.

"*D'accord. Je le prendrai,*" he calls back to Rozenn, and then looks back towards his dog. "Come on Sonny. Get in the car."

"*Bon!*" she replies with a smile, evidently satisfied with the result.

Rozenn, with fine and soft mahogany curls kissing her shoulders as they bounce in harmony with the spring of her step, marches back into the house and, with a dismissive shrug, mutters triumphantly, "*Tu prends le loup.*"

As man and dog move towards the somewhat battered, but trusted, Mercedes Benz estate, Sonny, with bounds of excitement, races ahead and, with the lithesome skill of one who could be more than equal to that of any gymnast, jumps up and through the already opened driver's window before hopping across to take his customary place on the passenger seat. The regularity of the procedure is reflected not only in his adeptness at being able to faultlessly execute the manoeuvre, but, more so, by the evidence of countless landings where powerful claws appear to have etched a record of each arrival into the once luxurious covering of leathered upholstery.

Unlike England — the land where he had lived from around the age of fourteen until the time of his divorce — this is a part of the world where it is still safe to leave a car unlocked. With a hint of romanticism serving to add a rather rosy hue to his recollections, he likes to think that this is a land which is more akin to that of his birth, which having been set amid the mountains and loughs of Donegal — was a place where everyone had known everyone. What's more, according to his father, people were able to leave the doors of their homes unlocked — and had they been fortunate enough to have possessed such a thing as a car, then they, too, would have been able to leave the keys hanging in the ignition without the fear of it being taken.

At least, with him having now adopted the same attitude to security, he has never had the occasion to suffer the frustration of not knowing where he has left his keys.

As he starts the motor, a clattering of dry tappets, accompanied by a belch of black smoke as the pressure of the engine pushes out an excess of diesel, suggests that a service is well overdue. With the engine warming and the oil circulating, the rhythmic beat of the mechanical workings settle … and the smoke is soon nothing more than that of a memory.

They move forward and onwards, briskly traversing the rocks and craters with the proficiency of one who has negotiated the track so often that the need to observe has virtually become redundant.

Once out and onto the smooth and relatively luxurious surface of an asphalted road, he starts to accelerate.

With worried thoughts racing through his mind, he wonders what Lucy could have done to necessitate the urgency for him to contact the police. Feisty she may be, but criminal? Definitely not!

His thoughts drift back to the time when he had last seen his daughter. Although it seems as if an age has passed, it was only a month or so ago when she was enjoying a lazy fortnight's summer vacation, *chilling out*, at his home.

Whilst she *chilled* and he busied himself with the routine of viniculture, she was, naively but endearingly, leading Rozenn astray by encouraging her to join her in absorbing the sun-drenched ambience of the cafés and culture of the nearby town.

She had finished the last of her school examinations and was quietly confident in having achieved a more than satisfactory degree of success. She had decided, however, that furthering her education in the formal setting of a college was not for her, and having made an impression whilst working part-time in the retail industry, she had elected to pursue a career in the fashion trade. In fact, she had already succeeded in finding herself a position, and as a result she had seemed quite content with her lot.

He had seen nothing about her demeanour to have given any cause for alarm. Apart from her scrawling a few jocular words on the back of some postcards for her friends, she had appeared sufficiently secure within herself to have relaxed and, what is more, to have switched off completely from all the trappings of her life in Devon.

The Mercedes surges forward as Tom, in an attempt to catch up with Philippe, significantly increases the pressure of his foot on the accelerator pedal. As the speedometer needle rapidly ascends the scale, he recognizes the irony … in that, for him to have been able to keep up with his *gendarme* friend, he has had to exceed the maximum permitted velocity.

With Philippe back in sight, he eases off from the throttle, and being cognisant of the need to respect the rule of law, and not wishing to be seen to abuse both the standing and good nature of his friend, he returns to the confines of the prescribed limit.

Chapter 11

Scattering his papers to one side, Philippe leans across the office desk as he reaches for the telephone.

He dials and waits patiently for the ringing tone as the connection is made

"*Ici* … It rings."

He passes the phone to Tom, sits and indicates for him to do the same.

"*Merci.*" Tom takes the handset and, with it pressed close to his ear, lowers himself into the chair which is positioned on the opposite side of the desk.

The ringing tone is cut short as the call is answered.

"D.I. Dowsett." Gruff and curt, this is the voice of a man who gets the job done and whose juniors dare not interrupt without good reason.

"Mr Dowsett? — I'm Tom McMurry … I'm ringing from France. You asked me to call?"

The detective inspector immediately drops the natural brusqueness in his tone and slips into a rather more tactful mode. "Ah! Yes. Mr McMurry. Thank you for getting back to me. You're a hard man to reach."

"Yes, I know. I'm ringing from the local police station — my home phone's been out of order. I'm still waiting for the engineer to get it repaired. So as you can appreciate, I've been *incommunicado.*"

With the explanation duly made, he waits for the D.I. to explain the reason for his need to be contacted.

Again, there's a moment of silence before the officer responds.

"I'm Detective Inspector Graham Dowsett and I'm overseeing the enquiry."

"Enquiry?"

"Yes. I'm sorry. Look …" As he prepares to issue some worrying news, there is a noticeable mellowing in the tone of his voice. "Mr McMurry … I need to speak with you … about your daughter, Lucy."

"Lucy? Why? Is she in trouble?" He gives no time for a response as, fearing that she may have been accused of something quite serious, he immediately launches the next question. "You mentioned an enquiry. What enquiry? Tell me — what's she done?"

"As far as we can tell, she's done nothing wrong. We're only concerned as for her welfare. Now then … Can you tell me? Have you heard anything from her?"

"No. Nothing … Why? Should I have?"

"Well, Mr McMurry…"

"It's Tom. Please … call me Tom."

"If that's what you prefer, then I'll call you Tom. Now, as I was saying,

Lucy has been reported missing." The detective inspector is blunt. The revelation, albeit brief, strikes with the force of hammer.

"What do you mean? … *Missing*!" Tom seeks clarification as the words float in his thoughts and he analyses the significance of the statement.

"Your wife — I mean your ex-wife. Anyway, she reported Lucy missing after she had failed to return home following a wedding party on Saturday night."

"Hang on a minute … You're telling me that she's been missing for two nights … and only now you contact me!"

"We did try yesterday, but your phone …"

"Oh yes, I'm sorry. Please — go on."

The D.I. continues. "Apparently there was a bit of an upset between her and her boyfriend, Joe. Do you know him?"

"Yes, and no … but I've met him. Anyway, what sort of upset?"

"I understand that he caught Lucy in a bit of a compromising position with another local lad, Marcus Warren, and, as a result, he gave the lad a bit of a thumping. Now, from what I've been told, Lucy took a bit of a smack as well. "

"What? Who hit her?"

"It's my understanding that Joe hit her!"

"What? What did he hit her for? Was she hurt?"

"Well, I can't be too certain until he's been spoken to, but it sounds like it may have been an accident. Apparently, he just hit out blindly. From all accounts, I don't think he knew who he was hitting."

"I don't care about that!" Instantly dismissing the intentions of the assailant as being of little importance, he is more interested in getting to the point as to what had happened to his daughter, and so he spells out what he needs to know. "What I want to know is … was she hurt?"

He accepts the priorities of Lucy's father and responds without delay. "According to your ex-wife, she was sore … but to the best of my knowledge, it was none too serious. There were definitely no notable injuries or broken bones, etcetera."

"Okay. Thank God for that. Thank you." The relief at the revelation is reflected in the tone of his voice, and with rationale having returned, he continues. "So what you're saying is that she was hit, and understandably she was pretty upset — but that doesn't explain why she's gone missing, does it? Surely, if she was that upset then she would have stayed at home with Gina … her mother?"

"Ah, well now, that wasn't the end of it. You see … after all this kerfuffle, I understand that she went on to have a bit of a fall out with your ex-wife and her husband."

"A fall out? What sort of fall out?"

"I'm not sure of all the details yet, but it ended up with her storming off and saying that she was going to find you. That's why I'm asking if you've heard anything from her."

"Oh hell! You're right — my phone. She couldn't have contacted me if she'd wanted to."

"Tell me ... how long before you get it up and running again?"

"I don't know?"

"Do you know anyone who can rush it through? I think that maybe under the circumstances, you can give them my name and number. If they want to contact me, then I can see if I'm able to explain the importance of it to them. You know ... Maybe, with me saying something, then I can add a bit of weight to getting it all done."

"Yes... Maybe."

He turns to his friend. *"Philippe!"*

"Oui?"

"Lucy, elle ne peut pas être trouvée. Elle est une personne disparue. C'est très important que mon téléphone est réparé. Est-ce que tu connais quelqu'un qui peut réparer il rapidement?"

In typical rural French style, there is always a friend or relation who can help in times of crisis. *"Oui, je pense si. Je parlerai avec mon cousin. Il pourra aider."*

"Est-ce que tu sûr?"

"Oui, Il est un des directors." Philippe is sure that the senior position which is held by his cousin will not be wasted. *After all, what are families for?*

"Inspector Dowsett?"

"Yes, I'm still here."

"Philippe, our local policeman ... he says that he has a cousin in the telephone company's management, and he's sure that he can rush it through."

"Excellent. If you have any problems, let me know."

"Look ... If it's of any help, I can get over there by tomorrow."

Tom is already beginning to feel as if by him doing nothing other than to passively wait at home, he will, in some way, be failing his daughter. He has a need to do something. What exactly ... he is unsure; but he wonders if he should make his way to Devon and join in with the search.

"No! I would rather you stayed at home ... in case she's on her way over to you."

"Okay. How do you think will she get here? She'll need her passport to cross the channel. Do you know if she's got it with her? What about money?"

The questions stream out, allowing little time for reply.

The D.I. cuts in. "I've spoken with her mother — your ex — and she says that since reaching eighteen, she carries her passport in her bag so that she can prove her age when she goes out for a drink."

"Actually, come to think about it, that was my idea. Anyway, you're right, she probably will have her passport with her. Still, if she has managed to get across the Channel, at least she knows how to find me."

"Good. So you understand where I'm coming from when I say that there's a chance that she could turn up."

"Yes, I do."

"Now, I can't force you to stay in France ... but bearing in mind what I've just said, then I think it would be a good idea if you did."

"For now, maybe ... but if nothing's heard in the next couple of days, then I'm on my way."

"I understand exactly where you're coming from, but, hopefully, it won't come to that. Now, so that I can keep you up to date, will you let me know as soon as your phone is reconnected?"

"Yes, certainly. I'll do that and ..." Tom pauses as he vainly searches his rapidly-numbing thoughts for another question. "No, that's all right. I'll leave you to it. Thank you ... and of course, it goes without saying that I'd appreciate it if you could keep me in touch, too."

"Yes I will. You have my word."

As both men replace their receivers, there is a knock at the Detective inspector's office door.

"Come! The door's open!"

"Sir ... I'm sorry to disturb you, but we have an update on the McMurry girl."

The constable's expression does not suggest good news.

Graham Dowsett sits quietly ... his eyes urging the officer to release the information.

The dog's found a shoe. It's already been confirmed as belonging to the girl."

"Where?"

"In the woods. Just off the lane ... nearer the village."

"Are you sure it's hers?"

The D.I. starts to rise from his chair as he listens for the answer to his question.

"Yes, sir. As I've said, it's been confirmed by the mother."

Unable to hide his anger at him having been excluded from such an important development, he snaps at the young probationer, who is nearing the end of his fortnight's attachment to the department. "Why wasn't I told of this before she was shown it?"

"I don't know, sir — I'm just the messenger."

"Mmm..." Unimpressed by the critical inference of the retort and unable to disguise a blush of irritation, he looks down at the papers which lie on his desk.

The constable stands silently as he awaits the opportunity to continue.

"Yes?" His senior sees that there is more to come and lowers himself back into his chair. "… and?"

"Yes, sir … and SOCO are, as we speak, examining the area where the shoe was found. I think they may have found traces of blood — but I'm not sure."

"Scenes of Crime are already there?"

"Yes, sir."

"Mmm… So tell me … Who the hell set all this up without informing me first?"

He is a man who, albeit in a managerial position, likes to keep his finger on the pulse and remain active, as is expected from an old-fashioned *operational*, policeman. Although his voice is calm, his annoyance is evident.

"Uniform, sir — Sergeant Cooper."

He sits back and opens out his wallet. Pointing at the displayed warrant card, he speaks, "Correct me if I'm wrong, but does that say *Inspector* Dowsett?"

"Yes, sir."

"I thought so."

He shakes his head, still wondering why his having been advised of the situation seems to have been little more than that of an afterthought.

"Okay — It's not your fault, lad."

Accepting that he may unduly be taking his frustration out on an innocent, he shows signs of a mellowing as he gathers the papers on his desk. "Ah well, I suppose I'd better get out there. As they say … 'tis better late than never."

"Yes, sir."

The constable backs away, and as he turns towards the door, he stops as his departure is abruptly cut short.

"Oh! And by the way…" He allows sufficient a pause to ensure that he has the undivided attention of his junior. "… I don't shoot messengers!"

He pauses again and then fires a somewhat veiled warning. "… Not unless, of course, they come with a twist of insubordination."

The constable glances back, and as their eyes meet, he accepts the subtle admonishment and apologises. "Yes, sir — I'm sorry."

Seniority acknowledges the apology with a nod, and with the balance of authority having been re-established, he is satisfied that the matter is closed.

Chapter 12

"Watch out, Sarge. Here comes the Growsett!"

The arrival of the senior detective is announced with a hushed and cautionary respect.

"Oh … Great!" A touch of sarcasm precedes the acknowledgement of the uniformed sergeant's responsibilities. "I suppose I'd better go and update him."

Careful not to contaminate what may well turn out to be a crime scene, he treads the few yards along the lane to greet the detective inspector.

With his car left in a state of apparent abandonment, Graham Dowsett ducks under the barrier tape and heads closer to the heart of the activity.

With a transparent exhibit bag in hand, the sergeant intercepts his course.

"Morning, sir."

"What have we got?"

"Well, sir … the dog handler's located this shoe in the gulley on the other side of the embankment. It's been identified as belonging to the *misper.*"

The senior officer is already aware. "Yes, so I understand. By the mother, if I'm not mistaken."

A nod from the sergeant confirms the fact.

Eyeing the bag with its solitary enclosure, he asks, "Just the one?"

"Yes, sir — the heel's broken."

"Yes, I can see that!" he snaps grumpily at being told what is, in his opinion, the obvious.

"Where's the other one?"

With a shrug of the shoulders, he replies, "I don't know — the dog's carrying out a search as we speak."

"And where is Mrs McMurry?"

"It's Smale, sir … Mrs Smale." The sergeant corrects the inspector. "It's an easy mistake to make."

Containing his feelings, the more senior of the two officers sighs and waits silently for his question to be answered.

"She's at the hall … She's with her husband."

"What are they doing there?"

His discomfort with the revelation is evident.

"Well, sir, they knew that we were doing the search from there, so, understandably, they wanted to be close at hand."

"Mmm…" He considers the emotions of relatives who hover around a scene of an incident to be a distraction from an investigation's need for clinical analysis. "Who's with her?"

"Kate — Kate Phillips."

Relieved that they are in the more than capable hands of a constable who had recently had a successful attachment as an aide to his department, he continues. "That's good. They're in good hands — I'll see them later."

Changing tack, he concentrates on the task ahead. "So, what's all this about some blood being found?"

"Well, it looks like she'd thrown the shoe into the woods farther up the lane — it being broken an' all that. But back here, it looks as if there may be traces of blood in the gulley. It's possible that the shoe probably came off in a struggle and someone else threw it away."

"The straps …"

"Yes, sir"

"They're unbuckled. Not broken … unbuckled."

He allows the sergeant to assess the implication of his observation.

"Yes, sir."

"Does that suggest a struggle?"

He considers the judgment of the detective, and, with his voice now subdued, he responds, "Well, not necessarily, I guess. You're absolutely right though … it doesn't suggest a struggle."

"Don't worry, *Sergeant* — it's an easy mistake to make."

He accentuates his words with a grin of self-satisfaction. No longer feeling that the sergeant had, somehow, managed *to get one up on him* regarding his earlier misnaming of Lucy's mother, he continues. "I trust you've done all the basics? Searched the home? Contacted her friends?"

"Yes, sir — it's all in hand."

"Good."

He looks towards the embankment and calls out to the *scene-of-crime* officer. "Good morning Ade … Is it all right for me to come over?"

He waits for authorization before edging even closer to where the scene is being examined and the evidence gathered.

The affirmative nod with a summoning wave of a hand guides him in.

As he approaches, he watches with interest as a protruding boulder is examined for traces of anything which could be of evidential value and worthy of forensic analysis.

"What do you think?"

He respects the experience and tenacity of Adrian D Williams; a man who is thorough to a fault. And with his extraordinary ability to read and analyse a scene of a crime, his value is incalculable.

"Have a look at this." He steers the attention of the D.I. towards what appears to be traces of blood.

"If this is her blood, then the rock hasn't moved … so it looks as if she either *fell* onto it … or her head was *bashed* against it. Now … if you look below it, in the earth, you'll see that it looks as if there's more blood which has congealed."

"Do you suspect foul play?"

"It's a possibility, but no more at this stage. But, erring on the side of caution, I've treated it as such; so everything's been photographed in situ', and now I'm just picking through the detail. I'll see what else I can find."

"Good. Is there anything else?"

"Yes, there is. If you care to take a look at the top of the bank, there appears to be some small holes. I think it's likely they're from the heels. At the moment it's difficult to be certain 'cause it looks like this may also be a route taken by some wild deer. I'm not sure ... but it looks like their hooves have turned the soil. I'll have definitive answer later on."

"If they are from her heels, then it may be safe to assume that she stood there of her own accord? Am I right?"

"Possibly ... but I can't be sure. One thing I do find odd is ... if it is her blood on the stone and in the earth, then you'd assume that this is where she was attacked — so why would someone take the shoe farther down the lane to throw it away?"

"Interesting ... I'll think about that one. Okay. Thanks, Ade. Keep up the good work."

Content that the officer has control within the field of his expertise, he diverts his attention elsewhere. "Now then ... where's the dog handler?"

"Sir!" The sergeant approaches. "Comm's are trying to contact you."

He taps his jacket pocket as he instinctively checks for his radio. "I must've left it in the car."

He holds out his hand, beckoning for the uniformed officers radio.

He transmits. "Q.B. from D.I.Dowsett."

"Go ahead."

"You have a message for me."

"Affirmative. From the station-sergeant."

"Go ahead."

"There's a Joseph Hardy at the station ... enquiring about the *misper*."

"Hardy? ... Good! Keep him there — I'll be making my way back a.s.a.p."

"Roger. Q.B. out."

With the transmission completed, he returns the radio to the sergeant, and then glances along the lane in search of the dog handler. There is no sign of the him; so, prioritising the need to see Joe, he aborts his search and heads back to his car.

Chapter 13

The enquiry clerk unlocks the security door which separates the public foyer from the operational areas of the police station and ushers Joe into the inner sanctum of the building.

He is feeling increasingly nervous as he is, albeit courteously, clinically led along the corridor and then into a sparsely-furnished and artificially-lit waiting room. There is no outlook; just four pale-green walls which are peppered with a selection of posters — all of which serve to extol the virtues of both crime prevention and victim support.

"Mr Hardy, if you'd like to take a seat, an officer will be with you as soon as possible."

"Thank you."

He smiles in search of a reciprocal response from the man in uniform — there is none.

As he sits alone with only his feelings for company, he muses as to the reasoning behind his decision to visit the police without having been asked to do so.

Surely they will be suspicious of his uninvited arrival; but then, he rationalizes, they will want to satisfy their curiosity and speak to him, even if it is only for them to execute the necessary format of investigative routine. Besides, he surmises, it will look far better for him if he makes himself available to them rather than forcing an alternative scenario where he has to be hunted down, before being hauled in for questioning at a time of their choosing.

However, whether his decision is right or wrong, he is here … and it is far too late in the day to back-pedal. To change his mind and leave before being seen by an officer will only add to any suspicions that may be developing.

His mind flits back and forth between reason and dread; he cannot settle. The need to know what they, the police, know about Lucy and her present whereabouts is of prime importance; however, he also needs to know whether or not any complaints have been made against him regarding either his attack on Marcus … or the lesser and somewhat unintentional assault on Lucy.

As the sounds of footsteps echo along the corridor, his body tightens with trepidation, expectant of an uncomfortable period of questioning. Then, as they pass by and fade into nothingness, he sighs and waits quietly for the sound of the next approach.

The hypnotic rhythm of the ticking clock threatens to dull his ability to concentrate. So, in a conscious attempt to maintain the capacity to think with clarity, he stands up and paces around the room, thus stimulating his circulation.

The wait seems endless, and his impatience, atypically, starts to build.

"Come on..." he growls, as be becomes increasingly frustrated at having to wait without being given any idea as to how long for.

"Come on... Where are you?"

He opens the door and looks along the length of the corridor. Spotting a young constable, with his back to him, he calls out. "Excuse me."

The constable stops in his tracks and then glances back.

"Can you find out what's happening ... please?"

"I'm sorry?" The constable is clearly taken unawares. "I didn't quite hear you. Can I help?"

"Yes, I's hoping that perhaps you can!" He repeats his request. "I was wonderin' if 'e could find out what's happening?"

"If you can tell me who you are and what you're here for, then maybe I can try to find something out for you."

"Thanks. Look, someone's supposed to be comin' to see me 'bout me girlfriend — Lucy — Lucy McMurry. Her's gone missing, see."

"And you are?"

"Oh, me? I'm Joe. I's Joe Hardy."

"All right ... I'll see what I can find out for you."

Although not directly involved with the ongoing enquiry, he is fully aware of the incident. Knowing how important Joe is to the investigation, he diverts himself from his previous task to adopt a more active stance in being of assistance.

"Well Mr Hardy ... if you would be so kind as to go back into the room and take a seat, then I'll see if I can find out who's gonna be dealing with you."

"Thanks."

He chooses not to linger; but instead, he complies with the request of the officer and returns to the loneliness of the room to wait, satisfied that at least some wheels of progress have been set in motion.

Chapter 14

Nigh on ninety minutes have elapsed since Joe had first entered the police station, but now, as he walks across the car park and towards his vehicle, he is, to some degree, relieved.

The questioning had been conducted in a manner which, to some, would have seemed to have been a little too casual. There had been no precursory warning that he need not say anything unless he wished to do so. Neither had there been the formality of tape recordings or, for that matter, long-winded written records of interview. It had seemed that, apart from wanting to know if Joe had any idea as to Lucy's whereabouts, the D.I. had required little more than that of a general run down of his movements before, during and after the event.

He had, to his surprise, been treated as being nothing more than that of a potential witness.

He recalls telling the policeman that he was as worried about Lucy as anyone else … and that he had absolutely no idea where she could have gone.

He had suggested that she may have gone off in pursuit of Marcus, or, on the other hand, that she may have just wanted some privacy where she could explore the potential of her latest romantic interest.

Albeit a bit of long-shot, he'd even suggested that she could have decided to make her way to one of the *cross-Channel* ferry ports with the hope of making a crossing … and then a rendezvous with her father on the other side. But, although she had often said how much she had enjoyed her times whilst with her father at his chateau in France, and that one day she may wish to relocate and settle in the area, he'd made it quite clear to the officer that his submission was, to say the least, highly unlikely.

Intuitively, he knew that his questioner was not completely satisfied with the explanation of him having spent the night on the moor in his Land Rover. But, instead of doggedly pursuing him over the matter, he had managed to unsettle him even more by nodding silently as he appeared to let it ride.

With self-doubt on the increase, he begins to realize that, when it came down to it, surprisingly little had been said regarding his assaults on either Marcus or Lucy — and, if the truth be told, no questions whatsoever were asked about the specific incidents; the explanations he had given were general, freely offered and without any need for probe or prompt.

As he pushes the key towards the driver's door lock, he pauses — and with the added discomfort of a nervous fluttering in his belly, he observes, with some concern, how his hand has uncharacteristically developed a slight, but definite, tremble.

Steadying his hand, he pushes the key into the lock and opens the door.

Once sat within the familiarity of the well-worn seat, he sits back and, with his eyes closed, allows his thoughts to race back to the interview.

Struggling to make sense of it all, he chases his thoughts, and as he does so, he rapidly comes to the conclusion that the lack of questioning was not, by any means, a sign of incompetence; it was the way of a man who is nobody's fool. In fact, he concludes that he is, without doubt, an extremely able tactician who knows exactly how to reserve his right to return for more, without having already prejudiced the line of his investigation.

It is unlikely to be the end of his involvement, and as such he is fully aware that he is not being let off the hook so that he can carry on with his life unhindered.

It is more that he has been granted a pause in proceedings whilst the police *further their enquiries* at their own pace.

When they are ready, and only then, will the questioning resume.

What's more, it will, in all probabilities, be tape-recorded in the more formal setting of an official interview room and at a time of the policeman's choosing.

He had felt somewhat frustrated by the impassive response of the detective inspector. After all, he had presented himself to the police so that he could be seen to being doing his bit to try and bring the matter to an early conclusion. But no … the wily old fox had other plans, and running to the timetable of others was not one of them.

He turns the key and the engine fires.

His return homeward is plagued by thoughts of being arrested, interrogated and then locked away behind a heavy, reinforced metal door.

An attack on another person always has consequences; one of which involves standing before the courts as the prosecutors present their case … and the judiciary give judgement. An assault on a woman is unacceptable under almost any circumstances and is thus, *in his mind*, worthy of incarceration.

If he were in a position to pass sentence on the perpetrator of such an act of violence, he would not hesitate in making it custodial in nature, and so, he fears that others may think likewise.

With the self-imposed fear of imprisonment haunting his mind, he realizes that part of him wants to avoid the intensity of further police investigations and the inevitable accusatory finger-pointing from the villagers. But then, another part of him wants to face his demons and uphold what is left of both his own integrity and the reputation of his family.

Confused and distressed, he enters the more familiar territory of the family spread. He slows … and then stops.

He wonders if Lucy's family are at the farm looking for him. Could he face them? He knows the answer … *Not yet!*

Even if they are not there, then the barbed comments from his father will, no doubt, lead to conflict. Again, he needs time to himself. After all, it will take time for him to come to terms with the shame of his actions.

He checks the fuel gauge. The diesel is low. A trip back to the outskirts of the city to refuel will serve not only to delay his return home, but also, to allow him time to rationalize his thoughts and steer himself away from a perilous course to insanity.

***

Marcus has finished his clerical duties for the day, and, as he walks out and towards his car, he considers the events of the past weekend. From all reports, the police have been active around the village for most of the day, and so, he speculates as to how they have progressed in their search for evidence of Lucy's whereabouts.

Whilst journeying home, he taunts himself with an image of a marked police car being parked outside his house, along with a couple of constables who — being reminiscent of that of a pair of orcas which prowl around a solitary seal which has been trapped on a drifting floe — are waiting patiently for him to return.

The police will want to know where he went after leaving the wedding do. They will also want to know if his whereabouts on the night of her disappearance could be verified. But, bearing in mind that no one had passed him while he walked alone along the lane and, what's more, it would have been extremely unlikely for someone to have seen him driving off from his home, then verification may not be forthcoming.

The only place that he may have been recognized was when, in an attempt to negate the effects of the alcohol and in order to relieve his stress, he had bought a coffee from the vending machine which is near the entrance to the motorway services complex.

What about his feelings for Lucy?

The police are bound to ask. If he is to be honest, then he has none — well, after having experienced the manner in which she had used him to get at Joe, then certainly none of a positive nature.

The evening's earlier acts of passion were brief and enjoyable, but then, that was where it had ended. By demonstrating her ability to use him as a tool to callously inflame the latent rage which had lain deep within the normally placid Joe, she had extinguished any ideas that he may have had with regard to it being the start of a meaningful relationship.

Thoughts of the incident, along with its painful outcome, still manage to send a shiver of fear throughout his body.

He takes some solace in the fact that although his account will not be able to be verified, neither will it be able to be unconfirmed. So, with this in mind, he feels more at ease and is as ready as he'll ever be to face an inquisition.

***

With the tank replenished and the bill paid, Joe wanders across the car park and into the main store.

He is not looking for anything in particular; he is just idly drifting along the aisles, perusing the display of products in the hope that there will be something to catch his eye … and which will offer some much-needed comfort.

Although he enjoys a drink, he is not by any means a *drinker*. However, he eyes the rows of bottles which are displayed, somewhat enticingly, on the shelves and reads the labels … Whisky, Gin, Vodka, Tequila. *Ah,* he thinks — *Tequila.* As he examines the bottle, the warm, golden glow of its content, in a strange kind of way, reminds him of Lucy's treasured pendant.

He cannot resist the desire to reach out and hold it.

He makes his decision, and so, with his hand wrapped around the neck of the bottle, he ambles to the checkout and completes the purchase.

Chapter 15

Insecure and abandoned, the short-wheel-based Land Rover lies askew across the entrance to the empty field.

Clambering up and over the five-bar wooden gate, Joe pauses before dropping heavily onto the bare earth, which, having been compacted and hardened from the constant trampling of generations of livestock, has become impenetrable and has thus debarred the grasses from making their claim.

Giving little thought to nature's wonderful display, he ignores the beauty of the ruddy, burning orb which bids its farewells as it gently sinks behind the rolling hills of the undulating skyline … leaving only its ever-changing apricot light to briefly illuminate the curling wisps of cloud which slowly unfurl and stretch lazily across the darkening sky.

With his head down, his thoughts elsewhere and an unopened bottle of golden tequila hanging loosely from his right hand, he lumbers down the uneven slope. As he makes his way towards the twisted old oak which stands, as if as a marker, at the point where, with the field suddenly sloping off and falling into the natural cleavage of the hills, he can get his first glimpse of his refuge — a place where he can be private — a place of solace.

Nestling in the dell beside the copse, stands the ancient, slate-roofed, stone-walled building which — with its permanently opened access screened by the cover of the adjacent woodland — has, for many decades, been a welcome shelter from the ferocious winds and the accompanying driving rain which so often quenches the thirst of the soil … thus maintaining the continuance of lush and healthy pastures.

Approaching the entrance, he slows. Pausing for thought, he recalls how it was in this very place where he had, as a young child, listened to his grandfather echoing the teachings of his own long-gone forefathers by showing both he and his younger brother, Robert, how to find and then, chase off the mischievous — but rarely seen — pixies.

It was during the *dimpsy hour*, when the sinking sun had only just vanished from view and the radiance of the day had started to fade, that they would squeeze and turn their rubber boots deep into the patches of soft, marshy grass … squelching out the bubbles and then, aided by the light of an ignited match, seek out *them tricky little fellas*.

The old man had never been one to be reckless. In fact, he had taught both he and his brother to take care and to ensure that they never stand above a burning match. After all, when pixies were nearby, there was danger. There would be a flash of blue as a bubble burst to the surface and ignited. Only then, when the flame flared large and bright, would the *little fellas* be seen; but never for long. They would take advantage of the distraction of the flash to make good their escape before disappearing into the invisible world of magic and intrigue.

He takes comfort from these precious memories; but, equally, the recollection of the loss of his old mentor serves only to compound his despair.

If only Grandpa were still alive. He'd know what to do.

His words, silent to all, remain secure within the confines of his mind.

His Grandfather's wealth of knowledge, trawled from a lifetime of experience, could always be relied upon to steer a steady course through the chaos of a fractured routine — bringing order to disorder when all had appeared to be lost.

Joe's lonely thoughts reach out, desperately attempting to tune to another plane, as he searches for answers.

There are none. He concludes that the mystical level that he seeks can only exist in legend and the wishful thinking of man; a species which, cognisant of the finality of one's own death, often clutches for signs of an eternality in a new and spiritual life to come.

Unscrewing the top from the bottle, he sniffs the aroma before tasting its contents. Pleasant? Maybe for some, but it is not quite to his palate. But then, he is hopeful that its intoxicating effects will aide his attempt to escape his inner torment.

He swigs and swallows — his mouth smarting with the burn as the liquor hits the back of his throat.

With the encroaching darkness furtively quenching the evening light, he feels a shiver as the temperature starts to dip. He is in need of warmth.

Another swig.

Another burn.

He enters the building.

"Ah... Dozy Barn ..." he whispers. *"Peace at last."*

He sighs as he looks around at the walls which, although moist with the invasion of misty airs, give comfort with their solidity and their record of memories from times long past.

His eyes drift up towards the crossbeam, activating memories of how, in years gone by, this was the roost of a dozing barn owl; a bird whose very presence inadvertently dictated the naming of the structure as it had perched, unperturbed, whilst it scrutinized the movements of those who had entered below.

As if as an act of self-punishment, he swigs another — and then another — repeating the action until his feelings are on the brink of being numbed.

Stooping down, he gathers a mix of twigs and scraps of wood — remnants of broken fixtures and long-discarded tools — and arranges them so that they can easily be set alight. An old plastic feed-bag is torn into strips, some of which are scrunched into loose and untidy balls and pushed under the wood … whilst others are kept back to be used as tapers which will drip their flame across the makeshift hearth.

Once ignited, the heat of combustion shrivels the plastic, and whilst some of the droplets of burning blue fall to the earth, only to extinguish in the dirt and so leave no evidence of their existence, the remaining stay lit as they adhere to the wood on which they have settled. With the earliest flames having licked at the kindling as if foretasting a meal, they gradually take a hold and grow … gorging on the wood which has been stacked for their consumption.

The choking smell of burning plastic, with its unforgiving trail of jet-black ribbons of smoke, will last only until the flames move on and feed on ligneous fuels alone. In desperation to rid his senses of the unwelcome acridity of the toxic emissions, he scavenges around the barn in search of the more natural and less-invasive of burnable materials. Then, willing the flames to take hold and strengthen, he crouches down and positions his harvest on that which is already lit.

With the dusk sprinting towards the night and the darkness staking its claim, he seeks comfort and warmth as he huddles closer to the growing flames.

The fire awakens and, as if celebrating its sudden release from the need for nurture, snaps and crackles whilst tossing its flickering light against the stony confines of its secluded world.

He glances up and tries to make sense of the random patterns which, within the twinkle of an eye, seem to appear, then disappear as they gambol haphazardly along the wall.

Another swig, and the muted grumble of an oral release confirms that the effects of the alcohol have started to take their toll.

He scans the ramshackle remains of worn-out machinery and rural jumble … seeking something suitable to be used for a seat.

Eyeing a log which — hacked and scarred by the blows of a long-forgotten axe-man — lays redundant and almost hidden beneath the crumpled pile of polythene sacks and assorted lengths of ruddy baling twine, he achieves his goal and concludes his search.

The irony of him sitting on the chopping-block is lost. After all, there is no one to witness him closing his eyes as he tries to shut out the distractions and, thus, allow himself some time to forage through the events of the past few days.

He takes another drink as he stares deep into the flames.

Mesmerized by the bright and multicoloured, flapping tongues which proudly flaunt the gluttonous traits of an insatiable appetite, and thus an obsessive need to devour all that is near, he allows his thoughts to flit through the fires of his emotion and, in doing so, wonders if they, too, possess the same destructive force of that which is burning before him.

With the night taking hold and the flames burning brighter still, the dancing shadows mockingly taunt as they skip from wall to wall, abandoned and free.

Through watery eyes — stung with smoky wisps — he watches on as his tireless tormentors joyously twist and turn as they, as if having embraced one another so as to form a single unyielding force, without truce or pity drive him deeper still into the hellhole of sorrow and despair.

Recalling her words — *I think we should take some time out* — which had been closely followed by those which had been embossed with the stamp of finality — *It's over!* — he cannot help but to submit to the wildness of his imaginings. From the tangled mess of his confused emotions, he induces a painful and vivid image of Lucy gazing into the eyes of her new-found love, before underlining her feelings with a long and passionate kiss.

With the growing knowledge that his time with her has, without a doubt, gone forever, he stares idly upwards towards the roof and muses over the reasons for the presence of the loops of twine which adorn the ancient crossbeam.

Vague recollections emerge through the mists of time long-past; recollections which conjure images of the tools which were, in his grandfather's days, suspended up and away — no longer a danger once off the floor. With the purpose of the twine recalled, he takes another swig from the bottle and gazes back and into the flames.

Chapter 16

As he pulls up behind his brother's Land Rover, Robert kills the motor and pushes his window open, in order for him to be able to listen for sounds of life.

Apart from the distant and fading grumble of a passenger-laden jet, the chattering sounds of the Devon fauna are all that can be heard.

Jumping down from the tractor's cab, he lands with a thud and then examines the located vehicle. The driver's door is unlocked and, having only just been caught on the first catch, it remains partly open.

Apart from the presence of the vehicle, there is no evidence of his sibling's existence. So, in an attempt to try to establish an idea as to the time of the vehicle's abandonment, he spreads his hand across the radiator grill. Feeling no warmth and seeing the untouched condensation on each pane of the split windscreen, he knows that there has been no recent usage.

Peering above the gate and then across the field, he sees no sign of his brother. Although distracted by the haunting calls of a pair of buzzards which soar effortlessly upwards, having climbed onto the first of the day's thermals, he still takes time to pause and to watch — his emotions stirred with both wonder and concern.

He has often marvelled at the magnificence of these indigenous winged predators, which, in their own way, play their role as the farmer's friend by helping to control the population of rodents and rabbits alike, but, he also harbours a dash of unease. After all, it is in the oncoming months when — with the early winter lambing — the newborns will be at their most vulnerable and, albeit an occurrence of extreme rarity, will be susceptible to becoming an object of predation.

Resuming his gaze across the pasture, he notes how, apart from the tell-tale spoor of a wandering fox, the virgin morning dew has remained unbroken.

He calls out, "Joe!"

There is no reply, so he calls again, "Joe! Where are you?"

Maybe he has spent the night in the barn, he thinks.

Knowing that it is not beyond the realms of possibility, the thought compels him to investigate and confirm.

Striding through the sopping grass, he heads towards the solitary oak which, being at the line where the field slopes away towards the run of the stream, is the landmark from where he can gain a vantage over the stone-built shelter. He sniffs the air and detects the slightest hint of recently-burnt wood hanging in the atmosphere. It is obvious that a fire had been lit, and with this as evidence of recent occupation, he hurries his steps in the hope that his search may soon be over.

The barn is well within calling range. Again, he shouts out.

Apart from the frantic flutter of wings as the wary wood pigeons race to safety and away from their roosts, there is no response.

He hurries his step. And with an odd, but well-practised, expertise he quickly traverses the irregular lie of the land ... slipping and sliding as he rushes his way down the hill and towards the barn.

As he rounds the wall and views the entrance, he hesitates, then, with another call of his brother's name, he walks in.

Particles of floating dust fill the few beams of light which have managed to shine through apertures which had appeared when the slates, over countless seasons of climatic attack, had been dislodged from their proper place.

With the last remaining ribbons of smoke snaking out of the openings before drifting away on the breath of the morning air, he allows his eyes to adjust to the darkness within.

He scans the space, and then — with a jolt — he stops. Stunned into silence, he struggles to register the extent of the horror which hangs, noiseless and still, from the ancient crossbeam before him.

As if entrapped by the powerful grip of the stillness which so often encircles a death, he stares ahead — shocked and in disbelief. Then, in desperation, and whilst praying for the slightest sign of life, he focuses his attention ... first on the face ... and then on the eyes.

With his brother's head wrenched to one side and tilted downwards, still facing the remains of his final encounter with warmth, the impassive stare of partially-opened eyes — which, being no longer able to register the shades of darkness nor the brightness of light — begin to unnerve him.

But, it is that unbreakable bond between siblings which abruptly levers him into fighting back his fear. So, with the need for action suddenly driven to the fore, he gathers his strength and rushes forward and steps up and onto the chopping block. Then, with the utmost of haste, he severs the ruddy cord so as to put an end to the garrotting and, thus, release his brother from the immovable resistance of the ancient, oaken crossbeam.

With a balance of both care and urgency, he supports his sibling as he lowers his body to the ground. As the ligature is loosened from around his neck, he can see the depth of its cut. In his heart, he knows that he is too late. Yet, although his ashen skin is cold and lifeless, he feels that not only is it his duty to do so, but he must, for the love for his brother and to ensure that his conscience will always be clear, make every effort to exact his revival. Tilting his head back to clear the airways, he pinches the nose. The first-aid instruction which had been received so long ago may be misty ... but the essence of it all is still imbedded in his memory.

The inflation of his lungs is repeated thrice. He cannot recall the textbook number of breaths required, but, instead, he relies on the purity of his instinct and the rawness of his passion.

With one hand clasped atop the other, and with the heel of the lower laid heavily on his brother's chest, he puts his weight behind him and thrusts desperately in an attempt to restart the heart. With each thrust he hears himself praying for the heart to pump and, thus, recommence the circulation of his brother's re-oxygenated blood.

"One ... Two ... Three ... Four ... Five."

He counts each thrust, stops and then re-inflates the lungs from the breath of his own. Seeing no signs to suggest the resumption of independent life, he repeats the pumping.

"One ... Two ... Three ... Four ... Five."

"Come on!" he shouts repeatedly, and to the rhythm of his efforts, as he desperately tries to will his brother back to life.

There is no response. He tries again — inflation of lungs — then compression of chest. Time after time, he repeats the sequence.

With his adrenalin drained and his muscles exhausted, he stops.

He is unable to force a pulse, and his labours have gone unrewarded.

He pulls back, and — with a reluctant and guilt-ridden acceptance of defeat — he looks up towards the Gods and forces out the last of his energy in a spine-chilling howl of anger and despair.

"No...!"

His cries fill the air. As the tears pour down his face, he, as if in desperation to offer comfort and apology to his brother, pulls Joe's body towards him. Then, rocking slowly to and fro, he holds and cradles his head firmly and lovingly against his chest.

***

The article which takes precedence on the front page of the local newspaper attracts her attention.

BOYFRIEND OF MISSING GIRL FOUND HANGED

The manner in which the boldly-printed caption has been blazoned across the publication is, in its own way, accusatory, in that it carries with it the suggestion that the self-imposed finality of his being may well have been a sign of a guilty conscience.

She picks up the top copy. As she waits in the queue to complete her purchase, she reads.

The article does not express a direct accusation of guilt. But the fact that a police spokesman has stated that they have now got reservations as to the certainty of Lucy's safe return, along with the revelation that more officers are being imported from other parts of the Force area to extend and upgrade the search of the vicinity in which she went missing, there is a latent suggestion of a change of tack. The routine of a missing-person enquiry has taken on the mantle of that of a major criminal investigation, with the focus now being put on the locating of a body and the subsequent tying up of loose ends.

Lucy's disappearance is already the talk of the village, and it has now spread where it will, no doubt, satisfy the needs of the idle gossipers who will spread their fabrications like unfettered viruses among the masses of the city. Whilst glancing through the printed word, she cannot help but to overhear the flippant and disrespectful comments of the two young men who stand in the queue before her. The prejudgements of the tittle-tattlers — those know-it-alls who, in fact, know nothing of the lives of the people involved — have already begun.

"If you ask me, he's guilty as sin!" the taller of the two declares as he shakes his head and scans the article.

"What's that?"

The first points to the headline and continues. "I suppose you can take D.I.Y a bit far. I mean … self-trial … self-conviction, and then … to top it all — excuse the pun — self-sentence! He's saved the Country a fortune!"

"Self-execution, too. Now, that can't be bad either."

They allow themselves a snigger, and then, being next in line to be served, they present their goods, pay their money and leave — oblivious to the sensitivities of the young woman who has been standing in the queue behind them and who has, therefore, been well within earshot.

She cannot comprehend how anyone could find humour within this episode of sadness. She feels compelled to shout after them in rebuke, but, distracted by the shopkeeper's customary "Can I help you?" she hesitates and stands, open-mouthed — stunned into silence.

Shaken by the public disclosure of the demise of Joe and also the thought that she may never again see her friend — Lucy — alive, she stares blankly and silently at the lady who stands behind the counter.

"Are you all right my dear?" The lady has a genuine look of concern for the young woman as she asks the question.

"Yes. I mean … No … Oh … I don't know! I'm sorry."

She hesitates, then, becoming increasingly more numbed with sadness and less and less mindful to her immediate surroundings, she replaces the newspaper, turns about and hurries away from the shop, empty-handed.

In the loneliness and confusion of her sorrow, she recalls the bitter-sweet memories of her friend's bubbling excitement; those, oh-so-recent, carefree moments when they had blithely shared their romantic secrets in the privacy of the ladies room at the village hall.

As she rounds the corner, she merges with the other shoppers, disappearing amid the anonymity of the many whilst she continues to chase the thoughts which remain cocooned within the confusion of her grief.

Time does not linger,
Nor does it pause.
It cares not for the joy,
Nor the grief ... nor the cause!

Chapter 17

Delaying the arrival of first light, swollen cushions of charcoal cloud mass as they blanket the early morning sky, whilst the prevailing south-westerly winds start to pick up their pace and drive the Atlantic spray, mercilessly, into every nook and cranny of the rugged face of this, the most southerly part of mainland Britain.

As the rushing gusts accelerate and join forces with the impetus of oceanic might, they — having merged as if they were one — power a battery of white-crested rollers to, forcefully and tirelessly, smash themselves against the rocky and inhospitable base. As the *un-weighable* tonnage of each wave hits its target, enquiring fingers of the briny aggressor obstinately probe for the slightest of cracks and weaknesses in its ultimate quest to conquer and devour this stubborn and defiant obstacle of land.

Reminiscent of an invading force and relentless in its mission, the storm marches on, increasing it's vigour with every mile as it violently pushes and shoves, dislodging the lull that had once rested so peacefully before it.

The fauna have followed their instincts and have taken cover until the storm has made the last of its fearsome roars and then, as if in some victorious celebration, has finally rumbled away.

***

With the serenity of filigree branches silhouetted against a backdrop of radiant salmon smudges which stretch effortlessly across a flawless canvas of cerulean skies, Geoff focuses on the leathery, russet buds of the skeletal sycamore. He wonders how each growth, swollen with the embryonic presence of fresh foliage, yet still barely displaying a hint of green, knows when to open and thus avoid the ravages of a long and bitter winter.

Seduced by the tranquillity of the morning, he is oblivious to the extent of the ferocity of the encroaching storm. He is not only intrigued by the miracles of nature's complexities which are displayed within the flora which surrounds him, but he has become increasingly excited at the impending prospect of experiencing the forthcoming joy of witnessing the miracle of new life in his own family.

The intricacies of nature, he thinks … *Wonderful.*

Boosted with adrenalin and a mix of excitement and trepidation to fuel his energetic start to the day, he begins to show signs of impatience as he flits between the house and the car, checking and double-checking that all is well. He prays that she is not going to suddenly step into the final stages of labour and plunge him into a state of absolute panic.

She is calmer than he. And with more than a little encouragement from her, he decides to get out from under her feet and prepare the car, ensuring that her bags are packed and loaded in readiness for their journey to the hospital.

With the approaching darkness now on the brink of substituting the clear skies of daybreak, he decides that she should be readied for the short, but potentially hazardous, journey from their forest-edged home and into the city.

Having experienced the destructive force of the hurricane winds of eighty-seven, he has no wish to gamble on them becoming a victim of this.

As if to confirm the wisdom of his decision, he feels the first sprinklings of light, icy rain prickle at his cold and tightening cheeks.

He listens and watches. And as the breeze moves from a hush to a roar as it rapidly ascends the steps of the *Beaufort scale*, it starts to thrust its way through the trembling branches and force the last of the few remaining leaves to shiver and flee.

***

Cornwall and West Devon having already been taken, the offensive continues unremittingly as it forges forward and leaves a trail of devastation and misery in its wake.

The black swans of Dawlish, as if sensing the imminent arrival of hell itself, take refuge as the surging of angry waves — with their salted spray dwarfing the Intercity train that edges ever closer to the station — start to gnaw ferociously at the ancient and weather-beaten sandstone cliffs.

***

With the anger-filled rattle of rain starting to crash noisily against the windows, and the accompaniment of a wind which commences the uttering of the first few bars of a chorus of intimidating groans as it rushes past the flaked and bubbled rendering of the chimney, she senses and shares his noticeable and increasing feelings of anxiety.

"Is there anything you need?" he asks, as he attempts to give the impression of calm.

Her contractions, although not yet arriving in quick succession, are being felt more often and with an ever-increasing intensity.

"I think you ought to phone the hospital." Her suggestion is made, conscious that, although this is *his* first child, it is not *hers;* additionally, it is often the case that second babies can have a nasty habit of surprising all with a somewhat hasty entrance.

"Right … umm… " The realisation of the arrival being near, if not imminent, pushes the calm aside as he abruptly finds himself on the verge of panic, whilst frantically looking around for the telephone.

"It's where it's always been! On the table … By the door!"

She finds it irritating but, also, amusing to see him in such a muddle.

"Ooo…" She puts both hands on *the bump* as another painful contraction hits home and coincides with the visit of a silent wave of melancholy as she recalls the events of that dreadful night when her beloved first-born, Lucy, had stormed off and disappeared into the clutch of darkness.

He dials and waits, with each second elapsing as if it were trapped in a parallel world where the need for haste is of little importance.

A female voice silences the ringing tone; reassured, he speaks.

Hearing his flustered exchange, Gina shouts to him. "Get on with it. Just tell her we're coming in … whatever she says."

"Did you hear that?"

The midwife heard.

"Shall I bring her in?"

Permission granted.

The maternity unit is always ready and waiting.

"That's great." The relief is evident in the change of his tone. "We'll be on our way in a few minutes. Thank you."

A wave-like rumbling from the chimney acts as a final indication that the time to leave has now arrived.

Standing on the porch, she hesitates; then, as she watches the lifting and bowing of the overhead wires and listens to the haunting moans of the racing winds which push through the strained strands as if they are in search of some elusive melody, she puts a reassuring hand on her tummy and comforts its precious content.

The time has come, and she has decided that she can afford to wait not a moment longer.

Precipitation is no longer just the uncomfortable falling of wild and wintry rain, but a torrential downpour of monsoonal waters which powerfully beat their pulse as they crash and splash onto the gravelled drive. The hurricane has arrived, and there is no time to lose.

Head down and hooded, she forces herself forward … and, avoiding the sting on her face as best she can, she hurries out and towards the car. Struggling against the wind, he jams the door open and beckons her on, urging her into the dry of the vehicle.

Both are sodden, but with Gina safely in, he slams her door and rushes around to the offside. As he drops into his seat and pulls his door firmly closed beside him, he fires the engine whilst she distracts herself and watches intently at the activity beyond the hedge. She is captivated by the presence of a mass of fluttering rooks which, with the violence of the storm and the security of their roost no more, have been unceremoniously flushed from the trees to scatter, toss and turn as they heroically attempt to flock, desperate in their attempts to make headway across the open pastures in search of shelter.

In the ever-darkening light, he flicks the switch and activates the exterior lights. He moves out of the driveway and turns to the right. Although it is in the opposite direction from the city, this is the route which will quickly take them away from the threat of the forest and onto the dual carriageway, thus, lessening the risk of them being struck by torn-off branches and crashing trees.

As they move forward, they start to plough through the unrelenting bombardment of driving rain; its swansong glitter of silvery shards racing down through the beams of glaring headlamps, self-destructively exploding against the bonnet and the already water-covered surface of the winding road.

The rush of howling winds cry out as if echoing the ghosts of cellists who — having been trapped in a jet-stream which denies them the final crossing from life to death — passionately bow their mournful song. With the near-deafening hollow booms of fallen branches crashing and shattering all around, the tension within the car rises. As they round the bend — a little too fast for Gina's liking — he, without warning, slams his foot hard on the brakes ... they judder and skid to a halt.

His route is blocked; a shoulder of oak — having been wrenched from its moorings — lies across the littered tarmac. The immensity of the bough dictates the futility of any attempt for him to single-handedly remove it. With the road impassable, he has no choice but to turn about and to take the less-inviting option of having to negotiate the confinements of narrower roads which wend their twisting way through the more threatening terrain of the storm-battered forest.

Allowing no time for natural drainage, the rapid and torrential fall of rain instantly fills the roadside gullies. With the wipers no longer able to attain sufficient speed, nor force, to clear the water from the screen, they cautiously, yet still with a sense of urgency, weave their way through the debris as they attempt to dodge the largest of the spent and strewn munitions of nature's war.

With a wrench on the steering, he feels a sudden loss of momentum as the wheels are grabbed by the billowing waters which, having been captured behind the heightening dams of sylvan wreckage, grow deeper by the second.

The white, central road-markings have all but disappeared beneath the raging torrent; he hesitates and stops to assess his options. Taking a few moments to survey the rage of swollen waters which, no longer restrained by the confines of the natural course of the once timid stream, flood uncompromisingly across the road, he weighs the risks.

Alerted by the sudden and unusually loud creak of living timber, he senses a threat; a threat which may well be chased by the deafening crack of a splitting trunk and the fall of a towering giant.

Having no time to spare, he looks anxiously for an alternative route to safety.

There is none!

Equally aware of the severity of their predicament, Gina, although preoccupied with the pain of another contraction, urges him on. With her support, the decision is made, and, with the rev's kept high, he ploughs determinedly through the wild and unforgiving waters. Three seconds seem more like three long drawn-out minutes when there is the fear of having to act as midwife whilst being stranded and incommunicado in an impotent and water-logged car. With this added incentive to spur him, he wills the vehicle through and prays that the engine does not succumb to the elements and silence with a stall.

As they emerge safely from the rising waters, they sigh with relief, and, with an exchange of smiles, they edge forward so as to continue their journey at a cautious but progressive pace.

But, having only travelled a few metres, they realize that the respite from worry is short-lived, for it is replaced with a rush of fear as a boom of seismic proportions signals the fall of a ton or so of ashen timber.

Through the misted and rain-lashed rear screen, they look back and, in shock and in horror, stare at the sight of the massive, prostrate tree which is now blocking the path over which they had only just passed. Gratefully relieved that they had made the decision to proceed, they both thank their primal instincts — for had they delayed, then, without doubt, they would have been crushed and lost amid the chilling statistics of time.

They glance towards each other and then, in silence, look to the fore and urge the vehicle onwards.

She clutches and gently rubs *the bump* as yet another contraction announces its arrival.

They drive on, desperately edging through the debris, accelerating only when it is safe to do so.

With the spur to the dual-carriageway clearly in sight, they glance at one another; with smiles and shared feelings of relief, they start to relax as their hearts slowly return to the more rhythmic beats of normality.

Confident that their route will now be clear, they head eastwards and towards the awaiting team. With the larger roads being far less hazardous than the country lanes, they begin to put the traumas of the journey behind them and allow themselves to turn their thoughts to the wondrous joys of being able to welcome into the world, a fresh new life.

***

Only three parking bays away from the brightly-lit entrance to the maternity unit, there is a space for them to leave the vehicle.

With the rain still lashing down, he wants to hurry her in, but she is not for rushing. So moving as fast as she is able, and with her coat pulled up and over her head for protection, he encourages her towards the lights and the sanctuary of the lobby.

The reception is composed, yet friendly and welcoming; after all, they have seen it all before. Calmly and routinely, she is ushered into the antenatal room in preparation for the moment of delivery.

With the knowledge that she is now in the capable hands of the professionals, Gina begins to calm, and resigns herself to simply go with the flow and accept their help; for they have an asset which is beyond any classroom based tuition — an undocumented qualification of wisdom which can only have been gained from their wealth of practical experience.

Geoff is, unsurprisingly, filled with a great sense of relief; he has succeeded in getting them to the safety of the unit, and he no longer has the worry of bearing the sole responsibility of having to care for a birthing mother and the immediate needs of a newborn baby.

***

There is mounting tension within the delivery room as the midwife concentrates her efforts on the task in hand.

"Good girl. Your baby's coming! I can see the head!"

Gina's grip squeezes and tightens on Geoff's hand while she searches for the strength to rid herself of the almost insufferable pain.

"Take a nice deep breath and puff. Good girl. Now … Come on … Push"

The midwife, with the added zest of urgency, gives her words of encouragement to carry on and not falter.

"I am pushing!" she screams out, emphasising the fact as she again tries to force the obstruction out from her body.

"One more time Gina … Here we come … I can see it now! It's nearly here! Oh, my! What a beautiful head of hair." She gives Gina a hint of the reward which is soon to come.

"And again … Good girl … You're almost there … Lovely … Keep going … You're doing really well. One more push and … Well done! You've just about done it. Here comes baby! Yes…! Yes…! Yes…! And … Out you come little one. Welcome to our world!"

With the baby having, at this very moment, entered this new realm of colour and light, there is a moment of silence as all await the joyous sound of the first breath being drawn.

The unmistakable cry of the newborn is uttered and tears of joy and relief quickly engulf the eyes of both mother and father.

Gina's eyes widen as she sees her baby for the first time, and, instinctively, she outstretches her arms, desperate in her need to satisfy her overwhelming desire to hold.

As the midwife lifts and checks all is well, the announcement is made with a smile. "It's a girl! Congratulations! You've got a beautiful little daughter!"

As she celebrates the occasion, she passes the newborn to Gina and quickly makes a note of the time before fulfilling her duties with the necessary checks.

Parental pride and the natural activation of their protective responsibilities are instant.

Both mother and father gaze in wonder at this helpless little person, whilst sharing the elation and treasuring every single one of these, never-to-be-repeated, precious moments.

"What are you going to call her?" the midwife asks.

Geoff, knowing that a decision has yet to be made, looks to his wife for guidance.

She allows her eyes to leave those of her baby for the briefest of moments as she responds, "I'm not sure. Maybe we'll have a few minutes to get to know her first … then we'll think about it."

Smiling warmly, and knowing that her answer is probably different from the norm, she returns her focus back towards her daughter.

With her thoughts provoked, the midwife responds. "I like that."

She pauses for a moment, then continues. "Do you know? You're right. There's plenty of time to join the rest of the world with all its labels. You just enjoy getting to know her for herself."

"Thank you. We will."

Gina, fully re-engaged with her daughter, slowly examines and absorbs every tiny feature of her face. "Oh, you are so like Lucy. Now, I suppose you'll have to have a name, so what would *you* like to be called?" she looks to Geoff, "What do you think? What shall we call her?"

"Well, I don't think she'd appreciate having my mother's name."

Gina looks intently into the little ones eyes. "No, I don't think you're going to be a Doreen. No, of course you're not."

"Mind you I think your mum's name is just as, umm…" He pauses as he thinks better of using the word *bad*, so, instead, he gives an alternative. "Dated. That's it — it's a little bit dated."

Her newborn's likeness to Lucy, lights the shadows of the past, and, like a slideshow of history flicking through her mind, she recalls the memories of before — that first graze on the knee which was closely followed by that *magic* kiss to make it all better. Then, of course, there were those joyful chuckles of laughter as she had delighted in seeing the Christmas tree in all its glory … before, excitedly, unwrapping the gifts which were scattered around the floor below.

Even the mixed emotions of sending her off on her first day at school, followed by the joy of seeing her happy face as she had, at the end of lessons, rushed out to greet her and tell of all the exciting happenings of the day — along with the gush of names of the multitude of new friends that had just been made — have come flooding back. Oh yes ... and that final vision of her when, with her spirits darkened with anger and with sadness in her heart, she had disappeared into the shadows of the night — still wearing her torn, yet beautiful, dress, has come hauntingly to the fore.

Tears rapidly fill her eyes and blur her vision as she holds her baby close. "Oh ... I love you! I love you ... and your sister, so much."

Knowing that the memories of Lucy, which were once hidden in the recesses of a not-so-distant past, have now managed to break through the apertures of time to make their mark on the present, he holds her tightly, and in silence, as he supports her whilst she negotiates a personal path through the mixed and confusing emotions of these bittersweet moments.

Chapter 18

Entering the new millennium has not been the disaster that some had predicted.

Six months into the year … and the world has not come to an end. Neither has it been a case of the *Millennium Bug* having wreaked havoc with the hard-drives of the planet's multinational computer systems.

The airliners are still flying and the traders are still trading.

In fact, business is looking good; his sales figures are up and there are more appointments in the offing. Even his journey has gone well. In the main, it has been uninterrupted and has already taken him from his Midland home, along the M5 and onto the dual-carriageway of the A30.

For the time of the year, it has been hot. Although the use of the air conditioning does not lend itself to thrift when it comes to the usage of diesel, it certainly does help with the provision of a more comfortable driving environment. Besides, it is a company car and, what with the tab for the fuel being picked up by his employers, the cooler air is well and truly appreciated.

With his appointment at Truro not planned for another couple of hours, he has plenty of time to relax and enjoy the drive. The business for the day will be completed later in the afternoon, and then he will be able to take advantage of the long summer evening with a leisurely stroll along the Hoe. His overnight stay in a Plymouth hotel has already been booked, and when today's appointment is concluded, he will be able to switch off until tomorrow.

The in-car phone sounds. He answers. "Hi, I'm on the road — I'll pull over and ring you back."

A sign shows there to be a lay-by a short distance ahead.

Once stationary, he returns the call. The office has made an amendment to his timetable for tomorrow.

Can he bring the first appointment forward by thirty minutes? Of course he can; this is business, and he is hungry for success. So, without question, he scribbles the new time on his pad and closes the call.

Slipping back into driving mode, he checks the mirror and engages first gear in readiness to move onwards. He hesitates and then stops. The call of nature is getting strong, and with an area of rough woodland beside the lay-by, he sees no reason why he cannot take advantage of its rural seclusion. After all, he is not sure how long it will be before he reaches a public convenience.

He gets out of the car, stretches and surveys the vicinity in search for privacy. A well-trodden path suggests that many others before him may also have had the need to answer nature's same call. Careful where he steps, he picks his way into the seclusion of a copse of spindly trees until he is sure that he cannot be seen. Although he has, whilst on his travels, seen many a man standing at the roadside blatantly urinating onto the verge, no doubt with a contemptuous disregard as to the feelings of those who are passing by, he has had an upbringing where respect for others had been put to the fore; therefore, discretion had been encouraged, especially when one's conduct may threaten to nudge the boundaries of social etiquette.

As the pressure of nature is being relieved, he looks around him. Although, bearing in mind the nature of his actions, it seems rather hypocritical, he is, nevertheless, disappointed, if not disgusted, at how much rubbish has been left to rot within such a beautiful area. As his range of critical attention extends outwards, his eye stops abruptly, and with his focus suddenly heightened, his heart begins to pump a little faster. Several yards farther down the slope, there is the unexpected distraction of colour glinting out from where the sun has kissed the coppery sheen of a crumpled mass of lustrous fabric which is partially obscured by the sweet-scented bushes of golden-speckled gorse.

Instinctively, he knows that something is wrong. Leaning his head to one side, he attempts to improve his view, and with the adjustment of both his focus and the angle of his vision, he attempts to assess the significance of what he sees. It looks to be a dress; an expensive looking item … and far too good to have been uncaringly discarded.

He moves forward … inquisitive, but with a feeling of unease … as he starts to suspect the worst.

When only a few feet away, he sees her — scratched, bloodied and still! Unnerved by the incongruity of the pallid flash of a naked leg and its shoeless foot peeking out from under the dishevelled fabric of what was once a striking and elegant skirt, he stands as if tied to the spot. With the rhythm of his heart beating loud, he struggles to think.

Standing alone, he is, for a few moments, torn between the embedded demands of his moral upbringing to try to help and the equally ingrained, fear-fuelled desire to cut and run.

His conscience wins the battle; so, with more than a little trepidation, he elects to take the honourable course of action … and stays put.

Tentatively, he steps still closer. Then, as the entirety of the form becomes clear, he stops.

He may not have had life experiences in which he has had to confront the harshness and cruelty of a violent world, but he has seen many a film, and so he assumes that there will, in all likelihood, be a lifeless face to be found hidden beneath the cover of the undergrowth.

He is afraid … and he hesitates.

He has no idea as to how he will cope with having to face up to the sight which threatens to test his nerve. But, plucking up the courage, he edges forward. His heart jumps another nervous beat and then, with his fears having been realized and without forewarning, it erupts as it thumps out its ever-loudening rhythm. The sight of her long, wavy hair obscuring almost all but a glimpse of her still and ashen cheek, drives him ever-closer towards reaching the brink of panic.

Her skin is pale — far too pale, he surmises, for there to be a glimmer of hope; but still, he fights his instinct to flee and, instead, forces himself to look more closely.

Apart from the hum of a massing of flies and the persistent crawl of scavenging insects which are already starting to stake their claim as they examine the darkness of her facial orifices, there is an eerie stillness.

He has no intention of going any closer, for he is not only repulsed by, but he is also afraid of the reality of death. In any case, he reasons, he can do no good; after all, it is already too late for any useful intervention from him or, for that matter, from anyone else.

Frozen in shock, he stands, stares and gathers his thoughts. Although he is, to a large degree, numbed, he is aware enough to be truly sickened as to how this young woman had, without doubt, been used and then discarded as if she were nothing more than an object which was no longer of worth.

Unlike the fictional characters of stage and screen who, unrealistically, seem to relish the opportunity to show their sensitive side and thus, rather melodramatically, *throw up* in every gruesome scene, he does not have the strength, nor does he feel the need, to urge. With the enormity of the situation hitting home, he becomes increasingly conscious of the fact that he cannot just leave her to be consumed by the ravages of the forces of nature. Instead, he must take control of himself and do something constructive. He turns about and rushes back to his car to find his phone.

Three nines are hastily dialled. Once answered, he opts to be connected to the police.

"I think I've found a body! It's a woman!"

As to why he had said *I think,* he is not entirely sure — the fact is that he *knows* that he has discovered a body. As he struggles to get more words out to explain the detail of his find, his voice trembles as it echoes the depth of his shock and bewilderment.

The control room operator is experienced and she calmly coaxes out the details. He has no idea which lay-by he is in, but he is certain that he has already passed the junction for Cheriton Bishop but has not yet reached the turnoff for Okehampton.

Travelling the road every day, to-and-fro her place of work, she knows, by description alone, exactly which lay-by the caller is in and assures that assistance is *en route.*

With the call made, and while awaiting the arrival of the police, he tries to make sense of the horror of his find and, also, to come to terms with the image of death which has already wedged firmly within his mind. Whether or not he allows his eyes to be open or closed, the picture is the same.

***

With the call received, the Volvo accelerates, and with a growl of intent the momentum forces the front-seat passenger back into his seat. With the flicking of a couple of switches, blue lights flash and sirens wail, and the outside lane of the dual carriageway clears as every vehicle moves over … allowing the emergency vehicle to go by, unhindered.

It takes just a few minutes to cover the ten mile distance when travelling at speeds which are well in excess of a hundred miles per hour.

As the lay-by comes into sight, the brakes are hit and the car glides safely to its nearside, then halts.

They know that they have found the caller, for he is nervous and moves towards them with urgency reflected in his step. As he approaches, and as if there is no time to spare, he hurriedly ushers them away from their vehicle and towards the undergrowth, steering them to his gruesome find.

The policemen, experienced and practical, do not hesitate as they push their way through the copse and then rush to the body and check for signs of life.

M.P.C Robbie Kerr holds his fingers against her neck and, with an air of professional calm, feels for a pulse whilst, at the same time, scanning her face — praying that he would not miss the slightest of any movement. He sees a twitch of an eyelid. He focuses, taps her cheek … the eyelid twitches again. As far as he is concerned, the first may have been down to his imagination, but for there to have been a second … then that's movement.

The air of calm is broken as he shouts to his colleague. "Ian … She's alive! Jeez, man! Quickly — we need an ambulance — now!"

His colleague breaks into the airwaves and instantly overrides and silences the chatter of the mundane.

"QB from Tango-Two-Zero. Urgent!"

"Go ahead Two-Zero."

"At scene. One female … unconscious, but living … Ambulance requested. Urgent!"

"Received. Do you need any further assistance?"

"Stand by — I'll get back a.s.a.p."

They know her chance of survival is less than fifty-fifty, but they are men of experience, and, although not as skilled as paramedics, they know what to do to maintain the existence of life.

"Tango-Two-Zero from QB"

"Go ahead."

"Ambulance on route. ETA — five minutes."

"Roger."

The officer re-assesses the situation and almost immediately transmits again.

"QB from Tango-Two-Zero."

"Two-Zero. Go ahead."

"For the log — this is no accident. And bearing in mind the severity of the injuries, can you arrange for another unit to attend to protect the scene? Also can you inform CID and call out Scenes of Crime?"

"Wilco. QB standing by."

The policemen work together. She is their responsibility and her life is in their hands until the arrival of the paramedics, who are trained to preserve and maintain life. Aware that the last of the senses to fade when a person drops out of consciousness is that of the hearing, and that it is also the first sense that returns, they keep talking, calmly reassuring her as they desperately search for more positive responses from their charge.

She remains silent.

Teetering on the brink of death, her pulse is weak, but she lives ... and that's what matters — whilst there's life, then there's hope!

The salesman, now on the periphery of the horrific scene, stands with tears in his eyes — silenced and traumatized by the events which are dramatically unfolding before him.

"Oh God!" he whispers, "Please ... don't let her die!"

She is, after all, someone's daughter.

Although he feels the pangs of guilt in not initially recognising that she was alive, he takes some comfort from the actuality that had he not made the stop and answered the call of nature and, moreover, had he not gone on to make the call to the police, she may well have lain unfound for weeks ... and, as a result, her demise would have been sealed.

At least there is a glimmer of hope in that she may well survive and, in time, recover and be reunited with her nearest and dearest.

He has children of his own, and, as such, he can only imagine how her parents will feel when the full extent of what has happened to their daughter is finally revealed.

It is the distant yet ever-loudening sound of sirens that awake him from his semi-conscious state of shock and fire him back into action. Sensing the need to allow the officers to remain uninterrupted in their efforts and also fuelled with a desire to do something of use, he rushes back and up into the lay-by. He will guide the paramedics in.

He knows that the location of the incident is obvious by the presence of the police car, what with its beacons still flashing for all to see, but he also knows that he needs a reason to escape from the horror. He needs to be far enough away for him to be able to avert his eyes from the bizarre, yet magnetic, draw of the macabre and, also, away from the terrifying prospect of having to witness the final moments in the life of this unfortunate young woman.

Chapter 19

Standing at the window, a deeply troubled and utterly despondent father gazes out and into the darkening skies which, as if they are in sympathy with the darkness that has engulfed his own heart, have gathered above the irregular roofline of the hospital's buildings.

The ominous arrival of fast-thickening clouds have all but dismissed the clear blue skies of an hour or so ago − it's as if any memories of their existence have become little more than that of a cruel illusion of nature's beauty.

Even with the benefit of an opened window, the air which hangs in the privacy of the isolated room of the *intensive care unit* is oppressively hot and has developed an unpleasant whiff of stagnation.

As he struggles to cope with the wild rage that lies deep within him, he is shackled only by the restraints of his overwhelming and exhausting mood of debilitating sadness. He stares at his daughter. With her wounds bandaged and a selection of cables and wires connecting her to an array of equipment which serve to maintain and monitor every part of her young life, she seems confined within a deep and lonely sleep − innocently unaware of the concern and love that surrounds her. He prays that she does, indeed, lie in peace, and that her resting countenance is not merely the deception of a slumber; a slumber in which she is being forced to relive the horror of the ferocious and degrading attack which had been so pitilessly imposed upon her.

With a short, but stern, inner self-rebuke, he checks and dismisses the pessimism of his runaway thoughts, and then, with a deep and lingering gaze, he studies the finer details of her innocent and undisturbed face. There are, thankfully, no expressions of anguish; in fact, he takes refuge in the thought that she looks to be fast asleep and tucked up safely in a place where she can rest and recover within the comfort of a much-needed peace.

Although the reality of her being ensnared in a condition of non-responsiveness should offer him little comfort, the thought of her being locked into a state of unconsciousness has at least, he hopes, protected her from the distressing and humiliating experience of feeling her body being subjected to a further invasion as a significant number of intimate samples were clinically, but necessarily, removed for the purposes of forensic evaluation.

The steady bleeping of the electrocardiograph machine, with its needle scratching out the trace of her heartbeat rhythm-of-life, gives some hope, if only by confirming the fact that she still lives.

He is hot … and he's tired.

As he looks at her helpless body and he is, yet again, rocked by one of the many, overly recurrent and extremely disquieting, arrivals of hopeless despondency, he becomes conscious of the possibility that maybe she will not survive after all, and her battle to live will be lost. As the dreadful thoughts taunt him, tears well up and into his eyes and then overflow and trickle down his cheeks. The saline taste as they touch his lips and the dryness at the back of his throat makes him aware of the need to quench his thirst, but then, he will not leave his only daughter alone.

All of a sudden, realising that he has allowed his positive attitude to wane and start to drag his thoughts down and into the powerful depths and negativity of a maelstrom of despair, he becomes angered with himself. He draws in a deep breath, halting the slide, for he knows that any concept of defeat must not be allowed to inhabit his mind. He *must* be strong and show no signs of weakness, for he is here for her, and he must not be seen to be drowning himself in his own feelings of desolation.

He knows his role. He is here to give her the strength to come home.

He sits beside her … his hand cradling hers as he seeks a response.

There is none.

He speaks … softly reassuring her that she is not alone.

Still … there is no response.

The door opens and he looks up — it's his wife; she has returned from updating her elderly mother by phone.

She gazes at their daughter and then back to him.

She can say nothing; for having been weighed down with the worries of a mother, combined with the terrifying prospect of having to prepare for a lonely and joyless end, her voice has been smothered into silence.

He shakes his head slowly, knowing that, although no words have been spoken, she is asking if there has been any progress.

Sitting on the opposite side of the bed, she gently takes her daughter's hand and rests it in hers. The circular motion of her finger on her daughter's palm takes her back to the early days when she would play … *Round and round the garden, like a teddy bear …*

The memories, vivid and bittersweet, will not be followed by the excited and joyous chuckles of a child — for today there will be no *one step, two step and a tickle under there.*

The door reopens and they are joined by a nurse who starts to check the monitors and examine the graph.

"Any signs?" she asks, as she glances briefly at both parents whilst checking on her patient.

There is more than a hint of hopelessness echoed in the tone of his voice as he responds with a shake of his head. "No — nothing at all."

"Well … at least she seems to be stable at the moment. I'll be back and check on her a little later."

Her voice, matter-of-fact and professional, strangely lacks the warmth which one would normally expect from a member of a *caring* profession.

He has no energy to waste on commenting on his surprise at the coolness in her attitude, and so, he simply replies with a short but, nevertheless, polite, "Thank you."

The nurse forces a smile as she leaves the room.

He looks back at his wife, and, shaking his head whilst still being unable to fully comprehend the reason for their situation, he asks despairingly, "Why? Why? Why her? Why our little girl?"

The grief which is shown in her facial expressions, mirror his.

Their tears, yet again, begin to fill their eyes before flowing out to trickle down their pale and fatigued cheeks.

The muscles in his arms start to tighten as his fists clench tight and his knuckles whiten.

"What sort of evil can make someone do this?"

There is no satisfactory answer to give and none is attempted — for not only does she share his grief, but she also feels the hurt of an additional pain; the pain which only a mother who has felt the first movements of life from a child within the womb, can possibly feel.

Their daughter had been out on a hen-night. From all accounts, nothing too raucous — just a group of girls having gone out for a glass of wine and a pizza. Once they had eaten, they'd linked arms and meandered, joyously, along the quayside in search for a place where they could dance the night away with their friends. They had just been letting their hair down by enjoying a bit of harmless fun, and that was all there was to it.

What had happened later, during the early hours and after the girls had all gone their separate ways, he cannot be sure. But he knows one thing for certain; there can only be one other person who can possibly know how much she'd had to endure — and that is the perpetrator of her subjugation. And, as yet, his presence and identity is still unknown.

"You need a break." She breaks her silence. Having recognized his weariness as much as she has her own, she puts his welfare ahead of hers and continues. "Look … We'll be okay. You go and get yourself a coffee or something. As I've just said … I think you need the break."

He is thirsty, yet he does not wish to leave his daughter's bedside. He pauses for a moment as he weighs up his desire to stay with the need to go and recharge himself. He makes his decision. The distraction of venturing downstairs to the café for a drink may, after all, be exactly what he needs.

"Maybe you're right. Do you want one brought up?"

"No, I'm fine … You go on your own."

He leans over to their daughter and kisses her on her forehead. "I'll be back soon, babes."

As he starts to wander out, his wife extends her arm and holds out her hand. He stretches out *his* and holds on to *hers* as he leans forward and pecks a single kiss onto her cheek. As he turns and walks away towards the door, she loosens her grip and their hands slip away from each other until there is just the tender touch of fingertips as the final sensation before the final and reluctant release.

As he moves away from sight, her attention instantly returns to her daughter and, so, she resumes the constant reassurance of her presence by both word and the gentle touch of her hand on hers.

He walks off slowly, dazed by the events that are destroying his family, and descends the stairs. As he enters the café, he sees people sitting in groups; some laughing and joking — some more pensive.

The lady at the counter is one of many loyal and unpaid volunteer workers who give the WRVS such a good name.

"How can I help you, sir?" Her smile is warm and genuine. Her eyes, still reflecting the brightness of a distant, yet not forgotten, youth, shine out like beacons from the wrinkles which betray the truth of her years. The words of his late grandmother, who, at the age of ninety-six, had been weakened by her years and had been experiencing her own final days, still echo in his mind — *Life is still sweet you know.*

"A white coffee … No sugar. Thank you."

She turns away and fills the cup from a glass pot of percolated coffee which sits on the hot-plate behind her.

Barely registering its content, he glances at the tariff as he grabs a handful of change from his pocket … and then stares blankly at the coinage that nestles within his palm.

She hands him his drink.

"There you are, sir … That'll be eighty pence…"

Instead of searching through the coinage himself, he spreads the handful of loose change across the counter, thus, allowing the volunteer to select and then take whatever is due.

"Thank you. I think there's more than enough there."

She nods in confirmation as she counts the money and then pushes the surplus towards him.

There are no empty tables. And although there are a few spare seats, he is not in the right frame of mind to share a space with another.

He needs air.

Walking through the concourse, and whilst still clutching the disposable cup of hot coffee, he makes his way towards the main doors. Once out of the building, he takes in a deep breath from the warm air which is starting to whip up and into a breeze. He takes a cautious sip of his drink. It's too hot … and so, he will wait and give it the necessary time to cool.

He steps onto the roadway and then turns and stands — oblivious to the approach of any traffic — and looks up to the window of the room where he knows his daughter still lies. His thoughts drift back to happier times.

Suddenly, as if the hammer of *Thor* has been hurled angrily across the heavens, smashing against anvil tops and sending metallic sparks haphazardly in all directions, an explosive kaleidoscope of blinding, electric blue flashes and a roar of thunder dramatically erupts in the blackened skies. As the sound drifts away, its rumbling tones echoing through the valleys of the distant hills, a sudden downpour of torrential rain cascades, monsoon-like, onto the flat roof of the covered footway.

Without pre-warning, he feels the hollow pain of desolation from deep within and — with the additional accompaniment of a great sense of loss — he instinctively knows that she has gone. With tears rapidly filling his eyes, he drops his cup, and as the coffee splashes across the tarmac it is, almost instantly, washed away by the flood of falling rain.

He rushes back into the building and hurries up the stairs — leaping two steps at a time. On entering the main ward, he hears a shout from behind — words which demand the instant clearance of the path ahead — *"CRASH TEAM!"*

Pushed to one side, he watches on as the doctors and nursing staff crowd into the side-room and, without delay, give their all as they desperately try to block her one-way journey along the path which leads from life … to death.

He knows his fears are all too real, and as he frantically clings to the fading hope of a miraculous intervention, he moves towards the side-room where he sees the form of his wife, ousted and distressed, crouched outside the door.

Cared for by the police officer who has been with them as a support throughout the day, his wife, with her head down and cradled in both hands, trembles despairingly. She looks up at him, and as her mouth opens as if she is preparing to speak, the quiver of her lips prevent her words from being released — for they are overtaken by a heart-rending wail and a deluge of tears.

The officer steps aside as she allows him the space to crouch down and draw his wife comfortingly towards him.

She buries her head into his chest, praying for an end to the nightmare and, at the same time, willing an awakening where all is still as it was … with the family safely back at home and together as one.

He listens quietly as she starts to murmur disjointed apologies.

She blames herself! *What has she done wrong?* She cannot think of anything in particular, but she assumes that it must be because of her; after all, nothing her daughter has done could ever have warranted this.

Over and over again, she begs to God for him not to take her little girl.

The continuous tone of the heart monitor is silenced — its need no longer required.

Staff Nurse Laity emerges.

Her expression alone, tells the story.

Words are not necessary.

It is over.

The pleas of a loving mother to the highest of all authorities have gone unheeded.

Staff Nurse Laity can give little comfort. "I'm sorry ... I'm so sorry."

Fifteen years of experience has not hardened her to the sorrows that she witnesses on too regular an occasion.

He stands upright — stunned into silence and traumatized by the finality of the revelation.

His wife slowly and shakily rises with him. Her eyes turn to the room.

Suddenly — as a surge of adrenalin pumps through her body, she forces her husband to one side.

"No ... You're wrong — let me through — I've got to see her."

She pushes past the staff nurse and forces herself through the throng of medical staff. Then, having grasped a hold of her daughter, she pulls her close, clasping her lifeless body tightly and securely against hers.

"Come on baby ... wake up ... Mummy's here."

There is no response from this ... her final sleep.

She looks up, helpless and imploringly at the medics — their silence is deafening. Then, as a rage takes hold and erupts from deep within, she screams out at them. "Don't give up! Do something!"

"There is nothing more that we can do — I'm sorry."

The doctor looks at his colleagues, indicating with the silent movement of his eyes that they should make their way out of the room and back to their normal routines.

As they start to wend their way out, she stretches out and pulls one of the doctors back with her left hand tugging at his sleeve. Their eyes meet for a moment. It is a moment, sufficient in length for her to realize that her appeals are all in vain. Still clinging on to her daughter, she releases her grip on him and reluctantly accepts the hopelessness of her cause.

The police woman edges away and into the privacy of the nurses' office. She has been given the use of the telephone so that she can keep her senior officers updated of any changes — and without the publicity of it being matter-of-factly broadcast over the airways of the VHF radio.

"Detective Superintendent Dowsett, please?"

She waits as the switchboard operator connects the call.

"Dowsett!"

"Sir, its Penny — Penny Adams — I'm at the hospital."

"Yes Penny. What's up?"

He has never been one to be bothered with the niceties of telephone etiquette. He prefers to get straight to the point.

"It's bad news, sir."

She takes a breath before she passes the information. "Rachel Allen, sir — she's just passed away."

"What you mean is … she's dead!"

"Yes, sir — she's dead."

"Okay … Thank you. Now then … I want you to stay with the parents until I get there."

"Yes, sir."

The disconnection is instant.

***

"Right you lot." He captures the attention of the team as he strides into the CID room.

"I've just had a call to say that, in the last few minutes, our young victim — Rachel Allen — has died."

The team is silenced.

Contrary to the beliefs of some, police officers are citizens. They are people and are, therefore, affected by the same emotions and concerns as the majority of those in civilised society.

"Right then! We've now got a murder investigation to sort … and with only five working days left, I'm certainly not going to want another unsolved mystery haunting me into my retirement."

The silence continues.

"So … Let's get it together. I want a result — if not, then I want to have something concrete to pass on to my replacement."

He finishes with a nod — a sign that he expects no less than that of their full cooperation.

"Yes, sir." They all answer in unison.

"And … ladies and gentlemen … you'll find my replacement is not a cuddly little teddy bear like me — so, maybe you can all give *The Growsett* something to be happy about. So come on … Let's get this case wrapped up! Okay?"

This time, the automatic and somewhat obligatory *Yes, sir* is complemented with an accompaniment of admiring smiles; expressions which not only show the respect for the man, but also an element of surprise at their boss's previously hidden sense of humour, along with his, never-before-heard, admission that he has always known of the nickname and its rather amusing connotation.

"Good — get on with it then!"

He turns on his heels, simultaneously summoning his inspector to join him on his journey to the hospital.

With the tide of each season
And the turn of the years,
The distance from sorrow
Grows not from the tears

Chapter 20

Both father and son enjoy the warmth of a summer's morning as they amble down the steep incline of what was once the spinal route for those who, in bygone days, had journeyed westwards and away from this ancient city.

Although he has traversed this path many times before, Bryn's eyes are drawn, as if for the first time, above and beyond the bridges which span the gently flowing waters of the river.

Looking past the mix of rendered and red-bricked houses — which, over the years, have crept upwards and outwards as they had surreptitiously invaded the hills before settling at the edge of a patchwork quilt of vibrant shades which still encase the pillowed landscape — his attention is captured by the almost magical, marble-white glow which shines, beacon-like, from the dark and densely-wooded skyline.

Struck by the fact that although he has for many years lived a little more than a stone's throw from the shadow of the eighteenth century Belvedere Tower, it is only now that he has become so aware of it's imposing, albeit distant, presence above the city.

He ponders as to how the forest in which it nestles has, over the years, become a place of sanctuary, far from the hustle and bustle of city life. After all, in the long and distant past, it was the city which had given refuge to those weary travellers who had dared to face the hidden dangers of its wild seclusion. It certainly was a risky business for those of the time to embark on the long, arduous, and often perilous trek through this ancient, tree-filled wilderness as they headed towards the elevated heart of Devon; a place where even the first trickles of water break free and take flight from the wild, bleak and uncompromising moors as they form rivulets which eagerly join forces — thus, growing in both strength and in power — as they escape through the winding valleys and towards the seas of both the English and Bristol Channels.

Veering off the main thoroughfare, they enter the more intimate surroundings of the covered impasse with its small, independent retailers.

The sound of traffic, with its stream of diesel-fuelled buses labouring noisily, upwards and onwards towards the city centre, diminishes as it is replaced by the more palatable sounds of the music which helps to provide an almost Parisian ambience to its street-styled café.

Above the shop door, and artistically fashioned from the neck of an electric bass guitar, a wooden cross-member supports a hanging, red and black logo-emblazoned board ... which leaves no doubt as to the nature of the business within.

They enter the shop and step down the two steps which lead into the main display area.

Although busy, the friendly acknowledgment and welcome from the staff immediately exudes a feeling of belonging. A quality which, in itself, cultivates a natural sense of loyalty in return. It is because of this, neither Bryn nor his son, would ever consider purchasing an instrument from another outlet.

A comprehensive range of top-quality guitars suspended on the walls, sparkle — their chromium and gold hardware reflecting the glow from spotlights which illuminate their polished and lacquered bodies.

This is the place where the young are able to indulge in dreams of being able to emulate the fame and stardom of their guitar heroes whilst they stand in awe, mesmerized at the sight of identical examples of the tools of the trade.

It is also the place where the not-so-young — those who have witnessed the passing of too many decades, and whose fingers are no longer as supple as they would wish — ruefully reflect on what could have been; if only they had not been distracted by the necessities of having to work to keep both home and family intact.

The muffled sound of the tell-tale hook of *Sweet Home Alabama* drifting from the double-glazed doors of one of the cubicles as a potential purchaser explores the sound and feel of a sunburst Telecaster, only adds to the mood.

Displayed with a hint of humour, fused with pride, the six-string electric — its body torn apart by fractures which serve to eclipse the imaginatively, and purposefully, created cracks of its mirrored front, acts as a shining example to all budding rock stars on how *not* to treat the craftsmanship of the master luthier.

But then, the owner of this instrument can, to some extent, be forgiven for the destruction of such a creation; after all, he is a master of the fretboard and has excited audiences of thousands, worldwide, with both his expertise and his creative genius on this *very* guitar.

The luthier — tall and slim, with a full head of shoulder-length wavy hair which, to a degree, belies his fifty-odd years of life — steps out and onto the shop floor from the privacy of the adjacent workshop.

When on the premises, he is always busy; but then, he has also developed the ability to juggle and prioritize the demands put on him without appearing to diminish the attention which is given to each individual.

It matters not whether they are the regular browsers — those who chat and joke as they amble through the aisles whilst looking around for new additions to the ever-changing stock … but, at the same time, half hoping that the irresistible is not, in fact, hanging on the wall, urging them to find an excuse to dig deep into their coffers — or, whether they are the newly acquainted — those who have only just discovered their *Aladdin's Cave* and now take their time to explore the inner confines of the premises as they, too, search for the instrument of the their dreams. Either way, they are treated with due respect.

Peering over the top of his lowered spectacles, he acknowledges Bryn and his son as he tries to recollect the reason as to why he had specifically hoped to see them.

"Ah..." He smiles as he lifts one finger, indicating the success of the recall. "I've got something to show you."

With a brisk about-turn, he re-enters the workshop and then, almost immediately, re-emerges with a flat slab of pale and grainy wood in hand. Holding it in front of him, angled so as to catch the light, he shows off its unique and distinctive pattern.

"What do you think?" His eyes flick between their's and the slab of wood, thus, grabbing both Jamie's and Bryn's attention before handing it to the younger of the two for his closer inspection.

"Is this for my bass?" Jamie asks as he examines the wood and tries to imagine it fashioned into the body of his new guitar.

The luthier nods. "Yes, it's all yours!"

More than a quarter of a century of guitar-building has given him an interesting and rewarding life. Knowing that his handcrafted instruments have been made, and are still being made, for some of the finest musicians of the time, Bryn is delighted and, to some considerable extent, honoured that *he* — the luthier — has been prepared to take time out from executing the orders of the famous, to build something special for his son's twenty-first birthday.

"Is it *ash*?" Jamie asks.

The luthier replies, "Yes, it is. But it's not any old *ash*: it's exactly what you ordered — *European ash*. Now, if I'm not mistaken ... I seem to remember that you'd said you'd like something local, so ... believe it or not, this came from a forest which is not too far from here."

"Really? It's from Devon?"

Jamie is intrigued as he excitedly embraces the idea of the use of home-grown materials.

The luthier nods with a smile as he takes pleasure in witnessing the authenticity of the excitement which is exuded from the facial expressions of his young client.

"It's heavy."

"Yep ... I told you it would be, but also ... that the sound will be crisp and clear. I take it that you're still sure you want the European Ash?"

"Oh yes, I'm sure. It'll build up my muscles!"

He laughs.

"I can carve out some chambers inside the body if you like? It will give a depth to the tone … and at the same time, it'll take away some of the weight."

Jamie tests its weight and re-examines the configuration of the grain. Then, with a nod, he accepts the offer.

Fascinated as to its history, he is enthused to ask for more detail. "Do you know which forest?"

"Yes — indeed, I do."

His tantalising silence begs for the follow-on of a question.

"Oh come on — where?"

"Well … if you stand outside the shop and look to the hills in the west, you'll not be too far off."

"You're joking?"

"No — not at all. I'm telling the truth. After the storms in the late eighties and the early nineties, a whole load of trees came down. Some were chopped up and burnt … and some were sold for timber. Anyway, I got hold of some of the best pieces for myself. Now I think this particular slab must have been hanging around my workshop for more years than I care to remember, but I do know that it's definitely from Haldon."

"Yeah?"

The luthier nods.

"Cool! So what you're saying is … it's as old as I am?"

"Oh no, this has got to be much older than you. You see, it would have already been somewhere around fifty years old when it came down."

Whilst he speaks, his smile fast-morphs into a grimace as he recognizes how quick the years have passed and, also, how that stretch of time has taken him so far from his earliest efforts to create a playable instrument.

Jamie tilts the wood from side to side as he tries to determine the configuration of the grain and envisage its look when it is finally shaped, stained, lacquered and then adorned with the hardware of the finished article.

Seeing the young eyes struggling to make sense of the pattern, the luthier nips back into his workshop and again, almost immediately, returns with a dampened cloth in hand. Helpfully, he wipes its surface and in doing so, he highlights the natural flow of the beautiful curves of its lines.

"Is that better?"

Jamie nods, and with a barely-restrained look of excitement, grins approvingly before announcing, "That's awesome! Can I see it in the daylight?"

"Help yourself. You can take it outside — it'll be much clearer in the natural light."

The luthier indicates to the arcade and then, immediately, diverts his attentions to a young lad who, being accompanied by his mother, is tentatively pressing the strings on to the fret-board of a bright-red, Stratocaster-shaped, *Fender Squire*.

The greeting of a smile and an offer of help puts both mother and son at ease. The guidance and attention of a friendly professional to assist her in the decision-making process of the purchase of this, his first guitar — is welcomed.

Father and son move from the artificial lighting of the shop and step out and into the walkway of the arcade.

So as to take full advantage of the natural daylight which pours through the glazed panels of the canopy which protects those who use the walkway from the unpredictable moods of the British weather, they negotiate a space between the marble-topped tables and hoop-backed chairs which sprawl randomly out from the entrance to the café.

Jamie examines the grain. Enthralled by the intricacies of its natural artistry, he, again, adjusts its tilt so as to achieve the best aspect with the clarity of natural light. Absorbed in his study, he steps backwards and, in doing so, unwittingly obstructs the path of a fleet-footed young lady. Although having noticed his preoccupation, she, with some impressive and evasive footwork, swerves to one side in an attempt to avoid making impact.

She fails.

"I'm sorry."

His apology is immediate and natural as he turns to face and address the victim of his clumsiness.

Instantly captivated by the bright and open sparkle of her sapphire eyes, his knuckles whiten as the wood is squeezed tight — a reaction to the irrepressible tremble that fires throughout his body.

Her long black hair, tumbling from beneath a turquoise knitted-beret and over a long and floaty silken scarf, frames a fresh and cheery look of innocence.

Spellbound, he stands in silence — for she has, in his eyes, a loveliness which he imagines could only have been spirited into existence by the gods themselves.

Their eyes meet, lingering for a moment as their pupils involuntarily dilate whilst each tries to absorb as much of the other as possible.

Their mutual attraction is both instantaneous and powerful.

Captivated by her angelic looks, his thoughts race, assessing whether he should politely turn away and add this to his ever-growing list of lost opportunities or stand firm and, with an air of self-assuredness, take the risk of opening his mouth and saying something embarrassingly clichéd.

With the impetuousness of his youth, the decision is made — the whim of the heart has overruled the staidness of reason.

Albeit barely audible, he utters just a single word. "Beautiful!"

She reads his lips. "Is that aimed at me ... or at that piece of wood?"

The enchanting lilt to her voice suggests an educated and somewhat privileged upbringing. She smiles, as she awaits his response.

Jamie averts his gaze, but his blushes betray any attempt to conceal the extent of his interest.

"You don't really wanna know the answer to that, do you?" his father interrupts.

Dismissive of the unwelcome irritation of the uninvited interruption, her eyes, momentarily, flick towards his and then back towards those of Jamie.

Bryn, suitably admonished whilst having still been in the flow of converting his thoughts to sound, continues with his words tapering to a whisper. "It could be too close to call."

In a desperate attempt to silence his father, Jamie answers, "Both!"

Naturally shy he may be, but he is careful not to lose this opportunity to take advantage of, what he hopes could be, a wonderful twist of fate.

"Thank you."

She accepts the compliment, and swirling on her heels and beaming with delight, it is obvious that she, too, is savouring the magic of this chance encounter.

Confidently and with her head held high, she moves away across the terracotta brick-surfaced floor. With her gait exaggerated, intentionally emphasising the swing of her hips and thus forcing the skirt of her cotton mini-dress to sway, seductively, over her snugly-fitted jeans, Jamie — awestruck by her beauty — can only watch in silence as she wends her way through the scattering of half-filled tables ... and towards the pink facade of the retro boutique which abuts the café.

Prior to entering the open doorway, she pauses and then turns back and looks directly at him. Their eyes meet yet again — the signals confirming their shared attraction.

She spins around and, as if wishing to add an air of mystique, steps into the boutique as he, simultaneously, edges back and into the guitar shop.

As the luthier retakes possession of the raw material of his trade, he asks, "Happy?"

"Oh, yeah! It's terrific! It's really great. Thanks."

Jamie's day gets better by the minute.

***

Half-heartedly, she fingers her way along a rail of hanging dresses whilst keeping a watchful eye on the arcade. Unusually for her, she has little interest in whether or not the garments are of a suitable colour, size or style; their present purpose is to conceal her intent and not to adorn her body.

Like an opportunist cat preparing to pounce, she awaits her moment. Perfect timing will be required if she is to orchestrate a second *chance* meeting.

She sees movement through the window as Jamie and Bryn approach the door. Coordinating her approach with precision, she steps out of the boutique and, not wanting to look too keen, adopts an air of nonchalance as she walks back, meandering between the tables and towards the doorway of the guitar shop.

Bryn exits first, his son following close behind.

Her timing is impeccable.

As the door closes and Jamie turns to walk away, she brushes past him … then stops and turns.

"Oh … I'm sorry!" She blushes as she wonders if he has realized that this collision had not been entirely accidental.

Their eyes meet again and they hesitate, neither of them knowing what they should say next.

He speaks first.

"Three or four?" he asks nervously. He is unsure as to why he'd asked such an obscure question, but the words had left his mouth and so he had no option other than to run with them.

Bryn hovers as he looks back at his son, pleasantly surprised at his forward approach.

"Pardon?" she replies quizzically.

With an ever-increasing self-assurance and with a blaze of humour lighting his eyes, he repeats his words. "Three or four?"

"Three or four, what … may I ask?" Albeit still puzzled, she is, all the same, intrigued.

"Marshmallows!" His confidence grows by the moment as he begins to enjoy the playing of this, somewhat bizarre, guessing game.

"Marshmallows?" she asks — still no closer to understanding what he is talking about and, what is more, where this strange encounter will lead.

Feigning a look of surprise as to her inability to understand him, he, with perfect timing, clarifies, "In your hot chocolate."

"In my chocolate? Oh … I take it that you're offering to buy me a drink?"

There is a hint of excitement in her voice, along with a sense of relief, in that there finally appears to be some rationale to his words.

"Yeah, I think … maybe, I am." He smiles openly — inwardly praying for a positive response.

The humour which had been reflected in his approach has succeeded in adding something special to the initial attraction.

She pauses, then with a nod, responds, "Four's cool."

"That's great!"

Turning his head, he looks across towards his father and calls out, "Dad … I've got my mobile — I'll see you later, okay?"

Having recognized that his presence is no longer required, Bryn nods in confirmation and then, with a knowing smile, turns away.

He phones his wife.

"Where are you?"

He listens to her reply and confirms the rendezvous.

"Okay, I'll see you there then."

With the conversation at an end, the call is terminated. With his hands in his pockets, he walks out and into the street, still mulling over the lack of convention of his son's latest *chat-up* technique.

Jamie leads her towards the counter of the café.

"What would you like to drink?"

"I think you've already guessed." She pauses, and then, with a smile, she replies, "How about chocolate with cream … and marshmallows. It's my favourite. Thank you."

"Great … Then that's what I'll get."

Noting that the tables are starting to fill as more people — some accompanied by tired and irritable offspring, whilst others are laden with bulging shopping bags — seek rest and refreshment.

"I'll get the drinks while you try to find us a seat … if that's all right with you?"

She nods as she turns to look for a vacant space.

She meanders past the tables, and on locating one which is suitable for two, she places her bag beside her and makes herself comfortable. As she sits alone, her mind is working overtime. She looks at him as he stands in the queue, confirming to herself the reality of her spontaneous attraction to him and hoping that his character matches his looks. She eyes her reflection in the window of the salon beside her. As she adjusts her beret, she plumps her hair with her hands, emphasizing the feminine flow of its waves.

Looking back towards the queue, she catches him gazing towards her.

Not wishing to be caught staring, he turns back towards the counter assistant and places his order.

As he waits for the drinks to be poured, he periodically glances towards her, as if checking that she had not had a change of heart and gone.

Drinks poured, he delivers them to their table.

Her hot chocolate, complete with toppings, is placed on the table in front of her, and as he positions his own cup of coffee opposite, he sits down.

There is a brief and uncomfortable silence as they both take a moment to think through their opening words.

She fiddles with her spoon, prodding the cream as she plucks up the courage to speak.

The silence is interrupted as he utters a somewhat predictable opening of, "I'm Jamie."

"That's nice … It suits you."

Anticipating a like-response, he waits as he picks up his coffee cup and, with both elbows on the table, leans forward and sips his drink. Whilst looking across the top of his cradled beverage and into her eyes, he says, "What's supposed to happen is that I say, *Hi, I'm Jamie* … and then *you* say, *Hi, Jamie, I'm* — "

He fills the pause with the look of the *little-boy-lost*.

She laughs as, with little more than a hint of embarrassment, she realizes that she has failed to identify herself.

"Oh, I'm sorry … I'm Tori."

"Tori?"

"Victoria." She pauses and, with her eyes revealing an inner humour, she adds, "Or…" mimicking her mother's voice as she goes on to emphasize both of her forenames, "Victoria Grace … if I'm in trouble, that is."

Recognising the behavioural similarity of his own mother, and who also uses his full name to ensure that there is no doubt as to whom she is directing a reprimand, he utters an empathetic chuckle.

Chapter 21

Several weeks have passed since they had first met. Although they have kept in daily contact by phone and have been out together on several occasions, Jamie will not allow himself to take things for granted, so, as is his way, he has arrived well in advance of the anticipated time of her arrival.

With a cup of coffee in hand and being only slightly distracted by the comings and goings of the staff and customers of the guitar shop, he flicks through the messages on his mobile phone. To the casual passer-by, he looks to be relaxed and content. But then, according to the old adage, appearances can be deceptive — and so, if his pulse and blood pressure were to be monitored, then, without a doubt, a very different picture would be painted. The fact is that beneath that veneer of calm, there sits a young man who is brimming with excitement as he waits in expectation for his girlfriend's arrival. What's more, although his eyes are down whilst he glances at the content of the screen, he is, in reality, doing little more than that of disguising the fact that he is, rather religiously, monitoring the count of the clock.

She is late — but then, he consoles himself with the thought that, unlike those of his parent's generation, there are very few of his contemporaries who would consider the agreed time of an appointment to be much more than a measure for rough guidance ... and from recent experience, he knows that she is no different. With this in mind, he will do as he always does; sit back, act cool and wait.

If he were meeting her anywhere else, he would not be quite as comfortable; the coffee is good and the relaxed surroundings lack the intimidation of some of the establishments which one would expect to find in the more central locations of the average city. In any case, if for some unexpected reason she does not turn up as arranged, then at least he can have a wander around the guitar shop and, if the luthier is about, check on the progress of his bass.

Although he is unaware of the fact, he has no need to be concerned; she is, at this very moment, hurrying her way down the hill, having been delayed by the need to shake off the presence of her *rather too inquisitive* mother.

The fact that she is *involved* with someone has not been too difficult for her mother to accept. She does, however, have some difficulty in the fact that she has been kept in the dark regarding his name. Tori's unwillingness to reveal the detail of his identity to her mother is not because she is ashamed of him, nor is it because she feels that she has something to hide, it's just that, for the time being, she wishes to keep it to herself.

There is no specific reason for the secrecy — it is simply that she wants to be able to enjoy some personal time in which she can be herself and, without feeling the constraints of any unnecessary parental interference, delight in the exploration of her newly-formed relationship.

Jamie glances up from the screen.

Recognising her silhouette against the daylight of the street, and seeing the way in which she then wafts into the arcade and approaches with a beaming smile, he feels a sense of relief.

Some of the old-fashioned values of his parents have obviously passed down the line, and, as such, he automatically stands and welcomes her with a kiss and an affectionate embrace.

"I'm sorry I'm late." She takes her seat.

"Late?" He also sits as he looks at his watch and lies. "I didn't notice."

"I had to get rid of my mum — she can be a little bit too nosey for my liking."

"You should have brought her along. I'd like to meet her."

"No, you wouldn't! Well, not unless you enjoy being interrogated and then judged to see if you are suitable to go through to the next round!"

"Really? It's like that, is it?"

"Yes, really … it is."

"Okay, so … changing the subject — how many marks will *you* give me?"

"Ooo… I don't know." She leans her head to one side as she teases him with a feigned look of uncertainty.

"Well, how about if I get you your usual hot chocolate and marshmallow fix? Will that be enough to help you work it out?"

"Oh! Well *that* will certainly raise the score — in fact, I think it could even get you close on top marks!"

He smiles, stands and then strolls off towards the counter so as to place her order, with a refill for himself.

Whilst sitting and waiting for him to return, Tori muses over whether the time is fast approaching when she will be able to take that embarrassing step to introduce him to her mother. She will need to warn him to watch his words as her mother can be rather sensitive and protective, especially when it comes to the welfare of her daughter. Some would say that she is over-protective, but then, she has her reasons. She delves into her handbag and takes out a ballpoint pen and a notepad. Tearing out two pages, she lays them on the table and writes on each, then sits back and waits patiently for her drink to be delivered.

As he walks towards her, careful not to spill the drinks, she lifts a leaf of the paper in each hand and presents them as if she were a judge presenting the scores in some television talent show. The number ten is clearly marked on each. He smiles, delighted to see that he has achieved top marks!

"Did you mean it?"

He looks puzzled.

She clarifies. "I mean, did you mean it when you said that you'd like to meet my mother?"

"Yes! Of course I did … It's no big deal though. Why do you ask?"

"I just wondered … that's all."

"Don't worry, if you think your mum's nosey, then you just wait 'till you meet mine. First, she'll smother you with kindness and stuff you full of chocolate cakes, and then, when you're sitting back nice and comfortable, she'll worm her way until she can download all that she wants from you! And guess what? You won't even know she's done it!"

"So she's nosey, too, is she?"

"Too right she is!"

"All right then — how about it?"

"How about what?"

"How about I ring her, and if she's still in town, then she can come down and meet us here?"

He hesitates for a moment as he comes to terms with the lack of warning, and then, as if *grabbing the bull by the horns*, he agrees. "Yes, Why not? As my old man would say, *There's no time like the present.*"

"Good, I'll call her now … before I change my mind!"

Chapter 22

The tell-tale, distinctive guttural purr which accompanies the classic thirty-year-old, low-slung Harley-Davidson, diverts Jamie from exercising his fingers on his elderly and well-worn bass guitar. With ten weeks having passed since he first examined the wood for his new instrument, he knows that its completion is imminent, and, like an expectant father, he is awaiting the call from the luthier for him to go to the shop to collect it.

With the distraction of him having been able to use this time to cultivate a relationship with Tori, the period of waiting seems to have gone by with surprising haste. Strangely, and somewhat paradoxically, even though they have known each other for a relatively short period, he feels as if he has known her forever and that their being together was somehow predestined. She has fitted in well with the band and their respective girlfriends, and with her regular attendance at the practice sessions, her critical, but constructive, observations have been appreciated by all.

Whilst the machine glides to a halt, the purring ceases as its powerful, twelve hundred cubic capacity, V-shaped, twin-cylinder engine clatters into silence.

Looking out of the window and onto the sparsely-gravelled earthen driveway, he is intrigued as he watches a leather-jacketed giant of a man, with his back towards him, holding the machine steady as he allows his petite pillion passenger to dismount. He observes attentively as she pulls her crash helmet from her head and then places it onto the backrest of the pillion seat. Her fingers pass through her black, russet-tinted hair, loosening any tangles as she allows her long and flowing locks to cascade over her shoulders … and then down her back.

Tight-fitting and slightly faded, her blue denim jeans tuck neatly into her calf-length, Cuban-heeled, antique-leather boots, emphasizing both her fitness and the perfection of her figure. As she pulls down on the zip of her leather jacket, she reveals a white, pleated cotton blouse of which the upper buttons are worn unfastened, thus allowing the top to gape sufficiently enough to display a tantalising, but respectable, hint of cleavage. Aged somewhere in her late-thirties, she has become accustomed to admiring looks from men of all ages, along with the envious glances from women who know all too well that there are many, who are not much more than half her age, who would be thrilled to have been blessed with a figure like hers.

Reminiscent of a dusty wild-west drifter who is relieving a tired and overburdened mule of its load, *the giant* unlashes and then releases the baggage from the machine — its height gradually increasing as the removal of each bag reduces the pressure on its springs.

She, his companion, stands upright and confident — a trait which in itself enhances her natural beauty. Then slowly, and with both hands, she massages the back and sides of her neck as she stretches, first to the right and then to the left, thus, relieving the muscles which have become taut with travel.

Tilting her head to one side as she fits the first of her gold, looped earrings, her dark-brown eyes survey the picturesque rural setting of the tastefully converted, stone barn. Casually, she looks up at the house, catching the eye of Jamie in the process. They exchange smiles and he, slightly embarrassed, hurriedly disappears from the window. Carefully and respectfully, he rests his guitar on its stand and then makes his way down the stairs to the front door, calling out to his parents while on the way.

"Mum! Dad! We have visitors!"

"Who is it?" his mother asks.

"I don't know — but he's big!" He pauses, then whispers, "*... and she's beautiful.*"

He opens the door.

The giant has unloaded the machine. There are three heavy, military-style canvas holdalls unceremoniously dumped on the ground around him. His helmet is off and rests, precariously, on the fuel tank. The sound of a door opening alerts him to the arrival of company.

Turning and looking towards the door, he robotically rolls a cigarette. As he transfers it, unlit, from hand to mouth, his blue eyes gaze out from his well-weathered, bronzed complexion and focus on Jamie. Immediately, he strides over towards him, arms outstretched and ready to greet with an encompassing hold.

He pauses as he glances over to his lady companion, and then, as he grasps her hand in his, he steers her towards Jamie.

"How's my little James William?" His voice booms out as he releases the hand of his lady before subjecting Jamie to an ursine embrace.

Jamie tries, unsuccessfully, to step back.

He is mystified by the presence of this full-bearded, straggly-haired being who refers to him by his full and proper name ... whilst in the process of squeezing the very air from his lungs.

Like crests of ocean waves breaking over a raging sea of auburn, his hair — wild and long and with streaks of white — imbues a look which is not too far from that of an ancient and mythological warrior.

Breathless, Jamie peers round the massive frame of the visitor and watches on as the Harley-D leans slowly to one side as its stand gradually sinks down and into the soft earth.

His attempt to alert *the giant* fails.

It is too late. Turning just in time to witness his helmet roll off the tank, closely followed by a sickening thud as his motorcycle falls onto its side, he grumbles his accusation, "Pesky little critters!"

There is no sign of shock, nor is there a look of anguish as he, quite unperturbed, returns to the machine.

The indentations on the colourful and enthralling artwork of the tank, accompanied by his somewhat laid-back response, suggest that this is not an unusual occurrence.

Jamie steps forward, symbolic of an offer to assist in the raising of the prostrate and incapacitated machine. There is no need. *The giant* bends over, grasps the handlebar and then, nonchalantly and with one arm, lifts.

It rises in submission, as if it dare not fail to comply with its master's wishes. With the Harley-D upright and secure, he turns back towards Jamie and shrugs.

As he walks, he limps. He has, at some stage in his life, suffered an injury to his left leg. Jamie muses over what may have caused the infirmity and concludes that the injury is more than likely to have been sustained as a result of *the giant* having become separated from his mechanical steed whilst on a distant and dusty highway.

Jamie's mother, having been disturbed while in the process of adding the final touches to her most recent artistic creation, appears at the door — paint-spattered and with her husband close behind.

There is an almost deafening silence as they register the face from the past. They look at each other in disbelief at the reality of the return of Guillaume the Bee.

Guillaume steps forward with arms outstretched. He embraces the two as if they are one, then abruptly releases them as he indicates to his stunning companion.

With a slightly put on, Spanish lilt to his voice, he introduces her.

"Meet Maria — my wife — my Señora."

He pauses, his face alight with pleasure as he continues. "She is beautiful. Don't you agree?"

Jamie's mother offers a hand in greeting, simultaneously looking her up and down approvingly. She nods in agreement, and guessing that Guillaume has not improved over the years, and will not readily see the need to comply with the accepted rules of etiquette, she takes it upon herself to continue with the formalities of introducing their new guest to the family.

"Hello ... I'm Beth, and this is Bryn, my husband ... and of course, you have already met Jamie, our son"

"Ah ... Jamie — my godson," declares Guillaume, proudly.

Beth looks at him, unimpressed by his exaggerated show of pride ... and more than a little annoyed by the fact that he has not seen his godson since he was a baby. But still, deciding that nothing good will come of her making an issue of the fact, she turns back to Maria, who acknowledges the introductions with an infectious smile.

"Gracias. Thank you."

As a show of respect, she switches from the language of her adopted home which, incidentally, is also that of her Hispanic roots, to that of her upbringing, and so, with a smile, she introduces herself. "I am Maria ... Of course, you know that. He's already told you that much."

Beth smiles warmly and, having picked up on an accent which is akin to that of those who come from the United States, she comments, "I guessed that you were from Spain ... but your accent—"

"No! I am originally from New Mexico. I was raised in a small town which is around an hour's drive from Albuquerque. But you are right — my mother has the Spanish bloodlines, but my father's family are all Texas born-and-bred."

"So, tell me ... how on earth did you two meet then?"

"Well ... we met in Spain. I was researching dance for my studies ... and I found flamenco."

"Go on — I'm intrigued."

"Well ... Gwilly found the bar where I was working, and so, one thing led to another, and that was it really."

"I must say, I'm not too surprised to hear that Gwilly found his way to a bar. Anyway ... putting that to one side ... you say you were a dancer?"

"Yes and no ... I mainly worked behind the bar, but very occasionally I'd do a turn to fill in if one of the girls didn't turn up. Nothing special though ... it would be just enough to keep the customers happy. We would try to give them what they wanted — that romanticized vision of Spain."

"So you danced the Flamenco?" she asks, with an edge of excitement.

"Oh, I guess. I mean ... it was not the true flamenco. It was just more the general style of dancing. By that, what I mean is ... it's the sort of thing that's seen in the movies. I guess it's what a lot of the tourists think flamenco is about, and so ... if that's what they want, then that's what they get!"

"Well, I think it all sounds quite romantic anyway. So, tell me, where are you living now?"

"We actually live in Spain. We have a place in the south — between Sevilla and Jerez."

"It sounds wonderful! I can just imagine it now — lazy days, stretched out by the pool ... and, of course, cloudless blue skies and the heat of the sun on my face — utter bliss!"

"Yes, well, we do have a pool. It's not particularly big though, but it's big enough for us. Maybe you should come over and stay with us sometime."

Beth smiles, delighted with the offer of a holiday and, also, for the opportunity to speak with someone who is from a world which is so far removed from that of her own.

She looks at the holdalls which are lying on the driveway and refocuses her attention away from Maria.

"I take it you're staying?" She aims the question at Guillaume — her eyes firm, but betraying a hint of affection for this engagingly amiable rogue.

Having known them well enough to be sure that, even at such short notice, they were not the sort to turn an old friend away, he grins, and then adds, "Well ... you did say I'd always be welcome."

"Yes ... and so you are."

She pauses as she assesses as to whether or not she should remark on how long ago that offer was made and how, after so many years, this is the first time that it had been taken up. She decides on the *not*. With a smile, she continues. "Oh, well, I suppose that you'd better grab your bags and bring them in!"

Her instructions, although sounding a little abrupt, are aimed at him ... and him alone. After all, she knows that she has to be resolute and that if given half a chance, he will shirk his responsibilities and allow others to carry his load.

"I'm afraid that you'll just have to take us as you find us."

Maria is ushered indoors as Guillaume, accompanied and supervised by Bryn and Jamie, collects the baggage.

Bryn addresses Guillaume.

"It has been a *long* time."

"Yea. Fifteen *long* years." He pauses for thought and then adjusts his estimation. "Okay, maybe it's closer to twenty. What's a couple of years between friends ... hey?" With a shrug, he grabs the three large holdalls in one hand and the back-pack in the other.

Bryn corrects him. "Almost twenty-one!"

"Hey man, as I said ... what's a few years between friends, huh?"

Jamie looks enquiringly at his father, who, reading his son's need for an explanation, responds, "Ah, yes! Jamie ... meet Guillaume — Guillaume the Bee. As you've probably already realized, he *really is* your long-lost and may I say ... wayward Godfather?"

Grinning broadly, the giant of a man lights his cigarette, inhales deeply and holds the smoke in his lungs for a few seconds before releasing it into the atmosphere. "Gwilly to my friends."

His grin broadens as the sweet, herbal bouquet carries in the air.

Recognising the scent of the illicit substance, and not wanting his son to be encouraged, nor tempted, to want to try and emulate his Godfather, Bryn snaps his order, "Gwilly! Put that out!"

Gwilly looks at him with a pleading, childlike expression … as if hoping for a reprieve.

"Now!" The response is short and firm.

His appeal has failed, so, suitably reprimanded, he complies with his old friend's demand by pinching the end with his fingers and extinguishing the burn. The procedure is completed and he tucks it away into his jacket pocket; a *joint* is not to be wasted — he will finish it later.

They enter the house — Bryn still shaking his head in mild disbelief at his old friend's indiscretion with regard to the recreational use of marijuana.

"You have enough bags with you."

"Don't blame me. Mine's the small one …" Gwilly pauses. "The rest are hers."

He dumps the bags in the hallway, half-hoping that Bryn will carry them upstairs and leave them in the *guest room*.

Jamie mutters, "Guillaume the Bee? What sort of name is that?"

"What was that, son?"

"Oh — it was nothing."

They move to the dining room-cum-lounge and Gwilly collapses into one of the two armchairs.

"Would anyone like a drink?" Beth pauses and then presents the choices. "Tea? Coffee?"

Gwilly places his order. "Yeah … a coffee would be great."

"White?" she asks.

He nods in affirmation.

"Sugar?"

"I wish you wouldn't call me that in front of your husband — he'll only get jealous!"

Her returning stare — silent, yet powerful — is not only a put-down, but it is also a request for him to provide a proper answer to her question.

Whilst ensuring that he has taken sufficient care so as not to have them presented in a way which could be deemed as being offensive, he raises two fingers as he states his preference. "Two, please."

"I've got no cake … but I may have some biscuits somewhere — anyone for a *bickie*?"

There are no takers, so she turns towards the kitchen.

"Can I give you a hand?"

Maria's offer of assistance is readily accepted. She hopes that it will give them an opportunity to get to know each other.

"I'll put the kettle on. Then I'll show you your room, and I'll get you some clean towels."

Beth is enjoying the unexpected role of playing hostess; what's more, she welcomes the opportunity of having some female company.

She fills the kettle and flicks the switch.

"Come on ... while we're waiting, I'll show you around."

Dutifully and somewhat proudly, Beth shows her guest the layout of the house.

They climb the narrow stairs and into the room which is to be Maria's and Gwilly's for the duration of their stay.

Maria, having spent many hours on the back of a growling motorcycle, welcomes the invite of comfort and sits, with a slight bounce, on the edge of the bed. Instinctively, she presses her hands into the quilt, as if relishing the gentle spring of the mattress and the promise of a good night's sleep ahead.

She smiles as she absorbs the room's cottage-style design and décor.

"This is beautiful. Thank you."

Beth acknowledges the compliment with a reciprocal smile.

Although she has had no prior notice as to the arrival of her guests, she always has fresh linen and towels. So, with Maria's assistance, the bed is made. Once satisfied that the bedroom is now in a state of acceptability, she shouts down the stairway. "Gwilly! Get off your arse and bring Maria's bags up to your room!"

"The kettle's boiled!"

"Never mind that — just do as you're told and bring those bags ... *Now!*"

Beth and Maria share a chuckle as they hear him grunt his response of reluctant obedience.

"I'm sorry that we didn't warn you that we were coming ... I hope it's not going to be a problem?"

"No ... not at all. We're delighted to see you both."

"I will ask that you say nothing to him, but ..." she pauses as she chooses her words, "he has been not too well recently ... and because of that, he's decided that he should make the time to see his friends again."

"Not well?"

She hears the sound of the baggage being hauled up the stairs and then on to the landing.

"Shush ..." she whispers, "I'll tell you when he's gone downstairs."

Having dumped the load in the bedroom, he has served his purpose and is then, accordingly, promptly dismissed.

As he leaves the room, ducking his head through the doorway, Beth and Maria catch each other's eye and exchange a quiet but nervous laugh.

"You said he's not well?"

"Yes, he doesn't want me to say anything to you about it, but as you are his oldest friends, I'll tell you anyway."

Beth waits in silence, and not without trepidation, for the revelation.

"He has been having radiotherapy treatment for cancer in his, umm…"

She taps the lower part of her tummy towards the groin as she searches for the right word.

"Stomach? Bowels?"

She shakes her head. "No ... No!"

"Oh ... there ..." Beth responds, as she sees that Maria is indicating to the area of genitalia.

"Yes — There!"

Beth says nothing. She is shocked. It is as if she has been shackled to the spot by the bindings of a deepening sadness.

"You mustn't tell him that I told you ... Please?"

"I won't say anything — I promise."

"Thank you. You see, this is why we are travelling to see all the places and the people that he loves. Of course, we're praying that the treatment has been good, but, at the same time, we think that maybe we should prepare for the worst ... just in case."

"Is that why he didn't warn us that he was coming? ... So that he didn't have to explain?"

"Yes, that's why. You see, he doesn't want you to be worried for him. He says that he wants things to be as they always were. After the last dose of treatment, the doctor told him that ... yes, there are many people who die *with* cancer, but there are considerably less who die *from* cancer."

Having paused for thought, she understands the doctor's point. "It makes sense — people probably do die from other things before any cancer can take them. Anyway I can assure you that I won't be telling Bryn — at least not until after you've gone home."

"Thank you. That'll be good."

Gwilly, having already lumbered down the stairs, is greeted by the sight of a seven-stone mass of wheaten-coated, Rhodesian ridgeback sprawled across the vacated chair. The dog, with his head resting on the armrest, lifts one eyebrow and watches Gwilly with interest. He makes no attempt to get up; for he has reclaimed his seat and has, therefore, no intention of allowing this newcomer to oust him ... and commandeer it for himself.

"Hey! I was sitting there!" Gwilly looks into the eyes of this mass of canine muscle.

As if making a statement of intent, the dog yawns — flashing a display of ivory teeth — before shuffling his body into a position of comfort.

Gwilly looks towards Bryn.

Jamie hears the click from the kitchen as the kettle switches off ... having, yet again, come to the boil. "I suppose ... if Mum and Maria are still sorting things upstairs ... then I'd better make the drinks."

"Yeah ... okay," Bryn replies, as Jamie leaves the room.

"What's that?" Gwilly asks, pointing at the dog and not used to being challenged by anyone — be it man or beast.

"Oh, *him* … He's been out the back … I've just let him in."

"Yea, but what is it?"

"*It* … is called Bill."

The tip of his tail starts to wiggle as he hears his name.

"Did you say … Bill?"

"Yes, that's right — Bill."

His curiosity begs the question. "Why Bill?"

"Why not?" Bryn offers no explanation.

Gwilly looks back at the dog. "Not after me then?"

"No! Definitely not!"

"Okay."

Gwilly adopts an almost childlike appearance of disappointment, but then, noticing that Bill's eyes are screwed tightly shut, he changes the subject. "Is he pretending to be asleep?"

"Yep."

Bryn sees the look of disbelief on his face and asks, "I take it you would like to sit down?"

Gwilly nods. "Yeah … That would be good."

"Well, go on then — push him off."

Gwilly steps towards the chair but then hesitates as the dog opens just the one eye and looks directly into *his* before closing it again, so as to resume the pretence of sleep; a pretence which — with the knowledge that his ruse will, in all probabilities, be short-lived — is betrayed by the twitches at the end of his tail.

"Will he mind?"

"Probably — give him a shove … he'll move."

To Bryn, the implementation of a *shove*, as he'd put it, would be no more than that of a matter of course — but he recognizes his guest's caution, and grins.

"Bill!" He tries to attract the Ridgeback's attention, but, as is often the case, he is completely ignored.

Assertively, he raises the volume of his demand and increases the forcefulness in his voice.

"Bill — I'm talking to you!"

The flicking of the tail quickens until it has the swing of a wag; then, as it pounds a thumping, rhythmic beat onto the leather, his eyes open wide and his neck arches around as if to assess the resolve of his master.

"Yes — I am talking to **you!**"

Bill watches and, as if frozen in time, he waits for the follow up.

Bryn barks his order. "**Off!**"

There is still no compliance.

"Well trained then!"

Gwilly's interjection of sarcasm is, apart from a disparaging glance, swiftly disregarded.

The dog watches intently as he stubbornly awaits the next command — the confirmatory command: the one which, when accompanied by the hardening of the facial expression and the tell-tale expanding of the chest, means that an act of enforcement is imminent.

Bryn, slowly and threateningly, rises from his chair, and then, with his eyes fixed onto those of Bill, he stands over him and roars. "I said, **off** — **Now**"

As he gives him a shove, Bill springs off the cushion, weaves past his master and then immediately dives into the other armchair and curls up tight.

Gwilly, quick to take his opportunity, repossesses his seat, leaving Bryn stranded between the two, individually occupied, armchairs.

Bill and Gwilly, satisfied with having shared the victory, watch each other in mutual admiration.

Bryn says nothing as he looks at each of them in turn, temporarily undecided as to which of the two should be moved. Asserting his role as pack leader, he again orders the dog to get off the chair.

Bill uncharacteristically obeys, then steps towards Gwilly and stands in front of him, as if willing a prompt vacation.

Their eyes meet yet again. The relinquishment of the right to stay put is not forthcoming, so he adopts another tactic.

Gently resting his head on Gwilly's knee, he gazes into his eyes, appealing for a compromise.

As Jamie re-enters the room, with a tray laden with mugs of coffee, he calls, "Mum! Maria! Your drinks are ready"

"Thank you — we'll be right down."

The response from Beth is immediate.

Jamie places the tray on the table and the pulls out a chair for himself.

Gwilly, shaking his head in disbelief, mutters, "I still can't believe you called your dog, Bill."

Beth walks in with Maria and, as she steers Maria and herself towards the table and chairs, she explains, "Bryn named him. Don't blame me. I think it's a stupid name for a dog."

"It's different. I'll give you that."

Gwilly looks at the dog and the dog looks back.

"No … I like it. Even if you didn't name him after me, I can pretend that you did. I mean, he's obviously a hound of my own heart — good looking, intelligent …"

"Stubborn … and idle." Beth finishes the assessment for him as Maria, enjoying seeing her spouse being, humorously but gently, baited in a way that only true friends can, beams with a smile.

"No, actually … I was going to say … relaxed and chilled — a sign of a mind with great acumen, I'll have you know?"

As Beth shakes her head in playful disagreement, Bill surreptitiously sidles his way up and almost on to Gwilly's lap. It is only when the last leg lifts from the floor, and he fidgets his bulk into a position of comfort, that his actions are noticed.

"How the hell did you do that?"

In expectation of being ejected, Bill wags the tip of his tail, but Gwilly, recognising the commonality of their traits, relents, smiles and then settles back, allowing him to stay.

Jamie listens to the chatter and the suggestions for the evening ahead, then, as a reminder to his mother of their previous arrangement, he interrupts the conversation. "Mum, you promised to drop me in town, to meet Tori."

"Yes, I know. I haven't forgotten. So what time are you meeting her?"

"Eight."

She turns to her husband and his old friend. "So … have you made up your minds? What are you both planning to do?"

"Nothing much … Maybe, we'll just have a couple drinks … nothing more. Why?"

"Well, how about Jamie and me pick up Tori, then she can join us at the *The Ferret*? I'm sure she'd *love* to meet Jamie's long-lost Godfather, and … I'm also sure that Gwilly would *love* to show Maria one of his old haunts. That, of course, is assuming that he's not still banned!"

"Ouch! That hurt." He smiles. "No, I'm not banned … I don't recall ever being banned from that one — a few others maybe — but not *The Ferret*. So … it all sounds good to me, and I'd love to meet the young lady."

A visit to the old pub; Gwilly cannot think of a better way to finish the day.

Beth adds, "Anyway … we haven't got a lot in … so, maybe, it would be easier if we ate out. If that's all right with you?"

The silence suggests an accord.

"The lady has spoken," Gwilly announces, "… and who am I to argue? We'll eat out."

Jamie had originally been hoping for a more intimate setting with his girlfriend, but the unexpected arrival of the *giant* had intrigued him. So, not wishing to miss out on an evening which would, without a doubt, become more entertaining as his godfather re-acquaints himself with both the village pub and the local brew, he agrees. "Yea, okay, that's cool. I'll ring Tori and see if it's all right with her."

Beth nods, she sees no reason why there should be a problem and leaves her son to make the call.

Chapter 23

The entrance to the old thatched inn is marked by the presence of three men who, with smoke escaping from their mouths, stand beneath the sign of *The Ferret*, chatting like disorderly conscripts, banished to perform sentry duties in the chill of the advancing night.

Legislation has brought an end to the days of smoke-filled bars. So those who still have the need to gratify the demands of their addiction must now sacrifice the warmth and the comfort … and take a satisfying puff in the cold.

As Bryn lifts the latch of the ancient wooden door, he peers through the leaded panes of the small, eye-level windows.

Two men — one in a well-worn, checked tweed jacket and with a cloth cap worn as if it were a permanent fixture on his head, and the other in an equally well-worn, military-style pullover — sit on high wooden stools and lean on the polished wood surface of the public bar. They respond to the opening of the door and the sound of voices by simultaneously twisting away from their conversation with the landlord and joining him in scrutinizing the faces of those who are about to enter.

It is relatively early. But then, this is probably the best time to order and consume a meal. Since the introduction of the smoking ban, the hostelry has suffered. Prior to the legislation, the regulars would arrive after work and then stay until the call for last orders, or until summoned by their long-suffering wives. But now, many of them go straight home and do not venture out until later. It is not until after nine that the bar will start to fill, and it is then when the volume will increase both in numbers and in sound.

The low-beamed ceiling and well-trodden, floral-patterned carpet, along with the traditional décor of whitewashed walls adorned with gilt-framed prints of horsemen in their hunting-pinks in pursuit of a lone red fox, helps to maintain the character of an old English pub.

Bryn holds the door back, allowing Gwilly and Maria to gain first entry.

In order to procure a decent table, the trio had made their way to the hostelry in advance, knowing that Beth and Jamie will follow once they have collected Tori from her home.

The three men at the bar are stunned into a wary silence as they struggle to decide where to rest their focus. Is it to be on the warrior-like colossus? … or is it to be on the stunning looks of his lady companion? Whichever they choose, there will always be a feeling of vulnerability. To stare into the face of the one of such mass is one thing, but to stare at his lady could be equally as perilous.

The two who are seated, elect to turn their attentions on their host, for it is *he* who will be making the first contact.

"Good evening."

Bryn appears from behind his guests. The landlord, recognising him as one of the not-so-regular locals, then adds, "Haven't seen you for a while. How are things?"

"Things are good — thanks. As you can see, we have visitors. So, I thought I'd introduce them to the culinary delights of your good lady's fare."

"Excellent. She'll be out in a few minutes ... so how about I pour you some drinks?" He rubs his hands together as he awaits their order.

"Oh, yes — thank you. I'll have a pint of bitter and ..." He looks to his guests and waits for them to express their preference. Then, noting their delay as they peruse the labels on the bottles, he decides to simply let them place their orders in person. "Yes, and ... whatever Maria and Gwilly fancy."

"Gwilly? Now ... that's a name from the past."

The elderly man in the military jumper, looks him up and down, and Gwilly, looking somewhat bemused, peers back and grins.

The man continues. "After all these years — is it really you?"

Seeing that he is still unable to place him, the old man drops a clue as to his identity and holds out his hand in greeting.

"You used to work for me. When you was a mere bu'y ... you used to help out at the garage on the old road ... You'd serve the petrol to the *grockles*."

He waits for the penny to drop.

Gwilly's eyes light up. "Mr Gill?" He immediately offers the hand of friendship as his voice, reflecting his genuine pleasure in seeing this much older man, rises in volume. "You're looking well. Hey man ... it's really good to see you. So ... how've you been keeping?"

"I've been keeping well. How about you?"

"I'm good." He lies, then turns to his wife and, enjoying the opportunity to add some mystery to his arrival, excitedly explains in Spanish, "*Maria, esto es de Señor Gill, que él me supo cuando era joven. Trabajé para él en su garaje.*"

Maria is no longer perplexed by her husband's penchant for acting as a translator and, although she is bi-lingual, she leaves him to it.

"Mr Gill, may I introduce you to my good wife, Maria?"

"Ah ... I'm honoured. Well Gwilly, I must say ... you've always had an eye for a pretty girl." He turns and focuses his comments directly to Maria. "And I must say ... he has certainly excelled himself this time. *Usted es muy hermoso. ¿Usted es de España?*"

She smiles. "*Gracias ... ¿Habla usted el Español?*"

She is impressed by his knowledge of the language and asks as to how fluent he really is.

His reply is honest. "*Sé sólo unos pocas palabras.*"

Gwilly is more than a little surprised as to Mr Gill's linguistic knowledge.

"When did you learn to speak Spanish?" he asks.

"A while ago. After I sold the garage, we moved to Cartagena for a few years — we learnt a bit then."

"Cartagena?"

"Yes, that's right — a retirement in the sun, and of course…" He starts to drift off on a journey into some long-gone past. "… there were those long balmy evenings when we would sit on the veranda with a glass of sangria. And then, with the Med beside us, we would watch the sun set over the Spanish hills. Wonderful it was, too!"

"So tell me, why did you come back?"

"It was the CID! They finally caught up with me." He laughs, and then continues. "No, I'm joking. Seriously though, it was for health reasons."

"Health reasons? You were unwell?"

"No, I was fine. It was more about the health of the economy which did it. I could see a crash coming, so we sold up — luckily, we managed to get out in time."

He then looks back to Maria and, changing the subject, he asks, "So, how did you two meet?"

"Well …" she replies, with her home-state accent now resonating in each of her words. "It may all sound a bit boring — but I was working in a bar in Malaga and he walked in … we met, we got to know each other, and so … here we are."

"You're American!"

"Yes, I am."

"Well, Gwilly, you had me fooled."

He turns back to Maria. "So, where did you learn your Spanish?"

"At home … in New Mexico. We speak Spanish and English — depending on who's with us, of course."

"Of course. Well, may I say — it is a pleasure to have made your acquaintance."

Gwilly puts his arm around her shoulders and, with a beaming grin, he gives her a slight squeeze.

Bryn's pint is pulled and placed on the bar and as he does so, the landlord looks to Maria and Gwilly for their order.

"I think a red wine for my beautiful wife … and for me? I think, just for old-time's sake, I'll have a jug of your local cider. Thank you."

The onset of night nudges the exiled smokers back into the bar. Then, while the landlord pours the drinks, there is the clunk of the latch which alerts both he and his clientèle to the arrival of more to swell their numbers … and so add to the atmosphere.

As the door is held open, Beth and Tori make their entrance, closely followed by Jamie, who allows the door to close quietly, but firmly, behind him.

Bryn indicates to the landlord that the drinks which are about to be ordered will also be paid for by him.

Beth turns to her family and guests and asks, "What about some food? I'm famished."

The landlord, overhearing her need for sustenance, calls back behind the bar and towards the private zone of the kitchen. "Chrissie, can you help our guests with their food orders please?"

His wife emerges with a clutch of menus and a welcoming smile as she makes eye contact with the group as a whole.

"We also have our specials for the day up on the board … and there are also vegetarian dishes available if you wish."

She hands out the menus and, whilst choices are made, busily readies a table which can comfortably accommodate the sextet of diners.

Gwilly has been away for a long time, and so, there has been plenty for them to catch up on. Conversation interspersed with congenial banter serves to pass the time as they wait for, and then tuck into, their meals.

With the main course consumed, they remain seated at the table and, while chatting, await the arrival of dessert.

Jamie asks the question which has been intriguing him ever since his Godfather's arrival.

"Gwilly. How did you get your limp?"

He tilts his head to one side, and with a pained expression, he recalls the event. "Ah … the old war-wound?"

Jamie's and Tori's attention has been instantly captured by the excitement of a warrior's experience. While they peer into his eyes for enlightenment, they are blissfully unaware of the disbelieving shake of the heads of both Bryn and Beth. They know the truth! Bryn was present at the time of the incident, but with an element of curiosity, they allow their guest to continue with his tale … without interruption.

Gwilly leans forward, and with a glint in his eye, he gathers them in as if he is about to divulge some great and deeply-held secret.

"Well, I was in Zimbabwe — or Rhodesia — as it was then called. Anyway … it was during the *War for Independence* when my then lady-friend was taken prisoner by the rebel forces of the Frontline States."

He leans back, and as if the very summoning up of the facts had started to evoke some deeper sorrow, he, with a deep intake of breath, fights back the emotion and continues to tell the tale.

"I'm sorry. Well, as I was saying … she was their prisoner. So, I was put in a position where I had to do what was right. It was a dilemma ... I had to weigh it all up and decide whether I should risk all and go to her rescue ..."

He pauses, and then continues. "Now, I know what you're thinking — I should have gone after her the moment that they took her. But — hey — I was on their territory ... and so, I had no idea where to start. She could have been taken anywhere! I mean — these were very dangerous times. Not just 'cause of all the terrorists with their AK47's, but you had the crocs in the rivers ... and lions and leopards in the bush. And then there were bull elephants and buffalo all over the place — it takes a special type of guy to take on a challenge like that."`

Again, he stops and ponders before carrying on. "Anyhow, to cut a long story short, I spoke to a local police officer, Le Roux. We knew each other through my helping him to infiltrate a poaching ring on the Zambezi borders — after the Rhino they were. Anyhow, he told me that he had a message ... a group of men were seen with a white woman crossing into Zambia. Well ... It had to be her, didn't it?"

"So ... you went off to rescue her?" Jamie asks, willing the disclosure of some heroic act.

"No." His reply is short.

"No?" Tori is dumbfounded by his apparent disregard for his lady-friend's plight.

"Of course not! You see, I figured ... that with her being such an argumentative old mare, they'd soon get fed up with her and they'd end up sending her back anyway!"

Tori breaks the silence which had ensued his revelation. "So that was it? You left her?"

"Yep, that was it ... I went off and had a few pints with Le Roux."

"What?"

Tori is no longer just taken aback ... if truth be told, she is horrified by his attitude.

"Well it was extremely dangerous out there ... and what with it getting dark and all that ... we thought that, maybe, we'd be safer in the bar. Apart from that ... it was his round!"

"All right ... So you're winding us up? Right?"

Gwilly grins mischievously.

"So ... what about the limp?" Jamie, with the hint of a smile, returns to the original question.

"Young man! I'll have you know ... this is no joking matter. Here I was, in the middle of Africa — my lady friend a prisoner to a bunch of terrorists and you wanna know about my limp! All right ... I'll tell you."

Bryn interjects, "This time ... the truth!"

"The truth it is then. Well, here goes. It was when we came out the bar and, being a little bit on the inebriated side, I tripped over a stone and fell down the side of the hill, towards the river. I know it sounds far-fetched — the thought of me being drunk, that is … but it's true — I twisted it on a boulder … and it's never been right since."

Gwilly's face lights up with laughter as he revels in how easily he has been able to capture and lead on his young audience.

"Dad?" Jamie turns to his father, who shakes his head as he constructs his reply.

"No Son, you're right … he's still winding you up. The only bit which has some truth in it is the bit about him being drunk. Come to think of it … I think we both were."

"What, you were in Zimbabwe with him?"

"No son, I wasn't in Zimbabwe. It all happened a lot closer to home. Didn't it Gwilly?"

Gwilly smiles smugly and nods.

"Ah … Here comes the sweet." Beth espies the arrival of Chrissie with a tray laden with an assortment of desserts.

Gwilly looks to Jamie. "I'll tell you about it later."

Jamie nods as Tori puts her question. "Excuse me … how did you get the name, Gwilly?"

"Ah … my name? Now there lies another tale. You see, like me, my father was a handsome fellow, and, because of that, he had the pick of all the *mademoiselles* of the district. But there was one — the loveliest of them all — who would not, as would the others, just throw herself at his mercy. No … She was different — she needed to be wooed. Anyway, after much effort, he managed to charm this most beautiful woman — my mother — down the slippery slopes of a misty French mountain and …"

"Gwilly!"

"Yes?"

"Get on with it. Tell them the truth … or I will!"

"Okay. The truth."

Reprimanded, he, with a disappointed shrug, edits the tale and sums it up within the brevity of one sentence.

"He chatted her up in a café near Mont St Michel."

Noting the sceptical looks on the faces of his listeners, he explains, "No, really — my mother was on holiday with some friends … and he was helping out in the café. One thing led to another … and so … here I am. Oh yes, and before you ask — the name Gwilly? She gave me his name — Guillaume."

"So, he was French?"

He nods. "*Oui*! I think so. My mother came back to Devon. But then, after she found out that she was pregnant, she went back to Normandy — but she couldn't find him. Anyway, so that's why I'm called Gwilly the B."

Again his audience look a little puzzled.

"What about the *B*, you are asking? Well … the most famous of Normans — William the Conqueror — was also known as *Guillaume le Bâtard* … and so … I, too, am *Guillaume le Bâtard*. So … there you have it … Gwilly the B!"

He gives no further explanation as he digs his spoon into his bowl of ice-cream and strawberries.

A little embarrassed by the personal nature of the revelation, both Jamie and Tori look away as they, too, concentrate on their desserts.

When all are done and appetites satisfied, they relocate to the less formal seating within the setting of the, now much busier, bar.

More drinks are ordered and, following an initial trickle, a cascade of reminiscences of two decades past are shared — and for good measure, spiced with more than a few humorous anecdotes.

As the quantity of alcoholic intake increases, the stories grow louder and the visual accentuation becomes more and more animated.

With a lull in the conversation, the attention refocuses on Gwilly. He seems to be totally absorbed in watching the bubbles as they rise up through the burnt-amber hue of his sixth pint of local, farm-brewed cider.

"Pesky little critters."

He looks up at the others, and with an intensity that has not been seen before, he prolongs his stare. Then, with a glint of devilment in his eyes and the adoption of a dramatic exaggeration of the burr of an old-time west-country mariner, he enlightens those who care to listen. "It brings 'em out, you know — 'tis the apples that attracts 'em … but 'tis the brew that makes 'em turn the art of jesting into somethin' …" He clenches his fist and shakes his head as he searches for the suitable word. "… I don't know, something nasty or …"

"Gwilly. What are you talking about?" Bryn can see that the effects of the alcohol have started to take their toll.

"They'm at again … them little critters — 'tis they who turned the brew."

He looks across to his old friend with an appeal for support.

"You remember 'em, don't 'e?"

Bryn nods as he recalls that particular night in the long and distant past when they had both staggered away from a session of excessive drinking.

"Yep, you're right — it was weird."

"What was weird?" Jamie, intrigued, seeks clarification. Unlike the stories previously told, at least this one has the corroboration of his father — and so, it needs to be heard.

"Go on Gwilly. You tell 'em."

"Bryn, my dear friend — I thought we said we'd never tell anyone."

"No … it's okay. You can tell them."

"Are you sure? They'll reckon we'em nuts."

Seeing the look of fascination on the faces of both Jamie and Tori, and also frustrated by the long and drawn-out decision-making process, Beth intervenes. "That assessment's already been made, so get on with it you grizzly old bear — put us out of our misery and tell the story."

"Yes Gwilly, you tell us. I'm also quite interested." Maria has always been of the belief that he had injured his leg in a motorcycle accident; whether this was by assumption or by Gwilly's own explanation, she cannot recall. However, she is also interested to hear this version, so, with no more than a look, she instructs him to recount the detail of the event.

"Okay. You win."

As if to signal to all that there is *a need* for him to relate his story in a huddle of secrecy, he leans forward and beckons them to do the same.

"Well…" He commences his account with an almost professor-like and matter-of-fact emphasis to his words. "… We was in this very 'ostelry, young Bryn and me … partaking in the traditional and ancient practice of consuming the juice of the pulped fruit of the much-revered — *malus pumila.*"

Seeing the expressions on the faces of his companions, Bryn, like the straight man in a comedy duo, assists with a simplified and somewhat less poetic explanation. "We were drinking cider — it was cheap!"

Gwilly glances across at his old friend and, with a disapproving grunt, returns to the tale.

"As I was saying, we were showing our respect for the ancient ways of our forefathers."

"I thought you said your father was French?" Jamie cannot help but to *toss a spanner in the works.*

"My mother was from Devon — okay?" Gwilly, still inflecting the drawl of an ancient Devonian, stresses each word as his frustration at being interrupted begins to show.

Jamie nods.

"As I said, my father was a Norman and, I hasten to add … they make a damn good cider in Normandy, too. Okay? Now, may I continue?"

They nod.

"Thank you. Well, let's try again. As I was saying, we was being respectful to the ancient traditions when the bell tolled for us to vacate the warmth of the premises, and so … we had no option but to venture out and into the night."

He leans back as he appears to gather his thoughts. Recharged, he leans forward and resumes the role of *storyteller*. "I remembers the night well! It were crisp, but magical — what with the darkness being lit by the glow of the waxing moon, that is. Anyway, in order to enhance the beauty of nature's design, I rolled a smoke and relished its fragrant essence before we drifted off, homeward-bound." He pauses, and then starts to sing the chorus of the *Simon and Garfunkel* song of the same name.

"Oh, get on with it Gwilly!" Beth asserts her control. "You've got the voice of a bronchitic frog! Now get on with it!"

"Well then ... as we was walkin' ... the ground started to move up and down. You see, it were like we was trying to walk on top o' the gentle swell of an ocean. What I mean is, you put your foot down ... and the ground disappears as it starts to sink ... then you put your other foot down and it gets hit as the ground rises up to meet it."

"So you were paralytic?"

"No, young Jamie boy, you'm wrong. I can take me drink."

He looks wounded by the very thought of him being considered as being unable to consume a few pints of cider without becoming intoxicated. "It was the fact that it had been got at. By that I mean ... we was not drunk — we was pixilated. And, young man ... there's a difference."

He looks across to Bryn for support — a nod is support enough.

"Okay — so you were stoned then." Jamie is beginning to enjoy putting the his godfather on a back foot.

"Certainly not. I've told you ... it were they little terrors ... them got to the brew — *they* did it. Now — may I be permitted to carry on?"

He scans the audience and notes the concurring nods, not only from his immediate congregation, but also from those nearby who, having been unable to be ignore his words, have been drawn by the magnetism of both the narrative and its delivery.

"Now, I was a trifle perturbed about how easily I'd been affected by the illicit doctoring of my favourite brew ... so Bryn and me got to do some talkin' and also some thinking. You see, we realized that we needed the wisdom of the ancients so that, maybe, we could prevent a repeat of the occurrence."

"So where were you going to get this ancient wisdom?" Jamie asks, with a cheeky smile.

"Ah ... you may mock. But the answer was there, right in front of our very eyes. You see, as we walked along the lane, I looked across the fields and I saw the silhouette of an old ash tree standing alone and, in its own way, proud. This was it — *Yggdrasil* — the tree of the world ... the *Tree of Life* — a descendant of the very tree from which Odin had hung as he had endeavoured to gain the knowledge of *all things past* and *all things present*."

He can see that he is about to be interrupted. So, he forges onward, dismissing any intervention to his flow. "Now ... Odin knew that the tree absorbed the knowledge of all that it surveyed and all that it touched, and so, he reckoned ... that if he hung off a branch for nine days and nine nights, he, too, would receive that very same knowledge."

He pauses, stretches his body, and then, after arching his back, he leans forward and resumes. "Now ... I thought — *what's good enough for Odin has gotta be good enough for me.* So ... if anything's gonna teach me how to counter the activities of them *troublesome ones*, then it could only be that there ... *Tree of Life.*"

He pauses again. "Well, I climbed up the tree, and I, too, put my hands over a branch an' clasped 'em together. So, there I was ... hanging off the tree. I just hung there ... and I waited — I reckoned that, by following the path of Odin, I was sure to absorb the knowledge of the ancients."

He sits back and looks around at the gathering — teasing them into urging him to finish the tale.

"What? You actually hung off that branch for nine days and nine nights?" asks Tori.

"No. Don't be daft. I hung there for a good mmm..." He looks up to the ceiling as he tries to think back ... and then, in need of further assistance, he looks across the table towards Bryn.

"Three ... maybe, four?" Bryn assists and Gwilly nods.

"What — days?" Tori's voice reflects more than an element of scepticism.

Bryn interjects as he tries to bring the tale to an end. "Days? No — of course not! It was more like three or four minutes — and even that's being generous!"

Jamie struggles to keep a straight face as he asks, "So, in that case, what great knowledge did you gain from the experience of three or four minutes hanging from this ... *tree of life?*"

"Well ... I learnt — that for me to hang off a tree in the middle of the night whilst under the effects of the juice —"

"And the weed!" Bryn's additional interjection is met with a disapproving stare.

"As I was saying ... to hang off the branch of a tree whilst under the effects of the pixiefied juices was, to say the least, dangerous ... and the evidence of that is in the fact that I fell off — and that's when I did my knee in. Now, you may laugh, but what made matters worse was the fact that *the little critters* had got away with it — and that gave 'em the confidence to go on to play havoc with us for the rest of the night."

He looks around at the faces at the table, and at the bar.

"Now you listen here ... I ain't lying ... we was *pixie-led* all night. However hard we tried, we just couldn't find our way out from the field. We went round and round and I's sure that they kept moving the gate so we couldn't get out."

"What a load of —"

Mr Gill interrupts. "No, lad ... he tells it as it is ... 'tis always bin that way, and 'twill always be so."

His deadpan expression, along with the knowing nods of the elders in the bar, silences Jamie as he contemplates the tale.

"All right, so what about the limp?" asks Tori.

"Cocked up the cartilage — 'tis been a problem ever since. So, there you have it!"

He downs the last of his drink, and then, with a beaming smile, he announces, "Methinks 'tis time for a refill. What say you my friends?"

With all in agreement, they take their glasses to the bar.

"Oh …" Gwilly, still with a glint of mischievousness in his eye, addresses his godson, "I understand that you'm having a new guitar made — cut from ash, if I'm not mistaken. Is that right?"

"That's right," he responds, with puzzlement and more than a little suspicion, as he waits to hear what gems are to follow.

"Well, to my knowledge, 'tis the ash which is the *Tree of Life,* and, if I'm not mistaken, there's an old Devonshire saying which warns you of its perils. You see … 'tis almost forgotten now, but what it says is this — *in the ash which is hewn from the hallowed earth, there's the hue of they who lie beneath its turf.*"

As if they are all afraid to show their ignorance of his words and, thus, his seemingly greater knowledge, there is a silence in the bar; it seems that no one else is aware of such a legend. But then, by the authoritative manner in which he has related it, they are minded to accept it as fact.

"Gwilly…" Bryn breaks the silence, "for a man who tried to kid a young 'un that, if he wanted to find a yew tree, then he should look for the one all covered in wool, I have no problem in telling you that, as usual, you're talking a load of crap. Now … how about you shut up, stop trying to wind my boy up … and get the drinks in."

"Well … as you put it with such finesse, I suppose … it's got to be my round then. Am I right?"

They all nod.

"Fine … that's good with me." He turns to the landlord.

"Same again, if I may?"

Chapter 24

With their distinctive, plum-like hue, and scarred with a peppering of tiny holes, the blocks of carbon-tainted volcanic trap remain as a stark reminder as to the transitory character of the Earth's thin, and often brittle, crust.

Having been cast from the raging fires of the countless tons of molten lava which had once spewed violently across this land, they serve to reflect a far deeper history than that of those who had, so long ago, hewn the rocks and then built the imposing walls which surround this ancient fortress.

Set in the heart of the city centre, the public gardens, which now stretch throughout the bowl of what was once the castle's moat, may well have succeeded in veiling the evidence of the area's cataclysmic past. But then, on a more positive note, their presence may also be seen as being more of a testament to the resolve of life to survive, adapt and thrive.

The almost sheer ramparts of the stronghold are no longer a place for insurrection; for the ground on which man had once fought against man as he had desperately vied for control in his claim for its possession, is now little more than that of a peaceful and fertile retreat.

Although only a stone's throw from the city centre, the Gardens, somewhat surprisingly, have not only managed to remain distanced from the constant background din which so often accompanies the modern-day hustle and bustle of commercial activity, but, moreover, they have also been able to convey the deception of them being an idyll of rural isolation.

This is, without a doubt, a place to de-stress. After all, it is where both man and woman, young and old, can — with that wonderful feeling of being able to be at one with the ever-changing beauty of nature's creativity — stroll about freely and enjoy the atmosphere of uncontested peace.

Bearing the weight of his upper body on one arm, he sits — twisted, but comfortable — ensnared by the magnificence of the colourful array of flora that fills the borders.

Absorbed and with admiration, he snoops into the activity of an industrious bumble bee as it flits from flower to flower, opting only to enter those whose looks and perfume emit the silent, but indisputable, signal that they are truly receptive to its invasion.

With the light of the day catching each petal, and whilst each bloom awaits a visit from this sedulous winged-courier, the delicate glistening of the sheen exudes a subtle but enticing message of availability.

There is no need for ceremony, nor is there the need for introduction; for a bee is just a bee … and that is all there is to it. Besides, it is whilst it is on its promiscuous flight — routinely visiting each bloom in turn so as to greedily take its prize — that it unwittingly transfers the pollen from the flower of one to that of another, thus, ensuring the proliferation of future generations of floral beauty.

Its human observer turns away, lies back and stretches out to relax on the grassy slope.

As he closes his eyes, he relishes the warmth of the summer sun. After all, it is his day of rest and he is far from the mundane repetitiveness of trolley-control in the car park of his place of work. He has, in the past, held posts of responsibility; but now, although his present position may not make him the envy of others nor allow him to carry the status of being a pillar of the local community, he is at least able to console himself with the fact that it is an occupation which enables the payment of the important bills, thereby, freeing him from the threat of impecuniosity and the tedium of unemployment.

Basking in the ambience of his new-found retreat, his thoughts drift away from the issues and the needs of his everyday life, preferring instead to focus on the fresh and vivid image of pendulous sheathes of silken cerise which wait, in turn, to envelope a black and gold invader, which will then, without a doubt, crawl its way up and into the heart of the natural beauty of each tubular bloom.

As if excusing himself from the actions of his past, he takes refuge in the notion of it being nature's way; the way which — having been decreed by eons of evolution — ensures that the rewards of desire are taken with neither sentiment nor guilt. So, as far as he is concerned, with this being the law of nature, then there is no room, nor reason, for the burdens of moral judgement.

With the time drifting by, his dozes are briefly interrupted by the occasional sounds of others who are also making the most of this late but, nonetheless, welcome taste of summer.

His back begins to ache. In order to lessen his discomfort, he shuffles himself into another position. It is not that he has suffered injury, it is simply that the hardened ground has served to emphasize the effects on a spine which has, over the years, lost much of its spring.

Pulling himself up and into the sitting position, he arches his back whilst massaging its small with both hands. With the pain relieved, he checks his wristwatch and then stands up and looks around, confirming that the afternoon has all but gone.

With a need to stretch his legs, he strolls over to the path which runs along the upper rim of the ancient boundary wall. Then, whilst peering across the vista of the adjacent grounds of the more formally-fashioned gardens of Northernhay, his eyes are drawn to rest on the memorial which was, long ago, erected in honour of all those who had perished during the twentieth century conflict of the fourteen-eighteen, *war to end all wars.*

Fixated by her towering form, he's ill at ease.

Cast in a pose of triumph, she — with a dragon struggling against the restraints of defeat as her footstool, and her long-bladed sword of conflict held, benignly, downwards — is symbolic of the battle won.

Verdigris robes, tarnished by the elements and captured in a feminine flow, bring an air of pacification to the warrior.

Magnanimous in victory, her eyes are fixed heavenwards. And with a sprig of laurel — iconic in its association with victory and honour — held high, she celebrates the cessation of hostilities with the hope that the peace will be long-lived.

The sculptor's representation, although captivating, leaves him unsettled; for he has no time for a warrior queen — a woman victorious. It is not the role of a woman to fight; it is the man who should take the lead … with his woman, compliantly and dutifully, following on as he, alone, takes charge of their destiny.

He knows this to be true. For as long as he can remember, his father had imposed on the family the conviction of his beliefs; the detail of which he had, on many occasions, felt the almost evangelical need to defend. He would often take quotes — but more often than not, misquotes — from the teachings of whichever creed he had thought would have been the most appropriate for the time. He had laid claim to the belief that there had always been a necessity for society to promote and maintain a state in which there should exist the fundamental rule of masculine supremacy. A society in which women should simply acknowledge and, without question, embrace their God-given status in which subservience to their man is the norm.

He had always thought it strange that his father — a man who had never shown even the slightest of inklings of being that of someone of religious conviction — would have, somewhat bizarrely, found a way to use the teachings of a variety of faiths — often skewed with the ambiguities of ancient legend — to add credence to his cause and, thus, guarantee his position of being able to exercise both power and control.

There were those, however, who were in positions of real power and who had differing opinions. He can still recall the time when, whilst still of tender years, and awaiting the imminent progression from the village school to the secondary stage of his educational path, he had discovered that his father had been absented from both his family and his responsibilities by a judiciary which had, somewhat ironically, once sat sagaciously behind these same archaic walls.

Haunted by the memories of her own abuse, his mother had taken the opportunity of the enforced separation to evasively initiate the first of many moves which, in time, took them on a journey from village to village and town to town as they had attempted to thwart the efforts of *he who would seek*. Even as a young lad, he had known that his mother had no capacity to fight back. But then, he had also known that, although she had been lacking in physical strength, she'd had the strategic prowess to know when it was prudent to lie low and then … when to choose the best moment to move on and thereby avoid the attentions of the manipulative *brute*.

Both of his sisters — one being just a few minutes younger than him and the other, some fourteen months younger still — were equally as vulnerable as the other; so, instinctively and protectively, they had been groomed to follow in their mother's footsteps. They had been conditioned into knowing their role. As far as she had been concerned, and based on her experiences, the ability for them to have known their place was essential for their survival. It would be defiance — and not compliance — which would awaken the rage of a future spouse.

Looking back as to how things had once been, the evidence of the imposition of clearly-defined roles within the family had been blindingly obvious. After all, the submissiveness of his mother and sisters could never in a million years have been confused with the persona of that of a warrior queen. As far as he had been concerned, that was the way it was — and, according to his father, that was the way that it was always meant to be.

He turns, and with the memorial now behind him and no longer within his view, he moves away to claim a seat beside the pathway.

Once settled, he closes his eyes and again allows himself to drift back and into times long-past. During those early years, his mother would start to tremble at the mere thought that his father may have captured the sight of her allowing the briefest of smiles to have inadvertently escaped from her soul.

It had been obvious in the way in which his father had always reacted that he had half-suspected her of mocking him with her flirtatiousness. But he was wrong. She would never have dared to mock him. Nor would she have dreamt of signalling an interest to another. If the truth were to be told, although he would never have admitted it, his father would have been fully aware of the fact!

But then, even with the knowledge that she would not have had the nerve to have betrayed him, he had, without the slightest of justification and on more than one occasion, openly accused her of responding to the advances of others.

Whether these imagined flirtations were just the normal everyday examples of acts of simple courteousness from tradesmen or, for that matter, nothing more than a genial smile of acknowledgement from a friendly neighbour, it mattered not; for he had seen the spark of life return to her eyes and had, therefore, already decided on her guilt.

However, even with the perverseness of the jealous rages which had often brewed within him, he had on each occasion been quite successful in the mastering of the art of self-control. In fact, he had always been wily enough to stay calm whilst still in the public gaze. Was he foolish to suspect his wife of infidelity? Maybe, he was. But then, his opinion was subjective, and because of that, he would not bow to the voice of reason. Mind you, although he may have been stubborn, he was not entirely stupid. He had always been careful to ensure that the customary trials and punishments for any supposed indiscretions had been withheld until they had returned to the privacy of their home … and were, thus, away from the sight and hearing of anyone who may have considered it as their duty to have intervened.

Having learnt to read the tides of emotion with the expertise of a ship's captain, edging a precious cargo through the perils of a narrow and twisted channel, she had known when to submit. But then, she had also been well aware of the fact that for her to have offered the defence that she was absent of guilt would have been futile. A denial would only have served to delay, or even exacerbate, the inevitable onset of a harsh and pitiless execution of an already decided sentence.

Would she have willingly admitted to a betrayal? Of course not. She had known that to do so would have been a lie. The fact was, she had simply learnt to accept the consequences, and, whilst doing so, she had prayed that his actions would stop with *her* only, and that he would not then turn his anger towards the children.

With no respect for chronology, his memories drift back to his earliest years, when he had also been subjected to the cruel regime of his father.

Even at the age of eleven, he had not been permitted to show any feelings of sensitivity — nor had he been permitted to join his siblings in what was, in his father's mind, the unnatural participation in unmanly pursuits.

To be comforted in his mother's embrace, even when he had been feeling unwell or had been suffering with pain, was not to be tolerated; for this would have been beyond the limits of acceptability and, therefore, completely out of the question.

But then, he was only a child, and, as such, he had enjoyed the camaraderie of his sisters in play. So, whilst embracing the inherent need to belong, he had happily joined them in sharing the adventures of an imaginary world of innocence and fantasy. These were just games … played with no more than that of harmless acts of role-play, but it was, as he was later to discover, an activity which had been fraught with danger, for with it came a price — humiliation in front of his mother and his two sisters.

Their home had not been particularly large. And with the staircase having risen directly from the living room to the upstairs landing, there was little opportunity for the children to be able to find somewhere to play without interruption.

Still — even to this day there are times when the roars of his oppressive father can find a way to resonate in his mind. He often recalls how, on one particular occasion, the sound of his fury alone had managed to numb the senses. But then, what with him having been forced into being subjected to the unexpected, and at the same time, confrontational, bellowing-out of *Oi! What d'you think you're playing at?* and, *You're not a fricking girl, are you?* it had not been too surprising for him to have been left completely baffled and, as a result, dumbstruck.

As strange as it may seem, even with all his failings, his father had always been reluctant to use the f-word, and, more often than not, he would readily substitute its usage with that of the much more acceptable term of *fricking*.

However, having left that observation aside — as it is a matter of very little relevance — he muses with the notion that, maybe, because he had been too stunned to respond and was, thus, unable to defend the innocence of his actions, his is father had jumped to conclusions. He had obviously thought that lack of response had meant that there had, indeed, been something more unsavoury for him to have wanted to hide. Even though there had, in fact, been absolutely nothing untoward in the way in which he had interacted with his siblings, his father, for whatever reason, had evidently thought otherwise, and so, he had been determined to get to the *truth*.

With an almost nose-to-nose confrontation he had let rip.

So … come on then. Tell me! What's with all this frickin' girly stuff then? … Is there something wrong with you? Come on … Speak up! I can't frickin' well hear you!

There had been no subtlety about the man. He cared not one iota about the fact that his open aggression was being witnessed by his wife and their two young daughters.

Anyway, with the tone of his father's voice, along with the all too familiar look of wildness in his eye, he had sensed the presence of more than an underlying threat lurking beneath the already rippling waters. Because of that, he had remained too fearful, and too shocked, to have even dared to have uttered a reply.

He just listened in silence and, as if it were being indelibly etched into his memory, he had absorbed — word-for-word and inflection-for-inflection — much of what had been said.

Right then, so that's the way it's going to be, is it? … If that's the way it's gonna be then, maybe, you need to be taught a lesson! Huh? … What d'you think about that? … How about a slapping? Maybe I should knock some sense into you! I guess that would do the trick — what do you think?

His silence had continued as he had stared blankly into the growing scowl in the face of his tormenter; for even with the fear of him having to accept yet another beating, the rising in the level of the threat had still failed to succeed in the loosening of his tongue.

As it happened, his father had not, on this occasion, intended to serve his more usual dish of gratuitous violence. He had, instead, decided on another way to deal with the apparent weaknesses of his son, and so, with the forcing of a smile, and a twist of sarcasm, he had continued to probe as if he had been seeking to provoke an angry and defiant retort.

The trauma of that time had certainly left its mark, for each moment is recalled as if it were being played-out in real-time, and, what's more, with his father's words having been played over and over in his nightmares, they are remembered verbatim!

So, I suppose then, if you really wanna act like a little girl, then maybe I should give you exactly what you want, how's that sound? Huh?

His father had paused for a few moments, and then, having heard no grumblings of protest or, for that matter, anything at all to suggest that his son would break his silence, he had suddenly upped the volume and venomously spat out his words. *So … you've got nothing to say, Huh! Well … Maybe, I'm thinking that — deep down — you really would like to go the whole, fricking, hog!*

He had paused for a moment and then went on to announce, *D'you know what? Well I'll tell you what! — I've just decided that today's gonna be your lucky day! — D'you know why? Well, I'll tell you why! — It's 'cause today's the day that I'm gonna make frickin' well sure that you get what you've fricking well been asking for!*

With his words having been cast, albeit by chance, with an almost poetic beat, they had — like the lyrics of a song — been set firmly within his memory.

He can still summon the imagery of that first occasion when those of his family who were of the fairer sex, had had no option but to watch on in silent disbelief as he, without due explanation, had been dragged upstairs by his enraged father. Then, with the threesome having been ordered to wait downstairs and not to intervene, he had been forced into changing out of the customary garb of a boy and into the silken embrace of his sister's most treasured dress.

Being far too small to have been able to have fought back, he'd had no option but to comply. He'd just had to suffer in silence and resign himself to having to acquiesce to his father's demands.

The experience had left him haunted with memories of that awful moment when, for the very first time and through tear-filled eyes, he had stared down at the folds of the lustrous silks which had, incongruously, yet, somewhat gracefully, cascaded from his waist and down to the floor.

The impact of the event had certainly left him with deep and lasting scars. If the truth were to be told, even now, and however hard he tries, he will never be able to forget *that* dress.

What had made things worse was that, although at the time he had not been able to see it as such, it was, when worn by the girl for whom it was intended, quite stunning. Furthermore, by both the elegance of its cut and the quality of its finish, it had not been created to simply please the not-so-discerning tastes of a mere child — it had had been fashioned with much skill and, as he was later to discover, from out of the abundance of sumptuous and glistening material which had, many years previously, more than satisfied the ultra-fastidious requirements of a young bride on that special occasion of it being her wedding day.

With the benefit of hindsight, he is, even to this day, certain that his father had been fully aware as to what he had been doing; for even if he had raided the wardrobes of the wealthy and the famous in order to have accessed some of the most lavish of robes ever created, he could not have found a more suitable garment for him to have been able to use as the means to fulfil his purpose.

Besides, for his father to have had, readily at hand, an article of clothing which had possessed the very essence of ultra-feminine allure captivated within its profusion of full and flowing skirts, would have been one thing — but for the dress to have also been of a size which had not been too far off from being that of a perfect fit, then that would certainly have seemed to him as having been almost too good to have been true.

He must have thought that it had been gifted to him from the heavens.

It may not have been something which had been grasped by him at the time, but with a satin sash trimming the waist, he realizes now, that there was certainly a suggestion of it having been his intent for there to have been no easy escape. After all, not only had it been pulled tight, so as to give an emphasis to the slenderness of the waistline, it had also been firmly and restrictively tied-off with a large, looping bow to the rear.

Under normal circumstances, that final touch would have added a rather captivating charm to the look; but then, these had been circumstances which had been far from being normal … and, as such, it had added little more than that of a splash of absurdity.

The dress could not be easily removed as its bodice had been designed to be a close fit. Furthermore, it had the added complication of being secured by a row of satin-covered buttons which had needed to be painstakingly slotted through each of the many silken loops which had run down the length of its back. But then again, although it was far from easy for someone unfamiliar with the techniques required to be able to secure the fastenings without assistance or, for that matter, to tie and untie the bow to the rear … once on, it could be worn with ease, and without undue restriction to movement.

Yes … he may have been just a child, and, as a consequence of that, he may well have been lacking in worldly knowledge, but then, he was not a fool either. Even *he* could see that it had been made quite clear, in the attitude of his father and, in particular, in the shrewdness of the choosing of the specific dress, that there was to be no chance for him to have evaded the *punishment*. In short — he'd had no choice but to accept the humiliation and submit to the extraordinary and unreasonable demands of his father.

He had also known that — what with him having been aware as to how cruel his father could be — there was bound to be more to the punishment than just a private lesson of humiliation in front of the man. It would not stop there — of that, he was certain.

He knew that it would only have been a matter of time before he would then be forced to face the stares of his mother and the two girls.

The very thought of being debased in front of his family had filled him with absolute dread. He had considered using the fit of the garment as an excuse by claiming that he could not wear it, but then, that would have been a lie. It had, in fact, fitted all too well, and so much so, that he could make his way along the corridor without risking mishap.

He could not have got away with pretence, so he'd dismissed the notion almost as soon as it had arrived.

With the option of him lying being out of the question, he had considered whether he should have yielded to his instinct to take flight and make a break for it. But then, that would have been foolhardy at best and, moreover, it would have opened the floodgates for much worse. Besides, not only would it have been nigh on impossible for him to have found an opportunity in which he could have made his escape, he had also known that he would not have been able to remain hidden forever. Eventually, he would have had to face the consequences which, he had known, would have been far too severe for him to even imagine.

He could remember, quite clearly, how the architect of the punishment had stared at his finished product and, by the smirk which had filled his face, had appeared to have been more than satisfied with the result. Besides, his father must have known that he had needed the entirety of an almost flawless look to ensure that he would achieve his aim; for that reason, for him to have hoped for success in his attempt to subjugate and humiliate, he could not have allowed any signs of incongruity in his creation … if he had done, then the spell would have been broken and his victory denied.

Anyway, his father had certainly been well pleased with himself. In fact, bearing in mind that he had been enraged by the apparent lack of manliness in the ways of his child, he had, somewhat bizarrely and paradoxically, seemed delighted in the way that, by having enforced on his son the wearing of *the* dress, he had succeeded in implementing the deceptive shift from that of him seeming to be rather insignificant and inadequate in his natural role as a *he* ... to that of being a picture of submissiveness and elegance within the guise of a *she*.

To an outsider, apart from the style and length of his hair, a casual glance may well have failed to have detected the truth which had lain behind the deception. However, even under closer scrutiny — with some careful restyling of the hair, along with the distraction of the dress itself — the makeover, albeit rushed, may well have been sufficient to have masked the reality from many.

Whether the expectation had been for him to have had to simply stand in front of his mother and the girls whilst being all dressed-up — and as if he had been little more than that of a mannequin in a shop-window display — or, whether he had, in fact, been expected to have been much more animate and, maybe, with the gracefulness of movement — and with a swirl and a twirl thrown in for good-measure — gone on to have played the part of a girl in full, had been of little consequence. The fact had been plain; whatever the intent, the dress alone had left no room at all for there to have been any doubt as to the nature of his role ... he had been expected to adopt the persona of a girl. For how long? He'd had no idea.

Still, once he'd been sufficiently feminised, and was still in a state of shocked disbelief, he'd been jostled along the landing. Then, with a push and a shove, he had descended the stairway. Once having been returned to face the fold, it had seemed as if he had been thrust onto a stage before being cruelly exhibited as if he were the *Belle of the Ball*.

The role of an inert mannequin had certainly not been on the agenda. His father had made that quite clear!

Give us a twirl you little wuss! he'd growled, with a grin stretched across his face, apparently revelling in the fact that the punishment had undoubtedly ensured the absolute attention of not only his son ... but also of the family as a whole.

Even after the passing of so many years, he can still recall how he'd stood frozen, demeaned and traumatized, whilst trying to decide as to how best he should respond to the taunting demands.

If he had complied and then got it wrong, then the penalty would have been the same, if not worse, as it would have been had he stood firm ... and refused.

But then, he had never given cause for his hypothesis to have been tested.

Come on! Do as you're told! Give us a twirl! The flushes of rage alongside his words had reddened his father's face ... and that had always been warning enough. So, having already resigned himself to the consequences of him not knowing exactly what he had been expected to do — and, also, knowing that he would have been punished, whatever path he'd taken —

he'd just braced himself for the customary beating.

Mindful of the fact that any act of disobedience would not have been tolerated, and sensing that he was therefore in imminent danger of being beaten to a pulp, his twin sister, Katy, had, somewhat protectively, jumped up from her seat. Then, as if she had been a model parading the latest in fashions, she strutted across the living room floor — no doubt praying that he would have the acumen to echo her moves and, in doing so, save himself from the harsh realities of the infliction of pain.

The distraction had been enough to have allowed him to see reason. After all, he had known that there had been little, if any, options available for him to have been able to escape the full force of his father's wrath.

Even a hint of insubordination would not have been tolerated; so, in the hope that an act of compliance would have at least given him a chance to avoid a battering and a bruising, he had decided to make the effort to come to terms with his situation, and then, by following Katy's lead, he'd just gone with the flow and had done as he had been told.

Although ill at ease in what he had been coerced to do, and had been feeling confused and extremely vulnerable, he had done exactly as had been demanded and had copied her every movement.

It had certainly been far from easy; but even though he had been trapped and restricted within the unfamiliar wrappings of feminine attire, he had strode across the room and, in spite of everything, he had managed to put his feelings of embarrassment to one side and twirl to every order. But even then, this had obviously not been quite enough for his father, since it had not, as he had expected, succeeded in drawing the episode to a speedy end.

There had been no let-up. His father had persisted until he had been satisfied that there had been absolutely nothing left for him to have been able to demean.

Now, whether or not the words were exactly as he recalls, he cannot be too sure, but those which still echo in his thoughts are, in essence, pretty much the same.

Go on! Do it again! You've shown us that you can walk the walk and twirl the twirl, so now's your chance. Huh? Now you can be as girly as you like. You can show us exactly how pretty you can be!

His father had been merciless; he had taunted and goaded him to such an extent that it had reached a point where he had felt as if he could no longer maintain the will to live.

He can still recall, … when … having caught his mother's gaze, they had allowed their eyes to linger, and, within the brevity of that moment, he had willed her to put an end to his torment. As far as he had could see, if she, as an adult, could not draw an end to the proceedings, then he, as a child, had no chance whatsoever.

Furthermore, if that had been the case then he would have always remained as a prisoner to his father's cruelty.

He had instinctively known that she had, in her heart, wanted to rush to his aid. But, having detected the most minuscule shake of her head and the welling of tears in her eyes, he had been aware that, with her having been disempowered by her own experiences of being subjected to both psychological and physical abuse, that she, too, had been helpless and, so, could offer him no route for escape. His sisters, he recalls, had been rocked into a state of confusion and, as such, their looks had been mixed. It was as if, on one hand, they had been feeling a deep and real sadness for him … but, at the same time, they had been trying hard to contain an almost irresistible urge to break out into an open, but embarrassed, bout of laughter.

Suddenly, as if there had been the flick of a switch, the demands from his father had stopped. He had been left to stand bemused and speechless.

Stunned by his experience, he had continued to stand, frozen in silence, as he struggled to make sense of why he had just been subjected to the ignominy of being, in effect, re-branded and forced to accept the unfamiliar caress of the silky-smooth layers of material. The reprieve, however, was all too brief — the sentence had not been fully served. It had in fact been open-ended; for his father had not been the sort of man to give up easily and then let things lie. The truth of the matter had been that he had only paused, and then, as if he had suddenly seen a need to add insult to injury, he had reasserted his presence with the additional disclosure that his son would be made to experience, at first hand, the more customary roles associated with that of female subservience.

No doubt the intent had been to somehow shock him out of his *girlish ways,* and, as if it had been an attempt to make plain to him the actualities of the non-so-glamorous side of the average female's world, he had been made to take on the ways of a girl and, thus, perform the more feminine traditions of domesticity. With his father having seen no need for modernity — unless, of course, it had been to satisfy his own needs — the convenience of an electrically powered vacuum cleaner to help his mother with her daily routine had long been denied; so, with nothing more than the use of an old-fashioned carpet sweeper, he had been instructed to clean the carpets and rely on its revolving brushes to remove any bits from within the well-worn pile. Even after he had finished the sweeping, there had been no respite. For once the first of his chores had been completed, he had been made to dust and polish the mantle-piece and furnishings. Then, whilst still remaining dressed as if *he* were a *she,* he had been ordered to change the bed-sheets and to sort out the family's dirty laundry in preparation for it being washed the following day.

He had wanted to flee … but to where? He would not have dared to

leave the house and then try to make an escape down the road —
especially as he had still been trapped within the persona and garb of
femininity. The very thought that, had he done so, he would have been
recognized by others — and then, no doubt, had been subjected to a
relentless barraging of ridicule, with a lifetime of hell to follow — had been
enough in itself for him to resist any urge to run.

He had been given no choice. He'd had to accept the situation — play
the role and then pray for an early reprieve.

Once the chores had been fulfilled and the sentence had been served,
he'd thought that his father would at last have been satisfied and that it
would all have been over.

He'd been wrong.

The following evening — although he'd not been enforced into
adopting the attire of femininity — on his return from school, he had been
made to ensure that not only was *the* dress clean and pressed, but it was
put onto a hanger and then hung up ... not, as would have been expected,
in Katy's room, but, rather, on the rail of his own *battered* wardrobe.

No doubt, the intent at the time had been for its presence to have acted
as a reminder as to the likely consequences of any wanderings into the
preserve of the feminine world.

Anyway, with him also knowing that the dress could easily have been
examined and that the punishment for allowing any damage, be it through
acts of negligence or intent, would have been severe, he'd handled it with
the utmost of care. He'd done exactly as he'd been instructed to do. He'd
put it onto a hanger and hung it up — away from any hazards and
protected under the cover of a transparent polythene bag.

His father, having evidently relished in the apparent success of his
actions, had made it exceedingly clear that ... if there were to have been
even the slightest of misdemeanour or sign of weakness, he would, from
then on, be sure to enforce the implementation of more of the same
humiliating sentences.

He could have made the attempt to fight back, but he had known that
the shortcomings of an eleven-year-old boy against the experience and
strength of an adult would have, without any doubt whatsoever, led to a
battering. And, yes ... he had certainly known what a battering was. When
he had first heard the expression *battered wife* — on the news, and then,
later, in the overheard conversations of adults — he had immediately been
able to draw on his own experiences and observations for reference.

He had, on more than one occasion, heard his mother's screams of
pain. He had also watched on as she had winced with every move whilst
shuffling her bruised and reddened body from one room to another. The
patchy darkening which had often appeared around her eyes had never
been down to amateurishly-applied touches of cosmetic shadowing. It had

been of no coincidence, nor, for that matter, had it been of any surprise, to know that their arrival had always run hand-in-hand with the episodes of violence which had evoked her desperate cries.

Even she, as an adult, had been unable to defend herself against the actions of his father and, as a result, he had come to understand that — although she would have wished to have been able to — she could never have been expected to have successfully defended him, or his two sisters, from their father's fits of rage.

With his mother's, his sister's and his own self-esteem already beaten down and with no one else to turn to, they'd had no option other than to comply with his father's demands.

Even when out and away from the home, the *brute* could exact his control. After all, he had been fully aware of the fact that it would take only the fear of an early, and unannounced, return to prevent a straying from within the preset boundaries of acceptable behaviour. So, by not having given a hint as to when he would return, they would never know when it would have been safe for them to relax.

With the increasing frequency of the sentences having been passed — albeit for misdemeanours which he had been unaware of committing — his father would always ensure that the boy-girl transition had been fully made and that the subsequent humiliating parade in front of his mother and his sisters had been completed before he would exercise his power with distance-control. He would just wander off to the pub where he would, without any doubt, have been *one of the lads* ... and then flirt with the landlady and barmaids alike.

Chapter 25

With memories steadily pushing themselves to the fore, he utters a hushed and private chuckle. For although it may not have been what his father had expected, the all too frequent repetition of punishments had managed to desensitize him from the reality of what he had been trying to inflict on him.

After all, the humiliation of the first experience was bound to have been effective; for not only had it arrived from out of the blue, but it was also a far cry from anything else that he had ever had to endure. In fact, it had been meticulously orchestrated so as not to cause physical injury. Instead, it had been designed to systematically break down his spirit and, in doing so, ensure his compliance.

But then, along with the routine of it all had come the placid acceptance of the inevitable. He had soon begun to harden to the experience, and, what's more, he had come to realize that it did not actually hurt him to do exactly as had been required.

So, once he had come to terms with the reality of his predicament, then the effectiveness of the sentence had, in essence, been diluted — in fact — so much so, that he had found himself to be in a position where he could sense the winds-of-change and, so, turn the fears and the prejudices of his father to his own advantage.

He will never forget that pivotal occasion when — with the sentence having, yet again and for the umpteenth time, been passed — he had decided to change his approach; without an utterance of protestation nor an expression of resistance, he had calmly and obediently gone up to his room and readily donned the instrument of subjugation.

He had certainly known what was required of him, and so, through nothing more than that of having had the benefit of practise, he had become more than adept in the process of being able to switch his image to that of a girl.

He had, of course, been bullied by his father to such an extent that he had no longer needed to be schooled into how to complete the look. In fact, he had become so familiar with the process that he could, without any help, secure each of the buttons which had run in a row down the back of the dress and then, almost instinctively, add the final touch by knotting the perfect bow, before swivelling it around his waist until its loops had settled, neatly and gracefully, in their rightful place at the back.

Maybe it had been down to the fact that he had been boosted with some much-needed confidence, he cannot be sure. But whatever the reason, he had finally made a stand to take back an element of control in his life. Even now, he can remember how, when he had looked into the mirror, even *he* had been impressed! The thing was, when he had turned ... so as to be able to view the lie of the back as well as that of the front, he had seen within the reflection, not the incongruity of espying a defeated little boy dressed up in a manner which had been designed to extol the essence of femininity, but, rather, he had seen the somewhat unsettling, but strangely victorious, image of what appeared to be nothing less than that of a confident, and surprisingly appealing, young lady.

Taken aback by the look, he had stared into the eyes which had mirrored his own and, with a boost of tenacity, mouthed the lines of some imaginary confrontation with his father.

So that's it — you've won! You wanted me to look like a girl? Well, here I am — just as you want me to look — and I hope you're ready for it, 'cause here goes — like it or not — you're about to meet the girl that you think I want to be!

Although he'd had no desire to *explore* his *feminine side,* he'd been quite prepared to play the part in full ... if only as a means to an end.

Even to this day, he believes that, when there is a desire or need to achieve something, then, irrespective of the means which are used to pull it off, it is always going to be the outcome which will be the all-important factor.

He had felt that he'd had nothing to lose. His mind had been made, and so, with a growth in confidence, he had decided to fight back — not by shouting and screaming as he'd battled against a powerful opposing tide, but rather by swimming with the current and, whilst doing so, looking out for the moment when he could catch him unawares and break the mould.

He had decided that on this particular occasion, he would not be tearfully subdued and then forced into performing what had, by then, become a rather tiresome routine. Instead, he would make a concerted effort to take control of his destiny. He'd thought that if he could outshine the performances of the past, then the shock of it all could well reverberate throughout the home. Still, although the image had been good, it had still needed that little bit more if he was to make an impression to last.

Self-indulgently, and in an almost warped kind of way, he seems to luxuriate in the memory of what had then followed.

The fact had been that he had decided to *grab the bull by the horns* and give a display which his father would *never* be able to forget.

He recalls in the tiniest of detail as to how he had nipped into his mother's room and then hurriedly, albeit apprehensively, grabbed her only pair of high-heeled shoes. They were the colour of champagne — stylish and glossy — and with heels which were elegant, yet not too high for safety or comfort. But then, what was more, they had only been worn the once and had retained the unblemished look of newness.

He'd been certain in his belief that, by wearing them, he would have gained sufficient height to intimidate, and so, he would not only have attained the extra stature needed to shock, but he would also have been able to launch his father into a state of utter confusion.

Having been of an age where his own clothing was often discarded — not through the ravages of general wear and tear but more as a result of the speed of his growth — he had, by coincidence, reached the point where the shoe sizes of both he and his mother had reached a crossroad, and so, somewhat fortuitously, the fit had been just about right. He had anticipated that, with the heels being not too high, and therefore manageable, he would have had no difficulty in being able to walk; moreover, he would not have been at risk of an ungainly stumble.

He had hoped that, with his apparent and new-found willingness to surrender to the adoption of both the attire and the ways of femininity, he would have been able to have pushed his father into having to accept that his grip was, to say the least, fragile. After all, his father would have had to ask himself if his insistence on the repetitive implementation of the punishment had, in fact, done little more than to awaken the very antithesis of his desired outcome.

Even though he had been quite young, he'd had the wherewithal to realize that compliance with his father's wishes could serve only to negate the need for enforcement. And so, the need for him to be controlled would, almost certainly, have been lost.

Having seen no reason to stop at having just the one enhancement, he had looked around her room and decided that he could go a step further. So, without further ado, he had rummaged through the drawers of his mother's dressing table and searched for the jewellery box in which he had known she had housed her silver chain with its moonstone pendant. He had been certain that, with it hanging gracefully from around his neck, he would have had more than satisfactorily enhanced the look.

Although he had not had the time, the knowledge or the skill to have successfully *made himself up* from what little there was of her somewhat limited supply of cosmetics, he had, nevertheless, still been confident in his ability to make an impact. After all, he had presumed that — by him effectively combining his new-found aptitude in being able to achieve a convincing air of femininity in his poise, and along with the look of a youthful innocence which had, no doubt, been purposefully crafted within the trappings and loveliness of both the style and the fabric of the dress — he would certainly have been able to cause a stir.

Whether this alone would have been enough to suggest the presence of a young woman with class, rather than that of a child, *dressed-up* and ready to attend some special occasion, he'd been unsure. But, when he had glanced behind the door and eyed her summer hat with its wide and floppy brim, he knew instantly that he had found the ideal means to disguise any remaining absurdity which may have lain within the attempt to feminise the true nature of the boy.

With the shoes slipped on and the pendant provocatively displayed from around his neck, he had carefully positioned the headwear so that he could, beguilingly and with the look of an *English rose,* pick the right moment to peek out from beneath the gentle waves of a sinuous brim.

He recalls how he had, yet again, looked into the mirror and had smiled at the finished product. It was then that he'd seen that, by having complemented the flamboyant display of the forthcoming performance with a hint of virtue, he had, somehow, succeeded in amassing all the ingredients necessary for him to cause a shock … and in doing so, make an impression that would be guaranteed to last.

He had been sound in his judgment. After all, the decision to accessorize and enhance the original look had turned out to have been spot-on. It had been well worth the gamble!

Having ensured that he had not only looked the part, but that he had also looked at his best, he had stood at the top of the stairs. Then, with his head held high, and having just taken a long and deep intake of breath, he had brushed down the sides of the fabric with his hands and grasped the front of the dress from a point several inches above the knees. He had paused … taken another deep breath … and then, complete with its silky lining, lifted it, ensuring no mishap as he had slowly and purposefully made his way down the flight of carpeted stairs.

Even now, he remembers how, with each descending step, he could feel the ever-increasing pound of his heart beating out its rhythm, and then, once he had caught sight of his mother and sisters and had seen that they had, without exception, been stunned into silence, he had known that his efforts had been worthwhile.

Having seen photographs of his parent's wedding day, he'd known that when those same silks had been first cut and then carefully sewn together so as to have made the original dress, his mother would not have needed to have clutched hold of and then to have lifted its skirts in order to negotiate an obstacle; for it had been styled in such a way that it was carried above-ankle-length in front, before dipping gracefully to the ground at the back.

Funnily enough, the fact that he'd not had the advantage of having the raised hemline at the front and had therefore had to lift the skirts himself in order to descend each step of the stairs had, in a strange kind of way, actually enhanced the image of what could only have been described as being a demure, yet captivating, depiction of feminine modesty.

So, without even the slightest hint of his inner discomfort, he had, rather brazenly, strode across the room and, for a moment, he had stood in front of the family gathering. Then — albeit with a whiff of there having been present a touch of impishness behind the façade — he had peered, rather coyly, from beneath the headwear, put one foot behind the other and then, somewhat clinically, dipped his knee and curtsied.

Straightaway, and in order to deny his father any chance to realize the true nature of his actions, he had then swung into what had become, through the repetition of having to endure countless punishments, a well-practiced routine — one which he had refined to the level of near perfection.

Had his father known of what was to follow, then he would have, there and then, pulled on the reins of control and ensured that his son could not execute his somewhat curious but, nevertheless, well-thought-out stand of defiance.

But the fact of the matter had been that the man of the house had been unprepared.

So, without further ado, he had just upped a gear and, is if having suddenly thrown caution to the wind, he had proceeded to emulate the graceful carriage of that of a *fashion house* model — one who had been charged with the responsibility to flaunt all the beautiful attributes of, what may well have been, an exclusive and expensive gown.

With each stride, he had kicked the skirts forward and, by stepping with one foot directly in front of the other, he had managed to accentuate the movement of his hips. With his confidence boosted, he had started to smile, not with the look of a performer enjoying the attention of an audience, but more with a hint of self-satisfaction — a feeling which had been fuelled by the fact that, by the expressions on each of their faces, he had seen that he had, in effect, all but taken control.

As he'd approached the end of the room, he had, without hesitation, spun around, so causing the skirts to lift upwards and into a floating swirl before they desperately chased after him on his uninterrupted journey back across the floor. As he'd spun, he, with an irrepressible verve, had repeated the show, once, maybe twice, he cannot be sure, but he *can* remember his *coup de grâce* — the spinning of a spectacular, final twirl before coming to an abrupt halt ... allowing the silken fabrics to swing to and fro before falling, somewhat enchantingly, back into place.

With his audience having been stunned into silence, he had lowered his arms beside him, and then, with a grasp from each hand, he had simultaneously seized the shimmering fabric of the skirts and lifted them outwards and upwards before, somewhat mockingly, curtsying again. But, this time he had ensured that his actions had been accentuated with the audacious accompaniment of a defiant smile.

He had known at the time that he had crossed a dangerous line and had gone past the point of there being no room for return; but then, he'd had enough of having to quietly suffer at the hands of his bullying father, and because of that, he had needed to bring it all to a head. So, having made his protest, he had simply stood quietly as he had waited for both the eruption and then the retribution from his bemused and extremely disgruntled father.

It did not come.

Yes, his father had been angry. In fact, it had been much more than that — he had been fuming. But, in spite of it all, his father, for reasons of his own, had decided to resist the urge to explode with an open display of temper. Maybe it had been because he'd dared not admit, even to himself, to the apparent failure of his peculiar form of remedial therapy. After all, it should have been easy for him to have orchestrated the repetitive humiliation of his son in front of his family, and then to leave sibling rivalry, with an endless bombardment of taunting jibes, to do the rest.

But — as is often the case with, supposedly, *well-thought plans* — his strategy had not only backfired but, what's more, it had looked as if it had exacerbated the situation; matters had been made far worse than he could have ever have envisaged.

He had, in all likelihood, expected the embarrassment alone to have been sufficient to have spurred his son into turning against his siblings. Only then, with his heart filled with rage and his mind focused on their nastiness, would his son have been ready to admit the error of his ways and then beat a hasty retreat from his *sissy ways*.

Anyway, whatever the intent — it didn't work.

Lost for words, he had stormed out of the house, no doubt in search of a few mind-numbing whiskies and the company of the pub's regulars, who, being unaware of what had regularly gone on behind the closure of his doors, had never failed to welcome him into the monotony of their lacklustre world.

When the door had slammed behind him and he had been, without a doubt, well on his way to the tavern, there had been — he recalls — a hush, followed by the gentle, congratulatory, clapping of hands as his mother had begun to open up and revel in the unexpected comeuppance of her brutish spouse.

"*Come here...*" she had beckoned with a nod and an enormous smile. "*Give me a nice big hug.*"

He recalls how he had stepped forward and then quietly slipped into her embrace, and then, with the sudden onset of stress-induced exhaustion, he had snuggled up close and rested in her comforting and loving arms. With the wearing of perfume forbidden, he remembers how she had exuded a fragrance of reassuring cleanliness — the result, no doubt, of the early-morning routine of her frenetically scrubbing herself clean, as if ridding all traces of her husband's touch.

The instinctive motherly action of the soothing stroke of her hand, running up and down the contours of his back, had, at least, confirmed her love for him. Furthermore, he could also recall how he had felt that she had been truly at peace, with him safely wrapped in her arms. She had not seemed to have been, in any way, sickened by his flamboyant and convincing display.

Yes ... she had definitely seen through his pretence, and she had, therefore, known that he was far from being the character of his portrayal.

The truth had been, not too surprisingly, that the instances of him having to suffer the penalty of feminization had been so commonplace that he had become almost numbed to the smoothness and the luxurious feel of the fabric. Its touch had no longer served to sensitize, never mind delight his fingertips, as it had still done to those of his mother's.

He — as had his mother — had known that it would have been folly to have removed the garment before his father's return. But, strangely enough, he had not been particularly bothered by the ensnarement of the cloth, since it had lost its hold, and, furthermore, he had not wished to disturb the rare and magical moments which he had then been able to share with her.

"*Do you know?*" she'd said softly as she had lovingly and thoughtfully fingered the exquisite texture of the silken fabric. "*I made this for Katy. It was amazing really; there was so much material in my old wedding dress that I even had enough to make one for Rachel as well.*"

Her pride in the quality of her creative accomplishments had been more than apparent in the way that she had eyed and handled the garment.

"*Do you remember? ... They wore them when they were the bridesmaids at your aunt's wedding.*"

He had remembered. In fact, he'd had no difficulty in summoning up the memories. After all, having been obliged to stand around in the churchyard whilst the photographer had rushed about to shepherd his charges, so ensuring that everyone had found their *proper* place in the wedding-day album, he had been bored to tears.

He recalls how his mother had allowed herself the indulgence of drifting down the solace of memory lane. She had seemed to have been savouring the feelings of happiness which had surrounded her sister's big day, and albeit being only a temporary state of affairs, the release that the event had given her from the pain of her own experiences of matrimony.

She had explained how it had been her sister who had chosen the colour of the sash and that, although it had seemed to be such an unusual colour, she had thought that it would *reflect the autumnal colours in the churchyard*.

As if she had been enjoying a few moments of peace, she had sat back, and whilst, no doubt, continuing to cherish the image of her two daughters, all dressed up and proudly following the bride as she had gracefully made her way along the aisle to meet her spouse to be, she had closed her eyes.

Suddenly, having shaken herself away from the warmth of the images which had been plucked from the past, she, with a smile in her eyes, had picked up from where she had left off, and then, addressing all of her children, had continued. *"Now then ... my wedding gown was ..."*

Although he had not taken on board the specifics, he can still recall how she'd taken great pleasure in describing it in full, and then, with an almost childlike emphasis as to how superior hers had been to that of her daughter's, had jokingly continued by adding, *"I think mine was so much better though!"*

She had started to laugh. He remembers *that* vividly — for as sad it may have seemed, it was a rare treat to have witnessed her freely showing signs that she had still been able to display some feelings of happiness.

Feigning a semblance of interest, he had nodded and, without a word, he had allowed her to continue.

She had then gone on to describe, in detail, her wedding dress and how it was the *most gorgeous* dress that she had ever seen. He recalls her having said that, when she had walked up the aisle, she had felt as if she were a famous Hollywood actress, and that she had the whole world at her feet and a bright and rosy future stretching out before her.

She had pondered for a moment, and it was then when he recalls seeing the joy in her smile begin to diminish as she had started to question the reliability of her earlier skills of judgement. He cannot remember exactly how she had said it, but she had told him that she had come to the conclusion that she had made a massive error in choosing her *leading man*.

Then suddenly, as if having pulled herself away from the brink of falling into the abyss of sadness and despair, she had regained her smile, and added, with a heart-warming hug. *"And now my lovely and gorgeous little man ... even if you are dressed up and looking pretty in one of the most beautiful dresses in the world ... it doesn't matter."*

She had gone on to say that he had proved that he had the courage to stand up for himself ... and *whatever anyone else cared to think ... that was proof that he would always be more of a man than his father could have ever been.*

He remembers some of her words well, and, although he had not been too sure about being referred to as looking *pretty*, the recognition as to his courage and, thus, the support over his actions, had been most gratefully accepted.

His sisters, with their hands cupped over their lips so as to disguise their words, had whispered secretly to each other, and then, with a playful giggle, they had rushed up the stairs as if they had been on some kind of mischievous and clandestine mission.

The spell of tender bonding had been, in his opinion, somewhat prematurely cut short when, after too brief a time, the girls had rushed down the stairs, dressed up and ready to make light of the events of the evening.

Even *he* had laughed as they, too, had paraded across the room like models strutting the catwalk. Enjoying the freedom to flaunt their new-found adeptness in the displaying of fashions, they had posed and pouted. And then, with a spring in their stride, they had marched up and down, slowing only to turn with skirt-raising swirls, before curtsying as they awaited the expected cheer and round of applause.

Making the most of the spell of emancipation from the oppressive ways of their father, they had grabbed him by the arms and dragged him to his feet. They were going to have fun — they wanted an encore.

With the encouraging smile of his mother, along with the knowledge that it was just a game, without the awful burden of judgement, he'd defied his initial reluctance and then, without further inhibition, duly obliged.

He remembers her, sat with a sparkle in her eyes and a smile as broad and bright as he had ever seen, as she'd delighted in the unfettered joy of her children playing whilst she mused as to what could have been, were it not for the presence of her loathsome husband.

For a fleeting moment, he had wondered if, as she had watched the contentment of her three children happily exploring a self-made world of imagination, she had forgotten the fact of his gender and was privately savouring an impossible dream of a life as a *single mum* with three lovely daughters … instead of an existence, with the complications of a son who may well be forced to live up to, and adopt, the unpalatable expectations and traits of the father.

As the evening had yielded to the encroaching night, there had been no return of the man of the house. So, with the prospect of him and his siblings having to go to school in the morning, they had all made their way up to their beds. They had needed to grab some precious sleep before the inevitable late-night disturbance, and the subsequent awakening, which would, as usual, have been triggered by the ravings of the drunken brute.

Following the unusual occurrence of him having had a full night of undisturbed sleep, he remembers waking up and watching quietly as his mother had hung *the* dress — pressed, pristine and protected under its polythene cover — before, rather symbolically, shutting the wardrobe door.

There had been something different. He'd known that his mother would not have risked all by doing his chore for him unless, of course, she had no longer feared his father's presence. So, with that in mind, he had suspected that maybe, for some reason, the routine of oppression had been broken.

She had seen him wake and then, unwittingly feeding his suspicion, had said to him, *"Don't you worry. It will all be over soon."*

She'd gone to say that she would hang the dress up in *her* room and, with a bit of luck, he would never have to see it again.

He remembers how, in the silence of his puzzlement and relief, he could only nod in appreciative acknowledgement.

"And another thing ..." she'd continued, *"... I think that now that Katy's seen you in it, she's not going to be in any rush to take it back either."*

"Where is he?" He remembers whispering the question — not because he had been concerned as to the welfare of his father, but more because he had been afraid to say anything which, if it were within his earshot, could have been misunderstood and, thereby, resulted in further punishment.

As far as he could recall, she had not given him an answer ... she had, instead, simply left the room with a smile on her face.

As they had sat around the table for breakfast, she had been gathering her thoughts, and then, once she was ready, she had explained that she had received a message that their father had been *in some kind of trouble* and that he had spent the night at the police station.

She had not seemed unduly saddened with the situation — in fact, she had appeared to have become a little lighter in her step, and, what's more, it had seemed that she had, almost magically, become a little younger in her years.

Little did they know at the time, but this was the start of a journey on which his mother would set out on a road towards freedom, whilst his father would be sent on a separate road which would end with his incarceration.

The young man who had dared to flirt with the younger and more attractive of the two barmaids was on a life-support machine, having been smashed in the face and then jabbed in the neck with the angry end of a broken bottle.

He seems to recall that his father had eventually been charged with wounding with intent, as opposed to a charge of attempted murder, and then taken to a court for the near formality of a remand in custody.

He had not opposed bail. There had been no point. Even though he had intimated a guilty plea, he had known that he would, in all probabilities, receive a custodial sentence — albeit, not as long as it could have been had he decided to plead *not guilty*. His guilt had been irrefutable, and so, all he could do was to go for *damage limitation* in an attempt to reduce the time to be served. What's more, he had probably known that the guilty plea would reduce the term, and also, any time spent in custody before sentence would be taken as having been time already served.

Once his mother had learnt the detail as to the length of his imprisonment, she had been able to take steps to rid herself of all marital ties and ensure that there was no longer a trail for his father to pursue.

They had moved house, and having had it explained to them that this was the only way in which they could ensure their safety, he and his sisters had, compliantly, accepted the changes and adapted to their new home and school.

Even though he had been removed from the regime of his father, the damage had already been done.

The experience of having been subjected to both psychological and physical abuse had been forever-etched within his psyche. And although he carries with him emotional scars with deep-rooted issues, he is not the type of man to ever admit to a weakness.

His recollections flick forward to an evening, a while ago, when having returned to the area following a substantial length of time living away, he had found his mother's house and knocked on the door.

The stranger who had answered his knock had told him that she had, yet again, moved on; so, with no forwarding address having been left, he had little choice but to reconsider his plans for the future.

He had not been told that it had been the combination of the occasional and shady glimpses of the father in the son, along with her fear that one day, in the future, they could both return and re-impose the cruel regime of the past, that had prompted her into taking a course which had necessitated an unsettling, yet successfully evasive, frequency of relocations. Had he known her reasoning, then, perhaps, he would not have attempted to re-establish contact.

It hadn't quite clicked with him that she had felt good reason not to inform him of her new place of residence; but then, even if she had done, he still had no wish to quarrel with her. Anyway, he had wished that he had known of her whereabouts because — although he had carried a secret that he could never dare to tell in full — he could have then relieved her from her fears by furnishing her with the fact that he had known that his father had gone … and that he would never be able to return.

The truth of the matter had been that, following his release from prison, his father had made efforts to seek out his son. It was then, when he had finally found him living alone in an old mining village in the far west of Cornwall, that he'd had to accept the reality of there having been no bonds left between them. The old man's pathetic attempts to try and forge some kind of relationship — along with his feeble excuses as to why he had imposed his cruelty on his wife and his children — did nothing, other than to worsen the situation.

Having allowed the years of his *twenties* to disappear into the irretrievability of the chasms of time, he had matured. He was no longer the pushover that the old man had recalled. He had also been fully aware of the fact that the man who had betrayed him was also the man from whom he had, no doubt, inherited some rather worrying traits. He thinks back as to how things had suddenly taken a turn for the worse between father and son. Even today, he wonders if these traits had been, somewhat ironically, the very same traits which had made it all too easy for him to execute a much needed cull and then deposit the corpse — as if it were just a piece of rotting garbage — into the darkest depths of an ancient and crumbling mine-shaft.

The execution had not been as easy to implement as he had thought that it may have been. Because of that, during the struggle, his father had left him with a permanent reminder of the fracas — that is to say, a couple of scars and a misshaped nose.

Strangely enough though, it had been the pain which he had received as a result of a particularly eye-watering blow that had given him the extra strength and the unrelenting will to grab hold of the steak-knife which had been lying beside the kitchen sink, and then to plunge it, deep into his father's chest. He remembers, quite clearly, how he had determinedly twisted it, as if in concert with the contortions which had filled the dying man's face.

As the years had rolled on by and the occasional passing acquaintance had sought explanation as to the cause of the injury, he had simply told them, rather dismissively, that — *with fifteen men a side scrapping over the right of ownership of an oval ball, one should not be too surprised to hear that a bone or two had been broken in the process.*

The account had never failed to satisfy the curiosity of the nosey. However, with no one left to care about him and with no one to report him missing, his father had, in effect, disappeared from the face of the world — it had been as if he had never existed.

Mind you, with the older man no longer in the picture, he did take the opportunity to make another effort to find his mother's address. But, with each push on a doorbell, he was greeted with either a blank stare of ignorance or a shake of a head to say that she was no longer in residence.

When her neighbours were asked for a reason as to why she had left, they would only say that they didn't know … *One day she was there, and the next, she was gone!*

Whether they were under an oath of secrecy or whether they were genuinely lacking the knowledge as to her whereabouts, he had not been too sure; but whatever had been the truth of the matter, he had been unable to find her.

Exhaustive enquiries with the civic authorities and traders alike — along with a comprehensive search of the electoral registers — had failed to find her. For, although he did not know it, she no longer answered to either the given name of her birth or by that which had been acquired through the formality of her marriage.

Maybe she has survived … but then again … maybe she has not!

Still, whatever the circumstance, he has absolutely no idea as to her or his sisters' present whereabouts. He has been left with no option, other than to resign himself to accepting that he may never know what has happened to them. Moreover, he has also been drawn to the conclusion that, when it comes down to it, he has a life of his own to lead, and so, there is little point in him wasting his efforts in trying to pursue the matter any further.

Chapter 26

The shops will soon be closing ... and he is happy. The reason for his happiness is simple; he has already collected his prize and is now homeward-bound with his guitar-case beside him.

He leans his head back and, with a sigh of relief, he rests with it supported by the rear-seat neck-restraint of his father's car.

It has been a strange couple of weeks, what with the arrival of his somewhat unconventional Godfather, Gwilly, and his rather captivating and considerably more balanced wife, Maria.

They had appeared, unannounced and from the depths of a long and distant past, and then, having made their impression — and as if they had been on some passing comet — they had picked up their bags and had gone again.

But now he has had the unsurpassable thrill of having just collected his long-awaited, hand-crafted electric bass; an experience which he will, without doubt, treasure for evermore.

The finish of twenty or so layers of expertly-applied lacquer which serve to protect and enhance the beauty of the navy-blue colouration of the flowing grain of ash, along with the warm glow of golden hardware, cannot be bettered. With the image of his acquisition firmly implanted in his mind, he closes his eyes. As he drifts into a state of contentment he becomes conscious only of the warm blush of colour which, as the rays of bright sunshine are periodically shielded by the passing of the roadside buildings and the bordering trees ... alternates between the tones of light and dark.

The hypnotic hum of rolling wheels, combined with the gentle purr of the engine, lulls him into a semiconscious state where his thoughts begin to morph into a vivid, visual and private revelation of his desire for success — if not the heights of stardom. Although just images of fantasy, they seem to be increasingly real as he melts into the depths of the twilight world of wonderful dreams; a place where, under the glare of a magnificent light-show, he breaks away from supporting his lead guitarist and then, with an element of self-assuredness, parades before a horde of adoring followers who, with their arms held high, rock exuberantly with the rhythm whilst his fingers thump away on the wire-wound strings of his custom-built bass.

With the instrument growling its presence and the rocking beat of the drums behind, he takes the lead ... bending, thumping and slapping the strings in a faultless rendition of his latest musical creation.

As he sinks deeper into a state of sleep, and whilst still revelling in the adulation of his fans, he is abruptly wakened with a jolt as his virtual world is suddenly returned to the everyday reality of city life.

The violent braking of the car, along with the synchronized sounding of its horn, is closely followed by the shouts of his father. "Bloody idiot! Watch where you're going!" Bryn yells through the window at the inattentive pedestrian … who immediately steps back and onto the safety of the pavement.

Momentarily and nonchalantly, she glances up at the car. She smiles as it pulls off again, before returning her full attention to her phone.

"That's right — get yourself knocked over … why don't you? Play havoc with my insurance … See if I care." Bryn grumbles, somewhat comically, as he lets off steam before recommencing the task of concentrating on the road ahead.

He glances in his mirror and, seeing her ambling along the pavement, he cannot help but to note how her ebbing figure still appears to be totally unconcerned … as if she is completely oblivious to how close she had been to tragedy.

Jamie, startled, looks out of the window and, searching for the cause of the disturbance, he asks, "What was that?"

"Just some moron glued to her mobile. … Silly cow … She should learn to look where she's going before trying to cross!"

Bill, their ridgeback, has taken possession of the entire luggage space. With both him and Jamie looking out of the rear window, it appears as if they are both focusing on the teenage girl who, obviously unperturbed by the incident, has now stepped off from the pavement and started to stroll back across the road, whilst merrily chatting away into her phone.

"I can see it now…" Bryn, bouncing each word with *Fawltyesque* emphasis, pauses, and then continues. "She arrives at the pearly gates … fifty years too early and oblivious to the significance of the presence of St Peter. And all she can do is whinge about the loss of a signal on her bloody mobile … Brilliant! Absolutely brilliant!"

Beth, sitting beside him, laughs out loud; not only does she recognize the aping of the fictional character of a somewhat beleaguered and henpecked hotelier but, additionally, she has been blessed with an artistic and vivid imagination which gives her the ability to readily visualise the scene.

They continue on their journey, putting the incident behind them almost as fast as it had occurred.

As they leave the suburban outskirts, they slip on to the dual carriageway and relax. Jamie, aware that his parents are in conversation, is happy to feel cut off in the back. Alone with his thoughts, he stares at the shaped hard-case of his new guitar, which is loosely wedged almost upright in the foot-well behind his mother.

The chromium-plated clasps that secure the lid tantalisingly invite him to unclip them, one by one.

His left hand creeps over and quietly unclips the first of the four. The temptation to continue is too great to resist. Feeling as if he is a willing victim of a seduction, he releases the second, the third and then finally, the fourth.

The lid loosens, barely opening in the process.

Gently, he expands the fissure and eases his hand through, allowing the tips of his fingers to caress the smooth and glossy sculpted curves of the freshly-lacquered arch-top body.

Forcing the lid open a little wider, an intoxicating scent of newness seeps out and excites his nasal senses. He peers in to view the beauty of his handcrafted instrument, but as the lid becomes obstructed by the back of the front seat, the restriction prevents sufficient opening for the contents to be seen with clarity.

He imagines how similar his feelings towards the wafts of fresh varnish, along with the first gentle touches on its smooth and glossy maple top, are to the joyous and warm sensations that new mothers and new grandmothers claim to feel when they snuggle up close to a defenceless newborn baby; or, alternatively, how they compare to the feelings of those who *do not do babies* but, instead, feel the need to crumble into a state of ecstatic peace when they absorb the smell of a fluffy, and not yet weaned, puppy.

This is *his* baby … and he is as excited and as proud as any new parent would be.

His hands, like sensors wishing to indulge in the delights of sensuality, resume their engagement with the gentle stroking of his fingertips against the glossy texture of this highly-polished instrument. Whilst doing so, he again closes his eyes, and in the hope that he will drift back into the earlier dreamland existence in which he was being idolised as if he were a legend of rock, he pushes away the distractions of the outside world.

As his thoughts start to wander, he becomes increasingly aware that the smooth, almost pleasing, sensations which are felt through his left hand are being mirrored by that of the right as — in an attempt to ease the effects of an unexpected arrival of cramp — he kneads the muscles in his thigh.

With his eyes half open, he drops his line of vision towards his right leg and focuses. He stalls and, whilst seemingly frozen in time, he tries to make sense of what he can see.

The heavy, blue denim of his jeans is no longer evident as being merely that of the cloth of the manual worker; it has, inexplicably, appeared to have morphed into something more delicate and much smoother to the touch.

Captivated by the dark-blue satiny sheen, he watches as it is smoothed by the movement of the hand which creeps upwards, over the knee and along the length of his thigh.

It makes no sense. As if to clear a misted screen, he blinks and shakes his head. The image has not gone — it is still the same. He stares at the hand, and, without warning, he feels a jolt. It's as if his heart has suddenly skipped a beat.

There's something not right with the hand! He blinks and pauses, allowing time to bring clarity to his vision and, thus, order to his thoughts.

Confusion mixes with fear, and as it takes its hold, the image remains firm.

It's the thumb — it's on the right of the hand as he looks down at it. It cannot be his right hand ... something's wrong. Panic tightens its grip as he realizes that the feelings of cool satin against his flesh are not, in fact, being felt through the sensory nerves of his own hand — they are being sensed through the muscles of the thigh itself. It is as if he has been touched by the hand of someone else!

The feeling, to say the least, is strange. As he races for an explanation, he cannot help to wonder if it is *he* who is going mad or whether something far more sinister — and, perhaps, from another dimension — has come into play.

He considers the options, and as if to clear any foreign body from the image-forming cells of the retina, he closes his eyes tight ... whilst praying that on their reopening he will see that it had all been quite innocent and was little more than that of a rather peculiar dream.

With his growing need to face up to his demons, he makes an effort to push through the barrier of his natural resistance to confronting the mysteries of the surreal. He opens his eyes and focuses.

Relief! As he sits with his own hand, as before, splayed out on the faded, blue denim of his jeans, he is reassured in the knowledge that the surreal has been ousted in favour of a return to reality. Perplexed by his experience, he rests his head back and onto the restraint, allowing time to contemplate his sanity.

Recalling the incongruity of the image of a stranger's hand stroking his satin-draped thigh, he searches for answers.

Worried that he may have, within him, hidden inclinations which are fighting to surface, he cannot help but to question himself as to why he should dream of such a thing. *Is it a sign of a perversion? ... or is it down to some hidden issue with regard to gender identity?* He dismisses the notions as quickly as they had arrived. Besides, he possesses no questionable desires, nor does he traits, and, with that in mind, he consoles himself with the fact that any inclinations must be so well hidden that even *he* has not be made privy to what they could be.

But then, he reasons, there must be something. Common sense dictates that there is always a rational explanation, but, for the time being, there are none that readily come to mind.

As he probes his deepest thoughts, his sense of relief — at first tested only by the tiniest ripples of apprehension towards the uncertainty of the unknown — starts to diminish as he becomes increasingly unnerved by a bewildering influx of images which seem to strengthen and become more violent as they resonate in his mind.

Suddenly, as if wishing to slam a door on his thoughts, he snatches his left hand from the case and promptly shuts it tight. With four rapid clunks, the catches are shut and the lid secured.

With the instrument shut away, there is an immediate cessation of the images. He sits back and tries to forget the experience by putting it aside while he distracts himself by gazing at the passing countryside.

He eyes the rolling skyline; its forested tops broken only by the solid and imposing man-made tower which dramatically, and almost mystically, changes with the angle and brightness of the light. There are times when it seems to glow like a guiding light for all to see, but then there are the occasions when it disappears; stolen by an illusion where a backdrop of featureless grey-white clouds absorb its form and smuggle it out of sight.

Calmed, he unclips the catches as he again falls to the temptation to admire his acquisition … and opens the lid.

Without warning, an overpowering and intense wave of terror begins to take control of his senses and, as if fighting for his very life, he starts to claw frantically at his throat.

He tries to call out to his parents, but no words are released.

"Wow!" The sudden exclamation of his father breaks the silence.

"What is it?" Beth asks, appearing somewhat shaken in herself.

Without answering the question, he exclaims, "If I could bottle this I'd make a fortune."

Again, she probes, "What is it? What are you feeling?"

"I'm not sure. It's like a really cold shiver ran right through me. It felt like all the hairs on the back of my neck were standing upright … if you know what I mean — really weird!"

Worried, she probes deeper. "Was it … was it almost like … spears of ice … That's it, spears of ice shooting through you?"

He looks back at her, noting the genuine but atypical apprehension that is reflected in her eyes, and answers, "Yea … sort of."

He looks back to the road. "Why? Is that what you've felt?"

He glances back to her for an answer.

Stilled and troubled by the experience, she responds with a silent, and uneasy, nod of affirmation.

They look ahead, wordlessly deliberating on their individual experiences whilst weighing up the likelihood of two people, quite independently, suffering the same.

Bryn checks his rear-view mirror and glimpses the sight of his son. He, too, appears to be suffering, albeit silently, but still in a severe state of distress.

He repositions the mirror to enhance his view and to confirm the assessment. "Jamie! Are you all right?" he asks, with more than a little concern, as he knows the answer is obviously a no.

Jamie's face — ashen, and with his eyes, wide and fearful — stares back through the mirror at his father's image as he grapples at his throat ... as if attempting to tear something away in his desperation for air. "I c— can't breathe," he wheezes.

Beth stares back. "What's wrong?"

"It's choking me. I can't b—breathe."

He's terrified and on the edge of panic. Sharing that same edge, she turns to her husband. "Pull over! Quickly!"

With the hazard lights on, he pulls across to the nearside lane and then up and onto the verge.

She stretches over and leans through the gap between the front seats to reach her son. "There's nothing there. What's choking you?"

"I don't know ..." His breathing is shallow, and although he feels his windpipe becoming increasingly restricted, he forces his words out. "It feels like s--something's squeezing my throat!"

The icy chill returns to engulf both his father and his mother with a vengeance — then, suddenly, and as if it had never been ... it goes.

She turns towards Bryn and, catching his eye, silently seeks confirmation of a link between their three separate and eerie experiences.

His expression confirms their shared but unspoken concerns.

"How are you now?" He asks as he starts to observe some signs of improvement.

"I think ... I'm getting a bit better ... I don't know what came over me. I'm sorry ... maybe I've had a panic-attack or something?"

"Tell me ... what exactly happened to you?"

"I don't know, Dad. I really can't remember."

He has no intention of releasing the detail.

"Has this ever happened to you before?" His mother starts to investigate the cause of the event.

Jamie shakes his head.

"Have you eaten something which is a bit off ... or have you taken anything you shouldn't have?" She does not want to be accusatory by openly using the word *drugs* ... but she needs to know. She needs to be able to establish the cause and then identify what may have instigated the strange reaction.

"No Mum. I haven't eaten anything *off* ... and I'm not interested in drugs. For Christ's sake, Mum … I don't even smoke!"

"What's that smell?" she asks.

"What smell?"

"That smell. It's like polish … or something similar."

"I think it's the guitar," suggests Jamie, "It's got that new smell to it — the varnish on the wood."

"Maybe that's what it is … perhaps you've reacted to it, somehow."

"Yea … possibly."

"If it's not that, then maybe you've picked up a bug … or it's an allergy or something. Now … are you feeling any better?"

"Yea. I'm fine — can we go home now? Please?"

"Are you sure?"

"Yes, I'm sure. I'm a lot better now — so, come on, let's go … Please?"

Bryn complies with the request and manoeuvres the vehicle back onto the carriageway and then accelerates to join with the flow of traffic.

As he drives on, he tries to reason as to how and why they had all shared the somewhat frightening and unsettling experience.

Perhaps, he surmises, Jamie had been affected by an allergy to something in the food that he'd eaten earlier … and that the reactions of both he and Beth were purely down to a psychosomatic response to being subconsciously aware of their son's distress. On the other hand, it could have simply been down to the effects of the varnish.

That must be it, he concludes. Everything has a logical explanation behind it, and if only people would take the time to think about things in a calm and rational manner, they would, like him, find their answers … and leave the supernatural to the writers and film-makers of science-fiction and horror.

Chapter 27

Sensing that they may well detect the telltale signs of her apprehension, and fearing that with even the slightest suggestion of her being discomforted by feelings of vulnerability they could be stirred into focusing their attentions on her, she takes care not to invite a reaction. So, by averting her gaze, she hopes to offer no excuse for any one of them to open up an unwelcome line for communication.

With her stomach tightening, she looks to the ground.

Urged on by an instinctive drive for self-preservation and the need to be forewarned of impending danger, she, with prudence to the fore, lifts her gaze so as to surreptitiously monitor their movements through the images which are mirrored in the row of adjacent shop windows.

The four young men, grouped, a few yards ahead of her — and on the opposite side of the narrow, partially cobbled and pedestrianized street — are showing signs of boredom. Subconsciously, they vie with one another for pack-leadership ... their voices, loud and intimidating, amplifying in the passageway which connects the quaintness of the quiet back-street to that of the far busier thoroughfare of the main road.

As she draws closer, she cannot help but to inhale the toxic by-product of their nicotine addiction, and as the obnoxious stench of their habit spreads out to contaminate even more of the once airy surroundings, she is irritated by the way in which she is, as a result, being denied of her right to breathe fresh air. The acridity of the taste, as the pollutants hit the back of her throat, generate a feeling of disgust which, with the added knowledge that these very fumes have already passed through the lungs of another, soon turns to nausea as that grisly notion wedges deep within her thoughts.

Normally, she would pause to gaze at the enchanting display of glittering crystals which fill the window of her favourite jewellers, but today she has no desire to linger. Instead, she prefers to quicken her pace, and so, with a façade of confidence to disguise the unease which urges her to pass and, thus, put distance between her and the unnerving foursome, she forges forward.

The sound of high-heeled shoes clicking on the stone slabs of the paving as she tries to avoid the discomfort and instability of negotiating the bordering cobbled surface, seems to magnify between the buildings and, in doing so, serves only to draw notice to the fact of her being both present and alone.

The wolf-whistle and the accompanying suggestive comments are obviously aimed at her, and they are certainly not welcomed. Instinctively, her hands go to her sides, tugging the fitted skirt of her two-piece suit downwards as if to confirm that it had not ridden up and, in doing so, inadvertently revealed more of her than she would have wished.

Her style of dress, although appropriate within the more sedate environment of her work-place, is rather more restrictive when she is out in the more exposed environment of the open street. The closeness of the fit would by itself hamper any attempt for her to make a quick escape if she were faced with the unwanted advances of those with dubious intent.

Although she has no need to attempt to satisfy some deep desire to show-off, she is more than aware of the importance of her being seen by both staff and clientele alike to have made the best of her appearance. Besides, it is taken as read that the manager and, as is stated on her own job-description, the deputy manager, should stand out ... not only to reflect their position within the city-centre fashion store but also to reflect the quality of the merchandise which the company has to offer.

She dresses in order to be smart, professional and comfortable. Moreover, she has absolutely no desire to try and arouse the interest of any passing Tom, Dick or Harry who happens to cast a glance in her direction.

The very thought of her being ogled by some *sick-in-the-head weirdo* gives her the creeps.

No — she should not have to put up with that type of behaviour! She has rights! As far as she is concerned, and in so far as she remains within the bounds of common decency, she has the right to be free to dress as she pleases. What is more, whilst being so attired, she also has the right to be able to walk through the streets alone ... and without having to carry the fear of being singled out as being one who may be receptive to the unsolicited advances of a total stranger.

Although, to some extent, she is experienced enough to be able to disguise her feelings to those of the outside world, the behaviour of these particular young men are beginning to rile her. Indeed, they have already managed to put her on edge. Maybe it is because they are behaving in a manner in which they seem to have assumed that by drawing attention to themselves — especially in such an insensate and boorish manner — she, or, for that matter, any other woman in her situation, would probably consider their actions as being not only manly, but also, in some primeval kind of way, attractive.

The reality, however, is very different. After all, she, like the majority of those of her gender and maturity, considers the display of this form of animalistic behaviour — especially when discharged from such an unattractive, immature and mentally inept source — to be, at best, an unwelcome irritation and, at worst, a precursor to something which carries with it the potential for malevolence.

It is unusual for her to finish work at this hour. The store, as a rule, closes for business at six. However, due to there having been a problem with the alarm system — and along with the fact that the manager has been away for the week whilst she attends a course — she could not shun the responsibilities which go hand-in-hand with her having taken on the role; so she had waited for the arrival of the engineer.

She can do without aggravation — she is tired, and having had a long and arduous day, she wishes only to go home and relax.

Preoccupied with trying to avoid the attentions of the young men who stand in a doorway across the street, she fails to notice the older man who sits quietly at one of the tables which are positioned just inside the open entrance to the coffee bar.

Although to a casual onlooker he appears to be benign, occasionally glancing up and into the street as he looks for inspiration whilst working at the newspaper crossword, he, too, had been alerted by the sound of her heels striking the stone.

By the tone alone, he had concluded that she was in a position of responsibility and in her prime, for he had perfected the art of being able to analyse the sounds of a person's footsteps.

This rather unusual talent had been honed, not whilst he had whiled away the hours in the confines of cafés and bars, but whilst he had sat out in the open public spaces of the piazzas and streets of the busy city.

He was then, as he still is now, a watcher of people. He recalls how, on one particular occasion some time ago, when he had been sitting on a bench with his eyes closed and embracing the warmth of the sun on his face, he had become aware of the mixed rhythms and varying tones of passing footsteps. Increasingly intrigued by the meld of their sounds, he could not help but to notice how the tonal quality of each heel as it struck the solid surface of the paving stones, was dictated by, and so reflected, the style and attitude of its wearer.

As far as he had been concerned, the tone of the strike was as distinct as any signature and, as such, as identifiable to the conversant as is the sound of each voice to the master of a choir.

Anyway, earlier this evening, having strolled down from the Gardens, he had sat at the table. And with his eyes fixed on the cryptic clues of the crossword, he had tuned in to the steps of those who had been passing by.

He had once read that a wolf in the darkness can pinpoint the sound of a human heartbeat from a distance of some fifteen metres or so. However, although he is not as finely tuned to the sounds of the beating of a heart as is the wolf, he is, nevertheless, proud of the fact that he, too, has been blessed with the flair of a hunter. After all, he is able to detect the sound of a woman's approach from a greater distance still; what's more, he can weigh her every detail with nothing more than that of the analysis of the rhythm of her gait.

The pace and the strike had been brisk and sharp. And, what with the fact that he had heard neither the sound of a scuff nor the accompaniment of a slap, the tone had suggested to him that the heel had belonged to the shoe of a rather healthy, agile and self-assured young woman.

Having made his assessment, he looks up for confirmation. His judgment is sound; she is, without doubt, a woman of poise, and what's more, she has something about her which he finds to be captivating.

He had already glanced up and dismissed those who had previously made their way along this ancient street as he had been able to evaluate and then conclude that they were of no interest to him.

He had also been of the opinion that they had all, to some extent, gone to seed. Although they were unquestionably female, with the excessive reddening to the lips and exaggerated shadings of blue around the eyes, they had overdone the process of prettification. As a result, they had, without exception, failed to deceive. If the truth be known, their integrity had been betrayed. Not just by the lie in their looks, but also by the truth of footsteps which could not mask the fact of there having been an undisguisable trait of the predator hidden behind the bows and frills of their deception.

However, he senses that this young woman is very different.

On the face of it, there appears to be no sign that she wishes to assume the traits of the promiscuous, and so, he guesses that she will, in the not too distant future, naturally pass on her sense of responsibility, along with the charm of her modesty, to that of her children. Hopefully, they, too, may follow her good example and continue to advance the ways of rectitude.

Although he suspects that she has an inherent confidence, he had not failed to notice the obvious signs of anxiety that had engulfed her as she had first seen the group of young men. The fact is, it was when she had tugged at her skirt and he had then glimpsed the slightest swing of the hips, that he had suspected that there may well have been another side to her personality; for, although her young, but mature, figure was emphasized for little more than an instant, it was enough to have stimulated a spark which would fire his greater interest. And so, as far as he is concerned … it was not his fault. After all, it was *she* who had cast the lure, and had she not done so, then, quite possibly, he would have allowed the moment to have passed, unquestioned.

Maybe he would have. Maybe he would not have. It matters not. The fact of the matter is that he had convinced himself that it was *she* who had been to blame, yet now it is *he* who is little more than a victim to her draw.

Having analytically watched her every movement, his thoughts start to run wild as he eagerly eyes the briefest of flashes from the sheen of her smooth satin slip, which, revealed only through the rhythmic opening and closing of the slash of her skirt, slides effortlessly against her skin as it flows with the movement of her thighs.

He is rapt in the image, and as he looks on, he cannot help but to feel the twinges of carnal desire.

Sharpening his focus, his senses edge beyond the level of simple excitement, towards the irresistible demand for sexual fulfilment. With his thoughts rushed and erratic, he probes his conscience in an attempt to justify the powerful surge in his desires.

On the face of it, she is a respectable young woman; he has already decided on that. But then, he has an inkling that, by the way in which she appears to give a welcome to the gentle touch of the fabric's feel of femininity as it, somewhat sensually, glides against her body, she must have her moments of weakness — moments when she will put aside the façade of respectable behaviour.

His judgement has never failed him before, and as far as he is concerned, it is unlikely to have failed him now. He will just carry on and follow his instincts; for he has concluded that she is, in all probabilities, not all that she seems.

Aware that she may soon be gone, he knows that there is urgency in his need to review the signs … and to then, if required, re-assess.

He weighs the evidence. *She certainly takes pleasure in the touch of the slip as it slides against her skin. What's more, she may, to a degree, feel somewhat enfeebled by the intoxicating seduction of its touch; after all,* he reasons, *she wouldn't wear it if she didn't want to feel that way. Of course,* he argues, as if acting in her defence, *it could simply be that the slip is integral with the design of her work attire, and that there is, in fact, no improper desire for her to be comforted by its feel. But then …* he cross-examines himself in his quest to find the proof of her guilt … *why would she be so at ease in the flaunting of the tell-tale signals of licentiousness whilst walking unaccompanied and, therefore, with a hint of vulnerability? Surely she would not have allowed the enticement of that provocative sway in her hips if she had not had the intent to allow her primordial signalling of subservience to signal availability and, thereby, attract the attention of the alpha male?*

These are questions which need answers.

Maybe, he had been wrong at the start and should not, after all, have given her the benefit of doubt with regard to her apparent need to feel the touch of seduction on her skin.

With the two observations taken together, his doubts are quashed. The evidence suggests that she is not as innocent as he had first thought; she is good-looking and most certainly has a lover. So, as a self-styled expert in the ways of women, he concludes that he had erred in his first assessment. In fact, on further consideration, it is more than probable that she — with the flirtatiousness of her ways along with her weakness in craving the feel of the caress of satin on her skin — will, in the end, use her feminine wiles for the purposes of deceit and betrayal.

With his doubts now validated and approved in his mind, he is satisfied; he will feel no guilt as he makes his move.

She passes by the young men and continues walking, her confidence regenerating with every step that separates her from them. Moving purposefully along the street, she gradually accelerates as she skirts the entrance to the arts centre before turning left and away from their view.

He checks his wristwatch; only nine minutes have elapsed since the hour of eight. Pushing his unfinished cappuccino to one side, he removes a pair of wraparound sunglasses from their case and puts them to his face. Although they are do not fit perfectly over the misshapen bridge of his nose, he finds them comfortable; so, composed and with his eyes obscured behind the shaded lenses, he rises to his feet and then walks out and onto the narrow street.

For a man of his years he appears to be reasonably fit; although the suggestion of a paunch and the beginnings of the premature whitening of his hair, along with a hint of reddening in his complexion, implies a slightly less than healthy liking for alcoholic beverages.

Careful not to draw unnecessary attention to himself, he moves calmly but with purpose; he needs to regain visual contact with the smartly-dressed woman.

He turns the corner.

She is nowhere to be seen.

He quickens his pace and hurries the few yards to the junction where the side-street adjoins the main thoroughfare.

He looks to his left and towards the heart of the city.

Again, she is not to be seen.

With the signs of his frustration beginning to show, he hurriedly scans each and every direction.

She is spotted.

A short sigh of relief confirms the sighting.

Her lone figure, unhurried but steadily, moves away from the city-centre.

He follows.

She has already passed the front of the museum and is now level with the entrance to the open-gated public gardens. Whilst still heading towards the clock tower, she slows, dips her hand into her bag and checks that she had not left her phone back in the shop.

A brief rummage and it's found.

She grasps it in her hand, pulls it out and then, having stopped for just a moment or two, flips open its top and glances at the screen.

Having confirmed that she has neither missed a call nor received a message by text, she replaces the phone and promptly resumes her course.

As she passes the railway station, she is blissfully unaware of the fact that he follows ... synchronously slowing and accelerating as he carefully keeps a respectable distance from his quarry.

The streets, which had earlier been streaming with the movement of shoppers and workers alike, have all but emptied. This is the in-between time — the time when those who would normally leave the city after their daytime occupations have, in the main, already departed, and those who enter for the evening entertainment in bars and clubs have yet to arrive.

The car parks are no longer packed to the gunwales, and the traffic wardens, or as they have, in recent years, been renamed — Civil Enforcement Officers, have gone home ... their services no longer required.

She is reassured by the latent security of the people who routinely go about their business, and with the knowledge that she has already put distance between herself and the four young men, her confidence has returned — it is evident in the way that she walks.

Her thoughts start to drift, and, with her handbag hanging loosely from its shoulder strap as she makes her way home, she unwinds from the trials and tribulations of her day.

The mobile phone rings. Slowing to almost a standstill, she removes it from her handbag.

She glances at the screen and smiles — it's from Chris.

Pressing the receive button, she flicks her abundance of titian tresses to one side and puts the phone to her ear. "Hi, I'm on my way home ... I got held up at work."

The pause in her progress as she answers the call allows him to gain a few extra yards.

Her step resumes, then quickens as she continues the conversation.

She has only recently moved in with her boyfriend, and the thrill of new love is still in her heart. To hear his voice lifts her spirits, and her sense of fatigue disperses.

As she moves onward — preoccupied with the distraction of her conversation — he crosses to the opposite side of the street.

Shadowing her, and with the darkness of his sunglasses disguising the focus of his attention, he is free to observe.

He peers over the shades and savours each tantalizing glint of shimmering satin.

He wants her. If necessary, he will have to assert himself on her, and armed with the notion that it will be for *her own good*, he is certain that she would, in the end, be grateful.

As his thoughts start to wander, he imagines how it would be to touch her and then, to hold her body close beside him as he runs his hands, slowly and purposefully along her youthful and supple thighs and then up and under her skirt.

Although he feels the blood surging through his body, he is unaware of the evidence in his veins which, having swollen to form ridges in his temples and cords in his arms, betray the secret of his inner excitement.

Enacting the scene in his mind, he envisions how her futile efforts to pull away would weaken and diminish, and with her pinned to the ground — fearful, but on the verge of submission — she would succumb to his muscular supremacy. Then, as she awaits the inevitable — and he prepares to thrust himself inside her — he can almost hear her ever-weakening cries being silenced as they are suffocated by the smothering of his mouth on hers.

Wallowing in these vivid imaginings of sensual delight, he cannot help but to summon up thoughts of himself squeezing between her thighs and, with his flesh touching hers, probing purposefully for the final and victorious entry.

He stalls as, with a sudden increase in the volume of traffic and in an effort to make herself heard above its invasive noise, she raises her voice.

Her words are clear — she *is* in love and, moreover, she is devoted to her man.

With her words echoing in his thoughts, he has doubts.

Maybe, he wonders, *his assessment was wrong.*

She is, it seems, smitten with her partner, and, with the benefit of what he has just heard, he realizes that the likelihood of her betraying her man is almost zero.

Having experienced the ordeal of being punished when he, as a child, had done no wrong, he is, even to this day, cognisant of the fact that the innocent need no reprimand. With his conscience to the fore, he stops and lets her go, unhindered; it is evident that she knows her place and therefore … she does not need to be subjected to *schooling*.

With the flames of his erotic fantasy now extinguished, he leaves her to disappear … unscathed.

Being oblivious, not only to his uninvited attention, but also, to the fact of his very existence, she will never know how close she had been to being scorched by the fires of hell.

As he turns about, he is chilled by an image — an image of hands squeezing around a pale and slender throat whilst delicate and manicured fingers desperately struggle to prise them away.

He is afraid of these recurring visions. They have troubled him for too many a year. At first, they had occurred only whilst he had been asleep. But, increasingly, they have taken to striking him during his waking hours and, in particular, when there has been within his view, the presence of an errant young lady who has been in need of *schooling*.

Removing his sunglasses, he welcomes the brightness of the light, for it is this that often helps to expel the echoes which haunt his soul.

Unsettled, he heads back towards the centre of the city, trying to distract himself with the recall of the times when, as a teenager, he would — with an upturned glass as a pointer and an alphabet of cards displayed in a circle — light-heartedly, and after the consumption of a few too many drinks, quiz the spirits on matters of little consequence.

He remembers, all too clearly, an element of success — a success which, real or otherwise, scared him then as it continues to scare him now.

Although outwardly he would always profess scepticism in the mysteries of the occult, privately, he had his concerns; for he had been certain that on more than one occasion, he had felt the touch of a presence.

As he returns along the walkway, he looks to his left … up and above the façade of those who trade their professions.

Registering, for the first time, the quartet of weathered faces which stare coldly out and across the street, he lingers for a few moments as he quizzically examines, in turn, the countenance of each stony form.

The severity in their expressions, albeit exacerbated by the residue of countless years of city traffic, leave no room for challenge or deception.

Suddenly, and with a chill rushing through his spine, he averts his gaze.

Agitated by the thought that the spirits of these ancient merchants may have, somehow, probed his deepest thoughts — and possibly, witnessed his misguided intent — he reactively hurries his pace and heads towards the anonymity of the more populated walkways of the High Street.

Striding forward, he explores the faces of those who approach, then pass … seeking confirmation that they had not shared the insight of the ancients.

The few whose eyes inadvertently meet his, turn their heads and step aside, ensuring the avoidance of a clash with *a man with a problem.*

He looks behind, checking for a *tail.* There is none. He glances back at the building and cusses at the unyielding stares of those stony-faced elders who — somewhat disparagingly — follow his every move.

He must make his escape.

As if trying to shake off a persistent and formidable foe, he again quickens his pace, erratically shifting his course as he scurries from walkway to walkway. Then, spotting the cover of the alleyway to his left, he takes refuge and disappears from view as if he were a wild and frightened rabbit fleeing into the darkness of some secret bolthole.

Chapter 28

"Jean-Paul, where is your Mother?"

"*Je ne sais pas, Papa,*" Jean-Paul replies with a shrug, then adds as an afterthought, "*Peut-être elle est à la maison.*"

"Son ... I'm speaking to you in English so that you will learn to speak it fluently. Okay? So ... from now on ... answer in English — understand?"

"*Oui ... d'accord.*" He turns away and grumbles his protest, "*Tu m'as compris ... quel est le problème?*"

As he walks off towards the rows of vines which he has tended with a passion from when he was a mere child, his father looks to the heavens and shakes his head in despair. "I give up!"

The boy certainly shares the traits of his mother. It is as if he has the ability to charm the birds from the trees one minute and then, within the blink of an eye, frustrate them into a premature and hasty migration with his mulish ways.

Still, his father can console himself with the thought that he's turned out to be a pretty good son, and even though he is still in his teens, he can run the business almost single-handed if needs be.

Tom knows that he has a son to be proud of — and even the stubborn streak of his may well be an asset in the years to come. Besides, it can be a hard and ruthless world, and so the ability to be able to stand one's ground may be all that stands between success and failure.

His reason to see Rozenn seems less important. Instead, he wanders off to enjoy the evening sunshine alone ... and at one with nature.

He stops at his favourite spot — a place from where he can readily survey both the silver-tinted greenery of his highly-productive spread of olive-bearing groves and then, with little more than the turn of his head and an adjustment to his focus, the revived and equally productive rows of vines which bathe on the sun-drenched slopes of his French retreat. As the abundance of pendulous ripening fruits absorb the warm caress of Earth's own bright and fiery star, it is as if they're preparing to offer themselves up as a just reward for his efforts which, with over a quarter of a century of devotion and attention, have successfully coaxed them back to a state of good health ... and ensured the continuation of their very existence. Interrupted only by the chirrupy song of the unseen cicada, he too savours the warmth and the serenity of the setting which, with the advantage of its elevation, is blessed with the most wonderful of panoramic views. Not being in his nature to take things for granted, he is always thankful to the good fortune which has permitted him the privilege to be able to gaze beyond the spread of his own somewhat modest acreage ... across the plain, with its scattering of sleepy villages and ancient churches, and towards the rugged and uninhabitable, jagged peaks of the far distant mountains.

A pair of ancient rocks, dated and scored with a name, mark the final resting-places of the paternal lineage of his present twosome of German shepherd dogs. This patch is kept clear of growth. It is reserved, not only for the laying to rest of his existing canine companions … but for his own interment.

Sonny — or *le loup* as Rozenn had, in what is now the distant past, taken it upon herself to refer to him as — had died many years before. He was just a few days past his eleventh birthday and had faithfully accompanied Tom through the trials and stresses of both his divorce and the loss of his daughter. Additionally, Sonny was also there for the good times — and being the *ever-helpful* companion, had readily disposed of any food which had come his way at the party which had followed the marriage of Tom to Rozenn.

The arrangement to keep a puppy in lieu of a stud-fee had suited him, since it was purely the desire to have the progeny of his beloved Sonny that had convinced him to embark on the dog-breeding trail.

Barter still survives within the traditional lifestyles of the rural community; somewhat ironically, it seems to be so much more civilised and refreshing than the clinical exchange of grubby notes and overly-handled cash. The continuation of the line was, for him, priceless. Having witnessed *Drifter*, the eldest of Sonny's progeny, growing up to echo the inherent traits of his father, Tom had been able to take some comfort in the knowledge that, even as he had been forced to face up to the grim reality of the loss of his faithful and dearly-loved companion, Sonny's genetic legacy was not wasted … and would thrive in the generations to follow.

The current incumbent of the post of top dog, being an unmistakable *chip off the old block*, and so a credit to the line of his grandfather, is himself showing the classic signs of age — what with the greying in the muzzle and the occasional stiffness in the hips. He is happy in himself … and that is all that matters. His own son has, on several occasions, made a rather tentative challenge for pack-leadership, but, as yet, he has met without success. However, the old boy is now no longer in a condition to fight off a challenge, and the youngster knows it. But, as if holding his father in a position of respect and secure in the knowledge that his inheritance is intact, he makes no issue of the matter. Instead, he appears to be content to patiently wait and then assume his place in the upper role when the time for ascendancy arrives.

Tom sits on a boulder and finds himself, as is the norm, talking to his dogs. Not just the two who are with him in both spirit and form … but, also, to the two who lie silently and beneath the soil.

Most people are able to visit and tend the graves of those of their family who are lost ... be it their mother, father, daughter or son ... but he has a dreadful and lonely loss: one which has no memorial — thus, nowhere for him to focus his grief or to sit in peace and say his goodbyes.

He often asks his *old friends* whether they have managed to find her among the myriad of souls that must wander through the mists of other planes. There has never been an answer ... and today is no exception; for, as the younger of his two companions presents a stone at his feet, and with a look in his eyes which plead for him to enjoy the simple things in life and play, he jolts himself back to reality. With the grasping of the stone and the sudden launch of a long and powerful throw, he spurs the dogs into a delightful pursuit. As he watches them run, each with the competitiveness of a single intent, he recalls how Sonny would have been be no different, and, in a moment of resignation, he reluctantly accepts the simple fact ... that life goes on.

Tom hears the call of his name. It is Rozenn.

"Ah! There you are. Are you okay?" Although naturally retaining the enchanting Gallic lilt in her voice, she often turns to *his* native tongue when she senses his pensive sadness. A sadness which can, without warning, cast its shadow over the brightest of days.

He turns to face her and tries, unconvincingly, to reassurance her. "Yea ... I'm fine ... thank you."

She knows that it is not true. He is far from fine, but she also knows that he will, as always, climb out of the rut before it can become too much of a problem.

She stands behind him and lays her hands on his shoulders, gently massaging his muscles whilst she, too, absorbs the peace and the beauty of the world which is spread around her. The relief from the physical tension which frequents his shoulders and neck is always welcome and, what's more, it goes a long way in assisting in the relief of the tension which is within his soul.

He breaks the silence. "I've been thinking ..."

She listens and waits for him to convey the substance of his thoughts.

"Do you know ... over the last few years, there have been several cases where a girl has been missing for a long time and then, suddenly, she's been found ... alive?"

She says nothing.

He continues. "There have also been a couple of times where a young woman has been found after she had been kept as a prisoner. Everyone had assumed her to have been dead."

He looks back towards his wife, searching for a reaction.

"*Oui,* It is so, but you must not think about this so much. It can only make you feel sad and ..." she searches for the word. "Helpless? Yes ... maybe helpless."

"I suppose you're right."

He stares out towards the horizon. She worries for him, and as if offering a display of moral support, she leans forward and whispers, *"Je t'aime"*

He tilts his head back and looks up at her and replies, "You too ... *Je t'aime"*

"You know, maybe I ought to go to England for a few weeks. I must try to sort this out once and for all."

"Pardon?" The word may look the same in both languages but, with the intonation in her voice, her reply can be none other than the version of that of the more gentile, Française.

Returning to the vernacular of her native tongue, he echoes his thoughts. *"Je pense je doit aller à pour, peut-être, deux ou trois et essaie découvrir si n'importe qui peut aider trouver Lucy. Je lui dois donner un plus d'hasard."*

"Je comprends. Mais et les affaires?"

She understands his need to resolve the mystery of his daughter's disappearance, but she also feels the need to express her concern for the maintenance of both home and business whilst they are away.

"Peut-être Jean-Paul?" He suggests that maybe their son could take charge for the period that he is away.

"Non, il est trop jeune. Tu devais faire ceci seul. Je resterai avec Jean-Paul pendant que tu es absent."

She believes that Jean-Paul is still too young to take the full responsibility of the chateau — what with the extent of its lands and the general day-to-day running of the business. So, although she would like to accompany her husband in his quest for closure, she has made her decision ... she will stay with Jean-Paul and leave Tom to make the emotional and painful journey alone.

"Est-ce que tu es certain?"

"Oui, tu devais faire ceci."

With the backing of Rozenn and the knowledge that the business will be in safe hands, Tom will make the necessary arrangements for travel. He will ensure that he keeps the date for his return to France open-ended; after all, he will not want to be rushed as he endeavours to finalise the mystery of Lucy's disappearance.

Chapter 29

Tom watches the steady disembarkation of vehicles which — led by a trio of old British motorcycles, each of which are mounted by a couple of fifty-something enthusiasts — snake away from the ferry and off towards the unhurried roads of Normandy.

There are no heavy trucks, nor are there any large coaches; they have been restricted by their size into having to embark onto one of the slower and more traditional ships which stoically ply their way, back and forth, across one of the busiest shipping lanes on the planet.

As he glances at the vehicles that surround him, he cannot help but to notice that his car is one of the few which are left-hand-drive and is on French registration plates. In the main, he knows that this route is travelled by those who wish to embrace all things French, but there are the few who have not been prepared to completely let go of their ties to the home country. Even with many years of cross-channel flitting behind them, some *Brits* still struggle to master even the must basic elements of the Gallic tongue ... and at times resort to a rise in volume when they are not fully understood.

He tunes the radio to a U.K. station and the sound of *Kirsty McColl* singing her version of *Ray Davies's ... Days*, fills the car.

Tom whispers along with the chorus while his foot gently taps the beat. As memories start to flood forward, he holds back the welling of a tear ... and his foot, almost with a suggestion of guilt, falls still. The link of the song with the carefree days of his long-lost youth was dampened a long time ago; it was much later, at the peak of his heartache and loss, when this infectious tune had re-emerged to echo in his mind whilst he had waited, in hope, for news.

Words, poignant in their effect and sung with a passion that makes him feel as if they were created for him personally, still hit deep and play havoc with his innermost feelings.

How could he forget any of the wonderful days that he shared with his daughter? Those were the *sacred days* ... the days which still are, and always will be, treasured in his thoughts.

An image of Lucy, with her infectious smile lighting her face, flashes through his mind; for he, too, has come to *bless the light* that had once shone so brightly on her. But it is always the words which follow ... *although you're gone, you're with me every single day, believe me* ... which always manage to hit home and bring a watery haziness to his vision.

Even with the passing of more than two decades, it is difficult, to say the least, for him to accept the notion that she has gone ... and that he will never see the radiance of her smile again.

He is distracted by the approach and purposeful movement of half-a-dozen men and women who, being dressed in high-visibility jackets, stimulate the starting-up of the vehicles as their drivers wait in anticipation for the signal to board.

The wave to move forward is given — the embarkation is on.

He is sixth in the queue, but there is no rush; seats on the high-speed vessel are not at a premium, and there will be no contest for a prime position. He will find a quiet spot and relax.

Once ushered into place and parked up, he makes his way up the pedestrian slope and into the main seating area and then reserves his place by leaving his jacket on his chosen seat.

With the purchase of the UK edition of *The Mail* and with a much-needed cup of coffee, he returns to his seat, sits back and flicks through the pages as he awaits the first signs of the voyage having commenced. He hasn't read a *truly* British daily newspaper for quite some time, and although he periodically keeps up to date with events on the internet, he still likes the feel of a real newspaper and the action of having to physically turn each page.

To some, it may seem strange for an Irishman — especially one who hails from south of the border — to consider himself as being not only Irish, but also British and European; but in an ever-shrinking world he wonders if the presence of borders are there primarily to protect the interests of the politicians and the elite.

With the change of pitch in the sound of the engines, accompanied by the movement away from the quayside walls, he is distracted from his thoughts and instinctively checks the time. The departure is on time.

With a settled sea allowing a cruising speed of around forty knots, he estimates that he should be on the road at Poole in a little more than a couple of hours.

As he glances from the paper to the sparkle of the sun on the gentle swells of the open sea, his mind drifts back to the day when Philippe had arrived to pass the message for him to contact Detective Inspector Graham Dowsett. This was the day when his life had been turned on its head and his sense of self-worth had been put into doubt. The thought that he had failed to be there for his daughter, and that he had also failed to find her in the weeks which had followed, had left him with a deep feeling of guilt.

He looks back to the paper and turns the page.

Tucked away and about a quarter of the way in, there is an article about an unnamed man who, having been arrested a couple of days previously on suspicion of having subjected a teenage girl to a serious sexual assault on the Penwith peninsular of West Cornwall, had now been absolved from suspicion and released.

Forensic tests, along with his irrefutable alibi, had proven his innocence, which, of course, must have given him an unfathomable amount of relief. But, with no forensic evidence available regarding Lucy's disappearance, Tom wonders what chance, if any, the police would have of proving someone's guilt if they had a suspect in custody.

No details regarding the nature of the attack had been published in the article, and the incident had occurred over a hundred miles from the administrative heart of Tom's adopted home county of Devon. Yet there was a suggestion that, as there were striking similarities in the modus operandi, there could be a link with an unsolved murder in which a young woman had been left for dead in a lay-by near Okehampton some ten years previously.

With the instigator of these horrendous attacks still at large, women living in Cornwall and Devon are again being warned to be vigilant … especially when out on their own.

Although at the time of Lucy's disappearance, the police had seemed satisfied that her abductor had taken his own life, Tom has always had his doubts. For over two decades he has clung to the hope that she would eventually be found. Whether she is found alive or whether she is found dead — the fact of the matter is … his need to find her is real.

He needs to know one way or another so that he can say sorry for not being there to protect her and, also, to give her the respect of having a proper burial.

Sailing past the waterside homes of the wealthy and famous, he prepares for the disembarkation; it will not be too long before they arrive and are in dock.

With the Sat-nav switched on and adjusted to read in miles as opposed to the kilometres of France, he adjusts the clock in the car to coincide with British Summer Time.

It has been a while since he had last driven on the left side of the road, and spurred with a hint of trepidation, he does what he did so many years ago and when he had first taken to the road in France. Although he is travelling alone, as he sits in his car awaiting the opening of the ferry doors and the accompanying flood of daylight, he audibly repeats the reminder of *driver to the kerb … passenger to the crown,* until he is sure that he has instilled the required change of mindset.

With the docking complete and the go-ahead given, the cars file off and, in an orderly fashion, head towards the kiosks of passport control.

There are no hold-ups. He joins the throng of traffic which heads away from the port and then out towards the primary routes where the new arrivals will disperse as they head for their destinations.

Chapter 30

He is in no rush. As he stands at the counter, he savours the warm aroma of freshly percolated coffee which drifts through the air as the *barista* prepares the previous customer's order.

Careful to maintain a respectable distance, she stands behind him. This is Britain, and the British *do* queues. In fact, she observes, that without her presence then there would be no queue, for he is at the front and now she at the rear.

She is slim. And for a woman, she is as tall. In fact, she is close on being as tall as he is; but then, she has benefited from a relatively minor, but not entirely inconsequential, deception — she has the advantage of having three-and-a-half-inch heels on her calf-length boots.

Glancing at his profile, she cannot help but to note how pleasant it is to see a man of his years who can stand upright yet look down and still maintain sight of his own feet.

His athletic build and tanned complexion, combined with a casual but well-tailored look, suggests a man who is not only self-assured but who has benefited from an interesting and wholesome life in a sunnier and more distant land.

Suited, he stands tall; a good six feet.

Crisp and light, with its fabric reflecting the ambience of the virgin sands of far-off tropical shores, his jacket hangs open and over the contrasting, yet complimentary, olive hue of his open-necked cotton shirt.

His hair, although showing the first signs of thinning, is, to all intents and purposes, full. Its tone, dark and rich, albeit with the slightest hint of silvery-grey, belies the truth of his years ... and with it emits an intoxicating aura of fitness and health; an aura which has served him well when in the company of attractive and more youthful women. Although he enjoys the attention received, his love, sense of loyalty and respect for his wife leaves no room for even the thought of transgression.

"Good merchandising ploy." With a smile which shines through her eyes, she attracts his attention.

"Sorry?" he answers, wishing to confirm both the content and whether or not he is the intended recipient of her statement.

"The pastries — they look delicious!" she replies, pointing to the glass-covered display of assorted croissants and pastries which sit temptingly on the counter beside the payment till.

He looks at the fare, then back to her. "Well ... it obviously works ..." As if confirming the success of the sales technique, he adds, "I've ordered the almond croissant."

With temptation getting the better of her, she states her preference.

"Well, in that case, I think mine's just got to be … the chocolate twist."

Compelled by the warmth within the café, she removes her jacket, no longer disguising the near-perfect form of her natural feminine attributes. Pretty she is not, but then, there is something of a mystery about her which has an appeal of its own.

The *barista*, somewhat opportunely, distracts him from the potential embarrassment of being caught with his eyes, albeit unintentionally, focused a little too low for comfort.

With the croissant plated and put on a tray, he observes the way in which she, almost robotically, conducts the latte-making ritual.

Having poured the hot, foaming milk into a tall, clear glass, she then taps it onto the worktop three times, thus, allowing the bubbles to settle. Then, with her left hand, she automatically reaches for the small cup which contains the hot coffee and pours it onto the milk. Mesmerized by the procedure, he watches as the coffee disperses throughout the drink, turning the white to khaki. She taps the glass one more time, before topping it up with a dash more milk. Prepared, his latte is placed on the saucer beside the croissant.

He picks up his tray, and as he turns to locate a suitable table, he catches the eye of the lady who has a liking for chocolate twists. He nods towards the croissants and pastries. "Enjoy."

"Thank you … I'm sure I will."

The expression behind her response has the twist of good-humour.

As he turns away, he overhears her placing her order.

"May I have a hot chocolate? And … may I have it with cream and marshmallows?"

The *barista* nods. "One chocolate and … anything else? Any cakes or pas —"

"Oh yes ….and a chocolate twist, thank you."

Hot chocolate … with cream and marshmallows. Her choice of beverage echoes in his mind. After all, this had always been the preference of his beloved Lucy.

Although many tables remain unoccupied, the one of his choosing is tucked away, offering a semblance of seclusion near the back, but to the left of the coffee shop's seating area. The warmly-lit décor gives an air of peaceful privacy … a retreat from the hustle and bustle of the city streets.

He sits quietly, his back to the wall, whilst absorbing the background sounds of a sleepy saxophone which *feels* its way through a soulful melody. Relaxed, he breaks into the croissant and then looks up, having been distracted by the movement of a tray — with a chocolate twist and a mug of hot drinking chocolate — being placed on a table which is opposite but slightly askew and to the left of his.

She pulls back a chair and sits facing in his general direction. With her drink and twist positioned on the table, she removes the tray and rests it against the wall ... so out of her way. A paperback book, retrieved from the black canvas bag which leans untidily beside her chair, is placed on the table in preparation to be absorbed.

Leaning forward, she spoons a marshmallow off the cream-capped drink and pushes it gently between her lips. She lifts her hand and, with a napkin, she gently dabs away any traces of the cream. Glancing over to him, she catches his eye and smiles. Her enjoyment is obvious as she savours that *melt-in-the mouth* moment. He returns the smile and looks away.

She opens the book. It's a novel. Although he cannot recall the name, he recognizes the face on the cover as that of the actress who had portrayed *Tess* in the BBC's television adaptation of Thomas Hardy's novel. One of the advantages of having satellite television is that he can, when the occasion demands, keep in touch with the *old Country* and watch British programmes whilst maintaining the climatic, financial and social benefits of his vineyard home.

Resting an elbow on the back of her chair, she leans back. Her hand pushes back her straight, rich-chestnut hair and holds it behind her ear, exposing the classic lines of the cheeks of her face as she becomes engrossed in the text before her. Her make-up is restrained — a hint of slate around the eyes and a blush to the lips. The rounded décolletage of her thin, blue jumper cradles a silver leaf pendant which is suspended delicately on a chain from around her neck.

Her right leg rests across the thigh of her left, and the three-quarter-length faded, blue denim jeans reveal the line of her boot, which moves in perfect time with the rhythm of the subtle background music of the city café.

As she reads, her hand moves from her head and rests with her fingers, unnaturally, outstretched on her left thigh, thus, overexposing the nakedness of the ring-finger and, as a result, indicating an apparent lack of any commitment to a monogamous relationship.

She pauses from her book and spoons another marshmallow from the top of her drink and into her mouth. Again she glances across to him and smiles before returning to her read.

Reaching a convenient place in the text, she slides the till receipt between the pages, as a marker, before closing the book and returning it to her bag. A further rummage through its contents results in the retrieval of a ballpoint pen and a small pocket-notebook, which is then duly opened ... and perused. She stops and looks blankly into nothingness ... her hands cradled around her drink as if searching for inspiration. She takes a sip — inspiration achieved. Pen to paper, her writing commences — pausing periodically as she looks up for further inspiration.

Whilst he consumes his croissant — a piece at a time and between sips of coffee — he feels certain that she is concealing an awareness of his discreet but, reassuringly, non-threatening fascination for her. Although she only occasionally looks directly at him, he senses that he is constantly being observed, albeit at the periphery of her vision.

She looks over to him, catches his eye, and indicates to what remains of the croissant and asks, "Is it good?"

He nods as he finishes his mouthful, before replying.

"Yes. It's good."

He sees no need to mention that, in his opinion, nothing can beat the taste of those which are made in the *boulângerie* of the village which is only a few minutes drive from his home.

"And yours?" he asks in return.

"Delicious," she responds, her smile blissfully reflecting the sweetness of its flavour.

"With the weather we've had this summer … it seems obvious that you haven't picked up *your* tan locally."

Her observation, although in the form of a statement, is, in reality, a veiled question — no doubt designed to eke out a response and thus be the start to a conversation.

"No … you're right … I live abroad."

Anticipating the next question, he confirms the locality. "Southern France."

"Sounds wonderful … If you don't mind me asking, what do you do?"

"Me? … I'm in business."

He immediately changes tack, cautious not to reveal too much about himself, and so, redirects the focus of questioning to her. "And you? Are you local?"

"Sort of — I've lived around here for six, or is it seven years, I can't remember exactly."

"So … what do you do with yourself, apart from flirting with men old enough to be your father, that is?"

The bluntness of his words, along with his infectious smile and the spark of mischief in his eyes, fascinate her and, accordingly, she cannot take offence.

"I people-watch." She looks at him, her head slightly cocked, as she awaits his response.

"Amateur psychologist? Mmm…"

She does not answer. Instead, she looks straight into his eyes and then, without further comment, averts her gaze.

He contemplates the situation … digesting the varying degrees of the subtlety of her body-language and, also, assessing how likely it would be for her actions to bear some relationship to her *interest*.

The forwardness of her communication, the over-emphasized stretch of her body as she had removed her jacket, the apparent engrossment in a classic work of romantic fiction and the contrived display of an empty ring-finger suggests an element of artifice ... with actions not to dissimilar to that of a spider which is weaving a web of entrapment.

He concludes that a link is likely and declares his hand. "If that *is* the case, then I suspect, that maybe it is *I* who has become the subject of your people-watching."

She laughs *with* him, as opposed to *at* him, as she realizes how life-experience has honed his instincts. "How did you guess?"

"Oh ... I don't know — maybe I'm psychic," he replies, with a teasing but knowing smile.

"Was I *that* obvious?"

"Have I sussed you out?"

She nods.

"Then, probably, you were. Perhaps it's just a case of *a little knowledge being a dangerous thing.*"

"Perhaps you're right — and I'm sorry if I've offended you."

"No ... You've not offended me, at all."

"Well, as I said, I really am sorry. Maybe I should explain myself. The thing is ... I'm trying to write a novel. This is my fourth attempt at the one story — and studying relationships ... and, in particular, how men react to women when in different environments, is helpful to my storyline. For example: does a man find a subservient woman more appealing than a woman with self-confidence? Or is it a turn-off? Anyway ... I place myself in a situation ... I act a part, and then I see where it goes. It's research."

"Mmm... Of course you could be playing a dangerous game!" he warns — instinctively protective, as a father would be to a daughter.

"Perhaps. But, you seem to be a really nice guy ... and now I'm beginning to feel a little embarrassed. I hope you don't mind."

"Do I mind that you're embarrassed? Or do I mind that you've tried to play me?" He doesn't wait for a reply. Instead, he puts her at ease with a smile, and answers, "No ... I don't mind at all."

There is a short silence as he decides whether or not he should enquire deeper into her intentions. His inquisitive nature dictates the option of further enquiry. "You don't have to answer this, but were you waiting to see if I'd picked up on something ... and then see if I'd try to chat you up?"

She nods, somewhat self-conscious at her own actions but, at the same time, happy and relieved that her initial assessment of his kind character appears to be accurate. "Yes ... I'd like to try and introduce a different angle to one of my characters, and I wasn't sure if it would work, in practice."

"Did it? Did it work?"

"I'm not sure."

He looks into her eyes and asks, "Then tell me ... what would you have done if I *had* tried to chat you up?"

Captivated by his gaze, she peers back and, as if plumbing hidden depths before daring to answer, she waits, then answers, "I don't know ... I really don't know."

"Well ... I'll take your response as a compliment, but ... I do have a wife ... and a son and, also, a daughter who is ... What I mean to say is ... a daughter who *would* have been ... just a few years older than you."

She is not slow to sense the well-disguised but noticeable pain in his expression. His thoughts, as if having been tossed across an ocean of time, are suddenly elsewhere. As he flits through an album of memories − in which the good seems to be so readily annulled by the bad − he catches himself sliding towards a world in which only sorrow and self-pity reside. Recalling the words of a singer who had once gained international fame in the sixties, whilst singing his songs of protest against the war in Vietnam, he puts the brakes on the slide. Their paths had met many years ago ... and by chance. He had been in his late teens and had been asked to assist backstage. The singer was not only performing, but he was also urging all those who had come to listen not to follow the path that he had taken − a lifestyle of addiction and questionable morals.

After the show, they had talked. On asking how he, the singer, had responded in times when gripped by despair and he had found himself slipping on a steep and dangerous downward path, he had replied in a slow and emphatic Californian accent *"Well ... I say to myself ... hey man ... you've been here before and you ... did ... not ... like it. So ... you're just gonna have to go right back up again. That's what I do ... I make myself go right back up again."*

Those few words have been an inspiration to Tom throughout his life, and because of that, he has been eternally grateful to fate for allowing the occurrence of such an unlikely encounter.

As the words of the singer reverberate in his mind, he climbs out of the hole, looks up at her, smiles politely and returns to reality. "You're clearly a bright young woman ... and I think you should have a bright young life. I think the time to live in the company of the more mature − I'm not too keen on ... old." He sighs ... then, with a half-smile, continues. "*Old* will come soon enough. Don't take life too seriously and don't ever accept second-best. Enjoy your life, and write your book − I'll look forward to seeing your face in the literary pages ... and then I'll think, *wow*, I met this woman *before* she became famous."

He observes her thoughtful silence as she accepts, a little reluctantly, the wisdom of his words. "Your children are lucky to have a father like you."

He nods — more as a gesture of politeness and an acknowledgement of the existence of her statement, rather than it being an expression of agreement with its content.

With his face no longer reflecting the character of a man who is truly at ease, he responds, "Thank you."

"Do you mind if I join you?" she asks, aware that talking across two tables cannot be conducive to privacy, nor can it be considered as sensitive to the feelings of others who sit within earshot.

"Sure. Feel free."

She joins him.

"I'm sorry if I've hit a nerve." Her apology is sincere and demonstrates a level of concern.

"It's okay — it's not you." He feels that, in order to confirm that she is not directly responsible for his sadness, an explanation is owed.

"The truth is ..." He pauses as he attempts to defeat the resistance which prevents the rest of his explanation from leaving his mouth. "What I'm trying to say is, my daughter went missing more than twenty years ago, and no one seems to know what happened to her."

She listens intently as she shakes her head in disbelief. Not that she does not believe him, but rather that she can hardly believe that she is talking to a man who has suffered and carried the pain of his loss over such a long time.

He sees the empathy in her eyes. "You're a stranger ... and I'm not going to burden you with my problems."

"Don't they say a stranger is just a friend you haven't yet met?"

Her response, although somewhat banal, suggests an invite to continue and that she is neither embarrassed nor offended by this release of his tragic and personal information.

The thought that it may well have been a stranger who had been responsible for the disappearance of Lucy, challenges the adage. Choosing to keep his views within, he, from behind the mask of a smile, conveys his gratitude for her understanding and sympathetic reaction.

Tentatively, she probes for more. "I hope you don't mind me asking ... but what happened?"

He does not answer immediately. Instead, he gazes down at his drink, in thought. Although one part of him wants to bury the past, another accepts that her disappearance will never be resolved if nothing is ever said or done. He looks up and returns his attention to her.

"No, I don't mind. I suppose you're in her age group and, maybe, some friends of yours could have heard something."

As he speaks, he finds difficulty in convincing *himself*, never mind anyone else, of the likelihood of any of her friends knowing anything of worth.

She acknowledges him in silence as she waits for him to continue.

There is a pause as he prepares himself to release the shackles that secure his deepest memories. "Well … Lucy, that's my daughter, was eighteen. Her mother and me had split-up a long time beforehand. She'd moved on and got remarried. Lucy, as is par for the course, lived with her mum and her mum's new bloke. I suppose, officially he was her step-dad." He pauses, not liking to think that his own role of her father had been usurped by that *arrogant, alcohol-dependant sleazebag*. "Anyway … they'd all been to a wedding do … and I understand that she stormed off after a bust up with her boyfriend."

She feels the energy from his pent up anger and looks at him in anticipation of there being more to his story.

There is no more.

"That's it. That's all we know."

She is surprised at the brevity of the circumstances. "What? … No trace? … No messages?"

"That's right. Nothing! Nothing at all. She'd just gone. Disappeared into thin air!"

"And the police? What did they think had happened?"

He feels discomfort with the thought of burdening her, a complete stranger, with detail, so, with that in mind, the fact of Joe's suicide is kept to himself. "I don't know. Probably the worst."

She tries to think of circumstances which could give some hope as to her still being alive. She struggles. "Maybe, she went to a friend … and after all the fuss, she was afraid to come back?"

Her suggestion is weak and she knows it.

"Maybe … she was taken by the bloody fairies?" he snaps back, sarcastically.

Instantly, he is overcome by a wave of guilt as he realizes that she is only trying to be helpful. "I'm sorry — I didn't mean to snap at you."

"That's all right. No offence taken." She knows that under the same circumstances she would be far less restrained than him.

"I cling on to threads." The delivery of his words become more stilted as if they have been disrupted by the opening of old wounds. "I see girls just like her … and I wonder, could it be? But, deep down, I know she's …"

He cannot say the word. *Dead* is too final!

She, too, is silent — it's hard to disagree with his conclusion.

"That's why I'm back in the UK," he explains, as he turns away from negativity and towards something which is far more constructive. "I'd like to see if I could get the media to take an interest in the case. Maybe they could broadcast an anniversary appeal."

"What … Like *Crimewatch*?"

"Yea. Something on those lines, I guess."

He does not sound overly hopeful of him achieving his wish. In fact, the very thought of a re-enactment of his daughter's disappearance, along with the grief of both her mother and him being broadcast on primetime television as a form of entertainment, fills him with dread.

"I'm hoping that someone, somewhere, will be able to shed some light on the truth."

"They often get success you know?" She tries to give him encouragement.

"So I understand ... but there is another thing which worries me."

"And ... what's that?"

"I've had no contact with Gina, that's Lucy's mother, since the immediate aftermath of her disappearance. And, if I'm honest, I still can't forgive her for accusing *me* of coaxing Lucy over to France ... and then hiding her. Mud sticks! Even now there are those who still point the finger at me. Why would I take *my own* daughter? She was old enough to come to me openly if she'd wanted to."

"Maybe her mother was also clutching at straws. Maybe she was hoping, deep down, that if she was with you ... then at least she would have been safe?"

"Maybe ... but then, the time and the money which has been wasted by the police in chasing up her baseless accusations would have been better spent in investigating the scene ... and checking out all the people who were there."

She nods. She cannot disagree with his reasoning.

"Do you know?" he continues, "... I often lie in bed and I think I can hear her calling me."

His eyes start to water. "I can actually hear her voice ... deep inside ... crying out for me ... her Dad. It sounds weird, but even after all this time, I still feel absolutely useless. I mean — I couldn't find her ... so I must've failed her. A father should be there for his little girl ... and, at the end of the day, I've let her down."

"No, you haven't. I'm sure you did all you could. It's not your fault."

"I can't have done enough. If I had done, then I would have found her. Do you know what hurts the most?"

She shakes her head.

"Sometimes, when I close my eyes ... I can't picture her. I can't see her face. It's as if I've forgotten what she looked like. Tell me ... what sort of father can't remember what his own daughter even looked like?"

She looks at him as he wipes his hand across his cheek, removing the irritation of a tear.

"It's normal. It's just a normal defence mechanism which is designed to save you from too much hurt." She pauses and adds, "It doesn't mean to say you love her any less. In fact … I think it means the opposite."

"Do you *really* believe that?"

"Yes, I *really* do. Your mind only needs to protect itself from memories which hurt. You love her and you always will."

He pauses for a moment as he takes in her words. "Thank you."

"You're welcome."

She gives him a reassuring smile, then adds, "You just keep searching … I think you deserve to find her, and, in any case, you certainly deserve closure."

"You're right. I'm sorry to have burdened you with all this."

"Don't be sorry — I invited it."

He knows she's right, but that does not prevent him from feeling a little uncomfortable with his display of vulnerability.

"Look for the signs. Wherever we go … we leave signs."

She asks, "What is more likely to end in success? For you to run around aimlessly looking for your daughter? Or for your daughter to *allow* herself to be found? All I can say is, read the signs and follow your instincts. If she wants to be found … then she'll leave the signs for you to follow."

Is there wisdom in her words? he wonders. *Or are they little more than that of an irrelevance?* As far as he can gather, she is sounding as if she is touching on the *mumbo jumbo*. If she is, then he cannot help but to wonder if she is not quite as *sound* as he had first thought.

Seeing the look of doubt in his eyes, she tries to explain. "Look … when you came to this place, you just wanted a coffee. Am I right?"

He confirms the accuracy of her observations with a slight nod of his head.

"Well … I *wanted* to be found by someone — and that someone just happened to be you. I *deliberately* left signs which you then picked up on. Right?"

Again, he nods.

"Well then … just look for the signs. Go back to the beginning … and look for them."

He remains pensively silent.

"Have you ever been on a train …" she asks, "and seen an old girlfriend, standing on the platform, alone and totally unaware of you being there?"

"No … But go on. I'm listening."

"Well, if you did … would you wave your arms and bang on the window to attract her attention?"

He nods and replies with no more than a tentative, "Maybe. It would depend on why we split."

"Okay … the ex-girlfriend thing may not have been a good idea. But what I'm trying to say is, maybe your daughter can still see you on that platform ... and *maybe* ... she'll want to wave her arms and knock on the window, hoping that you will see her."

She glances at her watch and, as if late for an appointment, suddenly pushes her chair right back, stands and, just before making her exit, leans over to plant a quick, but gentle, kiss on his cheek and whispers, "Look ... I'm sorry, I must go, and I *really do* hope you find each other."

"Thank you."

She smiles, picks up her bag and her jacket, and then turns. Without further ado, she walks briskly out of the café and disappears into the anonymity of the city street.

He stands up as if to shout after her, but realising that without knowing her name he could not call her back, he hesitates and sits back down.

It is too late. She has gone!

He sips the lukewarm remains of the coffee, pushes it to one side and then sits quietly as he takes time to reflect on the significance of this unexpected and strange encounter. With her depositing much food for thought, he takes time to weigh the merit of her words as they reverberate within his mind.

He whispers to himself, *"Maybe she's right. Just follow the signs. Look for the evidence."*

Sitting alone, his thoughts are all over the place as he questions himself over the futility of her advice. How can he follow signs which cannot be seen and, furthermore, which probably do not exist? But still, he will open his mind and, at least, give her the benefit of the doubt ... after all, he has nothing left to lose.

***

The worth of the meeting of two strangers which, at the time, seemed powerful and meaningful, has now, unsurprisingly, lost its impetus. He knows she had meant well, but the lack of life-experience reflected in her simplistic advice seems to have lessened the value of the experience.

Signs? What planet does she think I'm on? His thoughts lead him from a state of incredulity to a feeling of embarrassment as he realizes how easily he had allowed himself to have revealed his innermost feelings to this mysterious young lady.

It's time to shake himself down and to venture out into the growing bustle of the street.

He cannot help to notice how the city has changed over the years. Where there used to be a single, imposing and helmeted policeman patrolling the thoroughfares, now there are a pair of flat-capped, *police community support officers* wearing the uniform, but not bearing the powers.

He surmises that these must be the, somewhat infamous, *Blunkett's Bobbies* which he had read about a few years back. He wonders as to the success and effectiveness of this blatant *money-saving exercise. Surely*, he thinks, *one well-trained officer, endowed with all the powers of arrest, is going to be cheaper than two of these new officers who, although paid less individually, receive more when patrolling as one.* He much prefers the tried and tested ways of the past.

"Can you spare some change?" The voice of the beggar, who sits huddled on the pavement, is weak, but the image behind the façade is strong and intimidating. He has interrupted the privacy of Tom's observations. So, ensuring there is no eye contact, he ignores him and walks on by.

"Have a good day." Is there a touch of sarcasm in his good wishes? It is difficult to tell as the response is so routine that he suspects that he may well be devoid of any desire to express such a sentiment.

He continues on his way, absorbing the familiar and the unfamiliar alike. He recalls the times when, as a young man, he would wander the town with a friend or two, *killing time* whilst going from record shop to record shop where, in the privacy of a sound booth, they would listen to the latest releases of their favourite groups.

Yes, he thinks, *In those days it was groups — nowadays, it's bands. Even the description of a guitar-based foursome has changed ... and whatever happened to good old-fashioned R'n'B?*

He remembers the old rhythm and blues ... with the likes of *John Mayall and the Bluesbreakers,* along with the early *Stones* and a host of other young and wild, long-haired musicians filling the airwaves and exciting the senses. It was not the so-called R'n'B of today — *so why ...* he questions *...did they have to hi-jack the name? Surely they could have been original? Ah well...* he sighs *... I guess it's just a case of c'est la vie.*

His thoughts are, again, interrupted, but this time by the voice which booms out from the doorway of a shop premises which, having fallen victim to the recent recession, is no longer open for business.

"Get your Big Issue here! Form an orderly queue! Only one left ... before I take out another one, that is. Don't miss out, buy your copy today!"

At least the vendors of the *Big Issue* are, in contrast to his previous encounter, making an effort to make an honest pound and, in their own way, add an element of humour and character to the somewhat samey format of the city centre.

Things have changed ... and not all for the good. Back in rural France, they still try to keep a sense of history with their traditional, narrow, busy streets — each filled with the individuality of small shops, brimming with a variety of home-sourced products.

His eyes start to scan the faces of the people as he subconsciously looks for the familiarities of those from his past.

He cannot help but to notice a pair of women in their mid-twenties and sporting orange-tinted tans with blemish-free complexions. He keeps his desire to laugh to himself, for this lack of natural imperfection, combined with the even spread of *tan*, has given a clue to the deception; it has been sourced from out of a bottle. It makes him wonder if his home country has developed into a nation of deceit ... with the open begging on the streets by those who need not beg, and the sleight of hand and blatant dishonesty of those who should know better having become the norm. This is not just the preserve of the less well-off. From the what he has gleaned from the newspapers, it appears to be prevalent in the highest echelons of Government, and has slithered downwards to the minions at the bottom.

His observation seems to be confirmed, as a group of loudmouthed, young men — all dressed in an unflattering uniform of hooded-tops, baggy-joggers and designer trainers — swagger with exaggerated and agitated movements towards him. They don't seem to care that their very presence forces the elderly from the paths and into the street. The one in white — his clothes grubby with constant wear, leads the group as they strut around the street like *Jack-the-lads*, claiming ownership as they, weasel-like, look for opportunities to bully and steal. He concludes that these are not the unemployed. They are the unemployable — those who are of the criminal fraternity and who are not bright enough to see that their efforts to disguise their identity with hooded garments, ironically, only serves to draw attention to themselves, thereby, attracting the scrutiny of the security-guards and store-detectives who patrol the stores and streets of the city centre.

They pass him by without incident. He relaxes.

Having refocused his attention on the detail in his surroundings, he ventures into the newly-constructed centre, with its well-lit frontages and an abundance of restaurants and cafés. The quality of the window displays and the traffic-free environment emits a sense of well-being and obviously attracts people from far and wide to spend the honest spoils of their hard-earned efforts.

It is busy ... but in the alfresco ambience of cafés where — with tables spread across the pedestrian precinct and set against a background of tuneful sounds from a group of busking musicians — people enjoy their *tête-à-têtes* as they take in refreshments, there is a sense of calm.

The briefest glimpse of a raven-haired young woman amongst a crowd of people who are converging into the entrance of the large departmental store, seizes his attention.

His heart jumps a beat as he hurries towards the entrance and instinctively starts to call out to her.

"Lu —"

He stops mid-word as he realizes that for this to have been his lost daughter, she would have had to have held back the years of time way beyond the bounds of possibility. Lucy would be approaching middle-age and therefore would be some twenty years older the girl who he has just seen. He wonders if having been fuelled by his conversation in the café, he has allowed his deepest wishes to override logic and, in an act of self-deception, attempted to forge fact from fiction.

Chapter 31

She can see that the computer terminals are all in use. Those who wish to fill the next available position are sitting quietly as they scan the cubicles for the first signs of a vacation.

The Central Library had opened barely twenty minutes earlier. So, with the free internet access for the public having been set for a mere half-hour, there will, in all probabilities, be another five or ten minutes of waiting. After all, most will stay to the end of the session and then exodus as if as one.

She is in no hurry. It is Sunday. All she wants to do is to follow the usual routine of checking her mailbox ... followed by the sending of replies. Firstly, she will respond to her boyfriend, with an update on how she is settling ... along with the obligatory assurances as to how much she misses him. Then she will e-mail a letter to her mother, who, she hopes, will be able to relax back at her home in the Slovakian hills, knowing that her daughter is safe and well. Like all mothers, irrespective of their race or their creed, she worries about her children. Although she admires and understands her daughter's courage in wanting to venture alone to a foreign country and so, experience a little of what the world has to offer, she wishes that circumstances were such that the draw to greener pastures had not been so great. After all, her daughter has a boyfriend who has his future well and truly *in the bag*. All he needs to do is to graduate; then, with his degree secured, he will be able to take the first steps to becoming a lawyer within the lifetime security of his father's family practice.

With the promise of a life of privilege and with a guarantee of a home of their own, her mother has often questioned the wisdom of her wishing to leave.

"May I sit here, please?" The new arrival, in stilted English, asks the occupier of the seat which is adjacent to the only one which, apart from the presence of a bag, remains empty.

Detecting an unfamiliar accent in the voice, Lisa nods with a friendly smile and obligingly removes her bag from the neighbouring seat.

"Thank you."

There is a silence ... along with the occasional exchange of polite smiles as each awaits their turn.

So as not to disturb the man at the nearest terminal who appears to be buried in his research, they are careful to keep their voices down.

He has the look of normality and insignificance about him. But then, his apparent absorption in the content of the screen is a well-practised ruse which has, in the past, successfully disguised both his intent and his ability to retrieve discarded chatter from the open spaces that separate mass from mass. He listens and learns ... steadily collecting data which is, as a matter of course, duly indexed, stored and then readily available for when his need dictates.

The two young women exchange glances at each other's furry boots and, simultaneously, utter a muted laugh as they recognize that they are wearing the identical items of practical, but not entirely elegant, footwear.

It is often the most simple of things that one has in common that instigates the opening of a conversation ... and the wearing of the same boots is a rather unusual indication of their commonality.

Lisa breaks the silence. "I think we may have got our boots from the same place."

"I think you are right."

The reply from the girl from Slovakia is accompanied with a look in her face which suggests that she is fully appreciative of this opportunity for dialogue.

She sits silently for a few seconds and then restarts the conversation.

"I have been in England for only three weeks maybe. And I am still looking to find where everything is."

"I know how it can be. It is very difficult at first. I came here from Finland ... with my boyfriend. We found it difficult, but we had each other for company. You see ... we are both nurses at the hospital. That is how we met. We trained together. And you?"

"Oh, me? – I am from Slovakia. My boyfriend ... he is at the University. He is studying to be a lawyer."

"Ah ... yes, that is good. He is studying in England?"

"No. He is in Slovakia. I have come here to learn my English and ... how do you say? .... I wish to see some of the world before I am too old. Maybe then, I will go back and ... if I'm still sure, then we will be married."

"You don't sound so sure?"

The Slovakian girl shrugs her shoulders, confirming the presence of a few doubts ... but, also, demonstrating a reluctance to say any more.

"So, you are taking a break? Maybe it will give you some time to think ... yes?"

"Yes ... I am here for one year maybe. I work in a café in the evenings, and I have started to study English at the college in the day. It is good. I enjoy it very much."

"Have you made some friends?"

"Yes. Maybe I have just two friends. I started at the college late ... and they have their friends already."

"Do you go out with your friends?"

"Oh yes – but they want to go to the ... discotheque ... all of the time. I have gone with them once ... but I'm not liking the music."

"You do not like music?"

"Yes. I love music! I love rock, and I also love to dance. At home we watch the bands play on the stage — it is very good, and it is very exciting — but my friends who are here, like different music ... Not what I like."

"We like rock music also. Maybe ... if you are not working in the café on Tuesday, you can come with us to see a rock band in Exeter — it's at the SV club. It is not far from here — It is in the next street."

She trusts her instincts — so, although she does not know Lisa, she feels no threat from this stranger, and, what's more, she is definitely tempted by the idea of having an evening out. "Tuesday, you say?"

Lisa nods.

"I am not at the café on Tuesday. Yes. I can come with you."

"Ah ... that is good. We can meet outside the club at ... maybe, eight - thirty? You will meet more people ... and you will make new friends."

"Yes ... you can show me where we must meet?"

"Yes. I will show you later."

Realising that they have both forgotten to perform the most basic of requirements, the Slovakian girl smiles and introduces herself. "I am Anna."

"Oh yes, I am sorry, I forgot to say — I am Lisa. If you like, I will put my number on your phone? You can call me if there is a problem, okay?"

"Yes. That will be good. Thank you."

She passes her phone to Lisa, who duly enters her number before handing it back.

"My boyfriend is working today — so maybe, when we have done what we need here, we can go and get a coffee somewhere, and we can make plans for Tuesday. Okay?"

"Yes. That will be good."

***

Having listened in to, and then analysed the content of their conversation, he senses that there may be a malevolent deceit resting behind the façade of such an unassuming and rather innocent-looking young lady.

She's away from her Slovakian roots whilst her boyfriend is loyally slaving away as he tries to build the foundations for them both to enjoy a life of plenty. How would he feel if he knew that she was nightclubbing in the company of total strangers ... and, perhaps, seeking out thrills among the haunts of the purveyors of rebellion and the sounds of heavy metal?

He's heard enough. He has decided that she is on the prowl ... looking for something more exciting. What's more, it seems that she may be quite content to betray the loyalty of the man who is waiting in their homeland.

He disconnects from the internet, and with no more than a fleeting glance in her direction, stands up and vacates his seat ... leaving it available for occupation by the next in line.

Almost photographically, he stores her image in the archives of his mind, and then, without any indication as to his interest, he makes his way towards the aisles. From here, and under the pretence of him browsing through the titles which fill the shelves, he can watch.

Once certain that she has taken her place at a terminal, he wanders out from the building. Whilst sitting on the low wall which bounds the precincts of the neighbouring West Country Studies library, he settles to read his newspaper.

There is a brightness to the day, and there are many who seem to be quite happy to meander about the shops and browse as if they have no specific purpose.

He, unlike the others, positions himself strategically with a single aim in mind. He knows that the presence of a man sitting tranquilly on a wall whilst absorbing the warmth of the sun — which, with the gradual shortening of daylight hours, seems to be more precious than ever before — is not worthy of notice. In fact, people throughout the world have become adept in the art of avoiding eye-contact with those who sit alone in the city streets; for the slightest hint of curiosity can often get an unwelcome, if not intimidating, response.

He has no schedule to keep. He can just wait and watch whilst safely hidden behind a veil of anonymity.

***

Side by side, they walk down the steps. Lisa shows her the *club,* and then, unaware of his presence, they stroll into the High Street, across the main thoroughfare and into the modernity of the rebuilt, traffic-free precincts of the shopping mall.

He is in no hurry. Keeping a respectable distance, so that there can be no trace of suspicion, he shadows their route.

With their search for seating and the telltale aroma of freshly-ground coffee realized, they select a table and await the attention of the waiter.

Like a fisherman watching for the twitch of the line, he has perfected the art of patience … and waits for them to emerge.

With the passing of a little more than twenty minutes, they are out, and with the niceties of a wave and a smile, they go their separate ways.

Anna, at first, moves briskly, but as she glances at the glistening displays which edge her route, she slows, allowing herself the time to absorb and admire the styles and colours of the garments which have succeeded in catching her interest.

One dress in particular stands out above the others, and, as if having been arrested by the power of sheer desire, she stops and she stares.

Captivated by the simple, yet striking, creation which is presented alone and with effect within the tastefully and cleverly-lit display, she hesitates.

There are no gaudy embellishments nor sparkling trimmings to draw the eye. They are not needed; for the mere fact that one is able to glimpse the shimmer of glossy slate peeking through the intricacy of an overlay of beautifully-crafted burgundy lace is more than sufficient to allow the firing of the imagination ... and the senses.

Drawn by its appeal, she knows that she has no choice ... she has to try it on. So, without further delay, she takes her leave from the thoroughfare and enters the shop.

***

He does not stop. Instead, without showing any outward sign of him having any particular interest in the nature of the display, he just eyes the dress which has obviously caught her attention. Having made no more than that of a mental note of its appearance, he looks ahead and casually strolls on by.

He does not venture too far. He wants to keep an eye on the premises. He stops to peruse the menus which are displayed in the windows of the two restaurants which, rather conveniently, are positioned so as to offer him the advantage of having a clear and uninterrupted view back and into the well-lit shop.

***

She is blissfully unaware of being watched. If she had thought that the eyes of a stranger were well and truly focused on her, then she would have been left unable to relax to browse through the range of ladies apparel.

Flicking through the rails, she finds the identical dress to that displayed in the window and selects her size. She pulls it out for a closer look and allows a moment or two to feel the nature and texture of its cloth.

It is not as light as she had expected, but it does have a quality and a weight which will, no doubt, give the perfect swing.

Holding it up against her, she measures its length, and, being more than satisfied that she has the legs and the physique to get away with the disclosure afforded by the wearing of a mini-dress, she turns towards the mirror. Whilst she assesses the compatibility of herself with the garment, she becomes aware of the cheerful, yet not too intrusive, approach of a sales assistant.

"It is lovely, isn't it?"

"Yes, it is! It is very beautiful ... I like it very much."

The assistant, with an expression of sincerity, declares, "It is one of my favourites, too!"

As Anna continues to scan the dress for its style and the quality of its finish, the assistant, whilst indicating to the elaborate detail of the overlay, almost poetically goes on to accentuate its salient features.

"I just *love* the beautiful pattern in the lace, don't you? And, what with the *wonderfully* scalloped edges on the bodice … and the daintiness of those *gorgeous* little cap-sleeves. Well … it just does it for me. It is to my mind … absolutely exquisite!" She allows a second or two for Anna to absorb the essence of her words, and then, not wishing to break her flow, she continues. "I think it exposes *just* enough to be sexy…"

The emphasis on the *just,* suggesting the slightest hint of there being, within its design, an innate expectation for the thrill of adventure. "But, of course … not so much that it could be seen as being *too* revealing or *too* flirtatious."

She pauses with a smile as she notes her client's expression within the reflection of the mirror. Once satisfied that she has said all that is needed regarding the top, she steers Anna's attention downwards, and adds, " … And now … just look at the flare of the skirt! Well … to me, it is just as they say in the advert … *as figure-flattering as it is elegant."*

Figure and *flattering* — a combination of two words which can be persuasive when it comes to encouraging a woman into having a second look.

Anna, having not fully understood the meaning of all of the words which were used in the assistant's patter, makes her own assessment. As she absorbs the detail of the nipped-in waist and the enchanting fullness of the skirt, she smiles and, with a hint of hesitation, looks around her.

Then, as if her mind had just been read, her thoughts are suddenly interrupted with an invite of, "If you would like, there is a fitting-room just over there. You can try it on if you wish. Then, of course, you can feel exactly how wonderful it is to wear … and how beautifully it flows when you move."

The assistant may well have overdone the enthusiasm of her *spiel,* but it had been of little consequence. Anna has a mind of her own, and it is, simply, the style and the fabric of the dress which has been sufficient, in itself, to capture her interest, and so, fire her desire.

"Yes … Please … I would like to try it. Thank you."

She is ushered to the fitting-rooms and makes the change.

Knowing that her furry boots will unquestionably throw the eye, and that what she really wants is to see herself at her best when trying on the dress, she steps, barefooted, onto the shop floor. She is greeted with the spontaneity of a smile, along with an approving, "It suits you — It really does. You look absolutely wonderful!"

"Thank you."

Her response is made with the accompaniment of a look of joy as she revels in the compliment. Then, with her shoulder-length hair grasped firmly in her right hand and held up high and away from her shoulders and neckline, she scrutinizes her reflected image … twisting and turning as she examines all aspects before making her final decision.

With a gesture of her hand, the assistant encourages her to experience the comfort of its fit whilst subjected to the natural flow of movement. "Now … see how it feels when you walk."

She needs no persuasion; whilst releasing her hair with no more than a shake of her head, she walks proudly across the shop floor, turns … and then strides back again … with a smile much broader than before.

"Am I right?" The assistant knows she is right; as such, the question is no more than a probe for confirmation.

Anna nods her agreement, and, as if she wishes to be sure that she is about to make the correct decision, she turns and faces the mirror.

Grasping her hair and holding it up once more, she lifts herself up and onto her toes … and then lowers herself … only to lift up again as she adjusts her height, whilst determining the optimum length of heel which would be required to maximise the impact and, so, make the image complete.

She checks her bag, and eyeing her credit card, she smiles. She knows that by using it to make the purchase she will have no need to delve into her day-to-day funds. Instead, she will be able to clear the balance at a later date.

"Yes — Please — I will buy it. Thank you."

Still enjoying the feel of its swing as she moves, she skips back to the fitting-rooms and then, with an air of reluctance, makes the transition back and into the garb of everyday practicality.

With the purchase completed, she turns about and, with a spring in her step, heads for the exit.

Reflections in the glass show movement. He turns to confirm that it is she who is leaving the store.

It is!

Restraining himself from allowing others to detect the surge in his excitement, he, somewhat surreptitiously, keeps an eye on her as she walks on. He can tell that she is delighted with her purchase; she has an air of confidence in her step and a smile across her face.

I thought so — she's bought it! Although satisfied with the fact that his ability to predict the actions of others is still well-honed, he is annoyed with her. She has succumbed to the temptation of buying a dress, which, with the allure of an enticing sheen peeping through its lacy web, suggests the presence of nectar for the taking and, as such, advertises the true nature of her desires.

As far as he is concerned, this is a dress which, if worn in the bars and nightclubs of the city, may well elicit a debauched response from the drunken young men who — being on the prowl — will care not for the fact that she wears a ring of engagement. If she truly respects the values of fidelity, she should not have bought this dress ... and, what's more, she should certainly not wear it whilst she is away from her husband-to-be. But then, with her only having referred to him as being her boyfriend, she may have her doubts as to the strength of the tie.

With caution to the fore, he allows her sufficient time to put distance between them.

It's been an eventful morning; she's been invited to go out on Tuesday night with her new-found friend, Lisa, and she has now bought a dress for the occasion.

She walks back and into the High Street, pausing only to look at the selection of shoes which sit enticingly in the window of a high-quality and expensive outlet. With insufficient funds to indulge, she walks on before turning off and into the narrow walkway which passes the *Old Ship Inn*. Once within the precincts of Cathedral Green and with the warmth of the sun on her face, she, with a youthful spring to her step, continues on her journey along the ancient pathway which lines the cobbled street. She is soon walking under the ornate craftwork of the, nigh on, two-hundred-year old arched, iron footbridge and is, thus, within yards of reaching the peaceful setting of magnificent terraced buildings which line the well-tended gardens of Southernhay.

Having reached the junction, she stops. Then, tossing her hair back, she peeps into the bag ... as if ensuring that it was not a dream and that she had still got her beautiful prize.

***

He has a thorough geographical understanding of the city; as such, he is at a loss as to why she has chosen to take the longer route which skirts the precincts of the cathedral. The shorter path which connects the shops of the precinct with the gardens of Southernhay would have been more logical.

As he shadows her movements, he guesses that, with her being fairly new to the city, she probably feels secure within the familiarity of her first-taken routes. So, while she waits to expand her knowledge of where each path leads, she will, as a matter of course, continue to traverse those which are familiar as she travels between her home and the city centre.

***

She turns to her right and walks purposefully away and past the old buildings of what was once the Royal Devon and Exeter hospital. Her pace is brisk; not because she feels a need to try to shake off a threat from a shadow which stalks from behind — after all, she is blissfully unaware of its presence — but rather ... out of habit. It just so happens to be the way that she always walks when going from one place to another.

Whilst he follows ... he surveys. The locations of alleyways — and other places of seclusion — from where a hunter could furtively lie in wait for passing prey are noted. Outwards and onwards she proceeds, making use of the light-controlled crossings to negotiate the impatient traffic at the conversion of major routes. Once safely across, she heads down the hill as she makes her way to the terrace of Victorian houses which stretch down and towards the river.

Almost a third of the way down, she stops. With her key in the lock and a turn of the wrist, the door opens. She enters.

Once she has vanished behind the closure of her door, he smirks; he has found her *Achilles heel* — she is, like so many, a *creature of habit.*

He has heard her ... and he has watched her.

He is satisfied that she is in need of *schooling*; although he knows *when* the lesson is likely to be implemented, he still needs to decide as to how and where he will execute the necessary form of discipline.

Turning about, he retraces the route. He has time to consider his options.

Chapter 32

A relic of times prior to the amalgamation of the independent police forces of Cornwall and Devon — a time when every village had its own constable — the now privately-owned police house stands proud. With the embossed lettering of the Devon Constabulary still visible within the pediment which crowns the front doorway, he is certain that he has located the correct address.

He stands on the step, hesitates and then, having pressed his finger on the bell-push, steps back and waits.

"And what can I be doing you for, bu'y?"

The Devon drawl — deep and powerful — growls the words from behind a full and steely beard ... exposing a character which has turned the simple act of suspicion into an art form.

Tom looks to his right as he homes in on the sound of the gravelled voice.

With a muddied trowel in hand, a figure appears from the side of the house. Although well into retirement and no longer able to stand completely upright, he still possesses the air of confidence which is, so often, acquired by those who have served in either the military or the police.

"Mr Russell?" Tom asks. Then, seeking confirmation that he has successfully traced and identified the correct person, he adds. "The ex-policeman?"

"Maybe I am..." he replies, before adding with a further hint of distrust, "but then that could depend on whose doing the asking."

"Of course ... My name's, McMurry — Tom McMurry."

He waits for a moment as he wonders if his name has been remembered. Seeing no obvious signs of immediate recognition, he clarifies his identity. "I'm Lucy's father ... Lucy McMurry? Do you remember?"

The old man stares at him — silent and expressionless — as he registers the significance of the name.

Lucy McMurry; a name which has haunted him through not only the last years of his service ... but also, through much of his retirement.

This is not the nuisance call of a door-to-door salesman ... this a man who has a purpose and is clearly on a mission.

"I reckons 'tis best you come in then."

Immediately, and with no more said, he turns about and makes his way slowly and stoically towards the rear of his house.

Tom stands firm — not sure as to whether he should wait at the door at the front ... or to follow the enigmatic old man to the rear.

Shep stops and looks behind him. "Come on, bu'y. If you'm wanting to be speakin' with me ... then you'm best be keeping up!"

Tom, smiling with the notion that he may not be able to keep pace with a man whose steps are taken with sufficient care so as not to add to the lingering pain which appears to plague his lower back, follows on. As the trowel is put safely away in an old but recently creosoted garden shed and the muddied boots are removed, brushed off and then rinsed clean, he hopes that the methodical procedure is merely a sign of an organised mind ... and that it is not just part of a routine which has been learnt and perfected so as to negate the effects of the onset of dementia.

With his boots replaced by a pair of everyday shoes, the man steps out and onto the path. He smiles ... and then looking back at his well-tended and orderly garden, he silently invites his guest to do the same.

"It's nice. ... You've obviously worked hard on it."

Tom is not only polite, but he is also honest.

"I's quite aware of that, bu'y." He looks at the calluses on the palms of his hands ... and then back to Tom. "But, thank you anyway. You see ... me an' me late wife had an understanding — she liked doing the gardenin' ... and I liked sitting in it."

His eyes sparkle, exposing the humour of a man who seems almost proud to admit an element of chauvinistic idleness.

Tom envisages this wily old man, lazing in the garden while his good-lady toils ... endlessly planting, replanting and, at the same time, keeping ahead of the battle to keep the weeds at bay.

"Since her's been gone ... I thought I ought to keep it nice ... just for 'er, like. So now, I've neither the time nor ..." He stops briefly as a look of sadness drifts across his tired and rugged face, and then continues. "As I were saying, I've not the time nor the inclination to sit 'round idly. Things isn't quite the same now her's gone."

Tom looks at him and, recalling his own loss, nods. "Yes ... I think I know where you're coming from."

Shep looks back at him and, with an empathetic smile, responds, "Yep ... I reckons you probably do."

"Anyhow, you'm no doubt come y'ere looking for answers. Am I right?"

Tom, relieved to see that he is obviously still in possession of his mental faculties, laughs. "Yes, sir. You're right."

"Now then bu'y ... there's no need for 'e to call me *sir*. You see ... unlike some of me colleagues, I was never promoted above me level of competence ... and, may I add, neither did Her Majesty feel the inclination to offer me one of them there knighthoods." He rinses his hands under the outside tap, and then, having wiped them on a cloth, he offers the courtesy of a handshake. "So ... we'll have a bit less of the formalities ... if you don't mind? Right then — I's Shep. Shep Russell ... but you'm free to call me Shep."

Tom grasps his hand. "Well, Shep. I'm Tom ... and I *really* am pleased to meet you."

"Well then, let's hope that I can be of some help to 'e."

Tom nods.

Shep opens the kitchen door, steps inside and invites Tom to follow.

"Come on in ... We'll have a brew ... an' a bit of a chat."

"Thank you."

"Whilst's kettle's heating, we'll go through to the living room ... 'tis a bit more comfy in there."

Tom waits as he watches him fill the kettle and press the on-switch.

The task completed, Shep leads his guest through to the front room where he offers him a seat.

"I seems to recall that you was livin' abroad ... somewhere in France, if I's not mistaken?"

"Yes ... that's right ... I still am. I've come over on a whim really."

"So, where you'm staying to?"

"I've booked myself a room in a hotel in Exeter. I've got a sister living down in Cornwall — I thought about staying with her ... but, to be honest, I think she's too far away. In any case, I think I'm better off being closer to the city."

"Makes sense. Anyhow, I'll just go and make some tea ... I take it you'm all right with tea?"

"Yes. Thank you. White ... no sugar — thank you."

"I's got no cake nor 'ave I any biscuits to offer 'e. You see, 'twas always my good lady who would keep a stock of them kind of things ... and to be quite honest with 'e, since her's passed on I don't get enough visitors to warrant the expense. Now, you just sit there and make yourself comfy. I'll be right with 'e."

Tom complies, and as Shep turns and heads back towards the kitchen, he absorbs the surroundings.

He's always believed that much can be learnt about a person from the contents of their living space and, also, by the manner in which their possessions are displayed.

Perched on the mantelpiece, and in a position of prominence, there stands a photograph which, although it had obviously been taken many years beforehand, is unmistakably an image of his host standing proudly with his wife beside him.

Tom can see that this is evidence of a man with feelings; for although his wife may have gone in substance, she has obviously remained unforgotten ... and firmly within his heart.

There appears to be little room for fiction in his life; his bookshelf seems crammed with a collection of titles which are, in the main, factual, historical and geographical in nature. There are also, much to Tom's surprise, a smattering of books which suggest that he may also have an interest in the myths and legends of the ancient cultures from around the world.

Tom rises up from his seat and examines the framed certificate which hangs in the recess beside the fireplace — *Police Constable Robert John Russell had retired after thirty years of service* and — according to the *chief constable* of the day — *His conduct was* **Exemplary.**

Shep re-enters the room with a mug of tea held in each hand.

Tom turns towards him and, as if to apologise for being intrusive, indicates to the certificate, explaining, "I hope you don't mind, I was just admiring the certificate — pretty impressive."

Shep glances towards it and hesitates; there have been times when he has wondered if this rather insignificant piece of card would have been more fitting if it had been issued in recognition of him having completed thirty years of *shifts, hassle and not being there in the evenings to help his wife bring up their children.*

"You must be proud."

"Yep … I suppose I must be."

His words are unconvincing.

Shep places the cups on the table between the two armchairs and then sits down, beckoning Tom to do the same.

"Now then … I'm not sure how I can help you … 'twas a long time ago, see — but … I reckons I'd best be starting by asking you what you know already … if you don't mind, that is?"

"No, I don't mind at all. Well then … all I know is … that Lucy had been at a wedding do with her mother, and her mother's bloke … Geoff. Then, after a falling out with him and her boyfriend — that was Joe — she ran off … and that was it. No one saw her again."

Shep nods as he waits in silence for him to continue.

"I since heard that Joe hung himself. I don't know any more. I've heard nothing at all since then."

"Well … what you've said just about sums it up."

It is now Tom's turn to sit in silence — surprised by the brevity of the retired police officer's response.

"I apologise if I seems a bit forthright, but … back then, we'd drawn a blank. Now, I reckons that we'm only got one of two options as to what may have 'appened to her."

Tom listens — intrigued as to the simplicity of this man's approach.

"The first option is that her ran away … and then her got too scared to come back to face the music."

He pauses as he looks back and weighs the reaction from his visitor.

There is none.

"Now ... the second is that her's come to some harm ... and 'tis likely that her's no longer with us. Now, I know's there's no nice way to say it ... but her could very well be dead!"

Tom sits back and closes his eyes as the terrible word of finality echoes in his mind.

"As I said, I's not one to be doin' with riddlin' ... and no good comes from beatin' about the bush — so that's why I's come straight to the point with 'e."

Tom opens his eyes. He takes a deep breath and then sighs before responding. "Realistically? I don't think it's the first option. If it had been, I'm sure Lucy would have contacted me by now. Even if she'd not been able to get across the channel, she would have found a way to make contact. There's been nothing at all."

It's now Shep who listens in silence.

"So ..." Tom continues, "I feel that it's more likely to be the second option ... and she's come to harm."

Shep nods in agreement and leans forward. "Well ... if I were still in the job and was working on a case like this, I'd be lookin' for motives, suspects and opportunities."

Tom's thinking becomes more intense as Shep starts to reason like the steady old copper that he used to be.

"Logically speakin' ... if her's dead, then her's either died through ill health, accident or foul play. Well, from all accounts, her was a healthy young maid ... so I reckons we can rule that one out. In any case, if her had collapsed and passed away, we would have found her."

Tom concurs with a nod.

"Now then ... she could 'ave had an accident. A driver could 'ave knocked her over, panicked and then dumped her somewhere ... possibly miles away."

"Possible ... but a bit of a long shot, don't you think?"

Shep shrugs and then adds a dash of credibility to the suggestion.

"Think about it ... there's your maid, Lucy ... wandering through dark country lanes ... with people driving in cars, havin' had a little too much to drink. Some people can do some strange things when they panic."

"Okay ... I'll give you that. But I still think it's unlikely. To be honest ... I think we're both pretty sure that she's been ... murdered?"

As he speaks, he registers the significance of the word which comes from his own mouth; a word which conjures up an image of *his* Lucy — terrified and alone — as she frantically fights a losing battle for life at the hands of her abductor.

He tries to push away the harrowing thoughts of what she may well have been subjected to. *Was she abducted and abused before being disposed of when she was deemed to be no longer of any use? Or was she attacked and killed in an instant and her body hidden away and left to rot in a cold and abandoned grave?*

These thoughts have troubled him day and night for more than two decades; for his own peace of mind he needs closure.

With his eyes piercing out from behind a watery veil of grief, his feelings towards whoever took *his* little girl are clear. Given half an chance he would tear him to shreds. "To think that some slimy little bastard has taken my little girl ... and, what's worse, he's got away with it! Well ... that just makes me want to— No ... I won't even go down that road."

Shep can understand Tom's feelings, but he knows that the calm and collected approach will always be more productive than the one which is wild and reckless. "Now, as I said..." he continues, "... if I were still in the job, I'd be working out a list of motives and likely suspects."

Pausing for thought, he decides on which to mention first. "Let's look at the motives. Now then, as you know, people are murdered for many reasons."

"Go on." He forces himself to stay calm and to listen.

"To settle a grievance is one ... And I reckons that fear is another. What I means is ... they may be in fear of being attacked. Or, what is more likely, they may be in fear of being caught out for doing something which they know would result in them being dealt harshly with by the courts. Now then, if what they's done is so bad that they could go inside for a very long time ... then perhaps that could be just enough to spur 'em into needin' to dispose of a witness. Now ... if the only witness is the victim, then it's possible that the offender could panic and kill. Mind you, the ol' green-eyed monster of jealousy is also quite common in the old domestic murders. But then, of course, the one we all fear the most is the one when the offender is a psychopath ... and e's satisfying some strange and deep-rooted desires!"

Tom needs no elaboration as to the kind of person or, indeed, any detail as to the nature of the desires of which Shep refers. He needs only to turn on the television, whether it's a drama or the News, to see the way in which some people will brutalize others.

"Now then ... how abouts we look at the suspects ... and their motives. Top of the list was always her boyfriend, Joe — the Hardy bu'y. He's the one that everyone thinks were responsible. Them reckoned on it being down to him getting jealous after what happened, 'specially with him going on to do away with himself, the way he did."

"Jealous?"

"Yes. With him reckoning that she were *playing away from home* ... then jealousy could have been the motive."

Tom starts to recall the detail of the rumours — hearsay — which, at the time, he had not readily accepted. "I don't think she would have cheated on him. That's just not the way that she was brought up."

He looks at Shep in hopeful anticipation of him being in agreement.

Shep — remembering the night, and the vision of Lucy with Marcus, outside the hall — is unable to offer any indication of accord.

There is more to be told.

Tom seeks verification. "There were some doubts though, weren't there?"

A raising of Shep's eyebrows, accompanied by a shrug, is sufficient to indicate agreement.

Tom asks, "Was it ever proved? I mean, I know it was never officially proved, but ... unofficially?"

Shep shakes his head; his expression suggesting that, on a personal level, he was uncertain as to the guilt of the man. "All I can say is ... that in a *criminal* case you need to prove that the accused is guilty *beyond all reasonable doubt*. Which means — belt and braces. But then, in a *civil* case the evidence required is a lot less — a man's guilt is then decided on *the balance of probabilities*."

Tom nods, and assisted by Shep's tendency to put emphasis on certain words, he absorbs the knowledge of this experienced old man.

"Now — If I were still a police officer ... and I were gonna be arrestin' someone, I would need to be sure that I'd bin given the power to do so. I would be needin' to have *reasonable suspicion* that an *Arrestable Offence had been committed*. And also, that I had *reasonable suspicion* that the person in question *had actually committed it*. Do 'e get me so far?"

"I think so. Go on."

"Good. Now ... the *reasonable suspicion* to arrest could be based on the *balance of probabilities*. But then ... without going into detail, I would still have to find the evidence to make a strong enough case for a criminal court. Are 'e still with me?"

Tom nods, and so, the simplified lesson on law continues.

"Now then ... in Joe's case ... there may have bin enough for there to 'ave been suspicion that an arrestable offence *had been* committed, and ... at a stretch ... that he *may* have committed it. But without any real evidence, I certainly don't think there would have been enough to convict in the end. You see, as I've said, in a criminal court, the case must be proven *without any reasonable doubt* — 'tis a belt and braces job."

"So from the way you're talking, you don't think he did do it, do you?"

"Well ... I had me doubts then as I still have now. But then again ... 'twas not for me to say. I wasn't in on the interview ... 'twas CID. They was the only ones who spoke with him."

"Did they think he did it?"

"Some reckons he did — but I wonders if, perhaps, they spent a little too much time watching the rabbit which were in their sights to take too much notice of them who'd already disappeared down the burrow. Mind you, they reckon that with him committin' suicide an' all, that 'twas as good as a cough."

"A cough? Did he admit it then?"

"Not exactly. It was just with him killing himself that made 'em think he had something to hide. Mind you, as I said, nothing were proven, and I don't reckon it ever would have bin."

"Do you think he was capable?"

"He was capable all right — physically that is. He was a strappin' young lad. A damn good rugby player if you ask me. But there was one thing he never did — well not to my knowledge anyway — and that was ... he'd never play dirty. Did you ever meet the bu'y?"

"Yes, I met him the once. He was there when I came over for Lucy's eighteenth. He seemed okay, but ... when I heard he'd hung himself, I just couldn't believe it. I mean ... they seemed really happy together. It just didn't make any sense. But then, you don't always know what goes on in a man's mind, do you? Anyway, if it had been a jealousy thing, would he have gone to the trouble of hiding her? To me it just doesn't add up."

"Well, I's gotta admit, it surprised me, too."

"So you definitely have *your* doubts? What I'm saying is ... you don't seem to think that he did it. Am I right?"

"I haven't said he did ... an' I haven't said he didn't. But you'm right ... I still find it difficult to believe that he would 'ave. The bu'y couldn't lie to save his life. It just wasn't in 'im. I's pretty certain that if he'd done somein' to your young maid ... then he would have cracked and coughed. But then ... we'm both long enough in the tooth to know that there be hidden depths in us all."

Tom sits quietly, assessing the words.

"Put it this way ... if he'd lived and gone to trial ... I don't reckon we'd have satisfied the need to prove it *beyond all reasonable doubt*. In fact, I even doubt whether there would have been enough evidence for a charge. On *the balance of probabilities* in a civil court, maybe ... but I can't be too sure about that either. Look ... if it were rage and he'd done som'it daft ... then, you'm right, he wouldn't have been too careful where he'd left her. So, then I's pretty certain that we'd have found her."

"Okay, so if it wasn't him ... then who do you think it was?"

Impatient for a reply, he rephrases his question. "Who were the other suspects?"

"Well ... There was the Warren bu'y. He's the bu'y who took a bit of a pastin' from Joe."

"Oh yes ... I remember."

"Now ...when we turned up at the hall, he was outside ... with your

Lucy."

"What do you mean, he was *with* Lucy?"

"From what I recall, they was cuddled up together."

Tom had, over the years, dismissed the thought of his daughter having been disloyal. He had been more interested in finding his daughter than to delve into her indiscretions. "Actually, come to think about it, Mr Dowsett did mention something. All right, so where was Joe when she was with Marcus?"

"Joe? He was inside, lookin' for her."

"Okay. So do you think this Marcus may have had something to do with Lucy disappearing?"

"Difficult to say. I didn't know him or 'is family ... not like I did Joe's. But me and Sunset saw 'em together. We said nothing to Joe, but he found out about it anyway. So in the end, he gave him a good ol' smacking!"

"Sunset? Who's Sunset?"

"He was the *hobby-bobby*. A special constable. D'you know ... 'tis strange how you give someone a nickname and it seems to stick. Then after a while, you can't for the life of 'e remember how he come to have it ... or, for that matter, what were the proper one."

"Whatever his real name is, would it be worth going to see him and find out if he can remember any more?"

"I doubt it. He wasn't really involved like that. He was only a special ... a part-timer, if you knows what I mean. Mind you, he kept on about seeing one of them big black cats in the lanes up towards Haldon. Now then ... if I remembers rightly ... he reckoned he was driving around looking for your maid when he saw this 'ere big cat in his headlights."

"You've got to be kidding me."

Shep nods and confirms. "No ... I isn't kidding you. He reckoned he saw one of these big cats up by the forest. He could talk some rubbish mind ... and to be honest ... he was pretty gullible — dead easy to wind up."

He looks up to the ceiling and, with a wicked grin, relates a tale. "There were this one occasion ... when I was driving 'round a certain bend, when me foot slipped off the clutch and clunked the side of the foot-well. Well ... the bu'y must've been dozing 'cause he nearly jumped out of his skin. *What was that?* he'd said. Well ... I pretended I heard nothin'. Then, every time I went 'round that same bend ... I did it again. I let him think he was the only one who'd heard it. A bit cruel really, I know. But anyway, after a while I told him to stop winding me up — I made up some cock an' bull story about a ghost of a cyclist. I said he was killed by a car on the bend. The bu'y swallowed it hook, line and sinker ... silly fool. I never told him the truth, mind ... and I reckons that, to this day, he believes he heard a ghost!"

Tom wishes to pursue the original line of conversation. "This *big cat* thing? I don't think I ever heard anything about a big cat."

"He reckoned he saw one all right! He reckoned he saw a panther ... or somethin'. A load of bull, if you ask me. The boy must 'ave been daft in the 'ead. No malice in him mind ... but he'd never have made it as a regular. Mind you, 'e was keen — maybe a bit too keen, if 'e knows what I mean."

He stops as he thinks back across the two decades. "Anyways, I wouldn't have expected for you to have 'eard anythin' about it ... 'twas not the sort of thing CID would have taken seriously either. Anyhow, if word got out ... well, can you imagine how many nutters would be chasin' 'round trying to find the bloody thing? We'd have every Tom, Dick and Harry chasing 'round the countryside trying to bag it!"

"Do you believe that these big cats exist? It was a strange thing for him to make up, don't you think?"

"Well ... there's them who do ... and there's them who don't. And ... what with them tales of beasts on Dartmoor and Exmoor, 'tis difficult to know what to believe. Even Bodmin seems to have its own. Mind you ... them's they who reckon thems seen the *hairy-hand* of Dartmoor. Then there's them who reckons them's seen the ghost of Lady what's 'er name and 'er carriage of bones at Okey Castle. Just 'cause they say they saw it ... it don't mean it's true, do it?"

Tom's silence invites Shep to continue.

"Look ... I's not saying there's no truth in it ... 'tis just that I's a little bit sceptical about sightings all over the place ... especially when there be no proper evidence to back 'em up."

"So ... where's this Sunset now? Is he still a special?"

"Not 'round 'ere, he isn't. 'twas a long time ago ... and, like everyone else, he never kept in touch. Mind you, with all that cat nonsense ... I's reckonin' 'twould be lucky if he'm still in touch with himself."

He laughs, and then tries to recall the detail. "No. Come to think of it ... I's a feeling he went up country somewhere. That's it ... He'd decided he wanted to be a truck driver, an' I seems to recall that he may have gone up north — I can't be too certain ... but it rings a bell. Anyhow ... whatever happened to 'im, I certainly don't know where he's living to now. I's 'eard nothin' more from 'im."

"I suppose he wouldn't know any more than you do anyway?"

Shep shakes his head. "Can't see it bu'y. As I said ... the specials wouldn't have bin involved. Even us regular bobbies was cut out once CID got hold of it. Them likes to keep the freebies and the overtime to themselves, I reckons."

Tom sips his tea and thinks of what to ask next.

Shep breaks the silence. "I's remembered it now."

"What?"

"The bu'y's name. He were called Sunset — Sunset Strip; the bu'y was called Tripp."

Tom, in need of enlightenment, seems lost as he looks at Shep.

"Seventy-seven, Sunset Strip."

The older of the two men sings out the theme as he waits for a sign of recognition ... There is none. He continues. "Surely you knows what I's on about? Maybe not. Well ... 'twas an old TV detective programme, back in the sixties. Ring any bells?"

Tom shakes his head ... no bells rung, so he is none the wiser.

"Perhaps, 'twas a bit before your time. You see ... it were an old American TV programme about a couple of private investigators. Anyhow ... the boy was called Tripp — Special Constable Simon Tripp ... and his collar-number had a couple of sevens in it. So there you have it ... seventy-seven Sunset Strip. See?"

Tom nods as he answers. "Yes, I think so."

With his response having managed to have drawn a line under the saga of the nickname's origins, he changes tack. "Okay then ... going back to Marcus. What do you know about him?"

"Well ... not a lot, really. He was interviewed ... and 'tis my understanding that, in the end, nothin' come of it. You see, 'tis to my recollection that he went off along the lane back towards the village ... before Lucy, that is. So I reckons that he *would* have had the opportunity. And anyway, I weren't the only one who thought that way ... that's why he were interviewed."

"So he had the opportunity. Have you any idea where he is now?"

He shakes his head. "No. As I said, it were a long time ago, and to be honest with 'e, I've lost touch with who's who and where everyone's gone. In any case, I can't really say that I knew much about the bu'y. So, I's sorry to say ... I can't really be much help to 'e."

"I understand that ... but if I could find out where he is now, then I'd certainly like to have a few words with him."

"I reckons you would ... But then, I can't see there being any good coming from it. I mean, my gut feeling tells me he knows more than he ever told, and if e's kept it to himself for all them years ... then I can't see him letting it all out now. Now then, as I's not one to make allegations without something to back it ... I'll be saying no more."

He can see that Tom is disappointed. He weakens and offers a little more. "Look, bu'y, what I mean is ... what I think, is one thing ... but what I let known to others, well, thenk that's another. Okay?"

Tom nods, and Shep continues. "If I's to be honest with 'e ... if it couldn't be proven back then ... then it won't be proven now. So ... my advice is for 'e to leave it be."

Tom remains silent as he assesses not just what has been said but what may be hidden behind the words.

He has no doubt, whatsoever, that if Shep could have been pressed into saying who he'd believed would have been the mostly likely *offender* — assuming, that is, that an offence had been committed and that Lucy had not disappeared of her own volition — then Marcus would have been on the top of his list.

The silence is broken. "Mind you ... I's still a bit puzzled as to what you'm thinking you'm gonna be gaining after all these years."

"I don't know — I've been toying with the idea of trying to arrange for a fresh appeal on the local TV ... and, I suppose, I'm hoping that someone out there knows something which they're ready to talk about. You know, some fresh information of some kind."

Shep looks on in silence.

"What I'm saying is ... I think that it's quite possible that someone may have heard something since ... or maybe even remembered something they'd forgotten to tell your colleagues at the time. At the end of the day, I know I'm clutching at straws ... but I just need to know what's happened to her."

"'tis possible someone knows som'it — I'll give 'e that. There were a lot of people there ... and to be honest with 'e, any one of 'em could be in the frame. I reckon, as most of me colleagues have, like me, retired or passed on, then we won't be getting much out of they. Even old man Growsett's gone. In fact ... I seem to recall seeing his name printed in the obituaries of our local *NARPO* newsletter a while back."

"Narpo?"

National Association for Retired Police Officers. Dunno why I joined really. Never bin to a meetin' or coffee mornin' in me life. If you like, I'll dig out the details and then see if I can find someone who's still alive — maybe them'll be able to help us."

"Us?"

"If 'e don't mind, that is. I'd like to know what's happened to your young maid, as well. Anyway ... apart from that, it'll give me an interest, now's I's on me own an' all."

"You're more than welcome, and I'm sure that I'll appreciate any help that you can come with. Thank you."

Tom truly values the offer of assistance and writes down the number of Shep's mobile phone, just in case there is a need for him to be contacted.

Chapter 33

Whether it is down to the unpredictability of coincidence, or whether it is more of a case of him being subconsciously dismissive towards those which bear little resemblance to his own, he has, for some time, been aware of a rather strange phenomenon; it seems that whenever he changes his car, he is suddenly inundated with the sight of others which are of the same model and colour.

He had not simply made casual and mental notes of his sightings but, as if he had been collecting data for a vital statistical project, he had gone as far as to formalise his findings by keeping an accurate and regularly updated record. As a result, he knows where virtually every dark-blue, Peugeot 406 saloon car is normally parked. Whether he had seen it within the bounds of the city, where he now lives and works, or whether it had been in one of the towns and villages in the surrounding areas, the fact is … it had probably been listed.

If he is ever asked as to why he notes the detail of each vehicle which is identical to his … he would probably give no reason other than to say that he had felt compelled to do so and, therefore, just did it.

Although with the rolling of the years, the model of his car is no longer as commonplace as it had once been, there are still enough examples in regular use so as to not make them conspicuous amid the queues and bustle of the city traffic. One such vehicle, although unremarkable in its own right, has already come to mind. Having checked his records, he knows that he has, in all probabilities, selected the ideal candidate for his forthcoming ruse.

The car is exactly the same model, year and colour as is his own.

Apart from the fact that it is always driven by an attractive and well-presented young woman who, he has noted, regularly visits the store at about four o'clock, three times a week and on alternate weekdays, it is not the type of vehicle that one would expect to be worthy of a second glance.

She — the driver of the Peugeot — is more often than not accompanied by her small son who, based on the evidence of the badge which is emblazoned on his school top, is of an age which enables him to be on the register of the local primary school.

He had been quick to observe the fact that she does not wear a wedding ring. But he knows that she's a *good* woman and that she is in a relationship where the family comes first.

How does he know this? Well, he is no fool … and being in the almost invisible position of being employed in the lowly occupation of a trolley-man, he, if noticed at all, is often dismissed as being as insignificant as that of one of the trolleys. As he wanders amid the shoppers, with his ears tuned and his eyes everywhere, he is able to satisfy his desire to learn.

He recalls how, on more than one occasion, he had heard the boy ask of his mother, *What time's dad coming home today?* and then for her, with the warmth of a smile, to reply with something in the vein of, *I'm not sure, but let's see if we can find him something nice for his tea.*

He had surmised that with a young child and the child's father to care for, the car would be unlikely to be on the road during the hours when revellers and partygoers have come to life. While the nocturnal play ... they will be at home, tucked up in their beds and oblivious to the goings-on in the late-night bars and clubs of the city centre.

With all things considered, he had known that his choice would be good. He had decided that the time was ripe for him to make use of the knowledge which had been gleaned from such little evidence.

It is unusual for him to have bothered with the purchase of a Sunday newspaper, but today he has a reason — for it is from within the pages of sport that he will pluck the information required. He has no interest in the match reports, or even the results — he is concerned solely with the list of fixtures for the week ahead. In particular, he has an interest in the matches which are scheduled to be played on Tuesday ... and are within a reasonable and commutable distance from his home.

He checks the teams; ignoring those from Exeter, Torquay and Plymouth, he concentrates on those which are slightly farther away. He needs to put distance between the match and Devon, but he also needs to be on a route where he is not likely to be held up behind the hazards of slow-moving traffic.

Bournemouth and Yeovil are discounted. Not only because the 'A' roads, although good, are not quite good enough to ensure unhindered passage, but because he is unacquainted with the lay of either town. With a lacking in local knowledge, he knows that if he were to be unexpectedly diverted from his route, he would be put at a disadvantage ... and could then fail to make the journey on time.

There is to be a match in Bristol. He knows the layout of both the city and the ground well, having spent many a cold Saturday afternoon watching the successes and failures of what was once his local team. A match against Reading will not be far off from being considered as a local derby; as such, he would expect the assemblage of a healthy-sized crowd. As far as he is concerned, the larger the crowd, then the better it will be.

His attendance will necessitate not much more than an hours drive up the M5. He will be able to get to the ground a good forty minutes before the seven-forty-five kick-off.

With it having served its purpose, the newspaper, albeit in the main, unread, is no longer of any interest. Accordingly, it is put to once side.

The kitchen table is his worktop. The items which are required for him to realize his objectives are spread neatly across the wooden surface. The need for organization and routine in his life is obvious, for everything that he does reflects an air of order. Even the tinned foods which are stored in the kitchen cupboards are arranged by way of size. The titles in the bookcase are, rather predictably, stored by author and in alphabetical sequence. Some would say these are the signs of a man with *obsessive-compulsive disorder*, but he prefers to recognize his trait as being little more than that of him having been blessed with the advantage of a tidy mind.

With his innate desire to keep the things that matter in some kind of order, he knows that there is no better trolley-man than he. Unlike the times when he is away, be it on a rest day or annual leave, no trolley stands abandoned for too long whilst on his watch. Furthermore, his dedication to his task has been appreciatively noticed by those in suits. He is good at his job ... and they know it.

He scans the tabletop and methodically makes a mental note of what lies before him — a pair of reflective number plates, a selection of specially-selected stick-on numbers and letters, a cross-head screwdriver, some heavy-duty cable-ties, a blanket, a roll of plastic sheeting, a pair of scissors and a wide roll of silver-coloured duct tape.

There is something missing. He wanders out to his car and fumbles through the boot. He has it! A light bulb, with its glass slightly blackened from when the brake-light filament had blown.

He would normally have discarded the no longer serviceable item; but for no apparent reason other than it being simply an oversight, he had left it mixed up with the odds and ends which had collected in the boot.

He needs to ensure that his rear bulb will be operative for the major part of the night, and so, in order to ensure no lapse in his memory, he makes a written note — *Spare Bulbs*.

Tomorrow has been planned.

In the morning, he will be making a trip to a supermarket. Not his place of work, but, rather, he will choose one farther afield; one where he is unlikely to be recognized or remembered.

Not wishing to run the risk of having his registration number recorded as having entered the customer car park, he will be parking in a nearby street. As far as his appearance is concerned, he will not try to disguise himself; after all, that in itself could make him stand out from the crowd. Instead, he will ensure that his clothing, and thus his look in general, is appropriate. That is to say, it will be lacking in bright colours and logos. It will be non-descript.

The payment for his purchase will be made via the facility of a self-serve till ... and in coinage. This way, he will leave no fingerprints on any notes, nor will there be any record of him having visited the shop. What is more, by making use of the self-service facility he will avoid the need to make personal contact with a cashier.

The inconvenience of no longer being able to have a set of number plates made up without the authorization of documentary proof of ownership can be overcome. He has done it before … and he can do it again.

He has already replaced the fixing screws to both front and rear, as the old ones were showing signs of rust. Besides, with each of the screw-heads in danger of being chewed by the turn of a screwdriver, they would be difficult to remove in a hurry. There will be no such problem with the replacements. The removal and refitting will be a matter of routine.

As he sorts the numbers and letters and, with attention to detail, measures out the spacing so that they will not attract undue attention when he is finally on the road, his thoughts drift back, as they so often do, to the disturbing echoes of the traumatic events which had left their mark, thus, having made him into what he now is.

Looking back, those days were at best, surreal … and at worst, horrific.

The cruel and humiliating way in which he, as an eleven-year-old boy, had been mistreated had been unforgivable.

However, with the passing of time and the sympathetic support of his mother, he had eventually been able to file that series of events into what she had referred to as … *the extremely difficult and unpleasant life-experiences box*. She'd had an *extremely difficult and unpleasant life-experiences box* of her own — and from what he has since learned, it would have, in all probabilities, been bulging at the seams.

It had been a hard time for them both. But then, at least he knows that he had gone on to ensure that his father's actions would never again be repeated.

It was two, maybe three, years later — and after he and his sisters had already moved up and into secondary education — that things had taken an unexpected turn for the worst. It was then, when he had been secure in the belief that all was forgotten, that he had been subjected to an occurrence which had resulted in him losing the ability to trust.

Being twins, he and Katy had been placed within the same year-group. And although he has forgotten the exact date of the incident, he can certainly recall the detail of what had occurred.

He remembers it well. The whole thing had been sparked when Miss Bishop, their English teacher, had been fishing for volunteers to join in with the activities of the drama group … and in particular to find takers for the supporting roles of dancers in the school's forthcoming performance of *West Side Story* — the *Romeo and Juliet* tale of young love and ethnic tensions which had been set within the gangland turfs of fifties America.

It was then when Katy had breached her promise to never reveal the detail of their family's past. Maybe it was just a moment of thoughtlessness, but the fact had remained that she had blurted out to the whole class that … if there were to be a shortage of girls to fill the parts, then he, her twin brother, could stand in. She went on to tell them that she had seen on many an occasion that … although he was *definitely a boy*, he could be *very convincing* and *ever so cute* when dressed as a girl … especially, she had added, when he had been wearing the special dress — the one which had *pretty lace and silky petticoats for him to dance and swirl around in.*

No doubt having been boosted by the fact that she had suddenly become the centre of attention, she had then, without the slightest consideration for his feelings, gone on to add fuel to the fires of her indiscretion. She had told them that he'd had *plenty of practice* in the pretence of being a girl — and, what is more, he could play the part so well that … with just *a touch of colour on the lips* and the appliance of *a little make-up for the eyes*, no one would have ever suspect the *truth behind the façade*. He was certain that she would not have used those precise words, but the essence of the message was the same.

The truth? She had certainly told *a* truth, but it had definitely not been *the* truth. After all, she had known that he had never ever worn any make-up — and with regard to the wearing of the dress, she had also been well aware of the fact that he had not dressed up because he'd had some abnormal desire to be seen as a girl. The truth of the matter had been that he had worn the garment under duress; it had been used as a form of punishment by their vicious and cold-hearted father.

As one recollection inadvertently spurs another, he remembers how, when their classmates had pressed both Katy and him for further detail, his sister had soon realized that she had overstepped the mark. Then, having recognized the signs of anger building up behind his look of shock and horror, she had rapidly back-pedalled and retracted her declaration with the addendum of a rather unconvincing explanation as to why she had made her comments. She had said *It was nothing. I was only joking. It wasn't true. Really, I mean it … I was just trying to wind my brother up. See, look at him … he's all embarrassed. So, there you are … it's worked.*

It had seemed, on the face of it at least, that most had blindly accepted her explanation as to why she had said those things. Whereas, the few who had been more perceptive and had, thus, read more into the interaction between the siblings, had guessed that there had, in fact, been much more than a hint of truth behind the exposé of the events of her brother's past. After all, it had seemed strange for her to have, without foundation, made it all up!

It was when the girls of the class had all been grouped together that they had managed, no doubt with the deceptive reassurance of absolute confidentiality, to prise from her the finer detail of the somewhat peculiar incidents which had involved her brother and the wearing of dresses.

They had discovered a secret that they could not keep to themselves, and — as those who have yet to develop the art of empathy so often do — they had readily gone on to breach their promise. Furthermore, they had without hesitation gleefully spread their edited, albeit embellished, version to another ... and then to another. And so it continued — the word was out.

He had hoped that once they had realised that he had been the innocent victim of domestic brutality, they would have relented and let it be. But no — their distorted versions had not only succeeded in avoiding the truth, but they had also ensured the deliberate exclusion of the fact that he and his family had been subjected to the sadism of an unbalanced and violent man.

After all, they must have seen no scope for entertainment by simply accepting the truth; they had ignored the facts and invented a new version of their own. It had been an adulteration of the reality. They had created the myth that he had always possessed a desire to dress up and act as a girl. What was more, not being satisfied to rest with these mistruths alone, they had added to the mix. They had spread the rumour that he had intended to go on playing the role until he finally became of an age when he would be able to fulfil his dream and make the ultimate change into becoming, to all intents and purposes, a woman.

Like Chinese whispers, the falsehood of rumour had soon become a statement of fact ... and it was not long before he was being referred to as *Little Miss Give-us-a-Twirl*. The taunts didn't stop with the mere calling of names. There had been occasions when he had been walking home from school when some of the older boys, having been egged on by their female companions, would tease him with a blow of a kiss, whilst sardonically gifting him with a bunch of roadside flowers which had been spiked with a mix of unsightly weeds.

Somewhat surprisingly, it was the girls who were often the worst. Not only did they incite their boyfriends and their brothers to participate in the merciless acts of baiting, they would, themselves, take pleasure in goading him with offers to lend him their lipsticks. As if that were not enough, they would continue their taunts with a barrage of invites for him to join them in their customary weekend trawl around the shops. This is when they would try on the latest fashions and visit the cafés where they'd known that they would have almost certainly been *chatted up* by boys; older boys who had designs on achieving more than just a stolen kiss.

It had not surprised him that, being teenagers, they would use the tools of feminine beautification as a means to prod; for, having grown up with two sisters, he had known that as they had neared an age where their physical maturity had been starting to flower ahead of that of their mentality, they too had become adept in the implementation of the cruel and unwarranted sport of *tease*.

However, the final straw had been when, following the school's weekly cross-country run — and when he had, as usual, been one of the last of the runners to use the showers — he had returned to his locker to find that it had already been unlocked. Whilst he had stood wrapped with just a towel to maintain his dignity, he had discovered that his clothing had not just gone, it had been substituted. They had been replaced with a dress which, being of the hue of a rose and of a style which, with the flare of its skirts having been accentuated by the trimmings of elaborate frills and multilayered petticoats, had more than adequately succeeded in mimicking the vogue of Latino swing; a fashion which had been flaunted by flirtatious young ladies who, with a desire for excitement and rebellion, had jived the nights away within the dance halls and clubs of the rock-and-rolling fifties.

He can still remember how he had stared in both horror and disbelief at the garment, which — with its mass of brightly-coloured fabrics compacted to fit within the limited confines of his locker — had suddenly, when the door had been opened, sprung out and unfurled across the floor to lie still, and with an air of vulnerability, at his bared feet.

He had, without question, been shocked by its emergence. But then, this had not been down to the inherent allure of its fabric, nor had it been due to the exaggerated femininity of its design. The truth had been that there were pupils at the school who had felt the need to persecute him … and for no other reason than to take pleasure in the infliction of sorrow.

If they'd thought that their actions could have, somehow, trapped him into exposing some inexplicable need to embrace and adopt this potentially enthralling symbol of womanhood for himself, then they were wrong — they had failed!

In truth, he'd no leanings whatsoever towards a desire to assume the role of femininity. Their suppositions were, therefore, way off-target.

In later years, he may well have had his senses triggered by the allure of its fabric and design — but not for the reasons that they had supposed or, for that matter, for the reasons that they had hoped for!

With the memories of his past experiences so cruelly brought to the fore, he had been dumbstruck. As far as he was concerned, there was no beauty to be seen hidden in the lustre of its petticoats, nor was there flair in its frivolous design. He had been conscious of it having nothing more than the basic ingredients to become just another sadistic tool for subjugation. And as a consequence, he had been sickened and angered by its very presence.

Although it had been likely that the incident had started out as being little more than that of a practical joke — no doubt fuelled by the exuberance of youthful mischief — undertones of a more sinister nature were duly exposed. The perpetrators of this unwarranted act of heartlessness had gathered around to add insult to injury with an unremitting barrage of mocking jibes ... and the blockage of the paths for escape.

He recalls how they had grasped hold of the dress. Then having pushed him backwards, so that his back had been flat against the wall, they had restrained him sufficiently enough to allow one of them to hold it up against him ... and in a manner so as to demonstrate how he may have looked had he been dressed up and in readiness to perform.

With looks of malevolent intent, they had baited him. First with a verbal onslaught of sarcastic chat-up lines and then — as if they had been psyching themselves and those who had been watching — to a barrage of unremitting mockery. As he had struggled to escape from the living nightmare and, at the same time, had tried to preserve his dignity by not losing his grip on his towel, the taunting had escalated with an increasing bombardment of calls for him to put on the dress and give them a show.

Whilst he had stood, immobilised by the fear of what was yet to come, there had been a sudden tug on his towel. Then, with his only means of shielding having been taken and then cast beyond his reach, he had been left all but naked. So — much to the amusement of all — he'd had little choice other than to grab hold of the dress and welcome the covering that, with the fullness of its skirts and its mass of rustling petticoats, it was able to afford.

Even then, he was determined not to give way and submit to their demands. He was not going to *dress up*. With the option for escape well and truly out of the question, he'd just wrapped the garment around him as if it were no more than a bed-sheet — and whilst gripping it as tight as he could, he prayed that someone would intervene and rescue him from further humiliation.

Of course, he will never be able to forget the melody of the song ... *The Lord of the Dance*. Someone in the *pack*, having spontaneously *knocked up* a ditty for the occasion, had started to sing their own reworded version to the same familiar tune:

'He? She? What's it going to be?
A she who's a he, or a he who's a she?
He twirls and swirls, like all the pretty girls,
So it's going to have to be — he's going to be a she?'

It had not been long before almost all those present had picked up the lyrics and — with the additional challenge of trying to conquer the rather tongue-twisting element of the wording — had readily joined in ... and had sung along as if they were football fans baiting the opposition from the safety and anonymity of the home terraces. He recalls how, at the time, it had seemed as if the tune had somehow wormed its way into each of their minds and then, almost hypnotically, compelled each of them to chant over and over ... as if they were trapped within the confines of an everlasting loop.

The more he had reacted and struggled to push his way past to make his escape, the louder they had become. Ironically, it was only the volume of the singing which had instigated the intervention of the sports master — Mr McKenzie.

There had been no doubt that his arrival — along with the very real threat of detentions and possible suspensions for all — had only just occurred in time to save him from the distress of having been bullied into the donning of the dress. He'd known from bitter experience that had there been no intervention — and he had subsequently been forced into compliance — then this incident would have undoubtedly developed into acts of further humiliation. He would almost certainly, as had happened in the past, have been made to parade the newly-created persona in front of all ... and then been subjected to a relentless bombardment of cruel and belittling mockery.

He had been there before and so, had recognized the signs. He had known that he could no longer readily accept the situation, and this time he would not willingly go with the flow in order to keep the peace. What's more, the very thought of him being subjected to ridicule for the entertainment of the wicked and ignorant had made him even more defiant. But then, the sheer fact of the matter had been that if assistance had not arrived when it had, then he would have been outnumbered, trapped and placed in a position where he would have fought. But then, he would have lost, and his fight to retain even a semblance of dignity would have been in vain.

Mr McKenzie, however, had been quick to arrive. Having assessed the situation, he had been even quicker to secure the return of the rightful garb and then, with order duly restored, ensured that apologies — albeit issued under duress and, so, tainted with the underlying stench of insincerity — were duly offered.

None of them, not even Mr McKenzie, would have had the slightest inkling as to extent of the torment that he had suffered in the past ... and he had suspected that neither would they have cared.

Even now, he can recall how the sports-master, although instrumental in saving him from the jaws of his persecutors, was equally disingenuous as he, too, had seemed unable to completely disguise his own amusement over the incident. Although Mr McKenzie's intervention had ensured the recovery of the missing clothing and the return of the inappropriate attire to the wardrobes of the drama department, he'd had a grin which, having bordered on a chuckle, had been spread right across his face.

He had felt abused and angry. Apart from the sense of companionship and understanding which he'd still had with both his mother and the youngest of his sisters, he had also felt isolated, let down and demoralised by the ways of people as a whole.

The act of betrayal from Katy, his twin — whether intended or otherwise — had in itself gone way beyond the boundaries of forgiveness. But then, for her to have gone on to callously reveal the secrets of their family's sad and painful past, knowing that her so-called friends would be unable to resist retelling the tale to others, was totally incomprehensible.

As far as he was concerned, his dignity was in tatters and his life in ruins. So, it was then, after the incident in the changing-rooms, when in order to avoid further humiliation and the insufferable outbursts of mockery, he had started along the road to truancy ... and with it, an element of self-imposed seclusion.

He had certainly learnt some lessons that day; in particular, he had learnt to recognize the potential of treachery behind the deceptive smiles of the female of his species. Yes ... that day had been a turning point all right. It was then, when he had concluded that the human race — albeit often showing signs of sophistication and respectability on the outside — were, in his mind, little more than that of vermin ... and should, therefore, be treated as such. What was more, he had lost the desire and the capacity to care. So it was then that he had decided that he would live his life in the way of his choosing, and —as far as he was concerned — to hell with everyone else!

Still, those days have passed. So, with the falsified number plates completed, he moves his attention to the cable-ties.

On the night, he will not want to be distracted, nor will he want to be delayed by having to struggle in the darkness to find the aperture in order thread a loop. Knowing the importance of preparation he simplifies the procedure by partly threading the ends through the gap, thus, leaving them held on the first of the cable's teeth. Once looped they will be ready for when the time is right ... and will then, without difficulty, be able to be slipped over the wrists and the ankles before being swiftly and efficiently pulled firm.

The rest of the items need no specific preparation.

He sits back. Although he is happy that his plans have been thorough and well-thought-out, he mentally rehearses and visualises each stage, checking and re-checking for oversights which could thwart his mission.

He can see a weakness — the owner of the car to which the falsified number plates refer to is female and has a profusion of wavy, shoulder-length blond hair.

Although the likelihood of him being recognized whilst confined within the car is minimal, his silhouette — if viewed from the front, the side or even the rear — would, no doubt, give sufficient cause for anyone who knows the car to question as to why it is being driven by an unknown male. With this in mind, he concludes that it is not worth the risk of a call of concern to either its owner or, what would be far worse … to the police. He pauses and thinks. Then, with a solution in mind, he picks up his pen and adds to his list … *Wig —Blonde.*

Satisfied that all is now in place — bar the purchase of an item or two in the morning, that is — he sits back … and with an air of smugness, combined with the barely-restrained eagerness of anticipation, he starts to rub and clap his hands together whilst emitting a series of peculiar, high-pitched giggles.

Chapter 34

He is well prepared. He is also aware that the technique of triangulation means that the position of a mobile phone can be pinpointed to a specific location. Whether or not this can be done retrospectively, he is not entirely sure, but as a precaution he will ensure that *his* mobile phone is switched off once he reaches his destination. It will not be re-connected until later in the night when he returns homeward along the same arterial route.

The northbound carriageway of the M5 is, as is usual for this time of day, busy with the movement of both commercial and commuter traffic. He knows he has sufficient fuel for the return journey as, prior to joining the motorway, he had filled up the tank at the supermarket filling station … not just for the cost and the convenience, but because he was certain that the security camera would record the image of his leaving and, in doing so, record the fact that his nearside brake light was inoperative.

He had paid in the kiosk by credit card. The receipt, timed and dated, had then been tucked away in the zipped compartment of his wallet. There was to be no taking of chances.

The run has been steady, and as he approaches his turn off, he slows.

M5 — Junction Eighteen — Avonmouth.

He takes the off-slip and heads towards the Portway. Once having passed under Kingdom Brunel's, Clifton Suspension Bridge, he turns off and heads towards Ashton Gate — the home of Bristol City Football Club.

With their position in the Championship already looking dire, they must make the best of their home-ground advantage. Despite propping up much of the Division, they will still draw a good crowd, and so the chances of any one person being identified among the mass of faces will be unlikely.

He parks beside the nearest cash-point to the stadium. He draws out a little more than what is sufficient to gain entry and to purchase a programme. With the notes and the ATM receipt tucked in his wallet, he drives off towards the turnstiles.

On the approach to the ground, he spots a man who, donned in the red and white colours of the host team, is enthusiastically advertising both his wares and his presence as he hollers, "Programmes! Get your programmes here!"

Stopping just long enough to take the cash and then hand over the merchandise to the early arrivals, he continues to assert his presence.

The hollering stops as he pulls up and then makes his purchase through the opened window of his car.

A police officer has watched the transaction, but, having also noted that the stop was a little more than momentary and that the main thrust of the crowd has yet to arrive, he has ignored the yellow-line transgression.

Part one of his plan is now complete.

He drives off and back towards the motorway, taking a short detour to the pre-selected seclusion of a country lane where he will be able, without audience, to disguise the fact of his early return.

The forward planning of having renewed the fixing-screws for the number-plates has made the change-over quick and easy. Then, with the simple insertion of a new bulb, whilst ensuring the retention of the faulty item, he is satisfied that part two of his plan has been fully accomplished.

He checks his watch: seven-ten. The timing is tight, but he is not running late. He will still have time to travel back along the motorway and confirm the occurrence of the eight-thirty rendezvous at the *S.V. Club*.

Anonymous amid the steady stream of traffic, which, apart from the occasional straggler, cruises at speeds of just below eighty miles-per-hour for the entirety of the seventy-five-mile journey, he is just another traveller who is on an everyday journey and, as such, is of little significance.

M5 — Junction — Twenty-eight.

He indicates, and as he enters the boundaries of the city — from where the number which is now displayed on his vehicle is registered — he is a little concerned as to whether or not the car will be recognized by a friend of the woman, who, he knows, should be at home with her man and their son.

He is unconcerned as to whether or not the cameras pick up the presence of the car, but then, he does not wish it to be recorded that it is *he* who is the driver. He pulls over. Once away from the brightness of the street, he opens the glove compartment. Then, pulling down the windscreen visor in an attempt to mask his face, he fits the blonde wig over his head. It is a gamble; but then, he is up for it. Disguised, he continues towards the city centre, where he will ensure that he is out of the view of any prying cameras, and park in the leafy idyll of Southernhay Gardens.

He is on schedule! He removes the wig and stuffs it back into the glove compartment, thus, ensuring that it is out of the sight of any passer-by.

There is no need to rush. It is eight-twenty, and he has ten minutes to make the four-minute walk to witness the rendezvous.

Walking under the nineteenth-century footbridge, and with his head held down, he moves swiftly towards the city centre.

The dappled-shades of gentle light which radiate out from the antiquated lanterns — along with the preserved remnants of ancient walls, with overhanging branches stretching out from hidden gardens and private courtyards — creates a setting which sends a shiver throughout his body. It's as if it has tuned him into a world where lost souls have been trapped into roaming the periphery of these hallowed grounds.

Although reason dictates that there can be no life after death and that any reports of ghostly presences are nothing more than that of products of overactive imaginations, he cannot help but to have some lingering doubts; as such, he has come to keep an open mind regarding these things.

Logic tells him that it is nothing but humbug.

When his mind is focused, he is able to dismiss the illusion of superstition for what it is and concentrate fully on whatever is in hand.

This evening he is focused. He is able to single-mindedly stride onwards and through the narrow walkway which leads out and into the High Street.

The brightness of the city lighting hides little, and as he glances up the street opposite and towards the landmark structure of the Clock Tower, he sees several groups of young people making their way to the pubs and eating-houses of the city.

There is no sign of a lone woman walking with purpose towards the club.

He wonders if she has arrived early or, conversely, if she has changed her plans and will not arrive at all. But then, he reasons, it is likely that she is still on her way. With that thought to the fore, he knows that he will just have to be patient.

A young couple stand together on the steps. They look up the road and towards him. Although he is at a distance, he recognizes the woman as being the invitee. And by her demeanour, she is obviously awaiting the arrival of Anna — the girl from the Slovakian hills.

The columned entrance to the shopping centre will give him cover — he hops up the steps and waits.

While standing in the shadows, he is able to watch over the comings and goings of the club without drawing attention to himself. Furthermore, with the façade of him standing with his head downward whilst appearing to check for messages on his phone, he knows that no one will give him a second glance.

Lisa, the invitee, points towards the High Street and waves, signalling her presence to the oncoming figure.

It's Anna. She waves back. Although she is over five minutes late, it is of no consequence — to the young and the carefree, she is as good as on time.

Somehow, she seems different.

No longer has she the innocent waif-like looks of just a couple of days ago. Then, when he had seen her, she had been modestly clad in faded blue jeans, furry boots, a woollen cardigan and her hair hanging loose. But now, with her black leather raincoat over her new dress and a wooden comb holding her hair up and in place, she has the shape, poise and demeanour of a mature and confident young woman; to say the least, she is a very different prospect.

She is, by her appearance and the bubbly manner in which she presents herself, clearly excited about her chance to socialize and seems confident in her new apparel. He cannot help but to note how, lacking in reticence and within moments of meeting up with her newly-found friends, she is not slow to slip off her coat and flaunt the alluring design of the see-through panels of burgundy lace … and the captivating swing of the skirt.

Yes, she is extremely happy, and, as far as he is concerned, she is probably going to forget her fiancé back at home and make the most of this time to enjoy herself.

With the formality of her introduction to Lisa's partner completed, they disappear into the covered alley and towards the entrance to the club.

Once out from the shadows, he strolls across the street, thus, enabling himself a confirmatory peek to ensure that they have entered as planned.

A powerfully-built man is at the door, and, with the supplement of an admiring glance, he ushers her in.

It's safe. She is with her friends, and now, with her being past the point of payment, she will not see him. With a boost of adrenalin having given him a feeling of indestructibility, he, like a leopard eyeing its prey before making its final approach, cannot resist the temptation to walk through the alley and past the entrance.

He does not loiter; instead, he walks into the pedestrianized street. He knows of a recently-opened café from where he will purchase a strong black coffee.

With a long night ahead, an input of caffeine is needed.

***

Tori is running late … but it is not her fault.

Her mother had been preoccupied on the telephone. Then she had been waylaid by a sudden need to change her clothing — something other than the drabness of everyday wear. With the additional requirement of having to add the last subtle touches to her make-up, she had left it a little too late to be able to drive her into town … and still be on time.

Jamie and the band had arrived much earlier. There was equipment to set up, guitars to tune and sound-checks to be made. That takes time. But now, with it all completed to their satisfaction, they are waiting to impress. Even as a warm-up for the headline band, there is much kudos in performing at this level — and with an enthusiastic crowd wanting to rock, they are up for the challenge.

***

The staff are different to those who he has seen working in the daytime hours; there is no familiarity in their greetings. They don't know him, and, as it happens, he is glad of that.

As he carries his mug of coffee to his table, he looks out and into the street and catches a glimpse of a raven-haired young woman hurrying past the café and towards the alley. His heart misses a beat ... and then races. There is something familiar about her, but he can't quite put his finger on what it is.

He needs to check.

He places his cup on a table and steps out and onto the pavement.

He's too slow. She has gone!

Don't be ridiculous! he whispers to himself, *It's not possible! Come on man! You're imagining things!*

The noticeable drop in the outdoor temperature spurs him into returning to the warmth and comfort of the café. Once reunited with his coffee, he sits in thoughtful silence ... reflecting on how the earlier haunting ambience of the Cathedral's precincts has raised the spectre of memories, repressed ... and of issues, not yet resolved.

He is not stupid. After all, he has held positions which have carried responsibility and respect. But still, that does not stop him from feeling the effects of the conflict deep within him as he battles to make sense of his fears.

He believes that it is the logic and education of modern man that dictates that the rising of the dead is a notion too far. But he accepts that there is a deep and primitive inheritance which, shared by people from around the globe, seems to retain the primal need to believe in some kind of spiritual afterlife.

Maybe, he thinks, it is the inexplicable fear of an unstoppable vengeance from beyond the grave that fuels the doubts. Or, perhaps, it was when man had become reluctantly aware of his own mortality that the need had arisen for him to turn to the concept of ghosts and gods. But then again, it could also be that it is people of his own ilk — the cynics — who are wrong ... and that there is, in fact, some truth behind the myth.

He has no option other than to try and think of something else as a means of distraction. He must focus. Only then will he be able to dismiss the thoughts from his mind and, hopefully, push them back to where they belong — that is to say, irretrievably buried and forever hidden in the long and distant past.

Chapter 35

Gina feels more than a little self-conscious as she walks unaccompanied into the foyer of the rather exclusive hotel. She has an appointment with a man who she has neither seen nor heard from for nearly two decades. She is not troubled by the fact of who he is, but more as to why, after the passing of so many years, he has decided to probe into a past which carries with it so many painful memories.

The thought of her hanging around the foyer alone and with the eyes of others questioning the reason for her presence, fills her with dread. She glances across the room. She is relieved of her worries. He is already waiting, relaxed and confident, sitting in a chair ... and with an uninterrupted view to the main doors.

Having eyed both her entrance and her recognition of him, he, without a second thought, stands up. Then, with a genuine display of impeccable manners, he approaches and greets her with a smile and a welcoming embrace.

"How are you, Gina? How've you been keeping?"

"I've been keeping well, thank you. And how about you?"

"I'm good. Look ... I'm sorry about the short notice, but I felt that I ought to speak to you."

"That's okay. I had to bring my daughter into town anyway ... so I haven't been put out at all. In fact, it's probably better than *vegging-out* in front of the telly. Since we've had so many channels to choose from, there seems very little which is worth watching."

Tom agrees; then with a gentle swing of his arm he ushers her towards the lounge. "Now ... shall we go through and find somewhere we can have a drink and a chat?"

She nods, readily accepting the courteous etiquette which dictates that the man should treat a lady with respect and so, hold the door open for her as she enters a room. "Thank you."

"You're quite welcome. Have you eaten?"

She pauses before answering. She knows the reputation of the *gourmet-fare* which is served at this establishment. And although she wishes her answer could have been a *no*, she *has* eaten and so responds with a truthful, "Yes, I have ... but thank you for asking."

"It's no bother. How about a drink, then?"

"Yes, that sounds nice. I think, perhaps, a white wine ... that would be lovely, thank you. I can't have more than one though ... I'm driving."

He smiles as he asks, "Any preference as to—"

"No. You were always the expert ... you choose."

"Okay."

He steps over to the bar and gives his order.

"Is this to go on your bill, sir?"

"Yes ... on the bill, thank you."

He removes his room's *key-card* from his pocket, and the barman duly makes a note of its number.

"If you'd like to take a seat, sir ... I'll bring your drinks over to you."

"Thank you."

Tom returns to his guest and settles in the comfort of an imposing leather armchair which is positioned opposite and across the table from her. He sits back and collects his thoughts before speaking. "Now, as I said on the phone, I've been thinking that, maybe, we ought to consider trying to — how can I put it? Yes, that's it ... We ought to try to, somehow, resurrect the enquiry. I would like to see if we can reopen the whole thing about Lucy's disappearance. Perhaps we could try the papers, or even the local TV."

In anticipation of a response, he looks directly at her.

There is none. So he continues. "Well, I've been in contact with Shep, that's Shep Russell. I think he was the local policeman who spoke to you when Lucy went missing. Anyway, he's said that he would like to help us in any way that he can. He's also said that *he* wants to find out what happened to her as well."

She pauses before replying. "I'm not too sure about all this. And to be honest with you, I can't see how digging up the past is going to find her. Do you honestly think that there's anyone out there who knows something? I certainly don't ... and if they do, what makes you think they'll be prepared to open up now?"

"I don't know ... but I *do* feel that it's worth a try."

In silence, she wonders if she will be able to cope with the media attention. The thought of televised interviews and, possibly, re-enactments of that terrible night sends a shudder throughout her body.

He breaks the silence. "I know it's going to be hard, but I really do think it's worth a shot."

"Okay, maybe you're right. But can I sleep on it?"

"Of course you can — you sleep on it and I'll give you a ring tomorrow, if that's all right with you?"

She nods as the drinks are delivered to their table.

Gina looks at Tom and hesitates. She is uncertain as to whether or not she should disclose, firstly — the fact that she and Geoff are no longer together, and secondly — the detail of the final straw which had broken the back of their relationship. She decides against it and changes the subject. "So I take it that you're still living in France?"

"Yes ... I'm still there. In fact, while I'm in the UK the place is being looked after by Rozenn and Jean-Paul, my son."

"Jean-Paul? Very French, I must say!"

"Yes, well … I suppose he's spent the whole of his life there … and then he's got all his French family as well. So, I guess, to all intents and purposes, he is pretty much French. So … why not?"

"So, from what you say, you and Rozenn are still together?"

"Yes, we are. It's been a fair few years now … and yes, I'm happy with that."

"That's good. I'm really pleased for you." She detects a hint of disappointment in her own voice but hopes that he has not detected the same. But if he has, then he has kept it to himself.

"And you? Are things still good with Geoff?"

"No. We've gone our separate ways."

"Oh. I am sorry to hear about that."

"It's okay. It was a while ago now. So now … it's just me and Victoria, and we are managing just fine."

"That's also good to hear. I suppose she must be pretty-much grown up by now?"

"Yes, she is. She's turned out to be a really good girl."

She hesitates again as she assesses whether this would be a good time to reveal her secret … but he interrupts.

"So then, what does she —"

"Tom?"

"Yes."

"Will you bear with me, 'cause I'm going to tell you why Geoff and me split up. And then I'm going to ask you just to let me say what I need to say … and without any interruption, if that's okay with you?"

Intrigued, he nods and waits in silence.

"We had what you might call … an up and down relationship. At times it had become heated, to say the least. He found it difficult with my moods. You see, the truth is … I've never got over Lucy … and, so much so, that I've even had a few sessions of counselling."

Again, he nods as he allows her to continue uninterrupted.

"Well … as you've probably guessed, I've never been able to cope too well with things after she disappeared. So I started to blame him for everything. But then, during one of our rows, I told him that Victoria wasn't his!"

"Right …" He allows the content of the last sentence to sink in before continuing. "Okay … but, before you go on … I don't *quite* see what this has to do with me."

"Please … bear with me."

She pauses for a moment so as to ensure that he is fully attentive. "May I continue?"

"Sure. Carry on."

"Well … he stormed off, as usual. But when he came back, he said that he didn't believe me — and to be honest, I wasn't a hundred percent sure myself. So, like a fool, I told him that."

She can see in Tom's expression that he isn't impressed. "Yes … I know I was stupid. But then, I suppose, at the time it was my anger which was doing the talking."

Tom sips his drink as he waits for her to get to the point.

"Now, unfortunately Victoria was in the next room … and so, she'd overheard everything." She takes a breath before continuing. "Understandably, she was very upset, and she insisted that I tell her the truth."

"Which, I presume, you did?"

"Yes … and no. As I said, I could only tell her that I wasn't too sure."

"Really? — I bet she was really impressed with you then!"

With no more than a disparaging glance, she ignores the comment and continues. "Anyway … she demanded that Geoff had a paternity test, and, of course, we all had to agree."

"Ah well … it strikes me that you were on a bit of a hiding to nothing then. I mean, either she isn't his daughter, then I'm not surprised if he was a wee bit upset … or, on the other hand, she *is* … And so, you've been a complete *dillock* and owned up to having an affair when you were supposed to have been all lovey-dovey together! Well … he knew that you'd done it before didn't he? So, for what it's worth, I don't blame him for dumping you, whatever the results!"

She has no wish to listen to his uninvited judgements. So, with the insistence that she should be able to complete her story, she asserts her presence. "Do you want to know the result, or don't you?"

"There's more? Okay then … go on — you may as well."

"The result proved that he is definitely *not* her father!"

"Well, there you go. It serves you right. And now, you've paid the price."

She wants to retaliate, but she knows that he's right — and yes, she has paid the price. Although he is happy in his marriage, she senses that he still harbours an element of bitterness over the way in which their relationship had ended — and, to be fair, she can't blame him. After all, her relationship with Geoff had itself started out as an extramarital affair.

"But still …" he continues, "I don't really know why you're telling *me* all this. And to be honest with you, I can't see it as being any of my business—"

"Tom … " She rests both her hands on his. "Try thinking back to Lucy's eighteenth."

He slides his hands away and allows his thoughts to drift back through the passages of time. "Yes … okay. She had a party … and we all had a good time. We had a few drinks ... then I kipped on your sofa."

"That's right ... Geoff was away at the *hotel sulky-pants,* and, during the night, I visited you on the sofa. Don't you remember?"

He remembered. He had tried to forget it by dismissively putting it down to the old adage of *things happen* — but he *had* felt a little guilty. After all, he may not have been married ... but *she was.*

The penny begins to drop. He starts to recall how the combination of a few drinks within the almost forgotten ambiance of a family unit had led to a moment of indiscretion.

"When ... exactly ... was Victoria born?"

She laughs. "At last ... you've clicked, haven't you?"

"Are you saying what I think you're saying?"

"What? That you're Victoria's father?"

He nods.

"Well ... yes, I am. I'm saying just that. Victoria and Lucy are not half-sisters at all. They share the same parents. That is ... you are the father to both of them! So, there you have it."

"Are you really sure about this?"

"Oh yes. I'm sure all right. It could only have been one of two — and science has proved that it wasn't the other."

"Does she ... I mean ... does Victoria know?"

"What? That you're her father? No ... I've just avoided the subject for so long that I think she's given up and stopped asking."

He sits back, dumbfounded by the revelation.

She breaks the silence. "Do *you* think I ought to tell her? I mean you've done nothing wrong. And, in any case, you weren't *with* Rozenn at the time, were you?"

"No ... I wasn't. That came later. She just helped me through all the ... aftermath — if that's that the right word? I think it is. Anyway, she helped me through the aftermath following Lucy's disappearance." He breaks off for a moment, and then adds, "She'll be pretty upset when she finds out though. In fact, I'm not sure how she'll take it. And then, of course, there's Jean-Paul! I wonder what he'll think ... suddenly having a sister to nag him. Sheesh, I'm— Oh ... I don't know what to say."

He allows his thoughts to race through his mind, and then accepts that there should, in fact, be no problem. "No, you're right. She shouldn't be upset. After all, as you say, Rozenn and me weren't exactly an item at the time, so I can't see a problem. You should tell Victoria, if that's what you want."

"I've got something ... " She fumbles in her bag and pulls out her wallet-cum-purse ... opens it and produces a photograph. With the picture placed on the table in front of him, she announces, "Here you are ... this is Victoria — or Tori, as she now prefers to be called."

"Do you mind?" he asks, as he picks up the photograph for a closer examination.

She has no objection.

"Mmm… She doesn't half look like Lucy, doesn't she?"

She nods.

"Yes, she does. She's the spitting image of her."

"Do you know? When I was in town earlier, I think I must've seen her. I thought I was just imagining things. I'd just been thinking about Lucy … then there she was … in the crowd. And then she was gone. But now, looking at this, I know I wasn't going mad. It must have been Victoria that I saw."

She nods and poses the next question. "Would you like to meet her?"

"Of course I would — but only if she's been told in advance … and then only if she is happy to meet me."

"Fine. I'll see what I can do. I'll speak to her about it tomorrow. And I'm sorry about my attitude earlier. Anyway, I will tell her about you — and then, if she wants to meet you, then perhaps we can arrange something?"

Gina's confidence has improved with the relief of having shed the burden of her secret.

Presenting her empty glass, she asks, "Shall we have another?"

"I thought you were driving!"

"Well, yes, I am … but, I could always stay — "

"No … I don't think so. If I was single? Maybe. But not now. I'm married — I'm happy with Rozenn … and I really don't want anything to change that."

Even though she is still unable to completely extinguish the flame which still burns for her first love, she accepts the put-down without protest.

The years have drifted by, but sometimes, as is the case this evening, the memories bounce back and fill her with a yearning for a return to the excitement and freshness of their youthful romance. She remembers those early days so well. They were at college, away from their respective homes and on unconnected courses. But they had often shared the mid-morning facilities of the refectory to partake in the consumption of refreshments and a break from the intensity of their, sometimes tedious, lectures. She will never forget hearing the dulcet sounds of his Irish lilt for the very first time; it had caught her unawares and, in doing so, had engaged her full attention. Still carrying an image etched in the pages of her memories, she recalls how it had been his enchanting smile, along with the intelligent yet playful look in his eyes, that had ultimately reeled her in.

"A coffee, maybe?" he suggests as an alternative.

"No, thanks. Perhaps you're right. I think I ought to go home and, maybe, start making preparations for tomorrow's little chat with a certain young lady."

"Okay — you've got my number ... I'll wait until I hear from you. Now you take care on the way home, and umm ... I'll see you soon."

They part with no more than the simple courteousness of a friendly embrace.

Chapter 36

Having taken a walk away from the city centre and then along the quayside, he has not only burnt off pent-up energy but he has also killed some time.

But now, having returned to his car, he can see from his position in Southernhay that he has an unobstructed view along The Close and up towards The Green and its precincts. Midweek, and at this time of night, there is little reason for people to be out and about in the main thoroughfares, and those who are, are even less likely to have a reason to choose to walk along this quiet and shadowed route.

It is well past midnight and, he surmises, she will soon be making her way homeward.

In the silence of the night, sound travels easily. He does not wish to attract undue attention to himself, so he sits patiently and listens to the radio. The results and subsequent reports of the night's programme of football matches are broadcast and discussed.

Apart from wishing to hear the details of the one match in Bristol, he has little interest in the results in general. In truth, although he would prefer to hear of a home victory, the fact as to whether or not the team won or lost had mattered little. It is the knowledge of what had occurred during the match which is of importance to him. For this reason, he must ensure that he absorbs the specifics ... and sufficiently enough for him to be able to convince anyone who may be interested, that he was actually present and attentive throughout.

Once he has the information required, the radio will be silenced.

And now ... over to our reporter at Ashton Gate, where Bristol City have been playing ... The result is given, along with a brief summary of the match, which, detailing the circumstances of how each of the five goals were scored, is enthusiastically relayed across the airwaves. Even though they had found the back of the net twice, the home team had still suffered defeat!

Disappointed with the result? Up to a point, he is. But then, the truth of the matter is that it cannot be altered ... and so, he does not allow it to distract him from his purpose. He continues listening to the report, and as each scorer is identified, he notes the fact on the team-sheet of his programme with no more than that of a numbered tick.

With the report over and the attention of the station having moved on to reporting the play of another of the evening's matches, he presses the off-button, sits back and waits.

The radio has been deactivated for several minutes, and, then, whilst sitting back in a state of relaxed watchfulness, he becomes aware of the sound of distant chatter coming from the direction of The Green.

Although both voices are female and carry intonations from foreign lands, their accents are distinct and different.

He lowers the window and listens.

His sense of hearing has always been good, and having become adept in the skills of being able to eavesdrop on distant conversations — whether they have been within the precincts of the supermarket car park or through the background hubbub of the busy cafés of the city centre — he is able to pick out the relevant words of the exchange … and then use logic to deduce the rest.

"Are you sure you're are okay to walk alone?"

"Yes. Thank you. I will be okay. I have not far to go. It has been a really good night. Perhaps … I will be phoning you soon."

"Okay … If you are sure, then I will say goodnight."

"Goodnight."

It must be her. He feels a thumping in his chest as the adrenalin begins to make its presence felt. As he waits in silence until he has a confirmatory and uninterrupted view of his quarry, he draws deep and relaxing breaths.

As the power of his pulse increases, there is no voice of a conscience urging him to steer away from his chosen path. Instead, he is focused. And with an almost raptorial intensity, he watches her come closer with each unsuspecting step.

Unaware of her vulnerability, she, with an almost carefree gait, self-assuredly passes along the lane and under the overhead walkway towards him.

She may be unaccompanied and in a foreign country, but she has a confidence about her which fires his suspicions. He wonders if she has met someone in the club and had accepted an invite to meet him again and at a later date. Being away from home, she may well be seeking intimacy with another.

If his suppositions are true, then he has no doubt that it will end up with her going on to execute an act of betrayal.

He knows that he is right. She needs to be taught a lesson, and, what's more, she needs to be made an example of.

He watches as she checks her phone for messages. There are obviously none. With the phone having then been slipped back into her pocket, she continues on her way.

Her outer coat, with its close-fitting design complementing the style of the dress beneath, seems to enhance the very outline of her figure.

She is in no rush. She has enjoyed her evening.

She walks.

He watches.

Having been captivated by the way in which she moves, he has already embarked on a voyage of erotic imaginings — a voyage to a world in which he is able to relish in the prospect of what he knows is yet to come.

As she reaches the main road, she pauses. Being unaware of his presence, and with no more than that of a cursory glance having been cast in his direction, she turns to her right and then makes her way along the pavement towards the busy, well-lit complexity of junctions of the inner-bypass.

He fires up the engine and drives off in the opposite direction, dutifully following the obligatory course of the one-way system.

He is unconcerned that she is no longer within his view. Besides, he will be reaching the inner-bypass at a different point. He will then, without looking at all suspicious, catch up with ... and then pass her, before leaving her to continue to negotiate her route across the various sets of light-controlled pedestrian crossings.

He also knows that he has no need to rush. After all, he will have plenty of time to be able to reach his destination, park the car and be ready and waiting for her approach.

He arrives and pulls up at the roadside. Pressing the switch for the interior lights to the off position, he is able to ensure that they will not illuminate his face, on the opening and closing of the doors.

As he gets out of the car, he walks to the rear and clicks open the boot-lid. Then, ensuring that it is no longer completely shut, he allows it to rest on its catch.

With his coat slipped on, he pats its pockets, double-checking that he has all that he needs. The cable-ties are ready, and the duct tape has been turned over at the end. With that detail having been addressed in advance, he is sure that there should be no delay in its removal from the roll.

Standing with his back against the sandstone wall, and with the extra cover from the foliage of an overhanging tree, he remains secreted in the darkness ... and inconspicuous to all but the most determined of observers.

He waits ... and he listens.

It should not be too long before he hears the tell-tale sound of her heels *click-clacking* on the paving.

Silently, he runs through the opening line of his prepared approach, whilst hoping that, when the moment comes, he is relaxed enough not to frighten her off.

The sound of approaching footsteps with heels, as he had expected, clicking on the pavement, interrupts his rehearsal.

From the vantage of the shadows, he confirms that it *is* the target who approaches.

He sidles around the corner ... and, without looking too obvious, steps out and into the road.

Assuming the natural look of a pedestrian who is on a simple and routine journey from point A to point B, he, in a somewhat unassuming manner, walks towards her.

As he draws level, he asks, "Excuse me. I'm sorry to bother you, but can you tell me if I'm going the right way for the city centre?"

Seeing no need for suspicion, there is no sense of alarm in her response. After all, he had asked a simple question which requires nothing more than that of a simple and straightforward answer.

In the not so distant past, she, too, has had the need to request directions from passing strangers, and so, she detects nothing to raise her suspicions.

Besides, knowing how grateful she has been for the assistance of others, she is now, with the additional bonus of having an opportunity to practise her limited skills in English, more than happy to repay the debt and try to help another in finding his way to his destination.

She stops, and, with a smile, turns about and points in the direction from which she has just come.

"Yes ... I think I can help you. You go along that road, there. Then you go up the hill an —"

A diesel-soaked rag is forced into her mouth ... and she is silenced. Then, with a blade pressed against her throat, she is twisted around before being hustled and dragged backwards towards the boot of the car.

Hurriedly, he lifts the lid and thrusts her into the abyss of the black and empty space. With her face flush against the back of the rear seats, he is quick to grab her wrists and then yank them into a position so that they are both held behind her back. As he holds them both in the crushing grasp of a single hand, he slips the pre-looped cable-ties around her wrists and pulls them tight, thus, securing them so as to allow her no freedom of movement.

In a frenetic attempt to free herself from the nauseating taste and stench of diesel and also to liberate herself enough to be able to draw attention to her plight by screaming for help, she tries to spit out the rag.

She fails.

It's been jammed too far back into her mouth and, however hard she tries, it will not come free.

Silenced, she may be ... but beaten, she's not.

Twisting herself over and onto her back, she kicks out at him in both anger and desperation. Her ankles are instantly grabbed, and — with the ease of an expert in the capturing of a wild and unruly beast — they, too, are swiftly cable-tied and bound tightly together.

Having then been rolled back and onto her side, she is left to face the back of the rear seats.

It is dark, and although she cannot see his actions, she can hear the unmistakable sound of adhesive tape being torn away from a roll. Her neck wrenches as he grabs her hair. Suddenly, her head is yanked upwards and the rag removed. But before she has any opportunity to call out, it is immediately replaced with the silencing qualities of the duct tape. Although the tape is stuck firm and covers her mouth, the captor has ensured her survival; he has allowed sufficient space for life-maintaining air to be taken in through her nostrils.

She can feel his breath as he threads more ties around her already secured wrists and ankles; then, as he pulls her feet up behind her and speedily fastens them to her wrists with a linkage of two more looped cables, she knows that her nightmare has only just begun.

The boot lid slams shut.

She is in darkness. Silenced, helpless and trussed up to such a degree that she can barely move. She feels her heart pounding within her chest.

At least she can still breathe. Instinctively, she calls on her robust Eastern European tenacity to come to the fore, in the hope that it will serve to prevent her from falling apart as she faces up to the enormity of her plight.

She has no choice other than to lie still and wait passively. By reserving her strength and energy, she will ensure that she is ready for its expenditure when the opportunity for her to make her escape materializes.

Is she terrified? Of course she is. But then she is young, and she has always tried to enjoy life to the full. She has so much to live for, and she will not be the sort to give up easily.

Consoling herself with her belief that her moment will inevitably come, and she will not hesitate to take her opportunity, she swears that she will ensure that he will always regret having made his decision to have selected her as the one to tangle with.

As he steps back and walks around to the car door, he feels his foot nudge at something soft and leathery. Glancing down, he sees a small, fringed bag with an attachment of a long leather strap. He recognizes it as the one which she had over her shoulder. With him being acutely aware that there is always going to be a possibility that its discovery could prematurely alert the police to the fact of a suspicious occurrence, he decides that it would be foolhardy for him to leave it to be found. He stoops down and grabs it. As he gets into the car, he tosses it back and onto the rear seat behind him.

With the engine running, he leans over to the glove compartment and extracts the wig.

With the disguise in place, he flicks the on-switch of the headlamps and then calmly moves off and towards the main road. Turning to the right, and without any display of urgency, he accelerates up to the thirty limit. Having lowered his head on his approach, he passes by the cameras which capture the detail of all outgoing traffic.

With their rigidity restricting her ability to move, thus, thwarting the normal circulation of the blood throughout her limbs, the cable-ties have instigated the extreme and painful effects of cramp. She needs to escape. She wiggles her fingers and her toes in an attempt to reverse the agony. As the pain starts to ease, albeit only slightly, she accepts that her efforts to release herself from the restraints have met with defeat. She lies silently, listening to the sound of the engine and the steady rumble of the wheels as they turn on the smooth surface of the main road. She can do nothing other than to wait for the journey to end.

Besides, there is no point in wasting her energy, as it is only when the boot lid is opened that she will get her first opportunity to make good an escape.

He turns on the radio. It is still tuned in to the *5-Live* channel. It falls silent as he inserts a CD into the appropriate slot and awaits its activation.

As the music starts to play, he turns up the volume. Not so loud as to draw attention to himself, but loud enough for *him* to enjoy.

She is far too young to identify the song as being the 1965 top-ten hit of *Eric Burden and the Animals*, but she can hear it clearly as her captor sings along with the bluesy sounds of the chorus ... *I'm just a soul whose intentions are good ... Oh Lord; please don't let me be misunderstood.*

Even she — with her incomplete knowledge of the vocabulary and, thus, the subsequent lack of fluency of the English language — recognizes the incongruity of the lyrics when related to the gravity of her own situation.

He takes care not to be too precise in his adherence to the speed limit; to do so may in itself raise suspicion in the mind of a patrolling police officer as to the reason for the extra caution. He will drive sensibly whilst emitting an air of nonchalance, which, he is certain, would be expected from any man who has nothing to fear or to hide.

As he reaches the by-pass, he steers to his left, then depresses the accelerator and watches the needle of the speedometer rapidly move past the thirty, and towards the forty, as he heads towards the motorway.

She listens to the sound of rolling wheels and glimpses the recurring flashes of amber which, keeping in time with the clicks as the nearside indicator, signals his intention to divert away from the by-pass route.

She has no idea as to her location, but she is aware, by her own movements, that the car has negotiated a long, sweeping bend and is now heading downhill, and on a smooth and obviously well-maintained road surface.

He sees the red of the traffic lights ahead. He slows and manoeuvres into the lane which will take him under the motorway, away from the city boundaries and towards the tranquil setting of Woodbury Common.

As he approaches the junction, the lights turn to green, and he stamps his foot onto the accelerator.

Feeling the surge of power as the car is released from the shackles of inner-city restrictions, she is thrown back with the momentum. Once more, she tries to free herself from the constraints which have been forced upon her.

Again, the ineffectiveness of her attempts serve only to wastefully consume even more of her valuable energy.

Realising that she is squandering a valuable resource which would be better kept in reserve so that it could be put to use when it could make an impression, she closes her eyes and rests.

Taking the route for Seaton, he is soon away from the ubiquitous illumination of street lighting and the irritating invasiveness of the snooping lenses of roadside cameras. With the knowledge that the likelihood of him being pulled over and checked by an inquisitive country copper is, to say the least, minimal, he can start to relax.

He checks his rear-view mirror. There are no vehicles behind. He's not being followed.

He smiles, relieved that the hurdle of having to travel through the well-lit city has been cleared with relative ease. No longer in need of his disguise, he snatches the wig from his head and stuffs it into the glove compartment.

Now that the first stage of his plan has been executed, he grins. Contented in the knowledge that the *miscreant* lies bound, silenced and secure within the boot, his thoughts move on. He will soon be conducting some schooling!

With the CD player having been set to repeat, the incessant replaying of the single track has taunted throughout the journey. With the endless rendition of the same old tune, along with his off-key accompaniment, she is now starting to feel an additional anguish as it, torturously, eats away at her sanity. With the ability to physically block her ears from the sounds no longer possible, she tries, as a means for a distraction and also as an act of defiance, to hum a different tune.

There's a sudden braking, and as the car slows, she again hears the clicks of the indicators and glimpses the pulse of their amber flashes. The car drops a gear before turning to the right, and then, without stopping, it gathers speed as it commences its ascent up and along a winding route.

His feelings of excitement rise as he continues along his chosen path towards the Common. With the tree-lined embankments and the noticeable lack of other vehicular movement, he starts to gain a sense of seclusion. It will not be long. He will soon be putting his well-laid plans into operation ... and without the fear of interruption.

As the thoughts of what's yet to come take their hold and raise the rate of his pulse, he feels a tightening in his briefs as his body reacts to the thrill of expectancy.

Once out from the woodland shadows and beneath the sparkle of the starlit sky, he can see, reassuringly in the distance, the glow of city lights. With still no other travellers in sight, he cruises on ... and towards the approaching copse.

The car slows as he negotiates the sharpness of the meandering, tree-lined bends.

As the music is silenced and the brakes applied with purpose, she knows that he is close to reaching his destination.

Within seconds, the car has slowed to an almost standstill and then steered away from the road and into one of many car parks which had been created to accommodate the daytime walkers who enjoy the escape from city life.

Once away from the smooth surface of the road, he navigates a course across the pitted and rugged terrain of the car park; a clearing which had been hewn from a wilderness of heather and gorse. And having been left without a coating of asphalt, it pays no heed to the suspension and clearance of vehicles which are not designed for off-road excursions.

Utilising the beam of his headlamps, he swings the car around and scans the vicinity for signs of unwanted company. There is one other vehicle. A Vauxhall, with its windows steamed whilst its occupants are undoubtedly engaged in acts of passion.

He can afford no witnesses. So, carefully negotiating a route to dodge the deepest of the potholes, he proceeds away from the courting-couple and back onto the road.

Within a few seconds, he has driven back onto rough terrain and is now picking his way along a rough and bumpy track which edges him towards a new destination.

She listens to the splashes as each wheel drops in and out of pools of rainwater-filled depressions. Although she winces in pain as her body is tossed against the shell of the boot-space, she manages to retain the presence of mind to compose herself. She must be ready for that first opportunity when, hopefully, she will be able to initiate the ultimate act of defiance which, she prays, will ultimately allow her to escape and, thus, ensure her very survival.

As he reaches the end of the track, where it opens out into another purpose-built car park-cum-viewpoint, he can see that, this time, he has fortune with him. He has found seclusion. He is certain that the very presence of his vehicle may, as it did with him in the previous car park, encourage others to seek their privacy elsewhere.

Satisfied that all is well, and that he is unlikely to find himself sharing the spot with another, he stops the car and silences its engine.

With the orangey glow of luminosity radiating upwards above the distant city, he takes a few moments to unwind.

Preparing himself for the final onslaught, he lights a cigarette and draws the smoke deeply into his lungs before blowing it out ... with its blue-grey plume crashing against the windscreen before dissipating in all directions.

She listens as he calls.

"Anna! Can you hear me?"

She's shocked. He knows her name.

"You must listen to me. In a minute, I'm going to let you out. Do you understand me? Now, I want you to know ... that if you behave yourself, and then do just as I tell you ... then things will be a lot easier for you. All right?"

He waits for a response — there is none. So, with a childish and mocking titter underlining his awareness as to his being in command, he utters, "Oh! Of course — how stupid of me ... you can't speak, can you?"

His growing confidence, underscored with the volatility of insanity, fuels his sickly, muffled sniggering. Although she knows that her life is in jeopardy, she resists the urge to panic or struggle; there is nothing to be gained in any fruitless and energy-sapping attempt to release herself from the grip of the cable-ties. Instead, she lies composed and in silence ... patiently awaiting her moment.

In any case, the duct tape which had successfully ensured her silence throughout the journey is still firmly in place. So even if she had wished to respond, she was unable to give a reply to confirm to him as to whether or not she would be willing to accept his conditions.

With acute attentiveness, she listens for sounds which, although she has little doubt in her own mind as to what he wishes to do with her, will forewarn her of the imminence of his approach and the exactness of his intent.

"Anna! Can you still hear me back there?"

She remains still, allowing her silence alone to taunt him. She reasons that for him to feel in control, he must know whether she is still alive or, alternatively, whether she has succumbed to the effects of suffocation ... and died.

Her reasoning is sound.

She cannot silence the increasing pace of her heartbeat as she hears the click of his door. Then, with his weight no longer in the driver's seat, she feels the bounce in the spring of the suspension.

Every muscle in her body seems pumped in readiness for action. She listens as she waits for the clunk of the boot-catch and the subsequent opening of the lid. There is a pause.

The telltale sound of a rushing stream, splashing on to the compacted earth as he releases the pressure from within him, suggests to her that he, too, is nervous.

It's a supposition that, if right, she can use to her advantage.

He looks around him, re-checking the privacy of the location.

Satisfied with the isolation, he moves around to the rear of the car and presses the boot release.

As the lid opens, she accustoms herself to the reality of the light, which, albeit slight, is significant when compared with the entirety of the darkness of her confinement.

She can smell his cigarette-tainted breath as he leans into the boot-well and reiterates his assurances as before.

"Now then, if you wanna make things easier for yourself, then you must be a good girl, and you must do as I say. Do you understand?"

She tries to hum a reply, but her words are stifled by the tape and are, thus, beyond the realms of comprehension.

"Just nod if you understand."

She nods emphatically, ensuring that he is fully aware of the acceptance of his conditions.

"Good. Now I'm going to cut the ties behind you and then you can get out of the boot. All right?"

Again she nods.

He grabs a hold on her hair and then pulls her head around towards the scarce light of the night sky. With his hand held in front of her face, she can see that he is holding something. Exactly what it is, she cannot tell. So, being trussed and unable to make any reasonable attempt to escape, she waits for his next move.

Once certain that he has her full and undivided attention, he flicks a button with his thumb and, as quick as a flash, a long pointed blade fires out from its place of concealment within the handle.

As he turns the blade, allowing the distant glints of starlight to reflect off the highly-polished surface, he knows that he need say no more, for the threats implied in his actions are as real as the cold steel which wavers so menacingly before her.

He pushes her head back to, yet again, face the seats. Then, he grabs the cable-ties which have been successful in securing her ankles to her wrists.

A sudden jerk and the newly-sharpened blade of the knife cuts through the plastic, as easily as if it were being used to take a pat of butter.

The feeling of physical relief as she is at last able, albeit to a small degree, to straighten her legs is, simultaneously, annulled by the terror of what is surely likely to follow.

Again, he leans into the boot-well, and in a hushed but deliberate tone, he speaks into her ear, "Now Anna … I'm going to release your legs so that you can climb out of the boot. Don't try anything stupid or else …" He pauses, and with a flash of the blade, continues. "You know what will happen!"

With the vision of the shiny blade ingrained in her mind, and with her having already become accustomed to giving the required signal of understanding, she nods repeatedly.

With the formality of his warnings satisfactorily applied, he tugs at the restraints on her ankles and, once again, slices through the cable-ties.

The ability for her to now move her legs independently of each other allows a gradual return to the normality of a steady flow of blood and, thus, the consequent relief from her feeling the painful effects of the imposed muscular paralysis.

He rolls her over and then allows her to swing her legs over the boot lip and onto the solidity of the ground.

Still sufficiently bound, so as to prevent any realistic attempt for escape, she looks across the rugged tops of the fauna of gorse and heather … and then skyward.

She cannot help but to notice a familiarity in the vividness of the starry night. Chilled by the isolation of the location and, with it, the extreme severity of her predicament, she takes no comfort in the similarity of this sky to that which is so often seen over the hills of her homeland.

He grabs a hold of her as he makes his way around to the side of the car and opens the back door.

She can see the knife — he still has it grasped in his hand.

As the strength starts to flow back into her legs, and whilst they readjust to their new-found freedom, she starts to sense that here may be some green-shoots of hope.

He pulls her around, and grabbing the restraints on her wrists, he pushes close up behind her.

Waving the blade in front of her eyes, he reiterates his demands and his warnings.

"So far, you are being very good. So I'm going to release your hands and you will then do exactly as I say. Understand?"

Her acknowledgement with her usual nod is sufficient. He smiles as he lowers the knife and slices through the cables.

Still standing behind her, he immediately returns the blade upwards and rests it against her neck.

"You must listen to me. If you wanna live, you're going to have to pull down your tights … and your knickers."

She shakes her head. Afraid? Of course she is. But she has no intention to lie back and allow him to do as he will.

Sensing her defiance, and in order to prevent her fleeing, he pulls her closer towards him … and presses the blade, somewhat perilously, into her skin.

As far as he is concerned, albeit due to the lottery of conception, his gender has given him the preordained status of being physically dominant over the female. Yet, here she is, at odds with the dictates of nature, signalling a protest which will, no doubt, be followed by a futile attempt to resist.

There is certainly no place for a woman who tries to break the mould. So for her own good, he knows that she will need to understand that she must accept her role … and submit. But he also knows that she will not accept reason. So with that in mind, he is going to have to teach her a lesson. He will have no option other than to *force* her to experience the humiliation of having to comply with his will. Furthermore, he knows, through his own childhood experiences, that she will have no choice but to accept the inevitable.

He is no fool! He is standing right behind her and, therefore, she cannot see what he is doing. She is trapped with a man who is physically more powerful than her. What is more, he has a weapon. And with his blood pumping fast, his muscles are being refuelled.

He has the advantage! Everything is in his favour.

If she carries on fighting him, then she knows that she will soon tire. If that happens, then all will be lost … and the prize will be his.

She needs for him to drop his guard. There are no outside distractions, so she has no option but to appear to submit to his demands.

Cautiously, she starts to lift her skirt and coat as if they are as one, and then, in a spurt of defiance, she tugs at her undergarments and yanks them down, past her thighs … and below her knees.

With the grin of the victor spreading across his face, he savours the way in which she has edged closer towards subservience. Her lowered undergarments are now of use to him; they are, in themselves, restricting her ability to make good her escape — so he stops her from lowering them completely.

"That's good. That's far enough."

He spins her around to face him, and with a flash of burnished steel, he reasserts his position of strength

As she looks at the blade and then back into his eyes, he sees the embers of defiance smouldering beneath the fear.

For a moment, he hesitates. Then, with an almost surreal pang of guilt surging within, he recalls the similar look which was in the eyes of his mother when she, too, had been subjected to being violated by her man.

With the feelings dismissed as readily as they had arrived, he retakes charge of the situation and shoves her, violently, backwards and into the car. As he watches her fall helplessly and then sprawl onto the empty rear seat of the car, he feels a surge of blood rushing into, and swelling, his manhood.

He commands her to move back. She refuses! He waves the knife! She complies. Then, whilst he stands by the opened door, she watches on as he, calmly and arrogantly, unbuckles his belt and unzips his fly.

He lowers his trousers, and, with the look of a man who is about to seize the spoils of war, he leans into the car and readies himself for the launch.

She kicks out at him, but to no avail. Suddenly, he throws himself on top of her, smothering her ability to inflict injury.

Grabbing her by the throat with his left hand, he slaps her viciously across the face with the other. Immediately, he returns the swing of the arm ... and with the back of the returning hand he, yet again, slaps her hard across the other cheek. Feeling pain ... she complies.

He struggles to position his body in order to gain access and, thus, impose his masculine dominance. But her legs are as good as bound ... and so his efforts are thwarted.

He is excited. He will have to take a chance. He needs her legs to be freed.

Knowing that he needs to negate the restrictions of her underwear, he, with a mix of anger and frustration, slides off of her in preparation for her to be able to complete their removal.

Sensing a wane in his concentration, she readies herself to grasp at the first opportunity to escape.

"Get 'em off!" he snarls, as his anger starts to override his previous, cold and measured, self-control. However, mindful of his own safety and in order not to make himself susceptible to being injured by the kicking out of her feet, he does not risk an attempt to complete the procedure himself.

She edges along the seat and repositions herself by the opened door. She is seated upright and with her feet out of the car.

It is whilst she is in this position that she can prepare to remove the garments in a way that will not only maintain a semblance of decorum, but, at the same time, not risk heightening his sense of empowerment. After all, if she tries to remove them whilst she is still lying on her back, then the very nature of her movements may serve only to titillate his senses; furthermore, it may even suggest that she has become more willing to accept his rule.

With her shoes removed, she stands upright before bending down to remove the restrictive items from her legs.

Once off, they are deposited on the ground.

Then, standing upright, she, as if in an act of defiance, stares straight at him. Instinctively and without drawing any attention to her actions, she slips her feet into her shoes.

He grins!

Now that his predatory and self-indulgent instincts have been brought to the fore, the reason as to why she had been specifically selected has seemingly been forgotten.

He steps towards her. As he nears, she takes the initiative. Suddenly, and with as much force as she can muster, she butts him in the face, then, immediately, grabs a hold on his testicles. With her resolve to survive being uppermost in her mind, she squeezes as hard as she can — and then she twists and wrenches as if she were trying to wring out the last drops of moisture from a sodden sponge.

He screams out in pain and drops the knife. As he tries desperately to prise her hands away, she, with her confidence growing by the moment, digs her manicured nails hard and determinedly into his scrotal sac. With a sense of victory being within reach, she feels a give in the natural resilience of his skin as her nails sink in and slice through the protective sac of his testes.

With the sickening agony of the sac having been punctured, he grasps at her hands … desperately trying to free himself from her vicelike grip.

This is *her* time!

The victim has turned!

Now it is *he* who is on the back foot … and it is *he* who is vulnerable.

She twists again. Suddenly, she releases her grip and shoves him away.

Her fear has reverted to anger.

She cannot hold back. She follows through with a series of kicks — the first is on target and powers into his groin. He doubles over as the excruciating pain makes its mark.

Her secondary target, his face, is missed — but, somewhat fortuitously, she succeeds in delivering a ferocious kick to his throat.

She watches as he drops onto the ground, struggling to breathe whilst, at the same time, trying to cope with the agony of his injuries.

With him immobilised, albeit temporarily, she takes her opportunity and runs. Not in the obvious direction towards the road — that would be too much of a risk. In any case, she knows that he could easily catch up with her once his strength returns. So she clambers up and over the embankment, and as fast as she can, she runs along the pathway which stretches across the inhospitable landscape of the open Common.

As she runs, cloaked by the darkness, she tears at the tape which has enforced her silence and discards it without daring to stop.

She hears him calling. She remains silent. She knows that — with the fear of her being free to tell her tale — his adrenalin has overpowered the pain, and he is on the hunt.

"Where are you … bitch? When I catch up with you … you're dead! Do you hear me? You're f—g dead!"

To her left, there's a gap in the undergrowth. She takes the diversion.

Making good progress — what with the new pathway being of grass, and on a winding, downward gradient — she shakes off her shoes and then, instinctively, she carries them. It is far easier for her to run with the grip of bared feet than it is for her to make good her escape in heels.

She hears the car engine fire up.

Seeing the glow of the beams as the headlamps are switched on, she runs on, then stops and glances back. He is not, as she had assumed, heading for the road and then going away. The car is being steered to a position to allow the main beams to scan the scrub.

There is no doubt in her mind — he intends to find her.

She crouches down and scrambles into and under the cover of the gorse, surreptitiously crawling as far away from the path as she can before lying silent and still.

He is out from the car. With his torch in hand, he steps up and onto the embankment.

As the beam shines to and fro across the scrub, he has no option but to resign himself to the fact that he will not find her.

The Common is an expanse which, even in daylight, can make it nigh on impossible to find someone with the intent to remain hidden.

She is certain that, even with the assistance of a torch, the cover of the fauna will ensure her security and she will not be found.

Resigning herself to a long, cold and uncomfortable night, she curls up into a tight ball, conserving her energy and allowing her leather coat to protect her from the elements.

He is visibly enraged by the lapse in his concentration — his plans are in disarray, and he is angered by his own stupidity and incompetence.

She is out there, somewhere … hidden from view. With the vastness of the Common and the agonizing pain of his injuries, he is unable to conduct a search of any significance.

The longer he waits, the more vulnerable he becomes. The likelihood of him being spotted by the inquisitive occupants of a patrolling police car or a solitude-seeking courting-couple will increase by the minute. She is still out there — and he knows that she could well be the only person who possesses the evidence which could bring him down. He tries to console himself with the thought that, if it came to it, she would be unlikely to be able to describe him … and certainly not in sufficient enough detail to produce a useful photofit image. Neither would she be able to identify him amongst a crowd. After all, she'd only had brief glimpses — and even those had been in the dark of the night. With his worries on the wane, he makes the decision. He will cut his losses and leave the Common. He needs to lay the final stages of evidence in order to support his, preplanned, alibi.

As if to ensure that she is left with a final reminder of his self-proclaimed authority, he shouts out to her. "You were lucky this time … Bitch! I know where you live! Do you hear me? It's only a matter of time … and then … you're all mine. Do you understand? Comprendre? You're gonna be all mine!"

There is a far deeper purpose lurking behind his threats. He is hoping that, with the installation of the fear of his return, she may well suppress her wish to seek redress through the British courts. Instead, she may resign herself to putting the whole thing down to experience and return to her country of origin.

Deep down, he knows that his hopes will, in all likelihood, come to nothing. Furthermore, he is fully aware of the fact that he has lost the reins of control.

As he gets back into his car, his anger manifests itself with a tirade of cusses and threats.

With a final glance across the Common and the utterance of further curses, he fires up the motor. Then with the screech of wheels spinning, he races out from the car park, accelerating off eastwards as he commences the first leg of the long journey towards the motorway on-slip of junction twenty-six.

Chapter 37

Hearing the sound of his car fading into the distance, she is certain that he has left, and so, she dares to leave the security of her hiding place.

Whilst slipping her shoes back onto her feet, she scans the area … looking for clues as to her whereabouts.

Although relieved, she is shaking with the effects of her terrifying ordeal. So, needing to put some distance between her and the scene of the attack, she responds to her instinct for survival by seeking a route by which she will be able to ensure her escape.

Tentatively, and with her senses honed, she picks her way along the winding track. She has no idea where it will lead. It may be to a place of safety or, on the other hand, it may lead her into the clutches of something more sinister.

Responding to intuition alone, she hesitates.

There is something inside of her which is telling her not to proceed any farther. So, halted by her feelings, she listens intently as she weighs her options. Her abductor has long gone and, she guesses, the likelihood of his return is improbable … but not impossible.

Her decision is made. She heads back to her only point of reference — the car park. With her senses charged, she remains prepared for flight. For if there is the slightest hint of his approach, she will, without hesitation, dive back under the covers of nature and conceal herself until the threat is no more.

She fumbles in her coat pocket and finds her phone.

Flicking the screen open, it lights up.

Who can she call? Whoever she calls, whether it's a friend or the police, she will not be able to give her location.

She could venture onto the road and seek help from a passing motorist, but then, passing motorists are few and far between. Realising that she could inadvertently flag down the very man from whom she has made her escape, the option is dismissed.

Yet, she must do something.

As she clambers over the embankment and walks into the car park, she stumbles as her foot drops into one of the many water-filled depressions. With her feet and legs now cold and wet, her suffering is compounded.

Miserable? Yes.

Defeated? No.

She's a survivor. What's more, she knows that she needs to take care and not risk injury, for the need to be able to run is still firmly fixed in her mind. Her vision, although already accustomed to the lack of light, is enhanced with the added assistance of the illumination from her phone.

She uses the meagre light to scan the surface of the car park, and, within a minute or so, she manages to find and retrieve her discarded items of underwear.

Even with the severity of what has just happened, she will not allow the most personal of her garments to be left lying in the dirt ... for all to see when daylight returns. Having picked up her possessions, she stuffs them into her pocket before foraging around ... in the hope that he has abandoned her handbag, with its contents intact.

There is no trace. The very thought that he still has possession of her property fills her with dread. After all, he will have her keys — in fact, he could already be hiding in her home ... waiting for her to return.

She spots a large rectangular sign standing out against the city glow — a glow which taints the purity of the starry sky.

With the help of her phone's screen-light, she tries to make sense of the words, which, understandably, only reflect the language of the indigenous population.

Alongside the printed words, she eyes the images of the native wildlife.

As she looks at each picture, her eyes focus on the image of Britain's only venomous snake — the adder. The thought that she could well have been lying within touching distance of one or more of these reptiles sends a chill through the length of her body.

With the little light available, she manages to make out the words. Although she does not understand the meaning of *Pebblebed Heath, Estuary View* or, for that matter, *Woodbury Common*, she assumes that they may well be place names and are, therefore, vital clues as to her being able to pinpoint her location.

She has only one friend who may be able to help — so she makes her call. "Hello. Is that Lisa?"

"Yes, Anna, it is me."

She can tell by the shake in the voice that all is not well. "What is wrong?"

"I have been taken! A man has taken me in his car — and he has attacked me. He has tried to—"

"Anna, Where are you? Are you all right?"

"Yes, I mean ... No. I do not know. He is gone ... But, maybe, he will come back. He wants to hurt me ... Please — I need help!"

Although Lisa can hear the distress and fear in her new friend's voice, she remains calm. She does not waste time asking about the details of the attack or, for that matter, the identity of the perpetrator, but she concentrates on the more pressing detail of being able to establish her location. "Where are you?"

"I don't know. There are no houses ... but there is a sign."

Once again, she points her phone screen so that it can illuminate the sign. She reads the words out loud. "Pebblebed Heath — Estuary View — Woodbury Common. Do you know these places?"

"I don't know. Can you spell the words?"

"Yes I can..." She spells out each letter, allowing her friend the time to be able to write them down in order.

Lisa reads them back to her, and once confirmed as to their accuracy, she continues. "Good, I will phone for the police and tell them where you are. They will know the place, so you must wait there and they will come to you."

"Yes, I will wait, Thank you. Lisa ... Please ... make them come quickly, I am frightened he will come back."

"Yes, I will telephone them now. Can you text me a photograph of the sign?"

"Yes, I will try to do that."

***

In an attempt to put distance between him and the Common, and also to make good his attempt to establish his alibi, he swiftly winds his way through the lesser roads; roads that will eventually take him to meet with the westbound carriageway of the M5 motorway.

The pain in his groin is starting to ease, and he is able to concentrate on the matter of evading suspicion.

He needs to discard anything which could link him to the assault. So, without stopping, he fumbles in the glove compartment, pulls out the wig and drops it onto the seat beside him. When an opportune moment arrives, he will dispose of it ... once and for all.

Being aware that at this time of night, patrolling police-patrols are likely to be on the look-out for the wayward drink-driver, he, not wishing to draw attention to himself, continues along the minor roads which he knows will take him farther away from the Common, and onwards towards the M5, via the A30 at Daisy Mount.

***

Anna, having made her way along the track towards the main road, steps back into the shadows and watches the approach of a car. Her heart pounds as the car slows as it nears the car park's entrance.

She is not certain as to whether or not it is occupied by someone who is looking for her, or whether it is just a courting-couple who are looking for a place with sufficient privacy for them to be able to embark on an adventurous session of intimacy whilst under the romantic setting of a crisp, starlit sky.

The car, having no beacons or reflective markings to advertise its authority, is unlikely to be the property of local constabulary. But, much to her relief, neither is it similar to that which had been driven by her assailant.

She hesitates. As the car swings around, she resists the urge to make herself known, preferring to wait for the security which will come with the arrival of the police.

With the occupants being unhappy with the location or, on the other hand, put off by the pitted access to the car park, the car does not stop. Instead, it leaves the vicinity and continues; quite possibly in search of a more pleasing spot farther along the road.

Her phone rings.

It's Lisa. She answers, "Hello."

"Anna. The police know where you are. They are coming now. They should be with you very soon. How are you?"

"I am scared and I am cold. Wait … I can see a blue light … it is coming closer. Maybe it's the police. Thank you Lisa. I must go and let them see me. I will ring you later. Thank you. Thank you very much."

***

By-passing the market town of Honiton, he is feeling less stressed. He knows that he is soon to leave the dual carriageway and return to the more secluded and peaceful byways which stretch out across the county, northwards, through Dunkeswell … and then off towards his chosen destination — *Junction, twenty-six.*

Once away from the exposure of being on the main road, he approaches a sharp bend and slows. As he crosses the small, stone-sided bridge which spans the *Otter*, he tosses the wig out of the window. Knowing that it has fallen into the bubbling waters which flow swiftly and resolutely through the rural idyll of the Devon countryside before wending their way towards the briny and undulating seas of the English Channel, he feels a sense of relief.

***

It is not long before the arrival of the patrol car is supplemented by the arrival of an emergency ambulance and a dog van.

Lisa had done well!

Although she had wanted to know the extent of what had happened to Anna, she had prioritized — she had played safe; she had ensured that there would be no delay in the despatching of both law-enforcement officers and qualified paramedics.

***

As he travels north, up and across the Blackdown Hills, he pulls off from the road and stops. With due haste, he removes the good brake-light bulb and replaces it with the faulty one … and then substitutes the falsified number plates with the original, thereby reinstating the correct identity to his vehicle.

Cursing at his failure to have rid the world from the treachery of an errant young woman, he snaps the falsified plates into pieces.

He restarts the motor and moves forward, rapidly gathering speed as he hurries to his destination. Whilst on route, he disposes of the broken pieces of number plate along a stretch of a mile or so by tossing them across the adjoining hedges and embankments in the hope that they would be forever lost amid the undergrowth and the ditches of the woodland which borders his path.

The junction is reached. He accelerates up the on-slip and merges with the steady, but relatively sparse, flow of traffic of the motorway as he makes his way westwards … and back towards the Devon border.

***

The paramedics had been satisfied with Anna's explanation that — other than the marks of the restraints on her limbs and the bruising on her face — she had in fact suffered no substantial physical injury from her ordeal. As a result, they were happy to allow the police to take her to the sanctuary of the city police station, where a translator could be summoned to assist in the recording of the detail of her nightmarish experience.

With the security of a young, woman detective constable beside her, she feels safe.

She is taken, not to the police station, but to a special suite in an adjacent house. Comforted by a mug of freshly-brewed tea, she awaits the arrival of the translator.

Whilst waiting, she explains how she had fought off her assailant and, to the surprise of the police officer, laughs as she recalls the moment when she had squeezed his testicles tight and then punctured them with her fingernails.

The detective mirrors her laugh. Not only does she share the pleasure of knowing that the victim of what was, clearly, an attempted rape had issued her own form of punishment, but also, that her actions may well allow an opportunity for a sample of incriminating DNA to be extracted from a scraping from under Anna's fingernails.

Although her English is just about good enough to get by on, she understands that as far as her signing a legal document such as a witness statement is concerned, it would be preferable for her to be guided by the assistance of a linguist who is fluent in both English and the native tongue of her homeland.

***

He is nervous; he tunes the car's radio to the sounds of the local station, listening for anything that could suggest that she had been found … and that he was being pursued. There is nothing, other than the trivia of idle chattering, broken with tracks from the albums of musicians known only to those who enthuse over the sounds of *underground* jazz.

His thoughts leap from the plausible — that is to say, it is too early for the media to have picked up on the *story* — to the implausible, a scenario in which she has decided not to report the incident at all … but, instead, has decided to cut her losses and return to be in the bosom of her family back in her homeland.

In any case, he did not actually rape her — furthermore, she had not suffered any significant injury. Bearing that in mind, he wonders if she will just count her lucky stars and put it all down to being just a bad experience. Besides, she could never describe him — not well enough for an identification to be made by description alone, that is. So, with him knowing the way in which the police seem to react to many reported crimes nowadays, he consoles himself with the thought that they will probably just *kick the whole thing to touch*.

Seeing the sign for the *services*, he decides that it is time for him to make the all-important stop. Having planned that his presence would be recorded by the security surveillance equipment, and being cognisant of the fact that one of his brake-lights is inoperative, he drives into the parking area and, whilst ensuring that the rear of the car is in full view of a camera, he applies the brakes … and stops.

If he is questioned, then this will certainly help to confirm the alibi of him having travelled to Bristol to watch the match.

He allows himself the satisfaction of a grin as he considers how clever he has been. After all, how many *coppers* would think that he would have had the foresight to have changed the bulb in order to create the new identity … and then, after the deed was done, change it back again to recreate the old? Yes, as far as he is concerned, he is too clever for them all. Besides, with the knowledge that his alibi is still intact, he is feeling more confident … and, hence, much safer.

Unafraid of being seen, and with the need to make use of the toilet facilities, he locks the car. Before walking off, he glances through the rear offside window and then into the rear foot-well. With a grimace, he absorbs the sight of incriminating evidence — her handbag.

He looks around him … and seeing that all is clear, he unlocks the car, opens the back door and leans in. Without making his purpose obvious, he shuffles through the contents and finds her keys.

His face lights up. With a self-satisfied smile, closely followed by an air of calm, he returns them to the bag and then thrusts it, as far as he is able, under the back of the driver's seat until it is completely out of sight.

He closes the door and, although still feeling the discomfort of a nagging pain in his groin, he makes his way towards the entrance to the Motorway Services café and shops.

Chapter 38

To those who enter the precincts of the supermarket, he is just his normal self and, as such, warrants little more than that of a cursory glance.

Although smarting from his previous night's experience, he is still able to stop and watch the arrival of the customers in their cars.

He is back to routine and is already recognising those who have become more familiar through the regularity of their visits. He is composed enough to make note of those who are new to the store and share the commonality of lone female occupancy.

A woman in her thirties, captures his gaze. As she alights from her vehicle and makes her way across the car park towards the store, he stops working ... and watches.

With an almost engaging smile, he hurries across the roadway and intercepts her. Obligingly, and as if he were wishing to negate her need to divert from her destination by way of the trolley-park, he offers her the use of a trolley which he already has in hand.

She accepts his offer, and as if acknowledging the value of his helpful action, along with how his old-fashioned display of chivalry reflects so well on the store, she replies with a *thank you* and a brief but pleasant smile.

Had she seen the way in which he had eyed her up and down as she had walked off and towards the main entrance to the store, then she would certainly not have smiled at him ... nor would she have been quite so comfortable in the presence of his smile.

Although employed on the later of the shifts, his tiredness is obvious. When asked by both colleagues and management alike about his uncharacteristic lack in energy, along with the occasional, but noticeable, sign of him seeming uncomfortable in the manner of his walk, he had dismissed their concerns. His explanation had been quite plausible; he had been late home ... having been delayed by the effects of the, questionable, *freshness* of the prawns which had been in his take-away curry.

Mind you, he is quick to assert that as the week progresses, he will improve, and will, therefore, not be allowing his discomfort to absent him from work.

***

Tom's calm appearance belies his inner feeling of unease. He has already received the confirmatory phone call from his ex-wife, so it will not be long before he is introduced to Victoria; a young woman who, according to Gina, is his daughter.

Each of the twelve minutes, as if caught in a time warp, seem to hang as he repeatedly looks … first towards the doors and then back to his watch.

The wait is over!

As she enters the lobby, shadowed by her mother, he cannot help but to notice how she grasps a tight hold of the hand of a young man who is of an age which cannot be too distant from that of her own. He rises from his seat and greets them with a welcoming but cautious smile. Then, unable to resist focusing his attention on Tori, he is instantly captivated by the magnetism of her sparkling sapphire-blue eyes.

"Jeez!" he exclaims, as he absorbs how alike she is to his long-lost daughter.

He resists the urge to step forward and, as if she were the very reincarnation of his beloved Lucy, give her a loving hug … for he is afraid to scare her off by seeming too forward.

Tori, sensing his caution and equally afraid to take a step too far, holds back. Instead, she waits for her mother to step forward and break the ice.

"Hi, Tom."

"Hi, Gina … I'm guessing that this is Victoria?"

"Yes. Your guess is right. May I introduce you to your daughter?"

He smiles and steps towards Tori.

Not knowing whether to give her a hug or to just shake her hand, he elects to do neither. "Hi! How are you? Forgive me — I don't quite know what to say."

Reflecting the unnatural formality of the situation, Tori utters a nervous laugh and replies, "That's okay … How am I, you ask? Well, I suppose, under the circumstances, I'm good, thank you."

He glances across to her escort, and again, with the warmth of a smile, he introduces himself.

"Hi, I'm Tom … and you are?"

Tori answers on his behalf. "Oh, yes. This is Jamie — he's my boyfriend."

Tom immediately offers his hand in friendship, and Jamie, instinctively, echoes the move.

"Well, Jamie. It's nice to meet you."

He looks around the foyer and then, albeit politely, takes control.

"Shall we go through to the lounge? Maybe then we can be a little less formal and get to know a bit about each other … over a drink or something?"

There is an awkward pause as Tori seems to have found within herself a normally well-hidden trait of shyness; she is, uncharacteristically, lost for words.

Gina breaks the silence before it becomes embarrassing and accepts the offer on their behalf. "That sounds good. Shall we go through?"

Tori nods, and while still clutching Jamie's hand she follows her mother to the lounge.

***

It is only those with inside knowledge or those who have a good reason to be able to identify the vehicle as being an unmarked police car, who will be alerted to its arrival in the residential cul-de-sac which is on the outskirts of the County's administrative capital.

It is early enough in the evening not to risk encroaching on the preparations for bedtime, yet it is late enough for them not to interfere with the routine of an evening meal with the family.

With one male and the other female, the two detectives look like any couple who may be paying a visit to a friend ... and so, they draw no attention to their presence.

The bell is pressed, and after a moment or two, the door is opened.

"Good evening, sir."

The female detective initiates the introduction by showing her police warrant card. "I'm D.C. Jackie Clarke, and this is my colleague, D.C. Davison."

The man looks confused as he waits for an explanation as to why they have called on him.

Without delay, she states her interest. "I see you have a blue Peugeot on the drive and it's registered to a Donna Reynolds."

"Yes. That's right. It's Donna's car. She's upstairs at the moment, putting our son to bed. Is there a problem that I can help you with?"

"Possibly."

She is cautious not to be accusatory; her instincts are that this man seems to be secure in a family setting and may well be innocent of any wrongdoing.

"Maybe it's best that we don't discuss it on the doorstep, what with inquisitive neighbours and all. So, may we come in?"

"Oh, yes, certainly. Come on in. We'll go through to the front room if you like. Donna will be down shortly. As I told you, she's just putting our little 'un to bed."

"Thank you."

The police officers enter, and the front door is closed.

The man ushers them into the living room. Naturally concerned as to why the police would wish to visit his family, he seeks enlightenment. "Is there a problem with the car?"

"If you don't mind, sir, I don't wish to sound rude, but I think it'd be best if I wait until you're both here. Then I can explain it to you, both."

"Yeah, sure. I'll just go up and tell her you're here."

As he starts to go out of the room, she enters. She has heard the arrival of the visitors and is equally as curious as to the purpose of their visit.

"It's all right. He's just dropped off."

The two officers stand and introduce themselves.

Before being able to fire off any questions or impart any tangible information, they are halted by her inquisitiveness.

"So. What's this all about?"

"Please, bear with me. I need to ask you some questions first, and then I'll be able to explain. First of all — are you the owner of the Peugeot which is parked outside?"

"Yes, I am. Is there something wrong with it?"

D.C. Clarke does not answer her question. Instead, and without giving away her reason for the visit, she continues with her questions. "Can you explain what you were doing last evening?"

"Well, yes. We were home ... as we are this evening — and, for that matter, every other evening. Why? Why do you ask? What on earth is this all about?"

The officer continues without having answered her question. "When did you last take your car out?"

"This afternoon. Why?"

Her reply is weighed with a tone of puzzlement and irritation.

"And yesterday?"

"The same ... I collected Jake from school — then we went to the supermarket. I did my shopping, and then came straight back home."

"Anywhere else?"

"No! I parked the car in the drive and that's where it's stayed."

D.C. Davison catches the eye of Donna's partner. "And you, sir? Do you use the car?"

"No, I never do. I have my own. Mine's the silver estate which is parked on the road, opposite. Look ... can you *please* explain to us *exactly* what's going on here?"

"Well ... we've had a report that a dark-blue Peugeot 406 was connected with a serious assault, late last night. We've checked the security cameras and your car was seen in the vicinity."

Donna, indignant and more than a little impatient, reacts. "That's impossible! I've already told you. We were in all night!"

D.C. Clarke opens her folder and produces a photograph. She passes it over for them to peruse.

"This is a still. It was taken from a security camera on the Topsham Road last night. You can see the time and the date printed at the bottom."

The two detectives watch intently for signs of anxiety as the photo is examined. There is nothing untoward. Both Donna and her partner seem puzzled by the whole thing.

Donna tries in vain to make sense of the image, and then, in disbelief and with a shake of her head, she hands it to her partner.

D.C. Clarke explains. "Unfortunately, the reflection of the street lights on the windscreen have made it very difficult for us to identify the driver, but … it looks like it was a woman."

Donna's partner looks at it briefly, then hands it back to her before leaving the room.

Almost instantly, he returns with a magnifying glass grasped in his hand.

"Let's have another look."

He reclaims the photograph and then scrutinizes it with care. With his expertise as a legal executive in matters of contract law, he is adept in the art of paying close attention to the finest of details.

With a broad smile of satisfaction, he hands the photograph back to the detective.

"It's not our car!"

"Sorry?"

It is D.C.Clarke's turn to be perplexed as she waits for an explanation.

"The number plates."

"Yes. What about them?"

"They're false!"

He pauses as he allows the revelation to settle in the minds of the two officers.

"Ours …" he explains, "have got the blue GB logo on the end. And, also … they have the name of the garage that sold us the car printed underneath. These haven't!"

D.C. Clarke looks back at the picture and borrows the magnifier.

She confirms the observation with the silence of a nod and hands the picture to her colleague for his opinion.

"You appear to be right."

Her enquiry is beginning to embark on a different path from the norm.

"These are just plain old-fashioned plates. They've got no GB logo and there's nothing printed at the bottom."

She sits back and thinks. Her instinct for caution was right; her decision to hold back on making accusations had been well-founded.

She pauses as she collects her thoughts. Then with a sense of urgency, she makes her request. "I think I should have a look at your car. Maybe we can see if there's anything else which is different."

Relieved that the suspicion on them having been involved in any wrongdoing is as good as ended, Donna's partner readily agrees to their request and joins her in checking the vehicle.

***

The group have relaxed and are settling into a state of being comfortable in one another's company.

To an outsider, they would look as any normal family foursome would look when socializing in the more exclusive setting of one the city's better hotels.

They attract little attention.

The conversation is, in the main, light. But every so often there is a cautious *beating about the bush* as Tori — whilst desperately hiding her desire to just blurt out ... *Why were you never there for me?* — probes for answers.

Listening patiently as she tries to prise out the required information, he cannot help but to come to her rescue, and so, with the precursor of a quiet and sympathetic laugh, he volunteers the information.

"I'm afraid I haven't brought a C.V. with me. So, tell me, what would you like to know?"

Although a little embarrassed by her own transparency, she grasps the mettle and fires the first of her many questions.

As he lovingly describes his home, with its rambling buildings, recitals of cicada chirruping in the sunshine and rows of healthy and productive vines which stretch across the gently undulating landscape, she feels herself drifting, with the ambience of the setting, into a dream-world of a romantic and carefree existence ... far away from the cold and wet of the British Isles.

He explains how, after the disappearance of Lucy, his wife, Rozenn, and him had spent years devoting their time, money and efforts into renovating the property ... and, with the help of a few local characters, reviving the grapevines.

She is fascinated to hear that she has not only got a half-brother, who is a little younger than her and still in his teens, but that he is already learning how to take the reins — no doubt with the expectation of him, one day, and when the time is right, taking on the business and allowing his parents to embrace a relaxing and well-deserved retirement.

Gina sits quietly listening and, without giving her thoughts away, pondering over how different her life could have been, had she trusted Tom ... and not allowed Geoff to usurp his role.

If things had been different and Geoff had never been part of the equation, then Lucy would not have reacted as she had on that October night. Then, maybe, she would not have gone off. Mind you, if things had been different, then that *particular* seed of Tom's would not have been accepted by that *particular* ovum of hers ... and so, it would be fair to assume, therefore, that the random selection of genes which have made Tori the girl she is today, would not have materialized.

She resigns herself to the fact that however much she torments herself over her own actions, she will never be able to bring her firstborn back.

With this in mind, and with a loving glance towards her daughter, she counts her blessings.

Ah well … C'est la vie! she whispers, echoing the language of Tom's adopted home.

"Well." Tom breaks the focus which is on him as he hastily turns the tables. "And what about you? Hey?"

Tori looks towards her mother for guidance.

"Tell me, how did you and Jamie meet?" He knows that if he can get her to talk about a specific event, then maybe she will be more likely to open up about matters of a more general nature.

"Well … " She opens up as she goes into great length reliving the time when they had accidentally bumped into each other … and how he had then, disarmingly, uttered the *three or four* question as a means to get her to sit down with him and have a drink.

"Three or four?" Tom is bemused.

Tori enlightens him. "Marshmallows."

"Marshmallows?"

"Yes … In my drinking chocolate."

Tom, knowing that the drink had been Lucy's favourite, just has to ask.

"Chocolate? That's your favourite is it?"

"Oh yes … especially with cream and marshmallows … There's nothing better."

Tom pauses … and then moves away from the sadness of his recollections and turns towards her escort.

"Great chat-up line, Jamie!"

"I thought so. And, as you can see … it worked."

"Yes … it obviously did. Actually, I think it's great. I like your style."

Tori has already come to like her newly-found father. It is too early to know if she could love him as a daughter would be expected to … but, nevertheless, she feels quite comfortable in his presence.

She leans over to Jamie and whispers in his ear … as if she's asking for his approval for something. He nods.

Addressing Tom, she asks, "On Friday, after work, we're going up to Jamie's house … and we were wondering if you would like to come, too."

"Well … yes. But are you sure? I mean … I don't think I should impose if it's for something special."

"Oh no, you won't be imposing. It's just that Jamie and me are thinking about getting … Oops, forget I said anything. Just come up with us and meet Jamie's family. Will you? Please?"

Both Tom and Gina are equally intrigued as to their daughter's reluctance to explain her secret. Gina is the first to seek clarification.

"You're thinking about getting … what … precisely?"

"Mum … I was going to talk to you about it earlier, but with all this business about meeting my dad, I just couldn't find the right time."

"Well, maybe, this is the right time. So, I'll ask you again — what were you thinking about *getting*?"

Tori hesitates as she looks to Jamie for approval.

He gives the go-ahead, with a nod.

She reveals their secret, cautiously. "Mum! Please don't shout at me … but we are thinking about getting … engaged."

"Engaged!" she exclaims.

"Yes."

"To get married?" Gina questions.

"Yes — that's what *getting engaged* means, isn't it?"

"Well, yes. But you're so young."

"I know. But we were going to do it in a few months time — but now that I have a father, who won't be here for too long … I thought that it would be nice if we could have told you all together. I'm sorry, Mum … I really didn't mean to upset you."

Gina stays silent as she tries to process the disclosure. She's not particularly angry, but she is surprised to find out that, with them being so young, and after such a short relationship, they would actually be considering marriage.

"But … you've only known each other a few months!"

"I know … but we do love each other."

Tom interjects, "Come on, Gina. How long we were together before we—"

"Yes. Precisely! And, before you say any more, just look how successful *that* turned out to be!"

Gina takes a few more seconds to think, and then, with the subtlety of a marauding Centurion tank, she asks, "You're not pregnant, are you?"

"No — I'm not!"

Her response is as passionate as it is indignant as she cuts her mother's suggestion down. "And *Mother*, I would appreciate it if you could keep your voice down. It's a little bit embarrassing."

Tom cannot help but to let out a smile as he steers away from the spikiness of his ex-wife's responses. Then, skilfully, he avoids any further conflict with her by adopting the deflective strategy of openly confirming his acceptance of the invite.

"Okay. Why not? I've got to go and see a few people during the next few days. There's some things which need sorting before I go back to France. But yeah … I've got free time on Friday evening. So, if that's really what you want … then I'd be *delighted* to come with you."

Jamie thanks him and then turns his attention back to Gina.

"We would love for you to come as well. We were going to ask you first, but I think this meeting may have thrown a spanner in the works."

"A spanner? More like the whole toolbox, if you ask me!"

Gina, still shocked and surprised by the revelation, pauses and then responds with a silent nod, backed up with the olive branch of a smile as she resigns herself to the situation and accepts the invitation.

Chapter 39

As the evening approaches and the car park lies under the glow of artificial lighting, the customer-base alters. This is the time when those who have finished their day's work stop off to buy provisions whilst making their way home.

He watches with the noticeable fixation of a man who is brimming with an irrational surge of envy as a sleek and elegant Mercedes purrs into view. Having noted the national insignia which precedes the registered number, he cannot help but to express his irrational but, all the same, very real Francophobic prejudice. With more than a hint of contempt in his voice, he mutters, *"A posh frog … Whatever next?"*

Having seen that the exquisitely-crafted vehicle is occupied by just a middle-aged Frenchman and that it is not graced with the alluring presence of a lone and attractive woman, he is quick to lose interest. Dismissively, he turns away and carries on with the routine of trolley-control.

Tom checks his watch. He is early.

The arrangement had been made for Tom to meet up with Tori, Jamie and Gina at the in-store café. With no sign of them in the car park, he makes his way towards the main doors and enters. Having no need to enter the product-lined aisles, he, single-mindedly, follows the signs which will take him directly to his destination and thus enable him to make the rendezvous.

As he enters the café, he scans the faces at the tables and confirms that he is early.

With the purchase of a cup of coffee, he waits. From the vantage of his table he can see clearly across the car park and so, he is confident that their arrival will be noticed.

As he relaxes and watches the comings and goings of the shoppers, his attention is drawn to the strange, if not worrying, conduct of the man with the trolleys.

It is the way in which he stops and then, as if he has not a care in the world, stares at the legs and posteriors of the women who make their way between their vehicles and the store.

Scrutinizing the behaviour, he notes that whenever there is a possibility that he may be spotted by his target, he feigns indifference by simultaneously averting his gaze and holding his head downwards. But then, it is the shifty lifting of the eyes to steal another glimpse which betrays the unsavoury nature of his interest.

What is actually going through the man's mind can only be imagined and, he surmises, it is probably far from healthy.

Interestingly enough though, it appears that as soon as the trolley-man has allowed his thoughts to wallow sufficiently in the perversion of his imaginings and she — that is to say, his most recent target for attention — is no longer within his line of sight, he simply resumes his duties, periodically looking up and around as if seeking another to feed his fantasies.

With no more than his basic intuition to the fore, Tom readily perceives the potential for danger in this man. He may not have been tutored in psychology or psychiatry, but he instinctively knows that the man has a major problem. Moreover, he certainly wouldn't trust him anywhere near his wife, his daughter or, for that matter, any lone woman.

Tom looks away and concentrates on his surroundings. He stretches over and picks up a well-thumbed regional newspaper which has been lying on the recently-vacated table beside him.

He opens the pages, scanning the variety of headlines and not really expecting to see anything in particular to grasp his attention.

Page two shows a couple of very grainy images of a man seen in the vicinity of the abduction of a young Slovakian girl, just a few days earlier. The pictures which were taken from the closed-circuit television footage of different city-centre cameras are, to say the least, unclear. He suspects, therefore, that they will be of little use in ascertaining the identity of the person shown.

Although he has mixed views on the use or, to be more precise, the misuse of such technology, he wonders if things would have been different if the extent of modern-day usage had been operative in the *eighties*; and if they had been more prevalent, whether evidence would have been found which would have given the investigators some insight into what had happened to his daughter.

He scans the article. So as not to satisfy the needs of the voyeuristic, apart from the fact that she is Slovakian, the identity of the victim has been withheld … as has the detail of the attack on her. It is, however, written in such a way as to be able to evoke feelings of anger and pity in all but the most insensitive of readers. He is particularly saddened by the thought of how she must have felt … and how she must still be feeling. Knowing that he is still out there and thus free to return and silence her, must fill her with terror.

As he reads, he finds himself transported back to when Lucy had gone missing.

He wonders if, in her loneliness, she had suffered humiliation and fear. Had she called out for him, her father, to come to her rescue? He'll never know.

What he does know … is that with him having not been there to protect his firstborn, he had failed in his duty as a father. With the recall of those days becoming clearer by the moment, he feels the resurgence of melancholic guilt. So, in a conscious attempt to disconnect himself from his self-punishing thoughts, he closes the page, folds the newspaper in half and lays it onto the adjoining table ... hidden from sight.

Gina, having already collected both Tori and Jamie, enters the car park. Although busy, there are still many spaces from which to choose.

As she drives along the rows of parked vehicles in search of a suitable space, Jamie notices the tell-tale style and insignia of the French number plates which adorn a Mercedes, which is parked some fifty yards away from the store entrance.

"Is *that* Tom's car?"

Both mother and daughter eye the vehicle, and having agreed on the likelihood of it belonging to him, Gina swings her car around and abandons it untidily in a nearby space.

Tom watches as Tori, closely followed by Jamie and Gina, alights from the vehicle.

Subconsciously, still aware of the trolley-man's questionable demeanour, he casts his gaze across the car park and refocuses. As he had expected, the man has paused in his chores and is taking the opportunity to look across the car park towards both Gina and Tori.

As they make their way towards the main entrance, they stop. Gina hurriedly returns to the car as Jamie and Tori watch on.

They will not go on ahead without her; instead, they will stand and wait so that they can all arrive in the café together.

Tom refocuses his attention on the trolley-man. His attention is not on the lone woman, Gina ... rather, it is fixed on the younger, and accompanied, Tori.

Dismissively, he abandons the trolley with a well-aimed and obviously well-practised shove to one side and then watches as it glides into one of the dedicated trolley-bays. Showing signs of uncertainty, he edges closer to the couple and, with the cover of unattended vehicles, he betters his view.

He stops ... and, paying no heed to the conspicuousness of his interest, he stares. Tori glances towards him. Seemingly confused, agitated and concerned, he turns away and retrieves the abandoned trolley. Then, as if struggling to regain composure, he hurriedly connects it to the row of others which are being readied for the long push back towards the store.

Having recognized that the actions of the man are inconsistent with what he had assumed to have been his *usual* abnormal behaviour, Tom is intrigued.

In the eyes of the trolley-man, Tori is not just *any* attractive young woman. She is different, and her very presence has clearly unsettled him.

As the trio enter the café, Tom, with his customary display of gentlemanly etiquette, stands up and welcomes them with the offer of a drink and a bite to eat.

The drinks are happily accepted. The offer of food, however, is politely declined; it would ruin the anticipated fare of hospitality which Jamie's mother will, without doubt, be actively in the process of preparing.

In fact, it was because of the invite to Jamie's home that they had arranged to meet at the supermarket. Gina had wanted to purchase a bouquet of flowers and a box of chocolates as a token of her appreciation.

Still, having purchased and duly collected their choices of beverage he, with the fully laden tray in hand, returns to the table and retakes his seat.

The earlier actions of the trolley-man still echo in his mind, but so as not to cause needless anxiety to either Tori or her mother, he opts to keep his thoughts to himself.

He is not sure how to ask Tori if she knows the man. After all, he does not wish to disclose to her his reason for asking and, so, risk causing her undue distress.

As they chat together, Tom seems distracted by the activities in the car park.

There is no sign of the man.

In fact, there is now another man — much younger and clad in a high visibility jacket — taking on the role. Maybe, he muses, the *weirdo*, who he feels may have an unsavoury attitude towards women, has gone for a break … or even, for that matter, has finished his shift and is now making his way homeward.

Tori makes her first real attempt to engage in conversation, and with a somewhat naïve and superfluous question, she asks, "Do they have supermarkets in France?"

"Yes … they do. And like here … they're everywhere."

"Oh, really. And what are they like?"

Tom, bemused by the subject of her questioning, shrugs his shoulders as he gives his reply. "A lot like this I suppose. Noisy and busy … but to many, pretty much essential."

She does not know how she should follow on from her start — but being sensitive to the silence, Tom comes to her rescue and expands on his answer.

"To be honest, we only use the supermarket for fuel and a few basics … like dog food and cereals. But, otherwise, we try to use the local shops. And of course, there are the stalls in the weekly street-market. I suppose it keeps me in with the locals. Anyway, apart from that, the whole street-market thing is pretty laid-back and … nice."

Suddenly, realising that the oddity of Tori's questioning is in its own way fortuitous, he now has an excuse to discover the regularity of their visits. He wonders if the trolley-man had recognized Tori from a previous visit.

He looks across to Gina. "I suppose you use this place quite a bit?"

"No ... hardly ever. I usually go to the opposition. It's on the outskirts of town. It's much the same as here, but they've got certain things that I can't get anywhere else."

He looks across at both Jamie and Tori, who both, anticipating the question, shake their heads in response.

He targets Jamie. "What about you Jamie? Do your parents come here much?"

Jamie responds with a deadpan expression. "I don't know! I mean ... the food just appears in the fridge and I eat it. I shut the door ... and then — I don't know how it happens — but, I go back to the fridge the next day and ... it's sort of magically refilled itself. So then, I start again. A bit like the *Groundhog Day* thingy. It's great!"

Although he is not entirely sure whether Jamie is reflecting a touch of archetypical youthful indifference, or if he had been purposefully trying to add a touch of humour to the conversation, Tom, nevertheless, finds it amusing.

"Ouch!" Jamie winces as Tori jabs her elbow into his side — an action which, with her playful, *behave yourself* rebuke, suggests that his comments were, in actual fact, weighed towards him having been blessed with a wicked sense of wit.

"Thank goodness for that!" Tom says, with a feigned sigh of relief, "I knew you were kidding." He pauses long enough for them to look back at him quizzically, and then adds, "You see, I don't know of any youngsters who will remember to shut the fridge door after they've ransacked it."

"Touché!" Gina ends the contest with the declaration of a tie.

Tori has been mulling over the way in which Tom had questioned them over their shopping habits and asks, "Why the interest in where we shop?"

He felt it to be more prudent to lie. "No reason. Anyway ... you started it. So, let's move on. Come on, now tell me a bit about you. Your likes, your dislikes, your ambitions — anything at all."

"Oh, I don't know ... I'm just me." She opens her hands as a sign of her sincerity, and then, with a smile, continues. "So what you see ... is what you get."

"Okay. Maybe we'll get to know each other in due course."

Gina progresses the conversation towards a more serious and sensitive subject. "You said that you were going to try and refresh Lucy's case. How are you getting on with it?"

"Slowly. I've made some tentative enquiries with the local press ... but, to be honest, although they nod and shake their heads in the right places, I don't think they're going to be interested unless, of course, I can give them something new to latch onto."

"Is that it? Is that all you've done?"

"No. As I told you at the hotel, I've made other enquiries — I've been in contact with Shep, the old village bobby.

"Oh yes, I remember — I'm sorry."

"No problem."

"You may think I'm mad, but every night I talk to Lucy. I go over and over what happened. It breaks my heart."

"You're not mad. ... I'm the same. I have a spot back home where I sit ... alone and away from any hassle ... and I think. Anyway, back to the present ... Shep wants to help us in whatever way he can. That's something isn't it?"

Gina's expression tells its own tale. She is not particularly impressed, and neither is she convinced as to how he can help. After all, he has had plenty of time to bring all of his knowledge to the fore — and, at present, the enquiry is still no further ahead than it was on the night she went missing.

However, she decides not to dampen Tom's enthusiasm and elects to remain silent rather than to openly express the negativity of her views.

He has known her for too many years; because of that, he can read her silence like a book. "Maybe, he's got contacts — and, maybe, if the local press know that he's supporting us, then they will take on the story. In any case, I'm off to see him again tomorrow. Hopefully we'll be able to discuss the options available. He may be old ... and he may be retired but he's got a lot of knowledge *and* an awful lot of know-how."

"That's good. I hope it works out."

She turns her attention to the young couple. "Come on then ... let's drink up. We've got a couple of odds and ends to pick up to take with us, then we'll be off."

She looks back to Tom. "You can follow us, if that's all right?"

"That's fine with me. I'll meet you in the car park."

Tom is happy to comply. After all, he has not yet been made privy to the rather important detail of the address.

Chapter 40

The events of the previous evening had gone surprisingly well. Tori and Jamie have formally announced their intent to get married, and Gina, having already started to become accustomed to the news, is starting to get excited about the prospect of it all, even though the big day is unlikely to be soon.

The idea of her being able to help her daughter to make the arrangements and to select a suitable dress for the occasion has appealed to her. After all, she had seemed to be quite willing to steer the conversation back to the subject at every opportunity.

There had been a moment when she had been thinking about the forthcoming wedding day and how she would be able to assist her daughter in adding the final touches before walking up the aisle, when her thoughts had drifted back to that day when she had tended Lucy's injuries. Although it was following the fracas with Joe and Marcus and was, therefore, under very different circumstances, she had spent some precious moments helping her to touch-up her make-up before encouraging her to step, with her head held high and with a show of confidence, back into the throng.

Jamie's parents had been excellent hosts. They had been good-natured, amusing and more than welcoming.

They had that rare ability to make one feel as if they had been friends for years and, as such, had made them feel comfortable when in their company.

Bryn, Jamie's father, had seemed to enjoy playfully teasing his son by bringing up things from the distant but not forgotten past, knowing that they may have been the catalyst to cause him some mild embarrassment.

However, Beth, Jamie's mother, albeit unintentionally, did actually manage to cause him embarrassment; not by bringing up something which he would have preferred to have seen left in the past but, rather, by proudly concentrating on the positive — his natural flair for creativity in the medium of music.

She had insisted that he demonstrate his musical skills and at the same time show off his *pride and joy*; his custom-built bass guitar.

Now, although this is traditionally the time when, whilst hidden behind the façade of a smile, guests will often listen to a recital, politely and without criticism … Tom was genuinely impressed. He could see that the young man was good. In fact, he was very good.

He was also impressed with the craftsmanship of the instrument's creator.

The exquisite patterning of the bird's-eye maple through-neck which

— when integrated into the main body — was flanked and complemented by the long curving flow of the contours of the grain of ash, had given it a look which could not be bettered. A thing of beauty? Of course. But even *he* could see that it was more than that. It had that something extra … that certain *je ne sais quoi*.

Even as a layman he could appreciate the beauty of the thing. But then, with him having sensed that there was something more, something he could not quite get to grips with, he was also intrigued. Maybe it was the inexplicable feeling of warmth that it had seemed to convey to him as he had sat with it resting on his knee; or, on the other hand, perhaps it was just down to the lustre of its finish. Whatever the reason, he knew that it had an allure which had made him feel as if he had almost wanted to sit quietly and admire it.

In fact, he had considered it to have been so beautiful that he had wished that he had sufficient know-how to have been able to play it for himself.

Jamie had related to Tom's feelings. He had on many occasions felt the need to just embrace it … and so he would often sit quietly in his room with it cradled in his lap.

Put simply, it was indeed a very special creation.

***

Tom, having arrived at Shep's home, following a good night's sleep and a stress-free morning, is relaxed.

"Morning, Tom. Come on in … Make 'eself at home."

"Thank you."

Tom glances at his watch, and with barely two minutes remaining until the hour of noon, he continues. "You're right. It is still morning … well, only just. Anyway, how are you?"

"I's fine, and thank you for asking. I take it you'm ready for a brew then? I's havin' one — so 'tis no trouble for me to make another."

Tom indicates his acceptance with a nod.

The traditional ways of British hospitality intrigue him as much now as they have done in the past. He has often wondered how a beverage which has been made from a crop which is so alien to these isles has, in the perception of people throughout the world, become synonymous with the fabric of the culture.

Whilst he waits for Shep to return from the kitchen, he gets the feeling of *déjà-vu* as he re-examines the titles of the books which fill the bookcase.

The door swings open and Shep brings in the drinks.

Both men sit back and make themselves comfortable, each trying to decide as to how they should start the conversation.

"Shep?"

"I's listening."

"Do you ever go to that new supermarket? You know, the one between that old graveyard ... and where those retirement-flats have been built?"

"I knows where you'm on about. Them flats were put up where the old prefabs used to be. And if I's not mistaken, there were a few allotments there as well. Anyway ... to answer your question ... yes. I knows exactly which supermarket you'm on about."

"So, do you ever go there?"

"I reckons that maybe on the odd occasion I have. Mind you, 'twould have been some time ago. Definitely not recently. Why d'you ask?"

"I don't know. Maybe I'm just clutching at straws. But yesterday, I saw a guy who was acting pretty strange. Sort of creepy, if you know what I mean. Anyway, he works in the car park ... sorting out the shopping-trolleys."

"Go on."

"Well, I couldn't help noticing that whenever he saw a woman on her own, or even with a young child, walking from her car to the store, he would stop what he was doing and just stare at her. He'd just stare as she walked across the car park. He was blatant about it! It was almost like he was obsessed with watching a certain type of woman. I mean, he wasn't just appreciating the sight of a good-looking woman like most blokes would. He was different — sort of focused, if you know what I mean. To me, it was obvious what was going through his dirty little mind — and there's one thing I can be sure of ... It definitely wasn't good!"

"Well ... I's afraid there be no legislation that I's aware of which can prosecute a man for his thoughts — well, not yet anyway."

Before Shep starts to think that it is Tom who is being obsessive and becoming increasingly mistrustful of anyone, he responds, "Yes, I understand that. But when I was in the café waiting for Gina, my ex, and ..." He stalls for a moment as he deliberates as to whether or not he should add to the confusion and let on about the news of his newly-discovered fatherhood. "... *her* daughter, Tori — I mean, Victoria, to turn up, I saw —"

"Her daughter?" Shep interrupts.

"Yes. It's a long story, but ... Oh, what am I saying? No, it isn't ... it's quite a short story really."

Shep looks on with interest and waits for Tom to continue.

"Basically, Gina and me had a one-off thing on Lucy's eighteenth birthday. Anyway, I didn't know about it until now, but it turns out that the baby she had after Lucy disappeared was actually mine!"

"Her's yours?"

"So I've been told."

"Did her husband know anything about all this?"

"What? At the time?"

Shep nods.

"No, I don't think so."

"Well, well — the mysterious ways of us country folk, hey? Still, 'nough said. Best you carry on and tell me what else you saw."

"Okay. I think I've lost the thread of what I was saying. Anyway, what I'm trying to say is … from what I've seen, I think this guy is really weird. Okay, it may be that he's just a dirty old man, but there's something else. You see, when he saw Tori, he was different. It was the way that he looked at her. I don't know what it was exactly … but it was as if he'd been confronted by a ghost or something. I know it sounds strange, but I was wondering if—"

With a knowing nod, Shep finishes his sentence for him. "You was wonderin' if, maybe, he was thinking as if her were a bit too much like Lucy for comfort. Am I right?"

"Well, sort of. You see, you haven't seen Tori. The truth is, she's not just *similar* to Lucy; she's the spitting image of her. She looks exactly the way Lucy did all those years ago. And if it wasn't for the time lapse, you'd think they were one and the same. It certainly took me back a few years when I first saw her!"

Shep collects his thoughts, and then, before Tom can continue, he speaks, "Well Tom … I reckons that this is going to play on your mind — so, maybe, if we don't sort it out soon, then you'm never goin' to let it rest. Now then, I take it you'd like me to take a peek at this 'ere *weirdo chappie* an' then see if I can shine some light on who 'e might be. Am I right in my thinking?"

"Yes. You're dead right. Look, I know that I may be barking up the wrong tree … but there really was something about the way he reacted to her which made me start to wonder if—"

"No need to explain," Shep interrupts, "there's often good reasons for they gut-feelings we get. I'll tell 'e, them's feelings have certainly stood me in good stead during my thirty years in the job."

Having risen from his chair, he stands at the window … gazing out towards the driveway. "Now if you don't mind me saying, that's a pretty smart looking motorcar you have out there."

"Yes, it is. It's a Merc."

"Well, I reckons that maybe, 'twould be nice if you'm were to offer to take me on a little trip down to this 'ere supermarket, and then, perhaps I can be seeing if I can enlighten you as to the identity of this 'ere *weirdo chappie*, as you describe him. How's that sound?"

"It sounds pretty good to me."

"Well, 'tis no rush, so we'm best finish our tea first. Then we'll make our way down to the shops and see what's about."

***

Knowing, through experience, that there will be insufficient space in the staff car-parking area at this time of day, the trolley-man has left his car in a side street, a quarter of a mile or so away. He enjoys the walk. With the crutch of his last nicotine fix for the next few hours relieving his inner worries, he can take his time and amble his way towards his place of work.

He is able to use the walk to gather his thoughts and also to rehearse his answers in the event that he is, at some stage, routinely questioned by the police.

He has seen the images in the press; although he is confident that they are far from being clear enough for anyone to be able to put a name to them, he is still concerned as to the extent of the police involvement. What is more, he is becoming increasingly ill at ease with the thought that they have publicly stated that they are still in the process of trawling through the *extensive footage* of the security cameras which, being from both official and private sources, are situated at strategic locations throughout the city.

***

As Tom negotiates a path through the narrow lanes of the car park, both he and his passenger look out for signs of the trolley-man. He is not to be seen.

Shep looks at his watch. Feeling the first pangs of hunger, he suggests that a visit to the café will give them a vantage point for their observations whilst they partake in having some lunch.

Agreed. They make their way to the café.

Once the meals have been selected, Shep makes his apologies, and with a look of urgency, he makes his exit. He has a need to answer the call of nature.

Tom's position in the queue moves on. As he gives the order and pays the cashier, he cannot help but to allow himself a brief and private chuckle.

The crafty old sod, he thinks, almost admiring the cunning of his mentor, who has, somewhat conveniently, delayed his return sufficiently long enough for Tom to have paid for both meals.

Although nature's call may be genuine, he suspects that it may not have been as urgent as Shep had made it seem. If it was simply a case of him having executed the art of evasive tactics, then it had been a well-practised routine, which he finds rather amusing … and so, he can hold no grudge against the man.

Shep returns to rejoin Tom, who has already claimed a table which, conveniently, overlooks the car park. "Have you paid?"

"Yes. I've paid. It's all done."

"Hang on a minute …" He fumbles through his pockets as if in search of his wallet.

"Let me pay 'e ... Now, how much do I owe 'e?"

"Nothing. It's the least I can do for you, my friend. Please ... put your money away."

In fact, neither the wallet nor any money had actually materialized. In fact, by the way in which Shep just gratefully accepts the provision of his sustenance for the day, there is the slightest suspicion that a reimbursement had not really been on the agenda.

As they wait for their meals, they discuss *who* out of Shep's contacts, old and new, would be best placed to ensure an interest from the media.

Whilst systematically working through the options, they are distracted by the compulsion to scan the expanse of the car park.

It takes a while for the meal to be served, but even then, it is only once they have nearly finished, that the trolley-man is seen.

With due discretion, and so as not to alert others of his interest, Tom leans across the table and points him out. "There he is! He's walking across the car park. Can you see? He's over there ... heading towards the trolley-bay."

Shep looks up from his plate and peers through the window. "I sees him." His eyesight is not what it used to be, but rather than admit to it, he elects to do what he calls, *a Sir Francis Drake*. He will finish his meal, unperturbed, until the target comes closer to the building.

"Do you recognize him?"

"Plenty of time for that, bu'y. He isn't going anywhere fast. So I reckons 'tis best we be finishin' our food before it gets too cold. Rushing will only give 'e indigestion. We don't want that now, do we? Now then, when we'm done *then* we'll take a ganders. What d'you reckon?"

Tom is beginning to show the first signs of his frustration. But then, tempered by his needs, along with the fact that he trusts the old man, he has little alternative other than to just go with the flow.

"Did you watch any TV last night?"

"No. I was out 'til late, so I didn't see anything."

"So ... you missed the news then? Pity ... It showed a video of a suspect — or, to use the reporter's parlance, *a man who the police think may be able to help them with their enquiries*."

Tom, now more interested in what Shep has to say, responds, "What enquiries?"

"Well, it appears that, a few days ago and, I hasten to add, not too far from 'ere, there was an abduction of a young maid. Fortunately, her were able to make good her escape."

"Is that the same one who was in the paper yesterday? The Slovakian girl?"

"That's the one ... That'll be her. Now, I knows 'tis unlikely for there to be a connection with your Lucy's disappearance, what with all the time that's gone by, but this could get the local reporters keen to be gettin' your story across. What d'you reckon?"

"Umm... You've got a point. I think I can see where you're coming from." He pauses as he collects his thoughts, weighing up the merits of Shep's suggestion. "Yes, you're right. I suppose, if the public are interested in *that* attack, then they may also be able interested in what happened in the past, with Lucy."

Shep nods.

"Okay, my friend. So ... how do you think that we should go about it?"

The older man smiles.

Being referred to as *my friend* is nice — it suggests that he has been valued as someone in his own right and not just that of an old *copper* who has his uses.

"Now, I can go with 'e to see the editor of the local rag if 'e wish. You see, I reckons that, maybe, it'll give you some extra clout if you can give him the complete package. Tell him about Lucy, but also have the old local bobby on hand for them to make some use of. What d'you reckon?"

Tom welcomes the offer, and being unable to resist giving the compliment of mimicking Shep's broad, Devon brogue, he agrees. "Well ... I reckons you'm probably right, bu'y!"

Shep laughs, and as he does, his attention is suddenly drawn away from the café and back out and into the car park.

He watches intently as the trolley-man, pushing a train of trolleys back towards the entrance to the store, steadily approaches.

The old man's expression, now reflecting the more serious aspect of his character, changes as he digs into the archives of his memory.

Tom follows his gaze and also focuses on the common target.

"What is it? What are you thinking?"

"I's not too sure, bu'y. Just you hang fire a minute ... I's thinking." He concentrates on the target. "You know what?"

"What?"

"Well, there's something about him that's starting to ring some bells. I can't be too certain, but I reckons I should know him from somewhere."

"Who is he?"

"As I's said, I can't be too certain. I just needs a moment to mull it over ... if 'e don't mind."

Tom's attention switches to-and-fro the activities of the trolley-man and the thoughtful countenance of the retired policeman.

"Well, bu'y? I thinks I's right. I reckons I may have an idea as to who he is."

"So?" Tom waits for the revelation.

"So ..." Shep, with his eyes fixed on his target and having decided not to immediately reveal the name, continues. "... I reckons that if 'e's who I think 'e is, then there may well be a connection with him and your Lucy. Now, 'twill be a waste of time for us to confront him as to why he's been staring at Tori. An' 'twill also be a waste of time for us to be contacting the police just yet." He pauses for a few moments before making his suggestion. "I think it may be best if we try an' flush him out. A bit like flushin' rats from a sewer ... if 'e knows were I's comin' from."

"Okay. Go on ... I'm listening."

"Well, if I recalls correctly, he has a weakness — an *Achilles heel* if 'e prefer. Anyhow, 'tis 'cause of that that I reckons he could be susceptible to suggestion. Now, if we can confuse him ... perhaps, give him a bit of a fright ... then, maybe 'e's gonna be reactin' an' then do somethin' or say somethin' which will lead 'e to the truth."

"So, how are you going to do that?"

"You just leave that to me. Now then, how do 'e get on with your ex ... and the young maid, Tori?"

"Okay. So far, so good. Why?"

"Well, if you could make an arrangement for us all to meet up, I think I have an idea which may just do the trick."

"Come on, Shep ... tell me ... what have you got in mind?"

Shep just taps his nose, indicating that he will reveal his plans on a need-to-know basis. At this stage there is no need for anyone other than himself to know.

"All in good time, bu'y. All in good time."

"Oh, come on Shep. At least you can tell me who you think he is!"

"As I said, all in good time, bu'y. I knows what I's doing, so you'm best be putting your trust in *good ol' Shep*. Be patient."

Chapter 41

Gina is not entirely happy about the impending implementation of Shep's plan. But although she knows it is unconventional, she also knows that her daughter will not be alone and is, therefore, less likely to be at risk. Shep has made it quite clear that there can be no guarantee of his plan meeting with success. But, knowing something of his quarry's personality, he has a sneaking belief that however corny or simplistic the idea may seem to others ... it may well work.

He may not be academically qualified in matters of psychology but he is, nevertheless, quite the expert when it comes to exploiting the power of suggestion. Tori has taken Shep's tuition in the art like a duck to water. So rather than being nervous about her role in the charade, she seems to be relishing the challenge. What's more, with the additional zest of youthful exuberance, she dismisses the notion of failure with an element of contempt.

She has been fully briefed as to the *known* circumstances of her sister's disappearance. She has also been furnished with the details of how Joe had been suspected of *doing away* with her sister and how he had then — through a combination of both grief and fear — taken his own life whilst within the embrace and solace of, the now dilapidated, *Dozy Barn*.

With Gina's input, Tori has been made to look far more like her sister than anyone could ever have imagined. Although nature had done its part, it was not easy for Gina to complete, insomuch as she had to echo those precious moments when it had been Lucy who had been standing beside her in the ladies room ... whilst looking into the mirror as she'd allowed her — her mother — to lovingly brush her hair.

With her memories being so readily resurrected at the slightest hint of any similarity to the event, she knows that they will never be allowed to fade.

Shep had suggested that if they dress her exactly as Lucy would have been on the night of her disappearance, then that may have given rise to suspicion. It would have been too obvious. He had thought that, with the mere exploitation of them using the identical colour and fabric, they would be able to provide enough of a stimulus for it to spur the awesome power of autosuggestion.

It was Gina who had remembered the need for Tori to wear an amber pendant against the blue of the dress. On the night of her disappearance, Lucy had been wearing the matching pendant and earrings which she had received from her father on the occasion of her eighteenth birthday.

Anyway, a couple of hours ago, having made comparisons with photos of Lucy, Shep had given his approval to the way in which Tori had been transformed.

With an air of confidence in his voice, he'd announced, "Good! I reckons he'll be seeing what his conscience allows him to be seeing. Now then young lady ... 'tis up to you. If I's to be honest, I's pretty confident that when he sees you ... his guilt will be doin' the business. He'll be gettin' all panicky."

***

As she drives towards the supermarket, she consoles herself with the fact that Tom has, if nothing else, spoilt their daughter with the gift of not only a dress, but also, a gold necklace with an amber pendant and a matching set of earrings ... just like Lucy's. He had not stopped with the purchase of what had been necessary for the act of subterfuge; he had gone on to purchase far more. As a result, she has been able to freshen up her wardrobe and, thus, she will be spoilt for choice when she has to decide what is best to wear when she's next goes out socializing with Jamie.

Tom and Shep arrive at the car park.

So as not to insinuate a connection between the two vehicles, Gina, Jamie and Tori have arranged to arrive separately ... and a few minutes later.

With natural daylight on the wane, the conditions are just as Shep had wanted; light enough for the trolley-man to readily spot Tori as she walks across the car park, but not quite light enough for him to be distracted by the presence of the two men who will be watching on as they sit quietly within the confines of the Mercedes.

As Gina approaches the car park's entrance, she slows and, whilst still on the main road, she stops to allow Tori to get out and to make her way, unescorted, through the pathway which cuts through the heathery boundary of the car park.

Gina, keeping a protective eye on the progress of her daughter, follows the roadway around. Once in the car park, she selects a suitable space and stops.

She watches as he shepherds his flock of meshed, chromium-plated trolleys out from the security of the mid car park drop-off bays and towards the main building.

He looks up. Seeing Tori ambling towards the store's main entrance, he stops ... and he stares.

She is alone, and he cannot resist the temptation to get closer and improve his view.

As she glances to one side and sees his approach, she begins to feel the increasing effects of her nervousness.

Part of her wants to accelerate and to reach the safety of the shop before he catches up with her, but she knows that if she yields to her instincts, then she will succeed only in defeating the objective of the ruse.

Seeing the Mercedes nearby, her inborn sense for self-preservation determines that she should place herself in a position where the confluence will be within clear view and earshot of both Shep and her father.

Measuring her pace ... she slows.

He will certainly be able to catch up with her, but only once she is within the close proximity of the Mercedes.

With her senses on full alert, she knows, instinctively, when he is closing the gap behind her.

The rustling of his coat betrays his presence.

He is almost upon her.

She stops and turns to face him.

Taken aback by her sudden reaction, he stops. Then ... open-mouthed, he stands and stares in silence.

She watches him, albeit with a feeling of much discomfort, as his eyes scan both herself and her attire. With the glisten of blue satin peeping from under her coat, she cannot help but to notice how his attention flicks, back and forth, between her pendulous earrings and her amber pendant.

He is, to say the very least, unsettled.

Bracing herself, she finds the courage. "Are you looking for me?"

He is cautious. She has spoken as if she already knows how he will respond, but he asks his question anyway, "Who are you?"

He is blunt, almost to the point of rudeness. He has offered no explanation as to why he has an interest in her identity. As he looks her up and down, his attention, almost involuntarily, keeps returning to focus on her amber jewellery ... and in particular, her pendant.

"Who am I? Don't you know?"

"No ... I don't think so."

"Of course you do. How could you forget *me*?"

"No ... I'm sorry, I think I must've mistaken you for someone else."

He lies. She looks as Lucy had looked. If he didn't know better, he could easily be forgiven for believing it to be her.

He turns to walk away ... but, on hearing her call out after him, he stops in his tracks.

"Have you seen Joe, yet?"

He is shocked. With a shiver running through his spine, he turns back to face her, and, whilst trying to contain his composure, he seeks confirmation of her question. "What?"

"Joe ... You do remember Joe, don't you?"

The line of her questioning chills him from the inside. With his eyes starting to water, thus, blurring his vision, he replies, "I don't know what you're talking about."

His words are composed but, underneath, there is an edge. He is nervous and, what's more, he knows that she can sense it.

"He's not happy with you ... But still, he's got all the time in the world to find you."

"What? Is there something wrong with you? Look, I dunno what you're talking about. And, in any case ... that Joe, who you're on about ... he hung himself — he's dead and gone ... End!"

The echoes of his own words resonate in his mind. Realising that he has erred by leaking the fact that he is well aware of who Joe was and, moreover, how he had come to his end, he feels vulnerable.

Feeding off his fears and doubts has given her the confidence to continue to play her part. Besides, not only does she know that she has *got to* him, she is now convinced that Shep is right. This man knows far more about Lucy's disappearance than he would ever care to divulge. With that in mind, she is determined to play her part in ensuring that he is worked ... until he snaps.

Knowingly, she shakes her head and taunts him. "Oh dear, oh dear, oh dear. We all have our little secrets now, don't we? Tut, tut, tut!"

With the truth of her inner feelings showing clearly in the icy look which fills her eyes, and which, somewhat menacingly, stare out from the façade of a clearly forced and contrived smile, she adds, "I'm so glad that I've found you at last. Anyway, now that we've been reacquainted, then I'm sure we'll meet again ... quite soon. Are you sure you don't recognize me?"

She waits for a response, but other than the slightest hint of a nod, there is none.

She continues. "Of course you do! You know exactly who I am, don't you?"

Not being used to being the target of intimidation, he becomes more and more irritated by the moment.

He looks around him; whether it is through the chance of sheer coincidence or the more sinister reflection of the eeriness of the moment, he is aware of there being little to no movement — it's as if time, itself, has frozen.

He is feeling alone ... Very alone!

Suddenly, as if woken from a trance, he reacts. "I've told you, I don't know what the f—k you're on about. So why don't you just piss off and play your stupid little games with some other f—ker?"

"Oh! Tut-tut — such foul language! This is no game — I promise you that. But, all right, if that's the way you want it, then I'll be seeing you later. Bye then."

"I can't be doing with this."

He turns and starts to walk away, muttering reassurances to himself as he goes.

Picking up pace and as if seeking a return to reality, he returns to the point at which he had previously been working. He tries to focus on stability — on the more usual movements of vehicles which now move within the car park.

She has not yet finished with him. She will add fuel to his suspicions. So, once his back is turned and before she could have reasonably been expected to have completed her walk across the car park, she ducks out of sight and hides beside the Mercedes.

A couple of seconds pass — then, once the coast is clear, she pokes her head up and calls out, "The name's Lucy!"

She ducks down, and as she struggles to hold back the urge to laugh, she creeps around the rear of the car to the nearside and then crouches beside the passenger door.

The trolley-man stops, and then, having registered the name, which as far as he is concerned should have been lost in the void of history … he looks back, as if to confirm that she really had called out a name from the long-gone but not forgotten past.

There is no sign of her. She has gone!

He looks puzzled, for he knows that it would have been impossible for the young woman to have reached the shop. Even if she had broken into a run, she would have still have been within his view. He cannot help but to wonder if he is starting to *hear voices*.

If he is *hearing voices*, then he wonders if he may have imagined the whole thing. But then he also muses over the possibility that she may have been neither real nor imagined.

As he thinks, the intensity of his anxiety increases.

He pulls out a packet of cigarettes. His worries over the incident far outweigh the consequences of being seen smoking whilst on duty … and in public view. Disregarding the rules, he puts a cigarette to his mouth and lights it. The flicker of the lighter's flame is exaggerated by the shake of his hand, but the cigarette is lit and he is able to draw a much-needed inhalation of smoke.

Even if he has not been made the target of the supernatural, he is, nevertheless, worried. It may be that someone has linked him to the disappearance of the McMurry girl — and, with that as a possibility, he has more than sufficient cause to worry.

Tom, so as not to alert the trolley-man to his presence, switches the interior light to the off position. Once done, Shep opens the passenger door, leans forward and allows Tori to squeeze by and onto the rear seat.

She lies low … remaining out of sight.

With light reflecting off the windscreen, the identity of the vehicle's occupants has been obscured. But with no wish to tempt fate, they keep their heads down.

The trolley-man is flustered. He starts to show signs of increased anxiety as he tries, without success, to reason as to how she could have disappeared from his view so quickly.

Unusually for him, he does not finish his cigarette. Instead, he throws it onto the tarmac and leaves it to extinguish on its own.

At first, almost weasel-like, he searches along the rows of parked cars. Unable to locate her, he heads towards the store.

The security counter is strategically situated to allow constant observations on all those who either enter or leave the premises. Visibly on edge, he distracts the security officer from the routine scrutiny of the closed-circuit television screens.

"Hi, Mazz … You didn't by any chance see a young woman come in a few minutes ago — late-teens, maybe early-twenties … with long black hair?"

"How long ago, did you say?"

"A couple of minutes."

"No, I don't think so. It's fairly quiet, so I think I would have noticed. Why? Is she pretty?"

"Oh no. It's nothing like that."

He has no wish to have to explain the real reason for his interest — so, instead, he tries to dismiss the enquiry.

"I just thought that I may have recognized her from somewhere, that's all. It's nothing important. Forget I asked."

"No … give us a few secs … I'll rewind the video. Then we can see what we've got."

"Are you sure?"

"Yes … It's no problem."

"Okay. Thanks."

With the recording of the comings and goings of the main entrance being played back, the trolley-man realizes that she did not, in fact, enter the building at all.

"Thanks again, Mazz — I must've been mistaken."

His confusion is compounded.

Mazz flicks the switch from playback to live. "Ah well … I guess that's what they call, Sod's Law! You see a pretty girl … you look away … and then she disappears into nowhere. It happens to me all the time. If you ask me, I think it's either spooky or we've both had an unhealthy dose of bad luck."

The trolley-man thanks him yet again and then hurries out from the store and back to the car park.

She is nowhere to be seen … and with time having moved on, he knows that a protracted search would be a waste of time and effort.

With his inner doubts, he wonders if he has had some kind of brainstorm and has imagined seeing an image from his past. But then, he reasons … *she was real … and then there was that bit about Joe. Now that was weird.* He knows exactly who Joe was; furthermore, he is also well aware of the connection with Lucy.

"My God!" He exclaims.

His thoughts fire off at random and at all angles. *It couldn't be, could it? No — don't be daft — If it was her … then she hasn't aged one bit! But then, she wouldn't have … would she?* The more he seeks rationale, the more agitated he becomes.

Yet again, he scans the car park. Being unable to come up with any logical suggestion as to what had just happened, he starts to accept the possibility of what he would normally have considered to be … impossible. *Had he …* he wonders … *met up with the ghost from his past?*

Unable to concentrate on even the most menial of tasks, he makes his way back into the store.

He will find his manager … and then he will sign off as being sick.

It's the only way. He needs to check things out. Not tomorrow — but now!

Only then will he be able to put it all behind him and carry on with his life.

After all, he has enough problems with the police activity over the Slovakian girl — and with that as his priority, he needs to concentrate on matters of the present … and not of the past.

A stomach upset is as good as an excuse as any. What 's more, it does not necessarily mean a prolonged spell away from his work.

He taps on the manager's door.

***

Waiting in the car park, and with their target having entered the store, Gina rings Tom for an update. Although both Jamie and her had visually witnessed the exchange of words, they had, rather frustratingly, been out of earshot. She has, therefore, a need to check on Tori's welfare.

"She's fine." Tom having reassured her, explains, "She's done really well, and from what she's told us, Shep thinks that he may well be our man. Oh … and something else … Tori's definitely spooked him. It's not over. So, let's all be patient and see what he does next."

"What if he finishes work? What shall we do then?"

Tom looks to Shep for an answer.

With the appropriate guidance given, Tom replies, "We'll follow him and see where he goes. Are you on hands-free?"

"Yes. It's off at the moment, but I'll put in on."

"Good. Now … when he's on the move … we can keep an open line and run a commentary. Okay?"

"Yes. Okay."

She does not sound particularly keen on the idea of her using a mobile phone whilst she is driving, but then, she can see the reason for compliance.

"Shep says, if he goes off on foot, then Jamie and Shep can join up and follow him, okay? We can then follow on in our cars. We'll just have to wait for them to give us an update."

Shep notes how easily Tom has slipped into a state of reasoned objectiveness, having adopted the practical stance of being in, what Shep has always referred to as, *operational mode.*

***

The premature ending of his shift on the grounds of sickness has been granted.

Having gone via the staff room to put away his reflective jacket and don his personal jacket, he makes his way out of the store, stopping only to light a cigarette.

With the tool for his nicotine-fix in hand, he, without deviation, makes his way across the car park.

With five pairs of eagle-eyes scrutinizing the faces of everyone who leaves the premises, he is recognized. But with him being unaware of the attention which is now firmly focused on him, he feels no need to be elusive.

Understandably, he is still troubled by his experience, but, in spite of everything, he cannot help but to gaze at the people who are innocently carrying on with their routine ways. Although he realizes that the girl should be well-gone by now, he cannot shake off the doubts which, having been agitated by his self-fuelled fears, suggest that she may not have been all that she had seemed.

The very thought of her … with her clear, blue eyes staring coldly into him from behind an enigmatic smile, yet again, sends a shiver down his spine. He is convinced that he has seen that same look before, and, as he recalls the image, he has difficulty in differentiating between what is now … and what was then.

His reasoning is simple — *yes … It was a long time ago. But, those eyes had pierced into his, then … and in exactly the same way as they had done so earlier.*

He has crossed the car park and is about to leave the precincts by way of the same pedestrian cut-through which had been used earlier by Tori.

Shep gets out of Tom's car. Jamie, seeing his movement from across the car park, takes his lead and alights from Gina's.

They hurry their pace, converging at a point just prior to the cut-through.

He is already walking away.

"Put your phone on silent! We don't want to alert him, do we?"

Jamie complies with Shep's instruction.

Their target is well ahead. Without warning, he stops … and then lights another cigarette from the last glows from the burn of the first.

"He's chain-smoking." Shep whispers the observation to Jamie as he points towards their target. "We've ruffled the bu'y's feathers all right!"

"Is that good?" Jamie follows Shep's lead in keeping the volume of his voice down.

"Oh yes, 'tis very good! You see, when them there scrotes have their feathers ruffled, then them don't think straight. Them start to panic and run on impulse. So, bu'y, then 'tis we who have the advantage … and 'tis an advantage that I intend for us to be keeping for ourselves!"

Shep smiles as he starts to enjoy this taste of an unofficial return to the buzz of the old days; the days when all that was needed was just a potent mix of gut-feelings, common sense and a bit of good fortune to fuel the success of the, now sadly discarded, old-fashioned methods of British *coppering*.

Tom starts his vehicle, and as he starts to move off, Gina follows suit, timing her drive so as to slide her vehicle close-in behind his. For the time being, she will let him keep the lead — and if he feels the need to pull over and wait, then so will she.

Tom's phone rings. He presses the appropriate button and speaks, "Go ahead, Shep."

"Tom? He's stepped into the road. I reckon's he's got a car. Hang on a sec … Yep, the indicator lights have flashed … he's unlocked it."

As Tom slows and rounds the bend, the last flash of its amber lights pinpoint the precise location of the Peugeot.

He pulls over and waits.

"Okay, I can see it. What sort of car is it?"

"'tis a Peugeot. I can't quite get the full registration, but I reckons it's on an S plate."

Gina pulls up behind him and dims her lights.

Jamie's eyesight is far better than Shep's, and so, without hesitation, he steps a couple of paces forward. Having achieved his aim, he steps back and grabs Shep's phone so as to relay the registration number to his future father-in-law.

He returns the phone.

As the car's lights are turned on, the shape of the rear-cluster of brake and obligatory lighting identifies the model. "It's a 406 … Yep, definitely … dark-blue Peugeot 406 Saloon! Where are you? He's about to move off. Quickly! We don't wanna lose him … come an' pick us up … Now!"

"Okay. I'm…" He glances in his mirror and, seeing Tori looking at him from the rear seat, he corrects himself, emphasising that he is not alone. "I mean, *we're* on our way. Gina's right behind us. Get Jamie to get in with her … and he can update her."

"Will do."

As the Peugeot's indicator lights are activated, and the car starts to move forward, Tom also moves off and then hurries to pick up his passenger. With not a moment to spare, Shep climbs in … They're off.

The Peugeot slows as it gives way to oncoming traffic which, needing to pass a row of parked cars, is in the centre of the road.

"Look!" Shep, quick to realize the potential of an identifying feature when following a vehicle at distance, announces, "The nearside brake-light — it's out!"

Tom registers the fact as he checks his mirror to confirm that Gina and Jamie are still behind.

They are. So in order to make up ground, he accelerates.

"Hang back a bit. We don't wanna be blowin' our cover, now, do we?"

"Okay." Tom complies and eases off.

Chapter 42

He is driving on little more than instinct. Although he slows and accelerates in the right places, he is oblivious to the detail of that which surrounds him.

The more he thinks about his earlier encounter with the mysterious young woman in the car park and, in particular, the way in which she had seemed to disappear without trace, the more he questions himself as to the very reality of the experience.

Knowing that he cannot afford to make a mistake, he slows the rush of his thoughts. *She knew about Joe. Her Joe, she'd said. Oh hell, what am I saying? No way. It can't have been. Joe's dead! He was Lucy's bloke and he hung himself. But wait a minute ... How did she know who I was? There is only one person who could have known about it. No. No way – this is crazy! There's got to be an explanation. It can't have been her. It just isn't possible.*

Rattled by the incident, he remains silent as he chases the chaos which is within his thoughts. Then, as he starts to allow the primeval fears of man to wheedle their way in, he starts to question the logic of dismissing the illogical. With the encroachment of feelings of him being less alone, his body tenses as a chill of disquiet sends a shiver down his spine. As if needing to free himself from being taunted with images of the past inexplicably mutating into the reality of the present, he winds down the window so as to allow any lingering demons to escape out and into the shadows of the world beyond.

Again, he feels the shiver of that chill shooting down the length of his spine.

With thoughts of her having been released back into the real world starting to cross his mind, he begins to panic. *What if she's been found? Oh my God! That would explain it. She's come back to tell me ... she's been found!*

He brakes and pulls over to the roadside.

"No!" he shouts. "This can't be happening!"

He's angry with himself for allowing such idiotic thoughts to impose their will on the evidence of reason.

Trapped in a world of uncertainty and worry, he pays little attention to the headlamps of the vehicles which have been travelling some distance behind him.

Even though they have also stopped, with the distraction of his own angst, he fails to register the significance of their presence.

Regaining his composure, he engages gear and releases the handbrake.

The journey must continue.

***

Tom glances over to Shep. "What's he playing at? He's driving all over the place. Do you think he's seen us?"

"No. I reckons he's still ruffled though. And anyway, I wouldn't mind betting that he's been tossing things 'round in his head a bit ... and now he's wondering what he should be doin' next."

"Maybe you're right. I mean, he really does look to be all over the place."

"That's right ... he is. So, you just keep going steady. Don't you go spookin' him, and then ... maybe, he'll make a break for it."

Tom presses the redial button on his hands-free kit and waits for Gina to respond.

"Hi, Tom."

"Are you okay back there?"

"Yes, we're fine. How long are we going to be following him?"

"For as long as it takes ... Look, if you lose us, just remember, he's got a brake light out. So you don't have to stay too close. You'll spot him a mile off! Have you got enough credit on your phone?"

"I'm on a contract ... so there's no problem."

"Okay, we'll keep the line open. If we cut out, ring me back. I'm on pay-as-you-go and I'm not sure how much credit I've got left."

"Yes, I'll do that."

***

As he approaches the turn-off which will take him closer towards his home, he indicates to the nearside and slows. But then, instead of him taking the turn to his left and proceeding as normal, he hesitates. Drawn by the memories of the night of some two decades ago, he changes tack. With the indicator cancelled, he continues along the road ... He has somewhere else in mind.

The visions are insistent and will not go away. Feeling uneasy, he wavers as he reasons as to which of his instincts he should follow.

Part of him wants to make an about-turn so that he can return to the route which will take him back towards his home. After all, once in the security of familiar surroundings, he may be able to dismiss the evening's events as being nothing more than that of an uncomfortable coincidence. However, there is another part of him which needs to confirm that things are still as they should be, and that he has, in fact, no need to taunt himself with wild and absurd imaginings which ... if left to fester would start to take control of his life.

But then, with logic being put to one side, he feels as if the images of the past may well be trying to influence the present. Moreover, they are vying with him to repossess the reins of control.

Feeling pressurised by the constant replay of a medley of age-old events which, albeit not entirely forgotten, he had thought were no longer of relevance, his decision is made.

There is no place for the self-doubt; if he wishes to rid himself from the torment of unnecessary and unfounded worries, then he needs to sort this out quickly.

There is only one way for him to be able to oust the ridiculous, but haunting, notions from his mind; he must retrace the steps of the past and confirm that all is as it should be. He needs to know that the only disturbances are lodged within his thoughts.

Once he has established that there is no change to the way in which he had left things and that there is no such thing as a bridge of communication which can span the reality of existence and the fantasy-world of lost spirits, then, and only then, will he be able to, once and for all, smother the destructive echoes from the past.

***

"He's off! I told you he'd make a break for it. Follow him, but remember, don't you spook him! Keep your distance!"

"Yeah … okay, I hear you."

Tom's trust in Shep is compounded by the accuracy of the old man's predictions, to date.

"Gina? Can you still hear us?"

"Yes. We're right behind you!"

"Good. Let's see what he's up to, hey?"

He continues to follow their target, pacing his speed so as to keep an unvarying distance behind — so minimising the chances of them being seen.

***

The Peugeot picks up speed as it leaves the confines of the city.

Its driver, as if desperate to shake off the haunting images of the past, wills the feathered dream-catcher which swings gently to-and-fro as it hangs from the rear-view mirror to do its job. But these visions have got the fire and obstinacy of their creator and, therefore, they will not yield easily … even if confronted with the mystical ways of the ancients.

With the powers of the shamans having seemingly lost their potency, he wends his way through the narrow lanes of rural Devon, focusing his attention on the road, which, as the beams from the headlamps spread across its surface, lights up ahead. Yet, however hard he tries to distract himself from the unchangeable reality of history, his thoughts are soon hauled back into the mists of time long-past.

He can visualise her quite clearly. She was just a teenage girl who — with long and flowing raven locks, and dressed in the sumptuous femininity of a dark-blue, satin dress — had been limping along the lane whilst clutching a hold of the fastening-strap of a single shoe.

He had slowed as he had approached her; although she had glanced back at him for a moment, she had quickly turned her head from the glaring lights and, with an air of nonchalance, continued on her way, It was as if she'd been completely untroubled by the fact of his presence.

As she had turned to face him, the beams of the lights had caught the glint of amber and gold as her hair had swirled away from her ears before flowing back again to, once more, conceal the presence of her earrings in the process.

As he had pulled up beside her, he remembers leaning across the passenger seat and winding down the window to speak. *"Do you want a lift?"*

At first, without looking directly at him, she had just shaken her head and then simply ignored him.

"Lucy ... I think you do want a lift! Everyone's worried about you."

He was firm ... but not, in his opinion, too forceful.

He can still recall how she had stopped at the sound of her name ... and then, how she had looked at him. After the briefest of instants, she had relaxed, and with a glimmer of a smile, she had said, *"Oh, it's you. I didn't recognize your car."*

He had noticed how the amber pendant, suspended from its gold chain, had been resting at her cleavage. Although the pendant had drawn his eye towards her womanly attributes, he had also seen the blood on the side of her head. As far as he could tell, it was already clotted ... although there were still the signs of seepage. The wound was relatively minor, but was still in need of attention.

"It looks like you've hurt yourself?"

He remembers how she had not responded to the mention of her injury. Maybe she had been disorientated or even concussed — he had not been entirely sure; but one thing was for certain — she did not appear to have been functioning as she should have been.

"Are you all right?" He'd had to ask the question, even though he'd known that she'd been far from *all right*.

Having finally registered his words, through which she had undoubtedly detected the tones of his concern, she had silently and instinctively lifted her hand to her head and felt the dampness and warmth of fresh blood.

"Come on!" He'd wished to waste no more time ... neither had he wanted her to prod at her wound and so cause it to open fully. *"Get in the car and we'll try and get you sorted out. You're looking cold ... so how about I get you home?"*

"I don't think I'm ready to go home yet. Do you mind?"

Her smile had returned and, in an instant, it had shone as she'd succumbed to the attraction of a warm and comfortable car. She'd had enough and had seemed grateful to have been able to put an end to hobbling, with one shoe on and one shoe off, in the darkness and on the gritty surface of the country lane. After all, she had known who he was and, furthermore, she had clearly felt that she would be safe in his hands. She had no reason to have suspected that she could not trust him to look after her welfare.

He'd read her demeanour … and with it, her change of heart. So he took the initiative and, again, he leaned across the passenger seat and pulled the release for the door before giving it an opening shove.

He readily recalls the moment when she'd been about to get into the vehicle. As she had started to step in, she had hesitated, then stalled. He had wondered if she'd had second thoughts, but she had not. She had just taken time to gaze at the lone shoe. Then, seemingly more lucid than she had been only a moment or two earlier, and as if having come to accept the futility of her hanging onto it, she'd announced, "*Oh well, I suppose it was better when it was part of a pair! It's no use to me now!*"

She then turned away from the car and threw the broken item of footwear with as much force as she could muster, across the top of the hedge and into the copse behind.

She had started to regain her composure by the second, and so, his earlier thoughts of her being concussed had started to ebb as quickly as they had arrived.

It was then, when she had turned back to him, and had slipped herself onto the passenger seat, that he had felt the first real urges of his desire.

Maybe it was due to the look of her youthful maturity, along with the added appeal of her apparent vulnerability, or perhaps it was just the way in which her body had, and as if it were lubricated by the silky sheen of her dress, slipped across the seat before settling comfortably into place beside him.

Whichever, the upshot had been that he had certainly been affected by her presence.

With his recollections on the roll, he starts to recall the moment when, as she had sat in the passenger seat and had then removed the remaining shoe before massaging her throbbing ankle, he could not help but to feel the sudden increase in his pulse rate. But then — he recalls, and with some satisfaction — he had managed to disguise his feelings with the distraction of engaging first gear and then easing off the clutch as he had started to move off along the winding course of the narrow road.

As she had gazed out of the passenger window, no doubt contemplating the events of the evening, he had taken the opportunity to glance at her legs. They had been, somewhat modestly, directed away from him … with her right leg slung over her left and draped with the gentle flow of her dress.

He can still remember how, knowing how the caress of the sensuous material would have felt against her body, he'd been able to appreciate why she had been comfortable whilst held within its embrace.

As he delves deeper into his memories, he starts to recall the way in which he had felt an almost irresistible urge to stretch out his hand and to finger the alluring material so that he too could delight in the feel of its exquisite fineness. However, he also recalls how he had quietly fought with his inner demons and had only just managed to curb the pull of his desires.

With a conflict of feelings fired by the sight of the fabric, he had resisted the temptation.

The effects of his past, with its cruel enforcement of gender conformity, had never left him. As he'd marched through the various stages of puberty and then into the finality of adulthood, he had often wished that he could re-create those moments when he had felt cherished and wanted.

He had fully understood that the punitive regime of his father had been intended to harden him up.

Yes, there had been purpose behind the cruelty, for it had been designed to shock him into stepping towards the more macho ways of his congenital masculinity. But the fact was, whilst his father was out socializing in the village inn, having insisted that his only son would be left at home with his mother and sisters whilst still being made to remain, rather nonsensically, feminised … he had felt valued. After all, he had, for the first time, been able to delight in the feeling of contentment from the tenderness which had emanated from the empathetic caress of his mother's arms.

Bizarre? Maybe. But, all the same, he had remembered the feelings well … and had recalled them exactly as they were.

Maybe it was because his enforced, albeit temporary, change of persona had hidden the signs of the nastier side of the masculine traits that his mother had gained some respite from her fear that, one day, he would echo her husband's loathsome ways. But then, he surmised, it could just as easily have been that she had felt a sense of guilt … in that she had been unable to protect her child from the abusive and needless actions of her spouse, and so, all she'd had left to offer him had been her unconditional love, supplemented with comfort and warmth. Whatever the reason, she had treated him quite differently when he had been forced to adopt the role of a girl and − albeit with rather more than a hint of inner embarrassment − he had actually enjoyed every single moment. When it came down to it, while he had been in the persona of a girl, he had felt that she had been more loving and protective than she would have been had he been dressed in the more acceptable attire of that of a boy.

It had not been the wearing of the dress that had made him feel good … it had been the time which had been spent bonding with his mother.

Looking back on it all, he was not just angry with the controlling brutality of his father — and, incidentally, neither did he have any regrets as to his role in his demise and the unceremonious disposal of his corpse — but he was, for the most part, angry with himself. He had allowed himself to pass through the years of his adolescence … and then into the years of physical maturity, without ever fully conquering his acquired obsession with the medium which, strangely enough, had given him his first precious feelings of tranquillity and belonging.

The association with *finery* had not been entirely as his father had hoped. Being a tangible link to those treasured memories of the unconditional love of his mother, it had, in effect, sometimes been more of a comfort blanket, and not, as had been intended, a stark reminder of what it feels like to be subservient, vulnerable and utterly humiliated in front of those who were closest to him.

But, having also had *those* feelings etched within him, he had come to see *finery* as being a tool that can be used by some to beguile and control — it could cut into the spirit far deeper than any blade. What's more, it had the power to enrage and, at the same time, entice … and had fired a need for him to restore order to a world where boundaries have been blurred.

Yes, his mother's fears had not been without substance. After all, he had, in many ways, developed the traits of his father; moreover, he had certainly known his place in the scheme of things. He had also come to accept that ,because of his father's influences, he would never willingly allow a mere woman to be the dominant force in his life. It was not … as his father had so often said … *the way which nature had intended.*

Lucy had started to doze as he had negotiated the dark and winding lanes, and it may well have been because of this that he had found the time to probe the details of his own long-gone past.

However, the silence which had prevailed whilst he had been travelling along this — almost spiritual and, to some extent, troubled — voyage back and into the times of his childhood, had then been abruptly cut short … She had woken.

"Are you ready to go home yet?"

"No. Not yet."

"Why not?" he'd asked. *"They're bound to be worried about you."*

He had ensured that the tone in his voice had suggested that he'd a genuine concern for her welfare. It was, to some extent, quite true. He'd certainly had an interest in her … but not in the way that she had assumed.

"I don't know. I'm just a bit nervous about it. I don't know how my mother's going to react."

Even then, bearing in mind that he was much younger then than he is now, he had already possessed more than a passing interest in the workings of the human mind. When he was in his late teens and had been employed as a junior salesman within a branch of a, now defunct, national menswear outlet, he had learnt a little about the basics of psychology and the much-underrated power of suggestion.

Sales and marketing is all about reading people and knowing which buttons to push in order to make a sale.

It is also about learning *when* and *when not* to press for that all-important closure. Too early ... and the barriers may go up. Too late ... then, that speaks for itself — it's too late.

Either way, the sale is lost.

To be able to successfully reel-in one's prize, then one must know how to play with the line.

"She'll be all right, trust me!"

The subtle implant of the key words within his response was intentional. He had needed her to trust him; for he'd known that trust would inevitably lead to the lowering of her defences ... and with it, the opportunity for him to make his move.

Her returning smile had suggested that she had felt no reason to be wary of him; so, trust him she would ... and trust him she did.

But, even then, that was not enough for him; he had wanted her to *like* him. If she could learn to like him, then she would be more likely to trust him without reservation. He had also believed, as he still believes now, that an act of kindness — genuine or otherwise — along with a demonstration of the showing of a personal interest in another, can often soften the resolve of even the strongest of individuals. *"If you want to talk about it ... in complete confidence of course."*

She shook her head.

With his memories having transported him back through time, he revisits the conversation as if it had only just been had. *"How about ... I buy you a cup of coffee at the motorway services? Then, if you still want to, we can have a private chat in comfort? How does that sound?"*

"Coffee? No thanks."

It was a reply that he'd not expected.

"But..." with an almost disarming smile, she'd added, *"... chocolate with cream? Now that ... I will say yes to!"*

"Well then, chocolate with cream it is then."

"Thank you. Actually you're quite a nice guy really, aren't you?"

He hadn't expected that either; no one had ever referred to him as being *a nice guy*.

He did not recall giving her a reply, but he could remember how she had quickly returned to the privacy of her thoughts and resumed her gaze into the expanse of the star-studded skies. He had thought that she had, by his perception of there having been a hint of some encouragement in her words, been fairly close to have been considering whether she should make a pass at him.

How could she? he'd mused. After all, she had a boyfriend. All he had wanted was for her to like him. Not to fall in love with him. To like him enough to willingly lower her defences. No more than that.

Besides, she had already made a complete hash of the evening with her deplorable flirtations, so why should she not try to hit on another.

Surely, he had thought, *she'd had more than enough drama for one night.*

Although bothered by her adeptness for betrayal and, of course, her apparent flippancy towards the sensitivities of her boyfriend, he had found that he, too, had started to become rapt by the draw of her natural beauty.

He had been careful not to be obvious in the revealing of his innermost thoughts, but he had, yet again, started to make surreptitious and repetitive glances towards her legs. He could not help but to notice how, as she had unconsciously moved her hand to her hip ... and then down and along her thigh as she'd attempted to massage and ease the tenderness of her bruised and aching body, he had become both captivated and aroused ... especially as he had become absorbed in the watching of how the fabric of her dress had, with the gentle rhythm of her pain-relieving manipulation, ridden up and down her silky-smooth legs.

Chapter 43

With the narrowing of the road and the snaking of its path, Tom wonders where they are being led. "Any ideas?"

"About what?" Shep asks.

"Where he's going?" Tom clarifies.

"Not exactly .... but 'tis looking promising. You see, this was the adjoining patch to mine … an' 'tis not too far from where Lucy went missing."

The temptation to accelerate so as to maintain a view of the target when it rounds a bend and disappears from sight, is great, but on Shep's advice the temptation is resisted.

With the Peugeot temporarily out of view, Tom notices a bright, rotating amber beacon ahead.

He rounds the bend … and curses as he sees the reason for the warning; a tractor — with a heavy, unlit trailer in tow — has joined the lane from the gateway of a field … and is now labouring its way along the lane ahead of him.

"He's going to get away from us!"

"Well … 'tis a bit of an' inconvenience, I grant you that. But then … be patient. All's not lost. You see, there's a farm just 'round the corner, an' I's reckonin' that, maybe … that's where the ol' tractor's goin' to."

Shep, as Tom has discovered during the short time that he has known him, is rarely wrong, and, yet again, he has proven himself to be right.

The offside indicator which is above the tractor's cab starts to flash, and the vehicle, without altering speed, swings into the lane which leads towards the farmer's yard.

The road is now clear.

Tom pushes his foot on the accelerator.

Shep leaves him to it. This time Tom has been given the go-ahead to make up the distance.

***

As they'd travelled through the eerie ambience of the moonlit landscape, Lucy had appeared as if she had been feeling the uncomfortable effects of the chilling night. So in order to lull her into feeling able to relax, he had upped the temperature on the heater and directed the flow towards her feet — a simple action which she had seemed to appreciate.

She had sat back with her eyes shut; no doubt secure in the knowledge that her new-found chaperone would do what was right for her.

With her eyes having been closed, she had failed to notice the jerking movement of his right foot on the accelerator. But she did feel the jolts as the car stuttered and slowed … and then shot forward, before stuttering and slowing once more.

"What's wrong?" she'd asked, with the echoes of worry resonating behind her tone.

"I don't know."

He could not tell her the truth. There was nothing wrong at all — it was all part of a deception; a deception which had needed evidence in order to give it substance. *"I think I must've run the petrol a bit low a couple of days ago … I nearly ran out."*

"And?"

"And so … probably a bit of dirt's come up from the bottom of the tank … and it's blocking the jets in the carb."

"Oh."

She'd no idea what he was talking about; the workings of the internal combustion engine were obviously a mystery to her. All she had really seemed to care about was whether or not they would be stranded … and if so, for how long. *"Is it going to be all right?"*

"I think so. I'll try giving it a bit of wellie — that'll clear it."

He remembers slamming his foot on the pedal, and then the car shooting forward — its momentum throwing her back into her seat. *"There you are! That's cleared it. We'll be all right now."*

She had turned her head towards him, smiled, and then sat back and relaxed. *"Which way are we going to the services?"* she had asked as she'd noticed that they were still negotiating the country lanes and, more puzzlingly, were travelling away from the glow of the city lights.

He had told her, calmly and matter-of-factly, that he had decided to head for the A38 duel carriageway, via Haldon Hill. He would then make his way back towards the city and then merge with the motorway.

She had accepted his reasoning with a nod; then, seeming to be no longer troubled, she had closed her eyes and smiled, whilst luxuriating in the comfort of the warm air of the heater blowing onto her sore and weary legs.

***

As Tom and Shep negotiate the bends and continue to climb the steepening gradient, the country road is no longer bordered by the arable lands of farmsteads. Rather, it is edged by the envelopment of the vegetation of the hilltop forest. With the approach of a give-way sign and thus a junction, Tom stops.

Gina instinctively halts behind him.

There is no sign of the Peugeot.

Shep, with no more than the point of a finger, suggests that they should initially try the more popular route towards the dual carriageway.

"Okay."

Tom redirects his voice towards the hands free device which is clipped onto the vehicles visor. "Gina, can you still hear me?"

"Yes, I can hear you."

"We're just gonna take a quick look to the left. Maybe you could try to the right, if that's okay with you?"

"Yes, that's fine. We'll see you soon!"

"Call us if you see him … but don't — for Christ's sake — let him sus you!"

"Yes, Tom — I know what I'm doing."

Her intonation suggests a degree of irritation at her being treated as if she were stupid. Of course she would not confront the driver of the car; she would wait for Tom to return, and then … if anyone is going to be made a fool of, it would be him — it would not be her!

Tom wastes no time. Utilising the power of his Mercedes, he accelerates and leaves her trailing in his wake.

She is more cautious.

She turns to the right; with Jamie beside her, she systematically and efficiently starts her search for signs of the Peugeot.

***

Startled by the jolting of the vehicle, Lucy had been abruptly awakened from her dreamlike state.

She had been alarmed by the erratic movements which had accompanied the more worrying splutters of a dying engine.

"What's wrong?"

"It's the kangaroo petrol again."

He had remained calm and in control.

"What?"

"It's the dirt blocking up the carb again."

"Oh, really. Can you fix it?"

"No. Well, not without stripping it down and blowing the jets clear."

Again, his apparent knowledge of what to do if all else had failed had been designed to instil trust in his capabilities … and, ultimately, in him as a person.

He recalls how he had managed, as if by chance, to coast the car off the road and then into the privacy of one of the rambler's car parks.

"Don't worry. We'll sit quietly for a few moments … let it settle and then I'll try it again."

She had looked unconvinced, but it also been apparent that she had preferred to give him the benefit of any doubt … and so, she had stayed silent.

"Trust me, once it's settled, then a quick blast will push it through and

unblock it."

She had obviously been satisfied with the logic of his thinking; so, yet again, she turned away to gaze into the darkness whilst she collected her thoughts.

"Why?"

"Why what?" she'd queried.

"Why did you cheat on your boyfriend?"

If he tries hard enough, even now he can picture the look of annoyance as she'd tried to decide whether or not she would give him an answer.

"Well? Why did you?" He had been persistent in his search for a reason.

"To be honest … I'm not sure what business it is of yours!"

"Maybe none. But then, I'd still like to know."

"Listen — It's none of your business! I don't have to explain myself to you, so you'll just have to live with it! Now please, maybe you should get me home!"

She was annoyed. Then suddenly, like the flip of a coin, she raced beyond the boundaries of annoyance and into the realms of rage.

The defiance of this young woman had been like a red rag to a bull.

He could not have allowed her to stand up to him; neither could he have allowed her to exert *her* control.

His father would *never* have permitted that to happen!

They were alone; his pulse had been rising and she'd needed to be put back in her place. He'd had the advantage, and, as such, he had decided that she would be given no choice; she would have to accept the dominance of him, the alpha male.

With the invasiveness of his interrogation, she had closed her eyes and turned her head away … signifying her wish to put an end to proceedings.

His eyes had yet again been drawn to the enticing form of her body. Then, on impulse, he had laid his left hand on top of her right thigh and gently compressed the muscle.

Her reaction had been immediate and unforgiving. *"You dirty bastard! Get your hands off me — now!"*

Her right hand had grabbed a hold of his left and then pushed it away as she had frantically searched for the door release. He could not have risked her escaping … and to then report his behaviour to the authorities. So, without warning, he had unhitched his seatbelt and then launched himself across to his left. It had taken just a flick of a lever to collapse her seat and leave her lying flat on her back. Before she had been able to regain her composure, he had already lain on top of her; with the weight of his own body, along with his natural muscular supremacy, he had pinned her down … and kept her in place.

With his right forearm pressed firmly against her face, pushing her head into the cushioning of the upholstery, and so denying her the opportunity to spit and bite, he had immediately dropped his left hand onto her thigh. Without pausing, he had run his hand down the lustrous surface of her dress until he had reached the hem and thus the edge of the fabric. Once reached, he'd tucked his fingers under her skirt, and then, without caring for her feelings, he had run his hand determinedly back along the top of her thigh, forcing the silken fabric of the skirt to ride upwards and towards her waistline in the process.

Frenetically, as he had prepared to enforce the ultimate demonstration of his masculine superiority, he had probed and searched for the feel of her underwear. She was to be punished for her promiscuity, and he was going to be the one to execute the punishment.

Surprisingly, she had not screamed. She had been much stronger than that. She was deceivingly tough. He still cannot remember the detail of the threats which had snarled their way out from under the restrictions which had been imposed by his tensed forearm having been pushed against her jaw, nor can he recall the detail of her stifled, yet ferocious, curses. But they were certainly there and, what's more, he had been sure that they had been overflowing with venom … and were, unreservedly, meant for him.

He had been left in no doubt as to her mettle. He would never forget how she had kicked out and then, vehemently, lurched from side to side as she had struggled to protect herself from his sudden attack. But no matter how hard she had fought him, he had managed to remain in charge.

It was only when he'd grabbed a hold on the elastic of her tights and had then pulled them down until he had been able to grasp her knickers, did she start to dictate the turning of the tide.

The stench from the release of gasses in her fight-or-flight response was, in itself, enough to repel him. But it was when he had felt the warmth of acidic urine gushing over his bare hands, before soaking into the padding of the car's seat, that he had been truly repulsed. In fact, he had been repulsed to such a degree that it was *he* who had rolled away from *her*, and it was *he* who had hurriedly clambered out of the car.

This voyage of his recall through the events of the past has left him driving on instinct alone. But then, with the sight of the entrance to that very same rambler's car park now lying ahead, he is jolted back and into the world of the present.

He slows, pulls in to the side of the road … and then silences the engine.

The lights are extinguished.

There is something hidden within the forest which needs to be checked.

***

"Gina? Can you hear me?"

"Yes, I can hear you."

"There's no sign of him out this way. We're on our way back. Where are you now?"

"Oh, I don't know. How about you meet us back at the turn-off"

"Okay. We'll be there in a mo."

***

The car park is not quite as he'd remembered it. It is familiar, in that the entrance is basically the same, but the inner space has been extended to cater for the increased usage by those who want to escape from the hustle of the city and enjoy the raw and unfettered sounds and smells of nature.

He will check things out in a moment, but first of all, he needs to steady his nerves and collect his thoughts.

He lights yet another cigarette, and as he sits back in his seat, he tries to make sense of the evening's events.

His thoughts cannot help but to flash back to the supermarket car park and replay the surreal confrontation with the Lucy look-alike from the past … *What if it really was Lucy who had confronted him!*

Impossible? Maybe. But the thought of it is now playing havoc with his reasoning, and with even the notion of it being a possibility, there is, instilled within him, a sense of uncertainty … and with it, a very real and irrepressible fear.

He glances across the car park and towards the line of trees which veil the area which has, unofficially and for over thirty years, become the final resting-place for dozens of faithful and much-loved canine companions.

Becoming increasingly more agitated, he glances towards the roadside embankment.

A new growth has since sprouted from the remnants of the ash tree which had, so many years ago, marked the westerly approach to the entrance to the car park. In those early days, he had often returned to the area to ensure that nothing untoward or incriminating had been found. But then, immediately after the infamous Burns Day storm of 1990, he had again checked the area.

He recalls how the tree had been wrenched from its base and had left little more than a splintered and ragged stump as the only reminder as to its existence. As to what had happened to the timber … he had no idea. It may have been chopped up and used for burning, or, on the other hand, it may have been sold and then utilised for the creation of furniture or the like. The truth is … he didn't care then … as he doesn't care now.

The memories of what had happened beside that tree have remained with him throughout.

He had not meant for things to pan out as they had. But, all the same, the irreversible sequence of events had occurred, and now, however hard he cares to wish otherwise, the facts of history cannot be altered.

The ruddy glow of the cigarette brightens as he inhales the smoke and glances around him.

Looking across at the towering ash, he cannot help but to notice how, over the years, the new growth has — from exactly the same genome as the original — matured into a strong and unblemished example of the species. It is now a tree which has a solidity and doggedness which oozes feelings of both wisdom and knowledge.

With a sudden flash of images having been plucked from both his recent confrontation in the supermarket car park and the historical events of 1989, he is able to cross-match. The more he tries to reason, the more he develops the fear that, maybe, the resurgence of that tree from its torn and splintered remains is, in some way, a sign of a victim's ability to rise from the dead.

As the memories of Lucy's last night merge evermore into the present, he effortlessly re-forms vivid images of her having taken advantage of his rapid exodus from the car, by swiftly making an exit for herself. Although she had not fully conquered the obvious pain of her injury, she had, nevertheless, found sufficient strength to put her pain to one side ... and then run off towards the road.

With no shoes to protect the soles of her feet from the rough and stony ground, she had not been particularly fast — he had been able to catch up with her with ease.

A threshold had been crossed. She could not be allowed to escape.

He'd had no option. He'd needed to stop her, and so, he did just that; he'd stopped her!

He can remember, with clarity, how he had grabbed hold of her as she'd tried to break free ... and then how he'd pulled her back and wrestled her to the ground.

She'd had spirit! She'd not been one to have readily resigned herself to the consequences of fate ... She'd fought back!

From where she had been able to summon her strength, he'd had no idea. But whatever the source, he had found her to be a challenge, and, as such, she had been nigh on impossible to subdue.

She had twice succeeded in releasing herself from his grip. On the second occasion, she had even managed to clamber up and onto her knees as she had tried to stand and create the momentum for flight.

His strength, however, had proven to be superior; for he had quickly reasserted himself and then brought her back to the ground — face down and with a sickening thud.

He had forced her over and onto her back and, as his levels of testosterone had started to rise and the adrenalin had started to rush, he'd had no problem in excusing his actions — nor did he allow his revulsion at being urinated on distract him from his goal. Without delay, he had picked up from where he had left off; the means by which he had intended to impose his will ... and then take her for himself, had been re-instigated.

As far as he had been concerned, his actions were for her own good. After all, they would have led to her ending her days knowing that she had finally, if not voluntarily, had to accept her rightful place. She would have known that she'd had no choice but to have resigned herself to being subservient and compliant to the higher authority of the man.

People, like most animals, are much happier if they remain within the confines of acceptable boundaries. He was certain of that ... as was his father.

Although at the time he could not admit it, he had known that she could not be permitted to live to tell the tale. Exactly how he would carry out the act to finish her off, he had been unsure. He had decided that *he would have to cross that bridge when the time arrived.*

He was not going to be subtle in the implementation of his dominance. So, yet again, whilst he had held her down with the weight of his own body restricting the movement of hers, he had yanked up her skirt and, once more, tried to force down her tights and her knickers, as if they had been as one.

It had not been as easy as he had thought; for the very same weight which had prevented her from having the freedom of movement, had also, rather ironically, protected her from him being able to get into a position where he could force his intended incursion.

The removal of her underwear had been vital for him to succeed. Whilst they had stubbornly remained in place, her knickers and tights had, in effect, barred his entry and, so, had frustrated his efforts to impose the ultimate manifestation of his dominance.

As he'd leant to one side — in order to give himself the space for manoeuvre — she had taken her opportunity to scream out as loud as she possibly could. Then, kicking and gouging, she had struggled to set herself free.

He had panicked. He had no doubt about that. Although her screams would have been heard by no one within the isolation of the forest, he could not have taken the risk. Instinctively, his reaction had been for him to ensure that he would silence her once and for all.

He had grabbed her by the throat and, mercilessly, squeezed it tight. Even as her screams were being stifled into non-existence, she had still not relinquished the will to live. No doubt, knowing that this was going to be her last realistic chance to escape the inevitability of his brutal invasion which, in all likelihood, would have then led to him ensuring the permanence of her silence ... she'd fought on.

Her will to live, along with her determination to deny him the prize of self-gratification, had been formidable. Moreover, with him being fearful of a fracas which would have made him vulnerable to being scarred with some rather difficult-to-explain injuries ... she'd been able to bring things to a head.

With the resolve to survive uttermost in both her and him, the ferocity in his actions had erupted. She'd scrambled backwards, and he'd released his grip. Then, as she'd twisted herself over and onto her front — so as to be able get to her feet and run — he had grabbed a fistful of her hair.

Using her tresses like a handle, he'd smashed her head against the unforgiving surface of the thick and sturdy exposure of a buttress-root which had stretched conveniently out from the base of the tree, before curving and disappearing into the ground in its search for life-maintaining nutrients.

Immediately, she'd been plunged into a state of unconsciousness ... and, other than the occasional twitch of muscular spasms, she'd lain silent and still.

He can recall sitting on the ground, exhausted, whilst staring at her as he'd assessed the consequences of his actions. She could not injure him now, but he had needed to check for certain that she was, in fact, dead. So he leant over her and, with one hand, turned her head to face him.

She was alive. As she'd started to regain a semblance of consciousness, her piercing blue eyes had opened up wide and — with the glacial coldness of one who would never submit nor forgive — she had stared deeply, and hauntingly, into his.

It had not been difficult for him to read her thoughts, and he responded to her defiance by spitting out the words, *"No way are you going to get away from me — Bitch!"*

He still feels uneasy as the recollections of what happened next refill his mind.

As her eyes had started to close, she had whispered. And, having not heard her clearly, he had moved his head towards hers ... and then demanded that she repeat herself.

Albeit barely audible, her words were spoken with enough venom and exactness to make her vow fully understood. *"I will hunt you down until the day I die ... I will wait for you! Trust me ... I'll never let you escape!"*

There had been something hidden within the depths of her eyes which, over the years, he had failed to come to terms with. It's as if she'd been given an insight into the eternity of another world. And so, he had come to fear then, as he has done ever since, that her threats were far from idle ... and they would, one day, be implemented.

The extent of a man's fear is often reflected in the degree of his violence, and having become exceedingly unnerved by the feeling of an almost eerie certainty behind her resistance, he'd no longer had the stomach for carnal invasion; he had wished for nothing less than to ensure her immediate silence. Without warning, he had grabbed her around the face, then — with his thumb squeezing into one cheek and his fingers pressed hard into the other —he had, yet again, smashed her head against the tree's base until she had uttered no more.

He will never forget how he had just stood back and watched on in silence. Nor will he forget the way in which the ashen hue of the bark had darkened as it had absorbed the crimson lifeblood of her dying soul.

With the image having been pushed aside, his thoughts move on. Within the freeze-frames of recall, he pictures her body ... lain still and limp ... once her life had been no more.

With a jolt, he is back in the reality of the present, and with the burn of his cigarette nearly gone as it sears the edge of the filter tip, he flicks the butt out of the window and onto the ground.

Plucking up the courage from within, he decides that it is time to force himself to confirm that things are as he had left them. At least he can then put his mind to rest, once having assured himself that she has not — and in order to be able fulfil her vow for revenge — risen from the dead.

By checking his position on the road in relation to that of the castle-like tower, which — with its rounded, ghostly-white walls veiled by the surround of tall leafy trees — adds its own eerie presence to the forest, he confirms that he is in exactly the right place.

Chapter 44

Both Tom and Gina have returned to the junction.

With their vehicles parked alongside each other, and positioned in order that the driver's-side window of the left-hand-drive Mercedes is adjacent to the driver's-side window of the *Focus*, Tom asks, "Did you find anything?"

Gina's responds with a shake of her head.

"How far did you check?"

"Not far — you called us back before we'd even got our bearings!"

"I'm sorry. I didn't think." Having apologised, he redirects his attention to Shep and asks, "What now?"

"A systematic search — I reckon that's what's needed. We needs to carry out a systematic search."

Tom nods and turns back towards Gina. "Okay, then. Maybe you should follow us."

Shep interjects. "Hang on a sec. Before you young 'uns all goes rushin' off … I suggests, that if we see him parked up then maybe 'tis best if we all carry on past. We don't wanna be drawing attention to ourselves now, do we?"

They all agree.

"Now then … when we's all together, then we can walk back, all surreptitious like. If we do that, then he won't be suspecting anything', and then we can find out what he's up to — if that make sense with 'e?"

There is no argument. What he suggests makes perfect sense.

Tom and Gina nod, and with them both finding some amusement in the way in which Shep had managed to drop in such a word as *surreptitious* amid the colloquialisms of his rural drawl, they cannot help but to share a smile.

***

Closing in on the seclusion of what has been the final resting place for countless numbers of long-departed and much-missed canine companions, his heart rate quickens as he responds to the whiff of freshly-turned soil which is drifting in the air.

Perhaps it's a sign of another interment from earlier in the day. On the other hand, he wonders, *is it a sign of resurrection?*

Having been unsettled by the earlier experiences of the day, his thoughts are running wild. He wonders if he is edging towards the boundaries of fear-induced insanity.

With the light of the day having been replaced by the shadowy secrecy of the night, and not wishing to draw attention to his presence by switching on his torch, he makes do with the gentle glow from the crescent Moon.

He had buried her with neither words of reverence nor acts of religious ritual. He had left to her rot, alone and anonymous, amid the putrid remains of dogs; animals which had once run happily across this public wilderness whilst exercising both themselves and their human companions.

Kicking and shuffling his way through the tangle of overgrown vegetation which has, over the years, laid claim to much of the ground which surrounds him, he makes his way towards the landmark of an old horse chestnut tree.

As he locates a familiar rock, he, with his bare hands, rubs off the covering of lichen and moss to reveal its raggedly-hewn inscription.

COYOTE / A faithful old friend / 1981-1989.

Having located the spot ... and having seen that the earth is undisturbed, he, with a sigh of relief, whispers, *Jeez! Thank Christ for that!*

As he looks down at the untouched covering of the long-abandoned grave, he is beginning to feel rather embarrassed with himself for allowing his primordial superstitions to start to overrule the laws of both logic and common sense.

He had always prided himself on his organisational skills — and then, as is still the case now, he had prepared for all eventualities. So, together with the usual selection of tools and spares, he had equipped his car with a towrope, emergency lighting, snow chains and a shovel.

He remembers how, as he had raced against time to beat the arrival of daybreak, he had spent much of the night spearing his shovel into the hard and stony ground. Yet it was the incongruity of the beautiful sounds of a dawn chorus ... breaking through the early-morning mist ... as he had finally deposited her, face down and into the ground, that had always remained with him.

Lucy had not been particularly weighty, and the carrying of her lifeless body through the makeshift cemetery and towards her freshly-excavated grave had required little effort. It had just been the hastiness of the digging which had all but exhausted him.

This had not been a grave which had been excavated merely to conceal the remains of a single pet. It had been much deeper than that. In fact, it had been deep enough for there to have been room for the interment of more.

He can still remember how the old lady ... with her eyes filled with tears as she had systematically gone from house to house, knocking on every door as she had searched in vain for her much-loved canine companion.

She had, no doubt, suspected that he had been hit by a car and that his remains had then been carted off, like refuse, by the local council's waste-disposal department. During her failing years, she could not allow herself to fully grieve for her loss. The truth is, she had always held onto a glimmer of hope that, maybe, he had wondered off somewhere and had been re-homed. She had even hoped that the day would come when he would return. After all, she had seen films in which some people's pets had undertaken some arduous journey in order to find their way home.

With the passing of some six or seven months, she had passed away. He had known that to be true, as he had noticed two men in their customary garb of black suits and black raincoats carrying her casket to a black van which was parked outside her house. Some had said that, following the loss of her dog, she had died of a broken heart. But then, there were others who had been living in the same street who hadn't even noticed the fact of her having departed from the land of the living.

He knew that neither she nor her dog had deserved to suffer ... But then, some things are necessary. Yet, in a strange old way, even now, he feels a little heartened by the thought that they did not have too long to wait until they were reunited once more ... in spirit, if not in physicality.

He had also known that she had always let her dog out to answer the early-morning call of nature — unsupervised and before the majority of her neighbours had risen from their beds. Had she been a little less garden-proud and had, therefore, allowed her pet to do its business whilst within the bounds of her own premises, it would not have become such an easy target. But then, even a little old lady is not always as innocent as she may first appear. After all, she had often been happy to join in with those who would be heard to moan about the irresponsible dog owners who had allowed their animals to foul in public areas.

It had not taken him long to drive back to his home street ... and then, with no more than a brief whistle, to coax the dog away from the grassy verge and into his car. Once in the car, he had quickly made his way back to the forest so as to complete the deed.

With a thick layer of soil separating the two bodies, he had been sure that if someone had decided to dig at the spot, then they would have come across the macabre remains of the dog. Then, with their curiosity satisfied, they would have felt no need to dig further — thus, preserving the secret that lay much deeper below.

As far as he was concerned, the doe-eyed, black Labrador had well and truly served its purpose.

***

The Mercedes glides steadily along the lane, followed at a respectable distance by Gina's Focus.

As they approach the entrance to the car park, Shep breaks the silence.

"Look! There 'e be ... 'e's over there. On the right! — 'e's parked up ... just keep on going. I knows there's another car park a couple hundred yards farther on, so 'tis best we stop in there."

"Sure."

Tom turns his head slightly and directs his voice up and towards the speakerphone. "Gina! Did you get that?"

"Yes ... We've got it."

She sounds less than enthusiastic with the prospect of having to sneak through the darkness to spy on a man who, however weird he may have seemed to be, has done nothing substantive to suggest that he has had anything to do with Lucy's disappearance. But, then again, she has come this far, so she decides that she may as well just go with the flow and see what happens. "We'll follow you."

Tom eases his foot off the accelerator, and, as they round the bend, he sees the pull-in on his right. Coasting into the entrance, he extinguishes his lights and, as if she were on some kind of tractor-beam, Gina follows suit.

Stalling the proceedings, Shep dials a number on his mobile phone. The phone rings twice before being answered. "Good evening ... I's Shep Russell, I's an ex P.C. Now then, can 'e put me through to the officers who'm dealing with the attack on the Slovakian girl?"

He questions the response. "What d'you mean ... I've got to tell 'e what it's about?"

With the receiver pressed to his ear, he listens to the call-taker. As each word is uttered, he becomes increasingly more angry and frustrated.

"Look 'ere ... I reckons I's got the offender in me sight. So, if you don't put me through to the OIC or Comm's, then I's gonna have to be making a formal complaint against you. The way I sees it, 'tis neglect of duty. Now I reckons that you'm best be trusting me, when I says ... heads will roll!"

He smiles, and as he cups the microphone with his hands, he turns back to Tom. "Them's putting me through. You know ... sometimes you'm bangin' your 'ead against a brick wall trying to get the police to get off their arses and do som'it. It wasn't like it my day. Back then, you'd be hauled before the boss and given a *white-form* if you'd started cuffing jobs! You'd be walkin' round the *nick* as if there'd been a bell hangin' round your neck."

Tom is about to respond ... but is silenced with a *shush*.

"Yep ... I's still here."

He listens, then replies, "That's right, I's Shep Russell ... I's a retired P.C. Now, I believes you'm looking for someone who drives a dark-blue Peugeot 406 saloon. I understands it's in connection with an attack on a Slovakian girl ... up on Woodbury Common."

The communications officer confirms Shep's assumption.

"I knows you can't give me a result, but maybe you should make a note of the registration I's goin' to be givin' 'e ... Then you can do a P.N.C. check and log it. Oh, and by the way, I reckons it may be a good idea if you send a unit up to Haldon Forest. We'm up near the tower."

The officer is used to receiving calls from people claiming to know who is responsible for crimes, both past and present, and although he is still rather sceptical about the strength of Shep's allegation, he wants more detail.

As he starts to ask for more information, Shep interjects. "Now. You listen to me. I know's what I's doin', so just stop wastin' time ... and send a unit before we starts to take the law into our own hands!"

The hint of the vigilante has finally got the officer's attention. The go-ahead to pass the vehicle's registration number is given.

With the number having been relayed, Shep listens as it's read back to him.

"That's right, bu'y ... You'm got it right. Now, he's up here at Haldon. An' I can tell 'e ... 'e's up to no good. Now, before 'e asks, we won't be giving him a hammering — well, not if you gets your boys 'ere pretty smartish, that is! I take it you'm understanding where I's coming from?" He is understood. "Good. Now, we'm off to catch up with 'im, so you'm best be hurrying yourself to call out the troops."

Shep ends the call.

He turns to Tom and grins. "Now ... you see if I's wrong when I says that'll get 'em here. You see bu'y ... them don't like Joe public doing his civic duty — puts 'em to shame if the public do's their job for 'em ... An' what's more, if that happens ... then them can't even take the credit."

Shep targets his voice towards the speaker-phone. "Now ... listen everyone! The police 'em on their way. So, when 'e gets out the car, I want to hear no slammin' of doors ... and no idle chattin' either. We don't wanna scare 'im off now, do we?" He pauses and, hearing no words of dissent, continues. "Okay, let's go."

"Mr Russell!" Gina's voice echoes tones of doubt, for she is not entirely certain that the assumptions made by the old man are correct. But, if they are, then she is becoming more afraid as to how a gruesome find may, somehow, sully the way in which she had always remembered her daughter.

"Go ahead."

"I think I'd be better off waiting here for the police ... if you don't mind."

"No, that's quite all right. I trust 'e'll be all right on your own?"

"Oh, I won't be on my own ... Jamie has said he'll stay with me."

"And your maid ... Victoria?"

"Tori? I'm not too happy about it, but she'd like to go with you two ... if that's okay?"

Shep glances across to Tom, who accepts the proposal with a nod.

"Well … it seems like that's fine with us."

As expected, Shep's years of experience have come to the fore, and with him naturally assuming the role of leadership, he is the first to make a move.

***

Disconcerted by the sound of the snapping of a twig and the rustling of dead and dried leaves, he leans forward and peers into the undergrowth. Catching a glimpse of movement … and then a flash of amber, quickly followed by another, he steps back.

His heart misses a beat, and then — overawed by the image of Lucy's golden pendant glistening on the ashen hue of her lifeless body — it starts to race.

Again, like a beacon shining out from the depths of time itself, the colour flashes its presence, and, in readiness to take flight, he cautiously takes another step back and refocuses on the forest.

He spits out his demand. "What do you want?"

The flash of amber is now paired with another. And the more he tries to make out the detail of the source to the mystery, the more his eyes start to water, thus, thwarting his efforts to see.

He wipes away the tears with the back of his hand … and stares. With the meagre aid of the eerie light, he eyes the slightest hint of a raven sheen shimmering above and around the amber gems.

"Leave me alone!"

Reflecting a move from that of a state of anxiety to a state of outright fear, his voice has now increased in both volume and pitch.

"I can't do anything for you! It was all your fault! You shouldn't have betrayed him! You know that. I'd no choice. You had to be punished!"

His words carry through the air with a clarity which ensures that they cannot be misconstrued, and it is, therefore, no longer necessary for Shep to lead his charges on a long and protracted search.

He just needs them to home in on their target's fear-filled voice. But, in doing so, he also needs them to be careful so as not to alert him to their presence.

Closely followed by Tori, both Tom and Shep stealthily pick their way through the fallen foliage and abandoned twigs as they quickly close in on their quarry.

They know that they need to keep their nerve.

Once they have him clearly in sight, they will need to stand back and just watch and listen. Only then, will they have a chance of finally getting to the truth.

He is within view, yet he is absorbed in making his case to someone who is, under the cloak of the vegetation and darkness, hidden from sight.

"Don't just sit there … Say something … Come on … I know it's you. You've had your game, so do your worst … and get it over with!"

Shep taps Tom on the shoulder and points towards the bushes. He too has spotted a pair of amber flashes shining out from the backdrop of black.

Noting the point of the old man's interest, Tom stares into the darkness — then, seeing the same, he acknowledges the fact with a nod.

Mouthing the words as he tries to maintain his silence, he asks, "What is it?"

Shep responds with a demonstrative shrug of uncertainty.

He glances back towards Tori.

She has not yet plucked up the courage to venture too close.

He lifts a finger to his lips and, as if to suggest that they maintain their silence, he shakes his head. She understands.

Captivated by the jewel-like sparkle, the trolley-man does not dare to look away from what remains hidden within the darkness. He tries to force a reaction. "Lucy? I know it's you. So, come on out and show yourself?"

Other than the brief sound of yet another snapping twig, there is no response.

Gradually becoming accustomed to the continuation of the silence, his initial sense of fear starts to lessen. He steps half a pace forward. "Lucy, I'm not scared of you anymore. I know you're dead … and I knows you're buried. You've rotted away. So, whatever you think … you can't touch me. And there's something else …you're not real. You're not flesh and blood, so you can't hurt me!"

He steps another pace forward, and, in order to better his view, he crouches down. He flicks the switch of his torch and then shines it into the darkness.

Suddenly, with an angry snarl spitting aggressively out from the shadows, along with the manifestation of a mass of raven-coated muscle, he is rooted to the spot. With a pair of fiery, amber eyes firmly fixed on his … he trembles.

As it lurches forward and towards him, he throws his torch — with nothing but instinct to guide him as to whether he should opt for flight over fight, he turns tail and rushes back towards the place of Tom's and Shep's concealment.

With his back to the menace, he is unaware as to whether or not the torch has hit its target. Neither does he see the beast suddenly stop and stand, having been sidetracked by having glimpsed the slightest of movements from the direction of those who remain protected only by the fact of their near obscurity.

Cautious as to the identity, or the intent, of the unknown which lurks within the shadows, and realising its quarry has, in the critical seconds of that brief distraction, taken its opportunity to put distance between the pursuer and the pursued, the creature aborts its mission ... turns away ... and then slinks back into the darkness and out of sight.

Fuelled with the fires of terror, the trolley-man runs blind. Although he passes by with only a few feet to spare, he sees neither of the two men who are crouched and hidden within the cover of the bushes.

As he rushes through the darkness, he casts a cursory glance behind him. Seeing that his pursuer is no longer in sight, he refocuses ahead.

With a jolt, he stops!

Adorned in the silken finery of a warrior queen, and bedecked with a necklace from which hangs the glinting magnificence of golden amber, the raven-haired beauty stands still as she stares out from the shadows ... with a look that pierces the depths of his soul.

This silent and ghostly image exacerbates his state of panic.

Not wishing to wait to be trapped between the ferocity of the living and the vengeance of the dead, he veers off to his right, stepping up his pace as he smashes his way through the bushes.

With his need to escape taking precedence over all else, he has lost his sense of direction. In desperation, he fights his way through the constraints of the tangle of barbed and unforgiving undergrowth, which, as if in a frenzy of its own, seems to grasp at his ankles and his feet, thus, adding to his sense of there being an inevitability of doom.

***

The occupier of the motor patrol vehicle had been on the prowl in search of drunken drivers ... and, for that matter, anyone else whose actions had cared to activate his gut-feeling into recognising something which had not felt quite as it should. Being on the westbound carriageway of the motorway, and only a couple of miles east of junction twenty-nine, he had readily responded to the radio request for *any vehicle in the vicinity of Haldon Hill.*

A specific job to attend was all that was needed to break the monotony of his shift. With the power of the BMW at his command, combined with the authorisation of a gantry of pulsating blue beacons, he can easily exceed the prescribed speed limits ... and so speedily reach his destination.

He has already left the motorway and is, with graceful ease, sprinting along the outer lane of the dual carriageway.

As he approaches the sweeping bends which ascend the protracted gradient of Haldon Hill, cars and lorries alike pull to one side and let him pass.

***

Tom, having seen the near miss as the trolley-man had almost collided with his daughter, hurries back, so as to give her the support and the comfort required to lower her levels of shock.

"It's okay. He's gone. Now ... let's get you back to your mother, shall we?"

She nods with an uneasy smile, and, with her father's arms wrapped around her shoulders, they pick their way through the hazards of the dark and uneven terrain.

As the pair make their way back towards the cars, Shep hovers for a few moments whilst he stares, somewhat quizzically, at the stone which, allegedly, marks the grave of a long-departed pet — *COYOTE*.

He sighs, and with a wry smile on his face looks over and to where the trolley-man was last seen. *You'm no trickster, bu'y ...* he whispers, *you'm just a fool! ... Now, I knows who you are ... and I's not in the mood for playing your games ... So, if you can hear me, then you can be assured that I's comin' to get you!*

He turns about and, whilst deep in thought, he makes his own way back towards the car park, so as to rendezvous with the others.

***

Spurred by little more than the basic instinct for survival, and ensuring that he wastes no time by stalling to look behind, he forges ahead.

As he ploughs his way through the almost impenetrable mass of vegetation, he succumbs to a succession of stumbles; time and time again, he scrambles back up before forging on relentlessly as he tries to shake off the resolve of his pursuers.

Fleeing, with no goal other than to escape the menace which hunts in the shadows — and haunted with disturbing visions from both the past and the present — he screams into the darkness as he pleads for his release from the unrelenting torment.

Finally, he breaks through the restrictive tangles of the groundcover, and as he feels the firmness of the earth beneath his feet, his confidence gets a boost. Instinctively, he puts on a sudden spurt of speed.

As he runs for his life, he frantically tries to dislodge from his mind the flickering images of feminine beauty and big-cat ferocity melding into a ferocious and terrifying disciple of vengeance.

With bright lights rapidly approaching from the south, his sense of direction is restored and, having established the lay of the road, he adjusts his course.

Without hesitation, he rushes through the brush as he seeks the security of his car.

***

With the return of Shep, Gina is desperate to know, in detail, his assessment of the events. "So tell me, what's going on?"

"Well ... I can't be saying too much, but I reckons we'm actually close to getting to the bottom of what's happened to your Lucy."

"Really? Tell me ... what happened to her?"

"All in good time ... As I said ... I can't be saying too much. Now ... the bu'y's taken off in panic, so I reckon we'm best wait for the police. Then, perhaps, 'twould be wise to leave them to take it from there."

With his measured response, he has told her nothing.

Jamie interrupts. "Look ... through the trees ... I think I can see lights!"

Shep glances at his watch. "Well ... it looks like the cavalry's arrived ... an' we'm about to have some company."

***

With echoes of bloodcurdling snarls, spitting through a chilling display of sabre-like teeth, along with the icy stares from the wraithlike form of Lucy McMurry, he dares not slow.

He trips, rolls forward and then falls out and onto the inflexible tarmac of the road. As he struggles to regain his footing, he is, as if on the starting grid of a sprint, crouched with one hand on the ground. He looks up and focuses on the blaze of headlamps which are lighting up the trees of the forest.

He staggers to his feet.

It's too late.

As the car rounds the bend, he is blinded by the intensity of its lights — almost immediately, he feels the sickening blow as he is struck by the force of at least a ton and a half of metal which has been travelling at more than a mile a minute towards him.

His feet have left the ground; and, as if time itself has slowed specifically to allow him to suffer every frightening moment of the collision, he is aware of rolling, uncontrollably, upwards and across the bonnet before smashing his face against the windscreen. Whilst hearing the screech of brakes and rubber as the car slides to a hasty halt, he briefly becomes aware of the image of shock which is spread across the face of the driver.

His need to escape is still with him, and so, with what little strength he has left, he pushes himself up ... but then, he collapses and slides off from the bonnet ... only to crash back onto the road with a painful and jolting thud.

As he lies in the road ... unable to move ... and whilst bathed in the dazzling light of the headlights, he sees the additional display of blue lights, flashing their warning for all to see. Surprisingly, there is little pain as nature's boost of analgesic chemicals take hold ... but the ability to dispel the agony of fear is not on the menu.

Like a scene from a film of an extraterrestrial encounter, he watches as a group of figures emerge from the dark as they, slowly and purposefully, make their way towards him.

With the gravity of his situation, he is expecting urgency.

There is none.

His head is starting to fill with an undecipherable jumble of sounds, when, suddenly, the brightness of the light is muted by the presence of a worried look on the face of a young policeman.

He can tell from the movement of the officer's mouth that he is talking directly to him, but the increasing volume of the whooshing noises which rush about his head serve to deny him the opportunity to make sense of his words.

With no time to waste, he quickly loses interest in trying to comprehend the meaningless ramblings of the policeman. Instead, he allows the focus of his eyes to wander past him and, as if they have been drawn in by the power of some mystical act of sorcery, they settle, once again, on the icy gaze of the one who, he knows, has defied both the laws of nature and the forbidding permanence of death.

Oblivious to the presence of the others, he looks deep into the unwavering stare of her eyes. As his heart frantically pumps the blood in its fight to maintain his very existence, he becomes, unavoidably, aware of the ever-loudening sounds of a deep, rhythmic backbeat taking precedence over the muffled noises of before.

Without even a flicker of compassion, she fixes her stare and steps a pace towards him.

As the image of Lucy makes her approach ... he stares back.

He's scared; he cannot face any more confrontation ... especially with a ghost from his past. Knowing that he cannot run, he chooses, instead, to close his eyes ... and will an end to his suffering.

However hard he tries — and even with the distraction of him now feeling the pain of his broken body — he cannot dismiss the echoes of the curse which resonates through his mind.

Opening his eyes once more, he sees her standing over him ... resolute in defiance.

Resigned to defeat, he closes his eyes yet again, and as the sounds of voices start to fade, he is left to listen to nothing more than that of the erratic beatings of a heart which is clearly in distress.

With the gap between each cluster of life-confirming beats gradually drifting apart, he again tries to open his eyes. He fails. As he struggles to cope with the grim reality that it is *he*, the man who had once seemed to be invincible, who will soon be embarking on the path from which there could be no return ... he submits to the inevitable.

This is the path which he believes will lead him towards *the awaiting anger of the souls of all those who he had, so ruthlessly, subjected to the needlessness of his cruelty and degradation ... before forcing them to embark on their own one-way journey to extinction.*

The gap between each beat widens; with nothing more than the embrace of the lonesomeness of the final throes of life, he waits in vain for the pulse to beat one more time. It remains silent ... and still.

Knowing that he has entered the last few moments of his existence, he feels so alone and ... so very afraid.

Having passed the point of no return, and whilst he is still trapped within an eerie and deafening silence, he remains taunted with the fading image of Lucy McMurry's victorious smile.

As his lungs empty for the last time, and with little more than a rattle, he is overwhelmed by the encroachment of a darkness which signals his end.

How long he had been forced to endure the awareness of his own passing, no one can ever tell. But then, how can anyone be expected to know what goes through the mind of a person immediately prior to their death.

***

The policeman, having ushered Tori to one side, stares into the coldness of the dead man's eyes and checks for a pulse.

There is none.

"Quickly — give me a hand! We need to resuscitate him!"

No one steps forward.

"If I were thee, bu'y, I'd let him go. You'm be doing no good to man nor beast by bringin' 'im back. You see, I reckons 'twould be best to let him face his judgement alone and, maybe, at a much higher court than we could ever get 'im before."

As the constable absorbs his words, he sits back on his haunches and sighs.

Suddenly, the air is filled with the wail of sirens as the backup of paramedics and police make their final approach.

"Bloody hell — they're too late—" the constable announces, as he looks at the body which lies before him.

"No, bu'y. Them's not too late. In fact, the way I sees it is ... them's right on time. Now, if you ask me, I reckons they couldn't 'ave timed it better if they'd tried!"

As Tom looks on in silence, he wonders if Shep has always had the ability to utter ... within the brevity of a single sentence, the content and, with it, the complexity of a chapter.

"Do you know who he is?" the constable enquires.

Shep nods. "I reckons I do ... but just in case I's wrong, I think you'll find that a P.N.C. check on his Peugeot will tell 'e all 'e needs to know."

As the paramedics take control, Shep walks with the officer back along the lane and into the car park.

"QB from Tango-Three-One."

"Tango-Three-One. Go ahead."

"Vehicle check, please, on a blue Peugeot 406 saloon, registered number ..."

The details are passed over the airwaves, and, within a few moments, the result of the check is given.

"Tango-Three-One ... We had a call about this one earlier. Are you ready for details?"

"Go ahead."

"Tango-Three-one ... Your vehicle is a Blue Peugeot 406 saloon registered to a Simon Brett Tripp of 45 ..."

As the details are relayed back, Shep's suspicions are confirmed.

"I thought as such! *S. Brett Tripp ... Sunset Strip.* Well, 'e's one who won't be seeing any more sunsets ... that's for sure!"

"What do you mean?"

"I knew that Tripp bu'y. He liked to call himself Brett, but to me ... he were *Sunset*. He were a special constable ... many years ago. He was with me when we first went to investigate Lucy's disappearance!"

"Now bu'y ... I reckons you ought to come with me."

Shep leads the officer through the undergrowth and to the spot where *Coyote*, someone's faithful friend, had long been laid to rest.

"Well bu'y ... I reckons you boys is gonna be needing a shovel. Now then, I suggest that when they find the remains of the dog, which I's sure they will, then they don't stop with that. You see, I's of a mind that they ought to consider digging deeper. And ... if they'm still got doubts, then maybe, someone with a metal-detector may get a reading. I reckons 'twill be more likely than not that you'll be finding a pendant buried down there. I's one hundred per cent certain that this be the place where you'll be finding the remains of the young maid, Lucy McMurry."

He looks back towards the road. "Now, if it's all right with thee, I's gotta go and speak with her family and let 'em know what's happening."

The officer responds with the simplicity of, "Yes. You go ahead ... but before you go, what makes you think she's buried deeper?"

"Just ask yourself a question. Where's the joy in being so darned clever that, when it comes to it ... no one knows that it were *you* who were the smart one?"

As he collects his thoughts, the officer looks back towards the grave, and then, seeking clarification, he asks, "What do you mean? I don't understand."

"Well, I reckons that he didn't wanna get caught ... but then, there's still somethin' in him which makes him wanna boast." Having grasped the fact that he is still not fully understood, he adds. "Now, if you knows anything about ancient legends, you'll know that the North American Indians considered the coyote as being some kind of trickster. So, you see, I reckons that over all these years, he's been playing games with us, and, to my mind, I reckons he's left us a clue on purpose. He'm bin laughin' at us for not being as smart as he thinks *he* is."

The officer nods … and then lifts his radio. He hesitates and returns it to its holster. He has decided that it may be better for him to communicate on the more secure wavelengths of his personal phone.

Epilogue

The grisly task of exhumation is prolonged by the need to obtain and preserve anything and everything of evidential value. The procedure is, therefore, in the hands of those who have both the scientific expertise and the methodical approach to be able to complete the assignment with due diligence ... and without the risk of there being an oversight.

Gone are the days when the identification of a body was made, almost solely, through the hit-and-miss methods of having the remaining teeth compared with the dental records of previously-reported missing persons. After all, bearing in mind that the records were not always available, it could not always be relied on.

Nowadays, however, it is science which can provide the answers; thanks to the discovery of DNA — *deoxyribonucleic acid* — investigators are able to compare the more complex genetic information which is carried within the cells of an individual to that of any surviving family members. DNA fingerprinting has definitely hurried the process of being able to reach an indisputably accurate identification.

Owing to the body having still been wrapped in the fragments of what was left of her clothing, and had still been straddled with the golden relics of her jewellery, it had been evident that, even without the results of DNA testing, they were, indeed, the remains of Lucy.

From the initial observations at the scene, along with the more detailed examination conducted within the clinical environment of the laboratory, it had appeared that the microscopic remnants of her underwear had been found in a position which would have strongly suggested that they had not been removed whilst she had still been alive. The evidence had suggested that they had been in place at the time of her burial.

Maybe, in some small way, this will be of some solace for her parents. After all, they will be able to rest with the knowledge that she had not, in fact, been forced to suffer the spirit-breaking humiliation and lonely ordeal of being abused and then brutally raped, prior to her passing away.

Although the precise cause of her death remains uncertain, the fractures on her skull suggest that she had been a victim of an angry and frenzied attack.

The indications are that she had suffered a succession of blows which, with each having had the power and capability to slay in an instant, could only have been executed by a person who'd had both a mind and a soul fired with the venom of one with murderous intent.

***

Tom is well aware of the fact that the authorities will not be rushed into finalizing their enquiries.

The autopsies will have to be completed, and the coroner will have to determine the causes of both deaths. Whether or not the history of the dog is investigated, he has no idea.

Then, as a police vehicle was instrumental in the demise of Simon Brett Tripp, the *Independent Police Complaints Commission* will have to make its own enquiries and decide as to whether or not the driver was, in any way, blameworthy.

Files will have to be prepared and submitted. And decisions will have to be made. All in all, the wheels will turn … but in their own good time.

Knowing that his quest for closure, albeit devastating in its findings, has not been in vain, Tom feels an almost irrepressible need to return to France, where he can rejoin his wife and their son … and then lose himself in the routine of everyday living.

He will return, once his daughter's remains are released. With Rozenn and Jean-Paul at his side, he will invite a certain *wise old copper* to join them as they stand, together with Gina and Tori, to afford Lucy the respect of being laid to rest whilst her spirit is engulfed in an ambience of love.

With an appropriate memorial to mark the very beauty of her being, she will no longer have to suffer the ignominy of being left to rot in an unmarked and unattended grave.

***

With the unstoppable roll of the years, Tom has settled back into the unhurried lifestyle of southern France. Although he is rarely far from the pain of his loss, he has had closure. And, so, with the responsibilities of looking after his family and running his business, he has laid the past to rest and has moved on.

His relationship with Victoria has continued; in fact, it has blossomed … and she is no longer a stranger to his home.

Gina, through no fault of her own but, rather, through the long-term effects of her shattered heart, is not well enough to be able to make the daily visits to Lucy's final resting-place.

It is only when Victoria and Jamie visit with their two young children, Richard and Cassandra, and escort her to the cemetery, that she can share some precious time with the spirit of her — *never-to-be-forgotten* — first-born daughter.

By the quality of the headstone, and the power which is lodged within the few words which have been inscribed thereon, it is clear to all who care to stop and gaze … that *Lucy McMurry* was not only *much-loved*, but, what is more, *she will, for ever and a day, be sorely missed by those who had been privileged to have known her.*

David L Porter-MacDaibheid

David was born in the 1950's in Devon, England. As a young child, he was taken to Northern Rhodesia … where he spent his formative years. He returned to Devon during the 1960's and was educated in Exeter and North Devon.

His working life has been spent in both Cornwall and Devon … firstly, within the retail trade and then, within the public sector.

Prior to his retirement, he spent 14 years as a voluntary ambulance car driver, transporting patients throughout the county of Devon and beyond.

Although **The McMurry Girl** is his debut novel, he has previously published under the name David L Killick:

A Guide to Tracking and the Square Search … a dog training manual (*out of print*) and

The Magic of Milandi and the Smoke that Thunders … a children's book (*out of print*).

18445734R00209

Printed in Great Britain
by Amazon